UNUSUAL LOVE STORY

A. Amos

ISBN: 1523427981
ISBN 13: 9781523427987

Dedicated to:

Love, humanity and world peace!

CHAPTER 1
INCIPIENCE

Central Asia, *1948*

Miriam was almost seventy-four-years old, a lonely, impecunious widow who lived alone in a small village. Her whole family had been brutally killed during partition among India and Pakistan, because of migration riots between Muslims and Hindus.

She was working as a janitor and housekeeper in the community landlord's house. In return, the family used to give her leftover food and clothes. Her abode was completely empty, apart from two traditional woven beds, and a few cheap pieces of crockery. Her two-roomed house was made of mud and did not have electricity, only a lantern. Miriam's family had a tragic history and since she cleaned houses and worked as a janitor, most of the villagers considered her an outcast and didn't let her get close to them.

Even though she was a good Muslim, she was living in complete isolation. Her soul was empty, sad, and broken; however, she had always been an honorable, honest, incredibly hard working woman and never begged a single penny from anyone.

One day it was raining heavily with a gale force wind, and Miriam was walking toward her abode when she saw a man standing under the banyan tree. It seemed as if he was taking shelter from the rough weather. He was a stranger, and since it was a small village, everyone knew each other. When she came a bit closer to the man, he greeted her in an elegant, respectful manner. For a moment she was surprised, since no one in this whole village ever spoke to her in such a reverent way. She was happy, as it had been ages since she had the chance to speak to someone, so she approached him.

When she was nearer to the man, she observed him closely. He seemed around thirty years old. He was a tall and incredibly good-looking young man, especially his eyes. They were different from others. She had never seen such eyes in her life.

She greeted him and asked, "Greetings, would you like me to help you find someone's house?"

The man seemed watchful and replied shyly, "I'm just a traveler, and I was on my way to the next town. Suddenly the rain started, so I was waiting for the rain to stop. That's the reason I am standing under this cover."

Miriam was carrying some leftover food and thought the traveler would be hungry. "Would you like some food?" she said and raised her bag. "I have enough for two people and you're most welcome to eat with me if you would like."

The stranger's eyes grew vague with surprise, as if he had never experienced such kind words. Respectfully, the stranger thanked Miriam and accepted her invitation. However, at the same time, he requested that the only thing he wanted would be some milk. Poor Miriam was in shock with his strange request, although she felt herself under the strange obligation that 'Allah', had chosen her to be the host for this strange man.

Even though she did not have any milk in her house, she said, "Please come, I will arrange it for you." The rain was turning into a deluge now, so their pace hastened. As they headed towards her small house, neither of them exchanged a word. Miriam was gravely concerned about which house she should knock on to get the milk for her guest, but ever since she was young, Miriam had always kept her word, because that was one of the lessons her father had taught her.

He would tell her, "Remember Miriam, this is a truly important teaching your father wants you to know; you must always keep your word and be wise when offering and try not to give your word. However when you do give your word, you must fulfill it at any cost. Also, you can tell that the only difference between an extraordinary human and an ordinary human is the words in which they choose to speak. Lastly, always remember that those who value promises will never ever be let down in their lives."

Miriam was lost in her memories and despite the heavy rain she felt her father's presence with her, repeating the same words, as when she had been an eighteen-year-old girl vigilantly listening to her father's preaching. Her mind was set, and she made up a plan. She would drop the guest off at her home and go back to the landlord's house and request some milk. Not for a second did she doubt why this man would only ask for milk and not for proper food or water.

All her life she had grown up with Hindu and Sikh families and was aware of some religious requirements. Miriam was basically a broad-minded woman and always kept humanity first and religion second. Although because of her humanity, she had lost her whole family on that exceptionally sad day when one of her Hindu friends, Madhu had been left behind during her family's emergency escape.

Miriam and Madhu were childhood friends and they had been like sisters. On that day Madhu had been at Miriam's house to say one final goodbye when the fanatic Muslims had attacked the village. Madhu's family had somehow escaped without her. When they found out that one Hindu woman was still in the village, they had warned Miriam's husband Alam to hand her over. Alam had been a decent man, and he had simply refused. During the argument, they killed him and his two young sons and their wives; even though one of the wives had been pregnant, they showed no mercy. They kept Miriam alive so the whole village would receive the message of what happened when someone gave asylum to any non-believer.

That was one of the reasons why the whole village avoided her and looked at her with a hate filled eyes. She was living in her own world, with only herself and some good memories of her family. She requested that the stranger sit on her woven bed and told him to wait there and that she would be right back. She left the house and went to the landlord's house. The person who opened the door was surprised to see her out in such a storm. She was a loyal housemaid and he asked her if everything was fine and what made her return in such a storm?

"I need some milk, please," Miriam said.

The housemaid briskly went inside and got her a jar full of milk. Miriam accepted the milk and with humble thanks she left for her cottage. The rainstorm was terrible. In her whole life she had never experienced such a downpour. She was drenched but determined to fulfill her guest's wish.

As she entered her home, the guest remained in the same spot she had left him but his position had changed; he was seated in the pose of a Buddha, but seemed unbelievably relaxed and calm. The light of the lamp was making him look quite different and his eyes were shining, as if they were made from black diamonds.

"How do you like your milk, warm or cold?" in a very humble voice she asked her guest.

"Just the way you brought it," he said. "That is fine and thank you very much. My apologies for all the trouble I caused you. I have to admit you are very generous and at the same time a kind soul."

She removed the cover and offered him the pitcher. Once again he offered his gratitude, accepted the pitcher delicately, and took small sips from it. His eyes bored into her persistently.

"I still haven't asked your name, may I know what it is?" Miriam asked him humbly.

In an extremely decent manner he told her, "Raja." It meant 'King' in English.

"Nice to meet you Raja, my name is Miriam, and as you can see, I'm all alone in this world. You must have a great and wonderful family. Tell me about them."

"You are not alone anymore and from now on will never ever be," Raja, murmured mysteriously.

She thought she heard him say something, but was not able to understand it. However, after many lonely years, she was enjoying his company.

No one could sense and understand what loneliness was better than she, because being alone was strangely weird and a curse. Only a few who have been punished in that same category of isolation could understand.

She continued her conversation with the stranger: "So tell me, are you married? Do you have children?"

He answered, "No, I am also alone in this world and unless I find what I am looking for, I just simply prefer to be alone."

The storm today was not in the mood to stop or be kind, and the weather was becoming tremendously terrible.

Miriam said, "Raja, I don't think you will be able to continue your journey. You can feel at home here and are most welcome to stay until the storm ends."

Raja was quiet for a bit then replied, "Thank you for your hospitality. It is very kind of you. I think I have no choice but to accept your offer. I have to say: very few people of your rare kind remain, they really are the true form the way humans should be."

"Animals are notoriously famous and accused where as the real predators are humans. As they have no mercy, they hunt and kill each other, trying to seek minor opportunities to behead someone," Raja told her.

She listened to him avidly, while trying to connect his philosophies with her own story and how those brutal people whom she knew from ages ago had killed her whole family, and for what? The sake of religion! What wrong had her family committed? They had just been trying to save the life of a lonely woman. Tears involuntarily started rolling from her eyes. The memories were so barbaric of how those fanatic Muslims were playing god that day and killed her family and the memories tormented her.

The 1947 migration between India and Pakistan had been the worst human genocide ever recorded in human history, as Hindus and Sikhs sent trains full of Muslim corpses, which included children, women and men. From Pakistan they were doing the same with Hindus and Sikhs' families.

Later, the fanatic Muslims pulled poor Madhu by her hair and dragged her all the way to the ground. They took off her clothes, leaving her naked. What had really made Miriam cringe in horror was the way they had enjoyed making her walk through the whole village completely naked. They had mocked her and made fun of her in front of everyone. Kids, women, and men, young and old had spat on her face in hatred. Then they hanged her on the ancient banyan tree. It was such a horrible and shameful act that Miriam had forgotten the pain of her entire family's brutal murders. All Miriam had wanted to do was cover Madhu's body, but those goons beat Miriam with sticks and told her to stay away.

For three long days Madhu's body had hung naked on that tree. No one knew who had informed the police, but they finally came and took the body. She told the inspector the woman was Hindu and requested kindly that they arrange the proper cremation as per Hindu religion. The inspector had shaken his head and vanished with poor Madhu's body.

Like a flashback, all the memories ran through her mind, and Miriam found herself back in the moment when Raja' asked her about her biggest dreams which were still not fulfilled. It was a bizarre question, as no one had ever asked her something like this in her entire life. In a dreamy voice she replied, "I'm at that kind of stage, what can I dream now? And what can I wish for? I have not much left of this life, and all I wonder is, once I am dead who will bury me?" Raja seemed quite unsatisfied by her reply, and in a deep voice he told her, "Memorize one thing: all the time, while you are alive, always remember, keep dreaming! Wish for the whole universe, as the world belongs to those who dream and simply wish for the best for themselves.

"I know you must be thinking I am only one third of your age; however, what if I tell you a secret? Will you promise me that you will keep my secret with you until your grave?"

It was the first time she felt some kind of apprehension, as her guest was a stranger. He was calm, peaceful, and incredibly well-spoken. Raja seemed to be aware of many philosophies about the world, earth, and life.

Miriam replied, "Who will I tell? No one in this village speaks to me and the place where I work, they just give me instructions and I follow their orders. I can't say more or less. All I do is, when I enter I wish them time and when leaving I wish them time, and that is what my life is all about."

Deep in her heart she wondered what secret this stranger wanted to share with her. Why had he chosen her to share his secret, and who was this stranger? Millions of questions started to arise. Miriam was suddenly afraid of Raja. Abruptly, she started remembering his looks, and she started investigating her memories about his appearance. She remembered the most important part as she reminisced. When she had looked in his eyes, they were deep and anomalous; Raja was not blinking at all. That thought gave her chills down her spine. He had only asked for milk, and while he had walked all the way from a different village, he had never asked her about drinking water or food.

She was sure the guest she had brought home was not human at all. Either he was a devil or an ethereal although definitely not a person!

Miriam had grown up listening to various legends about people who encountered ghosts. One of the well-known tales was about a beautiful young girl who'd stood in the middle of the night and called out to people passing near her. As the legend went, it followed that those who saw that girl were surprised after one single glance at her face and were somehow mesmerized by her prettiness. However, the second they looked at her feet, they turned pale and terrified as if they had seen death!

Her feet were backward. Watching her feet made a myriad of people suffer heart attacks or extreme shock. Only the mighty hearted survived their encounter with her. But still either they ran extremely fast or fainted on the same spot.

Miriam felt trepidation as she wondered what evil she had brought home. She was a brave woman, as she had already seen so much pain, and she was not afraid of dying. She took the name of Allah and deep in her heart she recited, "Ayat al Kursi," from the Holy Quran. She felt strong in her mind, heart, and soul, and was ready for any kind of circumstances that could later occur on that stormy night.

Raja suddenly asked her, "Why are you worried or scared? Did I offend you or say something wrong? Fear nothing; I'm only here to give you a gift, which will take you into a different epoch, and you will fall in love with me for the rest of your life. I want to make you mine, and I want to love you like you have never been loved before."

Oh my Allah! "What is this man talking about?" Miriam asked herself deep in her heart. "Do you still remember how you used to look when you were eighteen years old?" Raja' asked her politely.

"Yes, I do," Miriam unwillingly replied.

Raja said, "You think you are older than me, well, the honest fact is I'm far older than you. Even I don't remember how long I have been living on this earth, and I've been watching you for a very long time, since the very first time I saw you as a child. The moment I first saw you; you were only eight years old. Then when you were eighteen that was the time I was truly amazed to see such a beautiful creation of God."

Miriam was really tremendously scared, as he seemed not more than thirty years old. "How could he have seen her, since the beginning of her life?

"Who are you?" Miriam asked, determined to discover who he truly was. "One thing I can understand, that you are not human. If you are here to kill me, you can take my life. I agree that a couple of seconds ago I was truly scared, but not anymore. However, I require your complete honesty as far as your identity is concerned."

Raja listened to her every word with great interest; he absorbed her, as if she were the teacher and he her student.

CHAPTER 2
THE PAINTER'S QUEST

He broke his silence while telling her; "All I want from you is to kiss me first, but with the depth of your soul, heart and mind, as I am the man you always dreamed to be with."

Instead, she tried to say something, but he continued to speak.

"Trust me on this one. Not only will you see my real identity, but at the same time you will see an entirely new person in you, a person you have totally forgotten."

Miriam felt as if she were in a strange situation, while wondering what kind of sick man he really was; at her age, she was older than his Granny, and he was requesting physical involvement with her?

"Allah," she said to herself, "What kind of situation have you got me stuck into? I can't even fight this young man, and what he demanding is simply quite impossible to even think about." She tried to look directly into his eyes, magical dark eyes that weren't blinking!

"What bad have I done to deserve this? I treated you nicely, invited you to my house, went out in the rainstorm to get you milk and this is how you are repay my kindness and my hospitality? I am the age of your grandmother. How can you ask me for a kiss?

What kind of perverted-minded man are you? I really don't care if you are human or not, but I will never allow what you are asking. Instead you should be ashamed of yourself. How can a man have such a low caliber?

Kindly forgive my awful decorum, however, I simply request that you immediately leave my house right now, or if you want to take my life, then go ahead!"

"I know what I'm asking makes no sense," Raja replied politely. His eyes shone in the lamplight, and still he did not blink at all.

"You always loved every one, but not a single soul loved you the way you deserved. I have been following you since the day you helped me. I know you don't remember that one day you saved my life. You were about eight-years-old, and I was passing by your house when your mother saw me, started screaming, and gathered the whole neighborhood. People came with big sticks, and they started searching for me. In order to save my life, I took shelter behind the wall. You were the only one who saw me climbing and hiding. With one glimpse, I knew you had a heart of gold, and you had never lied in your life. What surprised me is, for saving my life you did lie. When people came and asked you about me, you simply denied it, saying you had not seen anything."

While he spoke, she tried to remember the details from the past he was sharing.

Then deep in a corner of her mind, she started recalling blurry scenes and noises of people. There had been many and they had all been afraid. Everyone had been screaming to find it before it hurt someone. Like a flashback with images running in her head, she remembered she was in her parents' room, and saw a huge black king cobra briskly entering and then climbing the wall then went on the roof and vanished.

Those visions gave her shivers. So, the man in her room was not human but a king cobra in human form. Now the entire picture was clearer; no food nor water, only milk, and eyes not blinking. All the mystery was solved and her fear vanished.

The cobra could have easily bitten her, but he without harming her, climbed the roof and made his way out. She saw couple of cobras before, during performances by snake charmers, but none was as massive and graceful as he was. Instead of getting scared, she instantly fell in love with the beast. Miriam was an animal lover since childhood, and she loved that snake and did not want anyone to harm him.

Now, the same snake was sitting in her room, but in human form. Her fear was gone, and she somehow felt this creature was not here to harm her, but she was curious to know every detail about him. Why was he so keen to kiss her?

Miriam asked, "I can see you are fine and alive. I am glad you managed to escape that day. What really happened and how come you entered a human residence? As far as I know, king cobras are shy creatures and always prefer to stay in isolated areas. How come you ended up in our village, knowing humans will kill you at the first sight? I know many Hindus worship you, and they prefer not to harm you. However, you entered the site where Muslim residences were in majority. For Muslims, you are the most dangerous creature and killing you is the solution."

Raja said, "The year was 1882, and I were coming back from Lahore that day with my coachman. Strange feelings were bothering me, as if I was being watched by someone. Your vision can be in any direction, but your senses will make you aware of someone's eyes that are fixed on you, and you're followed by someone with evil desires to hurt you. I ordered the coachman to make the horses run as fast as they could and keep checks on the carriage following us. I'm blessed with a skill to envision the circumstances and environs. Deep in my mind I saw Abdul Salam, the most renowned sorcerer from East Bengal, following me and with his evil powers and sources, he figured out that I'm a king cobra in human shape. He managed to locate me and now was following me.

"East Bengal, in those days, was highly known for an elite team of sorcerers who maintained an excellent command of black magic. I was aware of Abdul Salam's powers, as number of my close followers had already informed me that he was on a mission to hunt me down."

"There were many rumors about Abdul Salam. Some informers told me his disciples saw him shape shifting into a crow. Just with one glimpse, I figured out he was not a shape shifter. There was no beast in him, but he might have shown some magical illusions to his disciples to spread the rumors about his powers. I had never ever seen such an ugly man in my whole life. I know the Lord gave his own face to every human born in this world; however some get involved in such evil works, and due to their devilish acts, their faces start turning from a person's into Satan's.

"A long time ago, I was sitting in St. Paul's Cathedral in London, where a guest priest was giving a sermon on the same subject. His words not only touched my soul but made a home in my heart. I have my own interpretation and wrote a poem on the same subject. Would you like to listen?"

Miriam was sitting lost and quiet while listening to his magical tale. He was eloquent, and the most well-mannered man she had ever met in her life and now he was asking permission, to share his poetry on devilish humans. She pinched herself to be sure she was not dreaming.

It was happening, everything was real, and he was sitting right in front of her. A king cobra in human form and with the heart of a poet, and he was waiting for her permission. Her fear vanished, and she wished to know every detail about his reality and his world.

Miriam said, "Kindly, please carry on; yes, I'm interested in hearing your poem."

The Painter's Quest

A very long time ago, there used to be a legendary painter
Whose name was Roberto Faustino and was extraordinary
In painting people, fantasies, visions and dreams
He was God gifted for giving life to his creations
Yet he was not satisfied and wanted to create a magnum-opus
One night he had a revelation; God was in his miraculous dream
While pleasantries God commanded him, to draw his face
Impetuously asked God, I only see light how can I paint your grace?
God with kind voice responded to him
Seek a man with benevolence, ingenuousness yet from a handsome race
Next morning, the painter was on his mission, he swiftly initiated traveling
The world, with a hope to find that one face
He traveled across oceans, walked on land
Even rode horses sometimes and spent cold nights in deserts
Saw millions of faces but not a single one he embraced
He'd lost his mind in search of a peculiar kind; on his failure he was amazed
On returning to his town's gate, he sensed his victory, as he spotted a face
The one he searched for in the whole world, he was only twenty-years-old
Something was unique about him and his eyes were divine and demeanor was like gold
Roberto requested if he could paint the man, shared his dream and informed him what had been told
The young man agreed with a smile, as he was surprised, yet at the back of in his mind he was scared and cold
It took two-weeks for the painter to finish his creation; the end result was splendid and bold

When the job was done, even the boy he had painted was stunned
Was overwhelmed and he fainted for few minutes
He never looked so good in the mirror
The magic of the painter made him pious and exceptionally vivacious
God appeared again in the painter's dream; and seem pleased with work done preciously
Promised to bestow good health, blessings and reward his future graciously
God instructed Roberto never to sell this work and then vanished from his dream
Time flew for the painter as God had commanded; never did he sell that painting
Twenty years later, God came again in the painter's dream
However this time his request was unusual
He told the painter, "I want you to make a face of the devil
Find the cruelest, most hideous face and he should be from an evil race"
As the painter was richly blessed since God was on his side
He followed the instructions and was again on an expedition of the world
To find the most malevolence face and to accomplish the will of God
Again his soul was blank and his heart was poignant
He wasn't able to find the face he was looking for
Again with languorous mind and defeated heart he traveled back home
As he entered the city gates and at the same corner, he found his muse and mate
The man was in his forties yet with his evil presence his eyes felt as if his soul was sold
He requested the man "he would like to preserve his face in his painting"
The man looked at him with eccentric eyes, said not a single word; instead he followed

It took him three weeks and the masterpiece was completed
During this whole process the man with the devil face was quiet,
and shared not a phrase
When the painting was done and Roberto showed him his face,
He started crying a river of tears, Roberto was concerned and dazed
With kind words he asked the man "What made you sad my friend?"
"You haven't recognized me, Roberto; I'm the same boy you painted
as God before
When you painted me I was chaste, so was my soul, and I was a
God fearing person
After that venture, I sold my soul to the devil, did all the evil doings
which were forbidden
I walked as man of the devil on earth; I committed sins like gam-
bling, adultery and even murder
Greed and lust overtook my soul and I walked on a different road
In me you found both faces, what kind of curse have I been through
to turn into such a shade."
Roberto hugged the man and said, "This time you better choose
right and be wise my friend.
Fear God and do good deeds, clean your soul, just kneel and pray,
we all depart who will live forever
I promise you he will forgive you and give you the face of the man
you were once before."

Miriam was speechless, lost in the depth of such an amazing poetic story. Being a Muslim, she wanted to argue on the subject. No
one could come close to Allah, and it was a sin even to think in
such a manner. However, since she was an open-minded Muslim,
she respected other religions the same as her own.

She looked at him and for a second and considered that, he
himself was a beast, and what did he know about Allah? So, according to his belief, he had written and basically was extremely

impressive and did captivating work. Especially the message, the whole world needs to listen and to understand.

Miriam said, "This was an interesting poetic story, and I understood your concept. So, you were telling me about Abdul Salam?"

Raja replied, "Glad you understood the essence of my poem. Abdul Salam was around fifty-eight. As I clearly mentioned to you, he was the most iniquitous human. Let me tell you something about his eyes, they were blood red. Intrinsically, eyes are like a mirror in which to view human souls. Concurrently eyes are indicators and you can study the health of the same person."

"Those with white, clean eyes are healthy people. Mostly white, clean eyes you view are among children as they are pure, healthy and their souls are like angels. Abdul Salam's eyes bore witness, ranting his malevolent identity and those who were spiritual and wise, were able to read him within a second."

"Abdul Salam devoted his life and time in worshiping the devil. While performing all types of devilish rituals, he managed to attain some evil powers to see the invisible, hidden things. What I find the most disturbing about him was that he preferred to sleep with virgins, so he could maintain his youth. The insane part was that after one month, he would kill that girl and eat her heart raw. By performing such a horrible ritual, he believed his soul would stay young forever."

"The humans who kill other humans in order to fulfill their filthy and devilish urges are not only animals; they, in fact, are the true face of monsters!"

"We wild animals and beasts are famous for being brutal killers; we only kill in order to feed ourselves."

"Capturing me or killing me would turn him into the most powerful man on earth. Some people want fame, few want money, and the evil types of humans want power and control over other humans."

17

"There are two types of powerful people in this world: those who are chosen by God and the others who choose to inflict themselves on others. Those who are chosen by God know their responsibility and are humble to serve their nations. On the other hand, people who take control of powers and become kings or dictators, show no mercy to anyone. No remorse of good or evil, they see things according to their mentality, which is based on pure sin."

"Abdul Salam was one of those evil people, and that day he was following me with his coachman, a snake charmer, and the paramount sketch maker of those days. He not only wanted to capture me, he wanted to record every moment of me transforming into a king cobra."

"As with his black magic, he was able to recite the malevolent words and, hearing those words, I wouldn't be able to control my powers, and rendered powerless, I would transform back into a king cobra."

"As per my orders my coachman turned my horses into Pegasus that day, and instead of running, they flew on the road. We managed to leave pursuers behind on a huge distance. As I drew closer to the forest, I instructed my coachman to drop me nearby forest and keep driving the carriage, and I gave him a point where I would meet him again."

"When I entered the forest, I transformed into a king cobra, and I started slithering toward your village. I didn't want anyone in the jungle to see me running. It was a safer and better process to be in my original form and move as fast as I could."

"That is where your mother saw me and started screaming and shouting. I was aware Abdul Salam would simply keep chasing my carriage, as he was so confident that I would not leave it."

"I ended up entering your village and that was the moment, while crossing your house, that your mother saw me and started screaming. After that it was like a circus. Everyone, with huge canes, was striving to kill me. You saw me and with your denial with regards to having seen me, you managed to save my life. I some-how managed to escape Abdul Salam, and I informed my coach-man to get rid of the carriage."

"That same night I was able to escape to India and stayed there for a few years. Abdul Salam never gave up his search for me; how-ever, I managed to enter my cave that was located in my Indian palace. That cave was completely protected with a magical seal, incapable of leaking any scent or vibration of my presence."

"Eventually, I discovered how some poor girl's brother had killed Abdul Salam after he had raped his sister and ate her heart."

"The problem with people such as Abdul Salam is that when they have great powers they ignore small details, such as their per-sonal security."

"As for them no ordinary human was able to touch them and that was the time when the young boy took the advantage and cut his throat. The young boy joined as a devotee and spent all his time with Abdul Salam. In a few weeks, the boy gained the trust of Abdul Salam, and one of the days, he got a chance alone with him and took his revenge."

"He took his head with him and left the city that night. No one knew what he did with the head."

"Abdul Salam's body was buried headless and still it's rumored that whoever walks near the graveyard where he is buried, myriad had witnessed a headless body in search of something. Some say he searches for his head, and a few say he desired the head of another human, so he could be resurrected."

"All I wanted was to come back and pay you my humble grati-tude, in the form of leaving you some treasure. Then vanish from your life for good. However, when I saw you, my world was changed; and so was my decision."

CHAPTER 3
METAMORPHOSIS

"When I came back and saw you again, you were all grown up and were the most beautiful human I had ever seen in my entire life. I have an ability to read souls, and you were the best combination, blessed with a gorgeous inner and outer persona."

"Even though I know what happened to your family, I never interfered. The reason was simple, as it was something that was meant to happen, and you were supposed to go through such pain. In life, we face huge losses, such as yours, where we think our world has finished and so has our life."

"However, those crucial moments are your tests and prove how strongly you believe in a higher power! Generally, weak souls start cursing Him by asking, "How could He do such things to us?""

"Suddenly their faith turns into illusions and their belief in a higher power begin to fade. They are unable to comprehend how something so severe could have happened to them. All it simply does is obliterate their faith. If a higher power chooses you to go through extreme pain, He has planned something exceptionally great for you in return."

"As in your case, you turned out to be an ardent follower. You understood the fate of your family members' lives and because they stood for a cause; they were killed for saving another human's life."

"You considered them as martyrs and according to your belief, martyrs never die. Instead, they go straight to Heaven and receive the best reception, since they died for a noble cause. Incredibly, few people are blessed with an ability to understand the harsh scenarios of life and be able to convert them into a positive reality. You are one of them."

"Simultaneously, you never stopped your prayers, connection with Him and being thankful. For me, people like you are meritorious and imagine how much the higher power loves you." Raja completed his speech while looking into her eyes."

Miriam spoke. "You are wise as a snake human and seems like you're a whimsical philosopher. What surprises me, is your thoughts contain and represent you like an angel rather than a king cobra. I like the way you praised the higher power as being a beast. You believe in Allah?"

"Yes," Raja replied, "I believe in a higher power, even the ant does. Imagine a tiny seed smiling before it flourishes into a plant and then turns into a huge tree. Have you ever noticed those trees bending sometimes during gale? The seed smiles because it praises the higher power before turning into a plant and when the trees are bending, they are worshiping and showing gratitude to the higher power. You humans have given many names to the creator, yet every living thing believes in Him."

"I'm honestly glad you're safe and sound. Now, while you're sitting with me, I clearly understand it's not only a legend that snakes can take the form of humans. Please tell me, are all types of snakes shape shifters?" Miriam inquired politely.

"Not all snakes are shape shifters, only the king cobra is, as the whole universe considers us to be a form of the Devil and the main reason mankind was thrown out of Heaven. Yes, our ancestor offered the fruit and he was punished, with his descendants by crawling for the rest of their lives on their stomachs. We continue to undergo that punishment."

"I would like to pay my humble gratitude for being concerned about my safety. Your words mean the world to me!" Raja replied.

"Like every living creature, we are also given assignments by the higher power. King cobras are assigned to be protectors of the hidden treasures in the world. Some humans are extremely greedy. They don't believe in sharing and all they want is the best life for them. The rarest type of king cobra is the one who completes a hundred-years of his life and can then transform into any shape or form he wants, and most of us prefer to be humans."

"We try to find one soul who deserves the treasure, and as I told you, all my life I have been observing you. Miriam, you're simply the best form a human should be.

"You've stayed away from religious conflicts, all types of greed and even with nothing, you always praised and thanked God. I know you believed your husband loved you. In fact, he did in his own way. Perhaps a woman like you needs to be worshiped as a goddess. I have seen as you were growing up. I never saw anyone as incredibly beautiful as you were."

While he spoke, she was suddenly lost in her memories. She had totally forgotten the girl she once was. He was not wrong. When she was fifteen she had always felt pleased while viewing herself in a mirror. What had time done to her? She was left with millions of wrinkles on her face, her long legs were no longer straight, and her body was slightly hunched.

She had such thick hair; she remembered those days and her elegant walk of grace. Oh yes, she remembered. Miriam wanted to go back in time and change everything, just like the old times.

She said, "Why are you doing this to me and hurting my soul, which is already lost in despair?"

Raja replied, "There is always a time, and, if God wants, he can repair everything."

The invocation had started; the myth was taking place as she was already feeling something magical. She was ready to go on.

He may not be a human, but his persona, his presence, and his oratory everything was simply and mysteriously strong.

She had always believed in love, where someone understood her soul and made her feel desired above all.

He was reading her mind and answering every thought like a rhyme, as she was feeling the fall.

Now was the time. He came a bit closer to hold her hand and made her feel as if he would soon crawl all over her. Miriam's breath was heavy, and she was able to hear her own heart beat. However, there was less concern about his chisel because her mind was distressed, but her soul was willing to give a try.

Deep down, somewhere in her soul, heart, and mind she felt as if she were eighteen again. Her decency was gone, as was her repelling and resisting spirit. The passion was about to begin, and, even if she was not eager, she was willing to give up and start the game he wanted to play. She felt a strange spark.

He was getting closer to her and she was not able to stop him. His eyes were melting her and still they did not blink. However, she was not aghast at all. The storm was getting deadly, and the voices from the skies were heard loudly as he held her hand in his and pulled her a little closer.

The grip of his hand was different, as she felt only flesh not a single sign of bone. However, she felt his passion and was ready for anything to happen. The minuscule light of the lamp, sound of rain and howling winds, created a passionate world. Her seventy-four-year-old heart was beating like it never had before. He brought his handsome face right up to hers without giving her a chance to take the next breath. He briskly locked his lips on hers. Something came from his mouth and went deep down into her throat. She felt a strange current and her whole body shivered intensely. For a few seconds Miriam felt she was dying and then, felt like new life was running deep down in her veins and she was not old anymore.

She had returned to the age of eighteen. How had he made this happen? She was just now in love with the man who came into her world, who gave her hopes, dreams, and above all, he not only changed her appearance, but had given her a reason to be a happy.

They made love all night and in the morning when the storm became calm and the light took control, she opened her eyes and saw him lying next to her, just staring deeply into her eyes. His eyes were the same. Still no movement in them but she sensed complete passion, safety, and protection in his presence.

He was truly a handsome man with a heart of gold. In one night they both felt like they had known each other from a million years ago. Their souls were together and they were meant for only one reason to love each other endlessly.

This was the magic of a soulful connection. Without any qualm or apprehension, she had accepted the heart of this man. They both remained lying in the same position and exchanged thousands of words through their eyes.

Then, he broke the silence and asked her, "Are you ready to rule this world as my princess?"

Miriam replied, "Yes, I will follow you wherever you go and will be your shadow and your personal ghost. All I have is just one humble request. Never ever leave me, my love, as this life is to serve you and worship you as my man. You may be a devil for the world, but for me you are my lord!"

"When we reach your new home, the first thing I want you to see is your face", he told her with a smile. "We will leave now. We will leave everything here. I have a palace for you and everything you need is already there."

Miriam touched her soft, fresh, young skin and was unbelievably excited. She was young. She looked into his eyes again and asked him, "What kind of magician are you? How can you perform such a miracle to give back someone's youth? How can you control time? What kind of powers do you possess?"

He replied with grin, "When we complete one hundred-years with a gift of shape-shifting, we are also blessed with black mercury, which is always under our throat. For this black mercury, many holy and evil men have worshiped for years. They fast for days and their demand and urge was to find the black mercury, because with black mercury you can be immortal and can set any age you want for yourself."

"Your body is cured for life from convalescence or growing old. It also contains powers from which you can sense directions of hidden treasures buried in the world. Those voracious people are always in search of me and they know by only killing me, they can possess such a supremacy. Now, you possessed those powers and the reason I blessed you with this gift is because I know you will always use your powers to do the right thing. I vehemently believe that your treasure is love and me."

Her eyes suddenly became wet with tears and she hugged him. "Please, promise me you will never let anything happen to you. I don't want any worldly treasures; all I need is you with me. If you are with me, we can stay and live in my hut for the rest of our lives and trust me, I will feel like I am the richest woman in this world. They have to kill me first to reach you," she said.

He held her back and kissed her gently. "Nothing will happen to me my love that I can surely promise. So are you ready for a magical journey to see the world?"

Miriam hugged him back, then asked him, "Yes, as I mentioned to you earlier, where you go I go. So when do we leave? I'm also concerned that the villagers will start getting nosy and they will wonder who you are and why you spent a night in my abode."

He smiled. "Listen, first of all no one will recognize you. Trust me, and once we are gone, all they will think about would be that you, as an old woman, got tired of their rude behavior and went somewhere and are never coming back. I tell you what will happen first. As the whole village will come to know you have vanished, they will start fighting over your house without even being concerned you could come back. One of the strongest families of this village would take possession of your house and for them that's what the whole world is all about."

Miriam quietly followed Raja and left the small mud house. They both started walking toward the main road. A few of her neighbors noticed them but simply ignored and thought that they were some travelers walking by their village.

She took a last brief view of every house and all the malicious people who lived inside thinking they were born humans but were worse than animals, and look at Raja who had been born as the wildest beast but was more human than anyone in this village.

The storm had stopped completely, and the day had turned beautiful with the sun smiling right back at her and a view of deep miraculous blue skies with clouds forming shapes to wish her a new life.

While on a quiet empty road, he told her, "As soon as we reach home, the second thing you have to do is study, and no excuse, because you're the owner of a fresh mind now. I have assigned a mentor for you. She will teach you the history of every country in this world, how to speak different languages, the art of protecting yourself, swimming, driving, and horseback riding and more. I want you to be prepared for the world because we will be traveling around the globe."

After a pause and while looking her right in her eyes, he said, "Listen and understand one thing. Wisdom is like an ocean and whatever drops you can absorb deep in your mind, do that. Secondly, she will enlighten you with the latest fashions, as now you are an extremely rich woman and you have to act like one."

Miriam understood every word he told her with complete concentration, and from time to time, she looked above the sky and thanked Allah for such a wonderful blessing.

After walking a few miles, she saw two cars and three men. One man was dressed in white while the other two wore black. They were well built and held guns. She became scared and held his arm firmly. He wore his dark-shaded sunglasses, and she was not able to see his eyes. He smiled at her and told her, "My love, nothing to worry about. They are my men and are waiting for me."

Then he said, "This big white car you see is called, a Rolls Royce 'Silver Wraith' made in nineteen-forty-eight. The black car behind it is for my security."

"Let me tell you something about the Rolls Royce, as it's the name of statement and the world's most expensive car. The company is famous, and they make engines for airplanes, which fly in the sky."

Raja tried to make her understand by moving his hand showing the flight of a plane and looking expectantly at the sky. Everything he was sharing with her was new. She had never heard of such material before. However, she was enjoying every bit of new information.

Miriam was entering a new world. She was happy and excited, and she was giving complete consideration every detail.

As they got closer, she saw all three men bow their heads in respect, without even looking toward them, and he opened the white car's back door. With great respect he made way for her to sit down first. In her whole life she had never sat in a car. It was her first experience and what a coincidence that the first ride happened to be in the world's most expensive car. What a way to start a new life.

After five hours of driving, the car passed through an extremely large gate with two guards who bowed their heads. A long driveway went through a beautiful forest, then she saw an enormous white marble mansion. The entrance door was massive, and it was made of exceptionally fine wood with elegantly handcrafted work, which gave the entrance a pompous touch.

The driver briskly opened the car door and Raja helped her out by her hand while showing her the house that was more like a palace. He then told her, "Welcome home, darling, and this is all yours now, my love."

While they were standing a girl approached them. She was modernly dressed and seemed sagacious. From her appearance, she seemed like a princess and owner of this grand palace. Miriam was fidgeting and was a bit shy about the clothes she was wearing. However, with Raja' next to her, his presence helped her not to be nervous and it kept her calm.

The girl came and bowed her head with respect in front of both of them then welcomed them inside. While gently shaking Miriam's hand, she introduced herself, "Hello, my name is Ayesha and I will be at your service, your highness."

Raja said, "Miriam meet Ayesha. She will be your mentor for the rest of your days."

Ayesha replied, "It will be my honor, madam, to be at your service."

The whole concept for Miriam was new. It was extremely hard for her to control her nerves. A huge house like a palace, so many servants and everyone bowed their heads before her.

CHAPTER 4
TUTELAGE

Once they entered the house, the magic and the view were simply indefinable. The hallway was massive and, as they walked further everything proclaimed the house's opulence. Then they went straight to the bedroom which was rather a large house in itself. The carpet was crimson and so were the curtains. The bed was king sized and finished with gold carvings, and the sheets on top were navy blue and made of the finest velvet and satin.

The massive bedroom became even more amazing when Miriam discovered the two medium-sized dressing rooms composed within. Both were for keeping attires; one was for Raja, and the other one, when she entered, amazed her by its vast collection of feminine clothes that was elegantly arranged. Below were few shelves that were neatly packed with sandals, shoes and various types of feminine foot wear. Miriam had never seen such a collection before. The feel of that room was as if someone had been already living there for a long time. For a moment she was concerned, scared, and worried that perhaps Raja had some other girl living with him before. Her heart started pounding, complicated by a thought that maybe he was already married, and this all belonged to his wife, who could come in any second and start yelling at Raja, whom he brought home and where did he find her?

She turned toward Raja asking him politely, "Do you have someone else living here?"

He laughed, and when he did, the whole universe seemed so stunning. Since he was an extraordinarily handsome man, and if his laughter could create such magic, what effect it must be having on other women around him?

"I told you I love you," Raja said. "Whatever you see here is for you, my love. All the clothes, shoes and jewelry, they are for you, my darling. I know your soul, so sizing you was not a problem for me. I enjoyed picking clothes that would have the privilege of touching your magnificent body and shoes that would fit your gorgeous feet."

She hugged him tightly and then he told her, "Let me fix you a warm bath to help you feel invigorated. Ayesha will be here shortly to assist you in selecting your attire for dinner."

With a deep kiss, he entered the elegant bathroom and fixed her a bath. The room was indeed a masterpiece of luxury, with a huge tub made of the finest marble and all the metal used seem to be gold. The toiletries seemed custom-made, as there were different sizes of soaps and each one had an 'R' engraved on it.

He was gone and she was left alone in the room. The first thing she did was view herself in the mirror. She had been returned to her youth but had never had an opportunity to see in detail just how she really looked. She took off all her clothes and stood in front of the mirror by herself. Miriam witnessed the magic of her youth, her beauty and elegance. Her skin was fresh like pure milk and her eyes had a different iridescence about them. Her hair had grown long and was jet black. The shape of her body was so beautiful that she herself fell in love with the beauty that she viewed in the mirror.

Miriam enjoyed lave as she never had before. The whole process was so invigorating, she really felt quite fresh and relaxed. As she emerged from the bathroom, she heard a knock on the door; it was Ayesha. She entered with a pleasant smile and announced that she brought Miriam herbal tea. Another maid followed behind and carried a tray of tea and refreshments. The maid poured the tea and then she was gone. Now she was left alone with Ayesha. Miriam was wearing a bath robe and Ayesha went into the closet room and started selecting clothes for her.

With every style, she gave her complete descriptions. "This attire is for an afternoon gathering and this is an evening dress worn with these sandals." Miriam was listening attentively to Ayesha's every word.

Ayesha said, "Every morning, whatever time you wake up, we will do studies. Then in the afternoon your one-hour grooming class will take place, and I will need to update you about trends, fashion and various issues, which will help you to understand the world of style and glamour. At five o'clock I will need another hour with you, where I will teach you about history, art and music from the world. Once you get comfortable with your education, you will start your physical training, like swimming, martial arts, horseback riding, and complete handling of various types of weapons. Workouts are extremely important for maintaining your health and beauty."

Miriam carefully memorized the schedule and was happy and excited that she would be learning about the world in a different perspective. It was distinct from her first life, which had been that of a poor village girl, now God had given her a chance to see the world from the perspective of a princess.

She wore an elegant dress that Ayesha had selected. One of her maids had been specially hired as her beautician and she made sure Miriam's hands and feet were neatly polished with a red hue, and she helped apply delicate makeup.

Raja returned and was looking elegantly handsome in a black suit with a white shirt and black tie. He approached her, kissed her forehead and with a gentle smile, held her hand and told her, "Let us go down for dinner."

He was still wearing dark glasses; it was then that she understood that only in her presence would he not hide his magnificent gaze.

The dining room was another world containing an exceptionally long dining table with two chairs that faced each other. A striking painting collection was displayed on an entire wall, which created a pleasing view.

In the center of the table were huge candelabra and near the door was a team of musicians who performed a fabulous, mesmerizing tune, yet only a cello, harp and violin were heard. The whole set-up was like being in a world all of its own. Raja pulled out her chair and requested that she take her seat. Then he walked around to the other end and sat opposite her. The music was pleasant and soothing. The head chef came and bowed his head in front of them, then welcomed Miriam in his own way without looking in her eyes directly.

"Madam, I'm the head chef of the house and my name is Anthony. Master never eats at home. The whole kitchen team only gets busy when we have delegations at the mansion. My whole team and I welcome you to the house, and it will be an honor to serve you with all our heart and soul. I have made various dishes as per Master's command, and hope you will enjoy the dinner."

Miriam nodded in a way to thank him. She looked at Raja, who sat emotionless. He seemed to not have any interest in the conversation. Within a few hours, she figured out that Raja kept a fair distance from the servants in the house.

However, all the staff she met seemed to have worked for him for a long time and judging by their eyes and style, one could easily determine that they were loyal and honest people. They were truly happy to work for him; it was an exchange of loyalty as Raja evidently took special care of each of his staff.

They both had a quiet dinner. Raja only had soup and what the bowl contained, she was not aware. Deep in her soul she wanted to cook for him, care for him, worship him and let him know the madness of her love that she had for him. Love could change a person's mind, and for Miriam the whole world was now like Heaven.

After finishing dinner, Raja held her hand and said; "Let me show you the whole house. Now that you own this house, every corner should welcome you and you should be aware of every detail."

The house was full of surprises. Every room she entered with him was a complete puzzle, with secret passages leading them to totally different parts. At the back of the house was an enormous swimming pool and a lush lawn.

In the distance, she viewed stables then there were big trees, as the forest was linked to the mansion. After the tour of the house he made his way back into the bed room and where he told her, "Now, where I will take you no one had ever gone and will ever go."

Behind the closet was a secret passage no one could even tell that there was a hidden tiny door. Even if someone removed the closet, they still would not be able to see the secret door.

He held her hand and they started walked down the stairs that were lined with lamps that were all turned on, by themselves. She didn't know exactly why; she was not at all scared, because she was enjoying every second being in his presence, in his world and hidden life.

Love had an astonishingly strong impact on the human mind. Once you are blind folded by love, the one who loves you could control you just the way he or she wants, and for pleasing him or her, you could go to any extent. That was exactly how Miriam's mind was totally under his magical spell.

After a long, quiet walk down stairs, she heard strange noises and gained the sense that something dreadfully dangerous seemed to be resided where she stood.

"Just don't scream whatever you see next, okay?" Raja requested her. She nodded, but deep down, her heart was beating fast, as if in any second it would explode.

As soon as he clapped, the dark cave started flashing lights from various angles it was nothing like a lamplight. On the walls she were many stones; like amethysts, aquamarines, rubies, diamonds, sapphires, emeralds, star garnets, turquoises, ambers, opals, pearls, citrines and others.

Some walls were only covered with platinum, rhodium, technetium and gold plates. Everything was visible inside the cave; it was like an ancient cave with a numerous amount of various types of snakes in a massive quantity. As the stone rays coruscated and connected with precious metals, the visibility they were created was a light from a different world. The cave seemed tremendously magical; Miriam was surprised to see strange species of snakes; some extremely enormous in size and a few tiny ones; as they were hard to be seen.

All the snakes bowed their heads. Then she looked at Raja'. He nodded slightly as if replied to them. He turned toward her and, while looking in her eyes asked, "Are you fine my love?"

Miriam nodded and felt relaxed and fearless. Since her childhood she had always been attracted to animals and had never harmed any living creature. This situation was new and interesting.

She took off her sandals and started walking between the snakes, while Raja remained where he was standing. She felt love from all the reptiles gathered in that cave as one by one each of them tried to pay his or her respect toward Miriam while touching her, and then moving away to give place to another.

A huge pipe opened from the top, dropping milk in a huge cement tub, which seemed deep, and the flow of the milk was abundant. There was a second pipe from which mice and rats poured down.

The third pipe was wide and where there was an ample supply of various frogs. She wondered whether someone from the kitchen was taking care of these supplies to feed all the snakes and guessed he wanted to show her the cave so his snake friends' supply would never ever be interrupted.

The cave had no entrance for rain, but she could still smell scent similar to the magical odor created by the beautiful combination of rain and earth.

She turned around and saw that though the snakes were nearby Raja, however not a single one tried to wrap around his leg or him; the whole view was mesmerizing for her.

It was almost as if they were speaking to him, with no sound between them, but with their presence, only they offered all details of an unspoken conversation.

While viewing the snakes and being in a world of serpents, Miriam felt as if she was dreaming it all, and that soon her eyes would open and she would be back in her small mud house again. She pinched herself to make herself feel that it was not a dream. Raja was still standing there, not speaking. No voice or sounds could be heard, yet she felt he was speaking to the thousands of snakes, greeting each one by one. What a strange world she now inhabited. However, for love she was willing to give her life.

Tragic circumstances God provided in her first life and now her second life, God made it handed over by her love of life and his world was magical and different from rest of the world.

One more thing was significantly different about Raja; she never felt any bones in his body. His whole body was boneless, yet he was extremely active and his speed moving around was phenomenal. His style of greeting everyone was simply a mix of Japanese bowing of head and an Indian Namaste. He always maintained a distance, and he never seemed interested in shaking hands with anyone.

After spending some time in the cave, they moved back into the bedroom. He held her hand and took her up to the balcony, where two chairs had already been neatly placed. The fresh air and the night's silence with a full moon watching over them made the evening marvelously romantic.

He pulled her chair close to his and, while holding her hand, he told her that he was delighted that she was with him. Then gently he kissed her. Miriam could see his eyes; they were alive and shining. She felt she could find all the love of the world in those eyes. He told her that the following day she would spend her time with Ayesha.

Raja said, "She is not only an extraordinary God-gifted teacher, she is also a great scholar and a philosopher. I know you will not understand now what I am trying to share with you. The reason I want you to learn fast is because if someone kills me, I never want you to be left alone in this cruel world without any wisdom. Education and knowledge will enhance your confidence, and that will make your personality stronger."

Miriam hugged him and placed her fragile fingers on his lips. "Please promise me you will never ever leave me, no matter what, and if that day comes, I want to die with you.

"This is a wonderful life you have given me, but all I really want is to spend every second with you. Please never talk to me about anyone hurting you or killing you, because they would have to go over my dead body to reach you."

Raja replied, "My love you don't have to worry about anything, but just for the sake of your happiness and safety, I have to prepare you in my own way. Let's go to bed now, because tomorrow you will have quite a long day. I have some work to finish, so I will see you during the day."

Ayesha's way of describing small details and making her understand was amazing. Miriam's fear was, what if Ayesha asked her how they met or what their love story was all about. She was surprised that Ayesha never discussed any personal issues with her.

Ayesha started her lessons by teaching her five languages at the same time, all alphabets and phonics, with the heading on each topic as following:

Hindi	Urdu	English	French	German
एक	ایک	one	un	ein

Ayesha made sure, she understood every detail with interest, not just memorizing. She made Miriam's education so such fun way that she enjoyed the whole process of learning with her in this great atmosphere of her education class.

Ayesha taught her about history and art, one painter at a time that started from Monet and Van Gogh to Leonardo da Vinci and others.

She did the same with music, helping her understand the preludes and symphonies of Beethoven, Bach, Wagner, and Mozart and many more.

In just one week she was a totally different person that was the magic of knowledge, along with Ayesha's superior process of teaching and grooming.

Raja came in and out during the days to see her, and spent time with her and obtained results from Ayesha on how things were moving. His actions were so humble, that she fell deeply in love with him every second she knew him more.

Raja told her he had many businesses. However, he preferred to maintain a low profile, and the whole country knew only that he was a busy businessman, and that most of the time he traveled around the globe.

CHAPTER 5

"PHILANTHROPIST"

In the living room were large, handmade portraits of various men. At first Miriam thought they must be Raja's relatives, but when she scrutinized them, she realized they all had one thing in common, and that was their eyes. They all had Raja's eyes.

Her heart stopped for a second. All those pictures were of Raja, but with different hairstyles and apparels.

Those portraits were from different eras. In some, he had mustaches and in others he had beards, and throughout each historical period, his attire was stylish and unique.

The whole set of paintings was like a family portrait of Raja, but she knew it was him in all those pictures.

How much knowledge Raja must possess, she thought. Surely he had much wisdom and she imagined all the different periods he had already experienced during his long life in this world.

Now Miriam was in a world of learning, and like an excited child she wanted to sit with Raja and ask him millions of questions about the countries and languages of which Ayesha was teaching her.

Raja showed her many pictures and shared many tales about the human mind that had been taken over by the Devil and by greed, how they killed their own kin and families and he spoke most of the languages in the world.

He carried himself like a true prince with his collection of watches, men's jewelry like rings and pendants, clothes, shoes and his vast collections of cars. Yet it was not only material things which presented him as a king.

He was eloquent, a proper gentleman, and his humble attitude made him exceptional among millions of rich people. He was king of kings and was responsible for his people's needs. Everything had to be top class for him.

She guessed he must have selected ordinary clothes when he visited her. If he had been dressed as a prince, she never would have been able to gather enough of her courage to go speak to him.

During their myriad conversations Raja became aware of her need to help poor people, and he guided her in the right manner.

Raja, on one beautiful sunny day, sat with her and, while gazing into her eyes, told her, "Listen, Sunday you will go with Ayesha, guards will be following you for your safety. I want you go to the underprivileged villages. Be yourself and appear as normal as you can. Make sure that crowds don't gather around you. No one should follow you or ask many questions. Help those whom your heart says yes, they need and deserve your support and assistance."

She understood the difference between scarcity and profusion. He gave instructions to Ayesha to take her to some of the deprived villages and whomever she felt like she could help, as per their individual needs and requests.

"Let her study their living conditions and give charity accordingly." Raja sensed and could feel Miriam's soul and knew that even if he gave her all the treasures of the world, he could never make her completely happy.

This was something that he knew she needed to feel alive. She was perfectly fit to be a great philanthropist, for who could help those who suffered and could feel someone's pain better than those who had been through such harsh conditions themselves? Sudden sparks in Miriam's eyes made Raja's day.

While Miriam was getting ready, she dressed as simply yet elegantly as she could.

Raja hugged her and told her, "For me, you take care of yourself while you are out there. I want to go with you but I can't because I want you to feel independent while participating in charity work and therefore by doing so, I know your soul will find its peace in a better way." Raja kissed her soft lips then said, "I'm very proud of you my love."

Ayesha took charge of the driver's seat in a red, 1948 Jaguar XK120, and was waiting for her in a driveway. While attending classes with her, she and Miriam became close friends, and as for Ayesha, she loved her benevolence, minimalism and humanity.

The guards were following in a Series 1 Land Rover 1948. Once the journey had started, and before reaching the village, Ayesha gave her a complete briefing on the conditions of the individuals and families they were going to meet.

Miriam's heart was stuck on the tale of a lonely widow who lived alone and still worked as a part-time housemaid.

Miriam was thankful to Raja for changing her life. She was also thankful to a higher power for such a miracle in her life. Now it was her turn to touch and bless someone else's life, because her man was now by her side and what could please her more than to bring healing to some desperate souls?

After three and half hours' driving, they arrived at their destination. All the village children started running after the cars and were happy just to see beautiful vehicles entering their small village. Most of the homes were huts and a few had been made out of mud.

Not a single child was wearing footwear, but they were all excited to see them. The whole village started gathering around them.

Ayesha was the one who made a short, yet powerful speech, introducing Miriam as her boss, who was concerned with the living standards and that she would provide assistance in solving their problems.

She told them they would visit everyone's house one by one. Ayesha had already done her home work and was aware of how many families resided in that one village.

Miriam spent time with every family, to listen their problems; however Ayesha noticed that she was not paying anyone a single penny. It was surprising, for Ayesha, as they carried some cash to distribute among all the families, but Miriam was just visiting house to house and had almost completed their whole tour.

The last house belonged to the old widow named Fatima, and everyone came out to welcome them, but the widow stayed inside her small mud house. Miriam knocked on her door and the old widow answered.

Without saying a word, Miriam just hugged Fatima. Affection in any form never needed any introduction, and that is what happened between them.

Fatima, without any hesitation, hugged her back as if she was her own daughter with whom she was reuniting after a long time.

Miriam held Fatima's hand gently and told her, "Consider me your sister or daughter. From now on you will be my responsibility and you don't need to drudge for anyone any longer."

Fatima was vigilantly listening to her with tears in her eyes. She was unaware of who this girl was and why she was showing so much affection and benevolence toward her.

Miriam told her, "You are my responsibility now. Allow me to take care of you as my own. Ayesha, can you give some money to her? Please make sure I visit her every month and we will look after her."

Ayesha stood and tried to understand what Miriam was planned to do with this old woman.

41

Then Miriam turned her head toward Ayesha and told her; "Please arrange a house maid for her full time. I think we can find an orphan girl or single woman who can live with her and look after her. Also, I will request to have her house rebuilt and filled with all the necessary household items required for her convenience."

Ayesha wrote every instruction down on a writing pad and nodded, telling her, "Please consider it done."

Miriam, while looking at Ayesha told her, "I want Fatima to be in charge of this village. Write down her our address and make sure if she sends me any message that it reaches me immediately."

She looked deeply into Fatima's eyes and informed her, "I'm taking responsibility for village and I urgently need your help and support to make this small village heaven. Would you be so kind to help me?"

Fatima, while wiping her tears away, nodded. Miriam understood her condition. Throughout her whole life, no one had given her respect or considered her worth for any suggestions. Miriam was not only trying to restore her dignity, but was making her feel like a special person who was valued in this world.

Miriam continued talking to her. "I'm making you responsible to inform me if anyone ever disrespects any woman here. I want to know if anyone beats his wife, any child is forced to marry to an older man; or if any girl's wedding is delayed because of dowry. If any kind of injustice, you feel, should take place with any woman, send me a note immediately!"

Miriam hugged Fatima again and went out the door. When they came out, Ayesha noticed tears in Miriam's eyes. Ayesha humbly asked if she was okay. Miriam nodded gently then told Ayesha, "Kindly inform the whole village. I made Fatima responsible of this village. I think we need to make a school here and we can arrange a small dispensary for their medical needs. Secondly, I need someone to come and redesign the whole village, as I want to provide them with better housing conditions.

"Provide sewing machines to all the women of the village," Miriam said. "Send someone to teach them arts and crafts so they can work from their homes. As far as their men are concerned, they will be used as laborers for building their own houses and, once that project is done, we will find proper jobs for them. Kindly will you start looking for jobs for them from now on?

"Or can you find out who owns the land they have their village on? If they own the property, fair enough. I want you to buy nearby land and turn it into farms, and I want them to be involved in agriculture and start harvesting rice and wheat."

Miriam continued, "You see, if we just give them money, they will finish doing a few things. However that is not the solution for their problems. We need to provide them with a platform where they can build their own destiny by their own will and hard work. I don't believe in just giving money once or twice to someone. My plan is to abolish their poverty."

Ayesha was truly impressed with her leadership qualities, confidence, judgments, and quick verdict.

Miriam took advantage of the weather and the convertible car, and swayed her hand outside while feeling the car's speed and the touch of the fresh air. Then she looked at the sun and felt he was smiling too, pleased for what she did. Her soul was at peace and she had never been so calm in her life as she felt today. Deep in her mind she considered how in such moments, you truly felt alive when you saw joy in some stranger's eyes because of you.

Giving was more pleasurable than receiving. If all the rich people start thinking the same way as Raja, no one in this world would ever be poor. Giving charity was not an option to sort out other people's problems; helping them to be surviving on their own was the only solution.

Miriam was glad. She was feeling languid and now all she wanted was to be in Raja's arms, so she could kiss him and pay her humble gratitude. Ayesha congratulated Miriam on her judgments and wise decisions. Miriam thanked her humbly.

When she arrived home, she was unable to find Raja anywhere. His car was parked outside. She thought that perhaps he might be down in the cave. She looked in the room then went down. He was there standing in the same position, and one by one the snakes came to him, touching his feet then making way for others.

Miriam took off her shoes and again walked between the snakes, as she felt strong connections with them and they did with her. She checked the supply of milk, rats and frogs. Everything was in order. She stood quietly next to Raja, wanting nothing more than to be in his presence.

Raja held her hand then kissed her. They started returning to the room.

With a smile, he asked her, "So, are you happy today?" Miriam replied, "Yes, my love, so very much, my darling, and it's only because of you. You have changed my life. Sometimes I wonder what good I have done in my life that Allah selected me and became so kind by blessing me with your love. I have no words to say how immensely thankful I am to you."

He hugged her back and, while staring into her eyes, told her "You never need to thank me, please remember that. Just love me as madly as I love you. My job is to care, love and respect you as long as I'm alive in this world, and even if I die, my spirit will be with you and will continue to love you until you join me.

"I have something for you." He held her hand, leading her toward the back of the mansion. As they came out, he looked at the swimming pool and told Miriam, "I think now is the time you should start taking swimming lessons with Ayesha. Also, I will instruct her to start your classes for martial arts and use of weapons, not because I want you to kill people." With a smile he continued, "Because I want you know how to protect yourself."

She nodded and they entered at the back of the mansion, walking through the lush green lawn and viewing the huge forest. Where was the end of the forest? However she never asked him.

He was taking her to his stable, where he owned more than ten pedigree horses. From a distance she viewed the headman, who stood holding a beautiful black horse.

Raja held her hand tightly and told her, "I have bought a horse for you and if you want him to be your devoted pal, all you have to do is feed him an apple every day.

"Horses are extremely faithful animals and they will love you until their death. He is one of the most expensive breeds in the world. You can name him whatever you like. All the horses are my pals, but the one I have named Champ, is very close to my heart. We understand each other on a different level."

"I never rode a horse before." Miriam expressed her concern.

I know about that, Jung will train you. He is known as the horse whisperer and I have taken his test plenty of times and all the horses I bought were untamed. Jung speaks to them better than me.

When they came close they saw Jung was holding Miriam's new horse while keeping his eyes low and his head lowered, in a sign of respect.

He wished both of them time and greeted Miriam, "Madam, you will really like this horse. He is one of the finest I have ever encountered." From his pocket, Jung gave an apple to Miriam and told her, "Please, kindly feed him this apple so he knows his soul belongs to you."

The black horse was truly a beautiful creature but he was uncomfortable in Raja's presence and acted as if he was scared. Raja went close, whispered something in his ears, and the horse immediately bent his head as if he was bowing in front of Raja.

Miriam took advantage of the horse's calmness and offered him an apple. He took the apple and came a bit closer to Miriam.

Jung requested, "Madam, kindly whisper his name in his ear, whatever you have selected for him and introduce yourself by telling him your name."

Miriam whispered in horse ear, "Son is what I name you and from now on I'm your mother, and my name is Miriam."

She named him 'Son' and the horse acted as if he loved the introduction.

Miriam said, "Jung, when will you start my training?"

"Madam, anytime tomorrow, just send me a message and I will bring Son right in front of the gate and you can start right away."

Jung seemed as if he knew horses better than humans. Miriam was amazed that the staff was a team of such talented people.

Miriam said, "Thank you, my darling, for such a beautiful gift." She kissed Raja passionately. "I thought Ayesha would teach me horse riding?"

"She will be with you during the whole process, though in presence of Jung no horse goes out of control. If I'm not with you, I can't take any chances with you. The only purpose I have in life is being with you. Otherwise who would want to live forever?" Raja said.

Miriam hugged him and kissed him passionately. "I want to love you like no woman has ever loved a man before. My purpose is just to serve you and worship you as my lord. My love, you are my whole world, my best friend, family and life. My time was up and I was all set to meet my Allah and now sometimes I wonder maybe I'm dead and I'm in Heaven with you and this is my afterlife. The meaning of Heaven is love, peace, and happiness. In your arms I feel complete and peaceful. Sometimes I wonder in which way I should say thank you to you."

Raja saw her tear drop, rolling down her cheek; he caught the drop with his finger.

While staring at the drop, he told her, "I can see rain of fire falling from the sky but only thing I never want to see is your tears.

My job is to keep you happy. Your tears are enormously precious for me and I just beg you, kindly never cry again."

Raja kissed her forehead and, while looking deep into her eyes, told her, "This is just the beginning of the adventure of our love story, which is yet to unfold. My love, within two months we are leaving for the world trip and first we're going to England. Your passport will be ready and all the relevant requirements are already taken care of. Spend some extra hours with Ayesha. Practice and focus on spoken English and gain control on horse riding. We will be visiting some deep, dark places in the world where only horses would take us. Just to inform you, one evening we will have dinner with the royals. By this I mean we will be dining with the Queen and her royal family in their palace."

CHAPTER 6
"XUSIS"

One more thing before we travel, I want to marry you." He was on his knees with a ring in his hand. "Will you give me the honor of being my wife?"

Miriam said, "Yes, my life and my love!" Then she hugged and kissed him.

Raja continued, "I know you are Muslim and we can get married as per your tradition. For me, I follow Christianity and the Lord Jesus Christ. However I believe in all religions which teach peace, love and humanity, as those are the true messages of God."

He was on his knees with an eight-carat, Asscher-cut red diamond ring in his hand. Miriam was dancing and prancing with such happiness, all the while saying, "Yes, yes". She kissed and hugged him. He was one of those men who would rarely smile. So whenever she saw his beautiful smile, her day became more beautiful.

Seeing him smile, and making him happy, was the main purpose of her life because he was a serious guy and was always lost somewhere deep in his thoughts and worries. Today she could clearly feel that he was happy, relaxed and in peace.

Then he asked her to sit on his lap. He brought her face closer to his while staring deep into her eyes. "You know I was not able to sleep the whole night because I truly was afraid to propose you. I was a beast before and I still can be a beast anytime I want. I was thinking how could a human love me and marry me? I wanted to marry you the very next day when I brought you home. The reason I delayed is I believe when two people love each other they should spend time together. Apart from knowing their good sides, each should be aware of ugly side too, and when they feel they can't live without each other, that's when they should marry each other. I wanted you to feel no pressure and all I want is for you to be happy and feel my passion of loving you."

Miriam said, "You met me in human form. I really don't care about your past because I have seen myriad humans in my life and, trust me, if I share their tales with you I know even the beast in you would be ashamed of the human race.

"I have never seen anyone so kind-hearted as you are, and I know my, Allah really does love me, because He blessed me with your presence and He gave me a new life. It all seems like a fairy tale. What more can a human ask for? You can be whoever you want to be because for me, you are my whole world and my whole life."

Raja said, "Thank you, my love. I promise you I will not only love you madly, I will make sure every single day of your life you feel like you are worshiped by me, and we both will enjoy life to the extreme."

"By the way, how is it that you never asked me to show you my true form, which is the snake in me? For when you first saw me, it was a very long time ago when you were a child. Are you interested to meet him again?" He smiled.

Miriam said, "Yes, and I would love to pet you with care and love and with an honest smile."

Raja told her, "Today when we go down into the cave, you will view something different. Maybe it will be a bit scary for you, but I have a reason why I want you to be aware of it."

"I have to give you complete details about a few of the snakes, how useful they can be and what kind of magical powers they have in them. The truth is no one in this world knows exactly the right quantities of our species. Some say there are like two thousand and seven hundred, and some say there are more than three-thousand total species of snakes in this world.

"The actual figure is more than six thousand two hundred, however now they are only two-thousand-nine-hundred left in this world. Snakes have been around from a hundred and twelve-million years. Most of the rare species have been killed by humans because of their greed."

While he shared this, she felt his sadness.

Miriam said, "My dearest love, please don't be sad, I wish and pray that every living creature should be loved and respected in full glory. It is hard to explain why people became so greedy. I want to understand every detail you think I should know about how to help and save them. You know how much I love to spend time with you, as the knowledge and wisdom I gain from you is beyond imagination. I agree, Ayesha is a great teacher, yet what you know, even she does not know these details. I love that you always teach me about humanity and you are always concerned about the development of humans, and on the contrary, whenever they see a snake, they instantly want to kill the poor creature."

Raja replied, "You know most of the world doesn't know that tobacco acts as a poison to snakes; just like cyanide works on humans; how those who were researching snakes killed them in Central Asia, keeping Naswar in any snake's mouth, he would die within minutes.

"Naswar is similar to dipping tobacco or snus. Tobacco is extremely dangerous. It is hard to imagine that humans use it for style or fashion and later they are addicted and gain nothing except serious diseases. Humans keep a pinch of Naswar next to the gum and they keep it for some time and once its tasteless they throw it out just like chewing gum.

"I want to introduce you to some of hidden powers few snakes hold. For you, they are always ready to give their life and it is not only because you are going to be my wife. The fact is, snakes are always ready to sacrifice their lives for mankind because sometimes only their venom can cure millions of chronic diseases.

"A snake will never bite a human without any reason. They only bite when they are left with no choice. This whole concept that the snake is the Devil is wrong. That creature, the devil that came as a reptile that was in the Garden of Eden, was more like a Komodo dragon and much larger in size.

"The Devil selected his body, and in return, God punished the lizard to crawl all his life on his stomach; hence that is also what the snakes are going through now. The Devil took complete advantage of the situation and stayed inside the snake, and could not imagine why God would create a bite of death, when God had already informed man about the snake's destiny, saying that man would smash the head of the snake and the snake will bite on the ankle of man. Still, he never clearly mentioned that the bite would bring death. The poison is from the Devil, because he made his own addition to the snake. The truth is, God has the ability and he blessed the snake, because there is no other animal on the planet that can be as useful to mankind as the snake."

Raja continued, "Seven-hundred years ago, one of the few species that were so rare are now extinct from the world. On the north of the Himalayan mountains was a hidden cave, and once you entered that cave it took you to a magical forest. In the beauty of that forest were infinitesimal effulgent plants.

"The light was so attractive that whoever watched it was mesmerized by its elegance and creation of God. However, instead of leaving the plants where they belonged, they just wanted to pull them out by their roots. As they were not aware that below the root lived a small snake called xusis, he sat on the roots and because of xusis the light spreads.

"Since ancient epochs, plenty of kings sent the best of their teams of people to find that glowing plant, but none of them ever returned.

"There was this one extremely greedy and cruel king from Eastern Europe, his name was Augustus the Second. He wanted to rule the whole world and for that reason, he had a team of sorcerers who could help him to find the treasures of the world.

"The head sorcerer was Ivan Qulin and he was aware of the powers of that plant. Somehow, he gave the wrong description to the king and told him that once you have that plant in your one hand and with other hand you could turn any metal into gold. Even if it's a mountain of metal your one touch will turn it into pure gold. His statement was intrinsically wrong instead the actual power was that once you tasted that plant with your tongue, you could become immortal.

"The sorcerer's plan was to get hold of the plant, kill the king and finally become the king himself in order to control the whole world. Ivan Qulin with his magical powers was able to find the hidden forest and made the greedy king send his finest team.

"The king selected a group of five people for the most dangerous quest of their lives, to obtain the plants. The team was made up of the top bravest, wisest and most devoted five knights who had years of experience in adventure traveling.

"After a crucial journey and facings various hazards, the group of knights managed to reach the magical forest following the map that was provided by the sorcerer. When the leader tried to pull the plant from the ground, he felt as if something had suddenly fled into the sky.

"When he moved his head to understand what it was, the small snake plummeted and landed right on his forehead. Bit him and within a jiffy he was dead. The same thing happened with the other four knights. One infinitesimal xusis they were not able to catch or kill, because it was faster than light.

"There is only one way to catch that snake. First, you would need to wear a damp batiste turban on the top of your head. Secondly, you must keep a mud pot on top of your turban so the turban will absorb the heat. The mud pot should be filled with burning coals. Hence, when xusis attacks, he would land with such a speed that the poor snake would bury himself deep in the burning coals. There is no other way you can ever get hold of that plant.

The whole world wants to live in opulence, but what they don't understand is that life itself is ephemeral, and if they only walk the right path, in the next life they will be blessed with whatever they wished in this world."

Raja told Miriam, "There are other sources to make gold and I will teach you how to make gold and silver. First, you will be taught the technique of making pure silver. It's very easy to make and I will tell you the technique and ingredients used in making silver. When you were down in the cave, you saw a couple of white cobras.

"There are two rare herbs that I have grown farther down in the cave below and all you need is five leaves of each of those herbs and one white cobra. Get a massive pot and pour some pure milk, as much as you like. Once the milk is warm, kill the cobra by placing a pinch of Naswar in his mouth.

"You can't kill the snake in any other form because hitting him will damage the skull and his venom would then leak. Drop the ten leaves and the snake in the milk and within twenty-four hours it will turn into pure silver."

Miriam asked, "Why, my love, why do you tell me all this? I really don't need anything; you know very well my life and world are only you, my dear."

Raja said, "My love, as I told you learn as much as you can, because you never know what tomorrow holds. Even I don't know what will happen tomorrow, for that is something only God knows. We should be prepared for anything and all types of circumstances. Only one thing will help us survive and that is our knowledge."

Then he held her hand and told her, "Let's go down and let me educate you more about snakes. She followed him toward the cave.

He whispered in her ear; "Listen, today I will change shape. Are you fine with that? If you are scared, I will stay in human shape or go alone. Once a month I have to change shape and be who I really am in order to make my existence felt among my followers, because I am still their king."

Miriam held his hand tightly and replied, "My love, you do what you have to do, because from me all you will get is love and support until my very last breath."

As they entered the cave, he stood at the same spot and within a few seconds his clothes started slipping down and he started turning into a huge, jet-black cobra. She stood behind and observed the whole process.

The cobra started to rise until he stood on the edge of his tail. This was impressive and totally new for her. She had seen many snake charmers displaying cobras, but not a single one of those cobras could stand on the edge of its tail and remain totally straight.

He was more than twenty-two feet tall. Among all the snakes his majesty, grace and glory could easily be felt. He truly was the king of snakes, as his presence could be sensed from miles away.

What he did was somehow intimidating for her. Raja bit another snake that was quite large as well. Within a few minutes that snake was somnolent. Then Raja started devouring the whole snake. She held her breath, as she was really frightened.

She felt bad for the other snake. Although when she looked at all the other snakes, they all seemed relaxed and calm, as if nothing had even happened.

She wondered, "How could Raja do such a monstrous act and hurt another snake? Since he was their king, how could he do such a horrible thing?" Within a few minutes, Raja' had swallowed the other snake and was back on his tail again.

Then she saw a large snake making his way toward Raja. Something was wrong with that snake's head. When he came closer, she was surprised to see that on top of his head was another tiny snake that was carrying a golden pebble in his mouth.

All the snakes were making their way toward this pair, because they seemed like important carriers with a special gift or message for Raja.

As they drew closer to him, the tiny snake dropped the gold pebble right near Raja's tail. He was still standing tall and straight, on the edge of his tail, and as swiftly as they had approached Raja, in the same speed they retreated and vanished.

On this trip, Miriam took a detailed look at the cave. There were few entrances, but she was not able to see the end of the cave. One thing was for sure, this cave was deep and seemed to connect with a different world, quite far away.

She was waiting for him to transform himself back into human shape.

She wanted to go up with him to her room, as it was the first time she felt a little frightened by this strange world. The huge king cobra that was standing on his tail was not her love, but was instead, a big cannibal cobra. It was tough for her to imagine him so brutal, cold hearted and evil.

She couldn't keep herself from asking the same question over and over again. Was he the same man who had been so kind hearted and the most loving soul she had ever met in her whole life? In two weeks she would be married to him, and for the very first in her mind she had million of questions.

The first thought was what if she got pregnant? What species would her child be, a beast or human?

Would her child ever grow older or stay the same age for rest of his life?

The black mercury he had inserted into her mouth to make her immortal would she also turn into Queen cobra after completing her hundred years as immortal?

If he could kill and eat a snake as being king cobra, would he be a human cannibal when he is in human form?

Love could make anyone blind. What had she done? She must have made her Allah angry. At her age, she was supposed to pray and be ready for her next journey. What had she accepted? Was she living in sin and favoring the Devil? She was so confused.

Raja was almost done with his routine visit and was back in human shape. After dressing, he picked up the gold pebble and he held her hand, they both went back into their bed room.

He took her to the balcony and they both sat quietly for a while. Then, while looking deep into her eyes, he spoke. "I know you have seen something which you shouldn't have. I do know this, you must be having thousands of questions that you need answers for. You have never felt this frightened being with me, and above all, for the very first time you have doubts about our relationship. Am I right?"

CHAPTER 7

"CONFIDE"

Miriam was quiet for a short moment with her downcast eyes. All of a sudden things had become difficult for her.

However, she loved the man, and love was blind. The way he took care of her, loved and respected her, no one had ever done that before.

She asked him, while trying to sound reasonable, "Why did you eat the other snake? He was alive and was one of your followers?"

Raja gently replied; "Listen, my love, in two weeks we are going to get married. I wanted to share my reality to you, whatever or whoever I am; this is my truth and my identity. I could have pretended I was just a normal human being and never showed you this side of me. But the truth is, I was a beast before and that is my honest reality. Even when I try my best it's not within my powers to take my reality out of my head. On the other hand, when two people fall in love, confiding the soul is more important than getting naked in front of each. I wanted to bare my soul to you in order for you to know the real me.

"I know humans are different and they can easily hide things, whenever they want. It's not easy for me to cheat you in any shape or form. I have my own way of loving you; maybe it's far too intense or maybe I'm insane. Love is all about honesty and truth. If a man doesn't share his heart openly with the woman he is with, then she is not the one he truly loves.

"King cobras are cannibals and they do eat snakes, and so did I in front of you. Some of the species are specially born for this reason. Their sole purpose for existence is to be food for us.

"I know you were trying to see the reaction of all the snakes in the cave. Not a single one protested or tried to save that snake. As you have noticed, if some of the snakes were giant they could eat me, but they don't because they know it's an act of nature. Those gigantic snakes are not cannibals. They can eat a whole cow or sheep but they will never eat another snake. It's not king cobras' fault. God made them in such a way and he himself selects food for all the living creatures.

"Everyone in this strange world has their own appetite. Different people have different views. Some think what you eat represents your personality and who you truly are. Some think enjoying life is to eat well and for them life is all about food. Some just live for eating, and a few understand life is not about eating. Life is much more than that. However, what to do with the time we are alive we have to eat, and survive and that is exactly what I did. We all have favorite foods and my predilection happens to be various types of snakes as being king cobra.

"Humans eat cows, goats, sheep, chickens, and fish. Don't you think as being humans they should not kill animals and eat them? Anything a human does, that is okay, but when in nature a lion kills a zebra, everyone feels sad for zebra. They don't understand God made zebras for lions and it is one of the items on their menu.

"The things rich and famous do are indefinable. If we expose one percent of the people whom everyone idolize, they will hate those idols more than Devil himself.

"One day I will take you to the world's most expensive chain of restaurant, located in every major city in the world. However, to own a membership they require at least one million rupees along with personal details from you.

"The specialty of the menu is human flesh.

"The restaurants are located in private mansions and the guests are picked up from their desired or given locations. They are blind folded until they finally reach the mansion. The total number of members is not more than ten. You will be surprised to find the world's most famous people in that restaurant; those elite people you often had seen on television, newspaper or cover of the influential magazines.

"Then you are taken in the one section of the kitchen, where they keep the live stock and what you're about to eat. Mostly it's one young girl and boy completely naked. You are delicately offered a tiny notepad where you can write the part of their body you would like to eat. The purpose of showing your live stock is simple, that you will be eating fresh meat right after killing them.

"Rich people will not welcome you in their circle unless you become like one of them. Which simply means you have to become extremely selfish, do things you don't like to do but for sake of fashion. The powerful elites who rule the world only show the commoners what they can easily absorb. Their secrets are beyond imagination not only for the world but for the universe.

"You must be thinking, who are those people whom they eat?

"More than millions of people go missing every year and they are never found or seen again. They are mostly used to pleasure other humans, and some are given on purpose by the world governments to various alien races.

"The worst part is even those who claim to be vegetarians are members of such restaurants, as they all want to rub shoulders with the rulers of the world and concurrently believe eating human flesh would make them spiritually strong.

"Even today there are many isolated villages in jungles where various types of tribes reside. They wait for strangers to enter their territories so they can hunt and eat them. Some prefer to cook humans and some eat them raw. It really is a strange and weird world out there. Once you start traveling and understand the cults, cultures and various religious acts, it will help you to understand the truth about human nature. Animals just follow their natural instincts, and there are no rules or regulations in the wild. You will be fine and have more tolerance toward such things.

"A few men in South East Asia even drink a live snake's raw blood just to gain sexual powers. They drink the blood as if they are enjoying holy water.

"In Europe there are a few very famous and expensive restaurants where they serve live animals such as black bear cub not more than six-months old. The table is designed in such a way that the whole body of the cub is buried inside the metal table from the neck down and only his head is visible.

"The cub watches the sophisticated, well-dressed humans, expecting kindness and mercy from them. He has no idea that they turn out to be his worst nightmare, as those human-looking beasts have paid a sizable amount of money for him. The waiter serves hammers and once the cub is properly locked in the table, they start beating his head with hammers.

"The cub screams tumultuously and in his own language begs them to stop because the pain is so unbearable for him. They are not the least bothered by his screams and pain, and keep hitting the poor creature on his brain, until the cub is dead.

"Then the waiter will come back and like a professional surgeon will start cutting his scalp 'til the brain of the cub is visible. Then those sophisticated rich people will start eating raw bear brain, as if they are enjoying a delicious pudding.

"As for such humans, they believe eating sacred animal brains will endow them with a special kind of wisdom and they will be closer to God.

"In the Far East they eat live octopus, fishes and shrimp; you have no idea what kind of crazy world you are living in.

"Do you think humans should do that?

He looked at Miriam's face and could easily understand from her reaction that she could throw up at anytime. As for her, this all was awfully disgusting and unbelievable.

"I know what I'm telling is making you feel sick, but please, you need to understand the realities of the humans and the world. Animals don't have intelligence and are not educated. They don't wear clothes or have the ability to act sensibly. They don't even have manners on who to sleep with; they have no concept of mother or sister. That is why they are called animals.

"Human beings have all the wisdom, still when it comes to the most dangerous beast among all living creatures, it is the human!

"I don't want to quarrel or argue with you. All I wanted to do was to help you to understand that in any relationship we think should be based on love, it should start with total honesty, and that is what I have shared with you. We all do have our dark sides, some so dark that we can't even share with our shadow, thinking that if our shadow will came to know such realities about us, it would vanish as if he never existed.

"I do have possession of some very dark secrets, however I can never hide a single thing from you, because I don't only love you; I feel you are part of me and are my own life.

"All I needed to do was to share this part of me with you. There is nothing I want to hide from you. I was a king cobra before. I lived a hundred years in that shape. How can I forget that, please tell me?

"I believe in love and you know I love you madly. In this whole world, my life and own true happiness I found in you.

"What can I do with treasures, palaces, mansions, castles, chateaus or jewels alone? For me, they are just material things.

"I was a snake before and always stayed on guard protecting those world's treasures. Although I still slept in small, mud holes in the earth.

"For centuries I waited to be with you, to find the one true soul I can call my own in this world, that one soul that I can share the good, bad or evil in me and still be your only love and you love me just the way I am.

"I confided the truth about my other side and I feel light and relaxed, for me love is above all this and sometimes it's extremely hard for me to tell you how passionately I love you!

"I have lived more life as a human than as a snake, so please try to understand that I feel emotions and I do have strong feelings about relationships, and I am truly so happy about starting my own family with you.

"You are also concerned what will happen if you get pregnant, so my love the answer is simple.

"One thing you need to know about me is I studied every minute detail about us being together positive or negative facts. When it comes to you, family and our love, you will find my romance simply antediluvian.

"As for your question; I make love with you as a human and you will bear a human child.

"You're concerned that the child may never grow and stay an infant for rest of his immortal life. Let me bring to your attention some serious facts. The child will grow 'til the age of thirty years.

"His age will be on hold after that period. He will never become thirty-one or even one day older than thirty. You also may worry sometimes that you accepted a gift of a new life from me and that it may be against your religion or Allah.

"So, my love, please understand one very simple thing. Whatever powers I have, God has blessed me with them. He created me, selected this life for me and he guided me toward you. He truly was the one who developed your love in my heart.

"I was a king cobra when I first saw you when you were just a small child. The way you saved my life I only prayed to God and wished to bless me with a chance so I can pay you my humble gratitude.

"You also may wonder whether I would start eating people. Why would I do that? When God blessed me and gave me a chance to become a human, I only studied to be a better man and do things that help other humans.

"I have studied all religions and I have tried to extract the best points from each one of them. I want to support the world and I try my best to make it a better place. I never ever want to hurt a single human, as human life is most dear to God.

"Still, my love, you are free to make a choice. If you have changed your mind about being with me in this house, I will show you a third level of the cave which contains treasures worth trillion of rupees. Treasures you can use for the rest of your life.

"Apart from this mansion, I have a few more manors, lands including forests and mountains, number of palaces in India, few castles in England and Europe, some gold and diamond mines in Africa, a couple of ships and several planes all around the world.

"All are in your name and I had already bequeathed whatever I own in visible shape as my lawyer has already transferred them into your name. Also, the two chateaus in south of France are for you.

"I promise you I will vanish from your life if this is what you wish, as I never existed. You can marry whomever you like because all I want is your happiness.

"For the rest of your life, never think that by leaving this fortune, I did some favor to you. All of this belongs to you, as you deserve the best and you know how to help others, I want nothing in return from you I just want you to be safe and blissful.

"I know every second my life without you would be a painful punishment. I can't even pray to die because I'm immortal. I will live with my curse and my gift, which is called life."

Before he said another word, Miriam briskly got on her knees and started kissing him. "You gave me this life and it is your responsibility now to take care of me. You are my man and if you leave, I will end my life that very second. I don't need anything else. I have no need of palaces or jewels.

"If you transfer me back into the old me, I will still be happy living back in my own mud house. That would be fine with me. However, the truth is all I want is for you to be with me. You can stay home and I will work and take care of you as long as I am alive.

"Never think I am ungrateful for what you did. Even if you had done nothing for me, I would still love you, because you were born to be with me, as I was born to love you, serve you, care for you and respect you as my own man and lord.

"I'm sorry if I hurt you in any manner, it was never my intention. I just got scared, please do try and understand that I am just an ordinary human and it was something very strange and new for me.

"I respect you more and love you in so many ways now, because of the manner in which you explained the details to me. You did confide in me and that is simply the bravest act I have ever seen from a man.

"You have never asked me about my previous life with my husband Alam and how he loved me. However, I feel like sharing it with you today. Those things which have always stayed in my heart and I have never discussed with anyone before.

"Alam's proposal was accepted by my parents without my consideration or even asking me. I was married to him but Alam was in love with his neighbor's daughter and all he ever wanted was to be with her. However, the neighbors were richer farmers than Alam's parents and they refused his proposal.

"The girl was very beautiful, but she got married to someone from the city and was gone. Alam, through giving hints shared his story with me.

"I always felt that something was missing in his life and he seemed disturbed most of the time. But whenever I tried to ask him he always changed the topic.

"Now I see you loving me, and I feel your smile and can read your eyes, what you want and how you want. I can understand the true meaning of being in love with someone with heart, mind and soul.

"Alam, my husband, was madly in love with the girl he wanted to marry and she remained in his system like a virus, which ate him alive day by day.

"Sometimes I used to think he was a dead man walking, as if he was alive yet his soul was dead. His attitude was completely discombobulated, as though he didn't want to live in this world; yet was stuck to carry on with his life with us.

"He was responsible, decent, and a nice husband to me. He never misbehaved, argued, or fought. Also he was a great father and with the children his love was phenomenal. He lived for them and I always saw the children were mad about him.

"Yet deep down Alam was a very lonely man. I never met the girl but I was really interested in speaking with her to know if she was as madly in love with him as he was with her.

"If you don't manage to be with the person you love the most, it is better to stay single rather than getting married to someone who you just live with as you not only screw up your own life, but the life of the person you marry.

"As far as my love was concerned, Alam was the only man I ever loved in my whole life because he was my husband and life partner. I came to know what real love is only after meeting you.

"Now I understand how people can live with one another and do endless compromises in relationships that not only messes up our lives, but at the same time our souls are lost too. These people are the victim of inferiority complex and feel that something is wrong with them.

"I lived all my life with that strange confusion and being in fear that perhaps I was not beautiful, my voice or body was not good enough to please my husband."

Miriam was in tears as she shared her heart with him. He held her close, and kissed and hugged her passionately.

It was a strange silence between them. But sometimes in silence, there were millions of unspoken words that people could exchange. That was exactly what was happening between those two very unique souls who were madly in love with each other.

Miriam continued, "I'm so very thankful to you for the way you made me understand complicated things in such an elegant and easy manner.

"I totally understand your approach for any relationship it is so much better to know souls and not just minds or bodies. I totally felt your soul. You, my only true love, can be the wildest animal in this entire universe and you can do whatever you feel is right.

"I have devoted myself to being with you, Mr. Raja, and all I know is, I truly love you and even if you say that I may die today, I would not think twice and would be ready to humbly give my life. Let's get married and start a beautiful life, just the two of us in our very own world.

"So tell me," she said with a smile to change the mood. "Will I always remain eighteen years old as long as I live in this world?"

Raja was one of those breed of men who rarely laughed.

However, her question brought a smile to his handsome face and when he smiled, she noticed his eyes shone with exuberance. He was an extremely attractive man. Mostly she felt he was the quintessential tough guy and minding his own business. Her heart always sensed his feelings were strong for her.

Miriam was realizing her aptitude of learning, perceptivities, and her command on various issues.

"My love," he said with a smile, "well now you are eighteen and I can't do anything to change that, unless you are not happy being eighteen." In an impish way he added, "It was not my wish, but yours."

"You never gave me a chance to speak. You just kissed me and there I was a brand new girl," Miriam replied with a smile.

CHAPTER 8

"LOPTI"

Raja took the golden pebble from his pocket and gave it to Miriam. She held it in her hand. The tiny pebble was extremely heavy and she viewed it from each side.

"That pair of snakes you saw today are part of a famous legend. Whoever sees this pair of snakes is very lucky, as they bring nothing but luck to the person who spots them.

"The name of this pair is Taruni. Now in this present time there are only twenty Tarunis left. They are always together. If you think the bigger snake was dangerous and weird looking, wait until you get the details of the tiny one. The tiny one is the new version of a dragon. I know I never shared with you about the species of dragons, but when we will be in Europe, it's a whole new chapter I need to teach you, while showing you some of their caves which still do exist but are invisible to human eyes. A little introduction of dragons they were giant flying lizards with wings and their power consists of spitting fire on a great scale.

"The tiny Taruni does have such power. It can throw huge fire from his tiny mouth and up until today the whole world is trying to figure out how he does that. I'm the only one who knows the details. How is it possible was that massive flames come out of such a tiny snake and why is he even more dangerous than the dragon?

"It is because his fire contains a powerful substance that just a tiny spark will ignite any living or dead material in a second. The poisonous fires he generates with this small golden pebble only a Taruni knows the art of handling and keep the pebble in its stomach. The Taruni contains a tiny spark and holds extreme poison in his minute fangs. However, when he holds the golden pebble inside his body the mixture he creates is deadly.

"Tarunis are the guardians of the golden pebble and, as I mentioned to you earlier, this is not an ordinary golden pebble. Just consider this gift above all that you have received so far. With this pebble, you have my life in your hands, and it is much stronger than the gift of youth and immortality I bestowed upon you.

"All I need is your full attention, as I have to prepare your mind and you need to know the powers, secrets and the true value of this pebble. It's worth far more than both our lives, as it's the tool which can open the gates of Hell if it gets in the wrong hands; it had been in many evil hands before and how they misused it, I will share with you. First let me tell you what this gold pebble is.

"I know Ayesha taught you about telepathy and I imagine with the right knowledge and training in telepathy, you can enter the mind of any person and read their thoughts. Imagine how you would feel if just by saying a small code word you could enter into the mind of every living creature in the entire universe.

"With this golden pebble, you can enter into the mind of any living creature, whether it's an animal, plant, human, fish or birds, anything which breathes and has life. With this golden pebble you can rule the whole universe. Once you capture the minds of living souls, they are your slaves and will do whatever you command them. The reason it's very dangerous is because if you control their minds and then forget about them, they will be like zombies, as life stays in them but they are not aware where they are and who they are. They will not eat, drink and will just be still while you command their frozen minds.

"All you need to do is wear the golden pebble as a pendant on your neck or on your arm. Cover it with a crocodile leather pouch to hide the golden pebble inside. The power behind this pebble starts the moment it is in the leather pouch and as soon as the pouch touches your skin. I will tell you the code that you have to recite and once you do that, the pebble will dissolve deep into your skin and will vanish from the pouch. However, the pouch should remain where you wore it for the time and in case someone steals or you misplace your pouch, you should have a few extra that are the same.

"You need to take care of this pebble and guard it with your life. Even if we lose everything, we would still survive. This pebble is worth more than the treasures of the whole world.

"From now own it's your protector and you will protect the pebble. It will follow all your commands, but you need to be very careful what you wish for, and especially if you have to give them very calculated and reasonable commands. It will not only hurt others but if you give the wrong command; you can hurt yourself as well.

"Even if you're standing on one side and on the other side there is an army to fight with you, you are untouchable.

"The name of this golden pebble is Lopti. When you want to use Lopti, you have to say these three words, 'Ya Pa Tok'. See now I said these three words. Just keep watching Lopti and you will see the changes that will occur in it."

Lopti's size became smaller and it turned completely black.

Raja instructed Miriam, "Now carry it in your hand and feel the weight of Lopti."

Miriam's eyes widened as she spoke, "This is lighter than a feather now. How is that possible?"

Raja replied, "Those entities which reside in Lopti, when given the code, will leave their abode and wait for further command. Within a second, the entities will control the mind and he or she will be under your command.

"One important thing, you must promise me you will never take it off, make sure you never lose Lopti. If it comes into the wrong hands of a person with evil powers, he will get hold of the code with those evil powers. Trust me, the whole world will be in extreme danger.

"Imagine everyone wants to rule the world and if someone finds out about Lopti, with what lack of restraint they will use it. For most, power means control rather than being kind or caring. Imagine leaders, kings, dictators and every single person who seeks to rule the world, would go war to gain such a powerful tool.

"You could make the whole world your slave. Not only humans, but every living thing in this world would be controlled by you. It's the most powerful mind controller and protector that ever existed on earth."

Miriam was scared while holding Lopti and she asked him, "Where does Lopti come from? How come such a tiny pebble is packed with enormous powers? What's inside this pebble that it changes color and becomes so light weight with a code?"

"There are many myths about Lopti as it's the only one in this world. Some say Lopti was the jewel of Medusa, while a few say it came out of a dragon heart. Well the truth is Lopti was fed to our ancestor snake in Heaven by the Devil.

"He later controlled the minds of Adam and Eve to commit the sin. When they both committed the sin, God became angry and, along with them, the same snake was thrown out of Heaven and with it Lopti which was inside the snake.

"The snake was feeling remorse as he understood he had been played by the Devil. Heavy with guilt, Lopti was hidden for myriad years. From that snake it was handed over to Tarunis. They were assigned by the king cobra to protect and guard Lopti 'til the end of the time.

"After the Tarunis the king cobra took the responsibility on his shoulders and became the protector of Lopti.

When the first king cobra on earth transformed into human form, he was guarding Lopti and he fell in love with a girl name Rsi and he share the secrets and powers of Lopti with her.

"Rsi's mind was controlled by the Devil and somehow she managed to kill the king cobra and became the most powerful queen and ruled the world. She fell in love with Vash, the bravest and strongest man in her nation, and shared the knowledge of Lopti with him. Later, he killed her and became the ruler himself.

"Love is a beautiful feeling. However it can be very dangerous as well. The problem is that when you love someone, you trust that person with your heart and believe he or she will never betray you. Well, the truth is, my love, expect the unexpected. They will not only betray you, they will tear your heart into millions of pieces and for the rest of your life, you will be busy gathering those pieces.

"Many Tarunis were killed by humans. They always found a way to kill them. Some were guided by witches, some used the help of sorcerers and a few even went too far and gained power by sacrificing people and later controlling their spirits.

"First Lopti went into the hands of a fake prophet who was not able to control Lopti, and he went insane for a few years and even tried to kill himself. He fabricated a cult religion and surprised the whole world. The world of snakes is set on the mission to keep the Lopti away from the hands of any evil humans.

"It is not easy at all, as the person starts gaining powers and control; his security becomes tighter and it's tough to reach him.

"However Tarunis is the only pair who can sense and find Lopti; together they both contain various powers. One of those powers is that they can smell Lopti; secondly, they both can be invisible;

and third, the bigger snakes do have wings and can fly. The reason the whole world has never seen them flying is because they are invisible in the sky. Fourth, they know one more code. On reciting that code, whoever possesses Lopti in his body, Lopti will leave the body and drop onto the ground and that is when they pick it and it vanishes from that person's surroundings. At the moment, the evil person feels his powers are not working, the first thing he will do is to search for Lopti. On not finding it, he will go crazy and will do everything in his power to gain it back.

"Lopti has been in the hands of many people. Some are fake prophets who cause humanity shame, and create cult religions in which people are forced to do things that are beyond imagination of an ordinary human mind. Several great conquerors, who wanted to rule the world. Some evil rulers, last but not the least the chancellor of Germany. This massacre of hatred resulted in the death of millions of innocent humans, all around the globe.

"He came from a humble back ground from a neighboring country. He was not even from Germany, so how was he able to control the minds of millions of Germans?

"They weren't only under his command, but at the same time worshipped him as a god. His order was like the word of God for them. The chancellor was a short, ordinary man. The world was not able to understand how he captured the minds of his nation and controlled them to kill without having any remorse. The world gave him many names. Some even compare him to the Beast that is clearly mentioned in the Bible in the Book of Revelation, chapter thirteen to eighteen: 'Here is wisdom. Let him who has understanding calculate the number of the beast, for the number is that of a man; and his number is six hundred and sixty-six'."

Miriam listened to every detail with complete concentration, the room was quiet as death. Only Raja's voice was heard, and deep in thought she experienced a flashback of what he was sharing with her. She asked him politely, "My love, would you be kind enough to give me more detail about the Antichrist, as I was not able to understand what was written about him in the Holy Bible?"

Raja kissed her forehead and was happy because she was involved in the whole process. Not only was her mind on the track with the learning; he felt her soul was deeply occupied too. He felt really proud of the woman and concurrently he raised his head and thanked God for his blessing in the shape of Miriam.

Raja, while looking at her with love, asked her, "Darling, you know who Jesus Christ is, right?"

Miriam in a respectful manner replied, "Yes, Jesus Christ (May peace be upon Him) was one of our beloved prophets. God blessed him with many gifts, including healing ill-people, curing the blind, and even raising the dead."

Raja said, "Perfect, so are you are already aware of the great things which Jesus Christ did for mankind, even suffering on the cross. So he could cleanse the sins of all the sinners in the world. Jesus only gave the message of love. On the other hand, antichrist means a beast in human shape, acting and pretending to be as innocent as a lamb. He will do everything against Jesus' teachings and will teach humans to kill, hate, lie, and commit all type of sins. He will have many followers, who are always willing to give their life for him as he promises them false Heaven."

Raja, while holding her hand continued, "With the passage of time, you will learn the truth. I don't want to rush you into these topics.

"The Christian world was sure the chancellor of Germany was the antichrist', as no human could be so brutal by killing so many people. Only five wise men were aware of Lopti and how the chancellor was misusing it. They knew he was possessed and the owner of Lopti. There had been several attempts to assassinate the chancellor, however every time he managed to cheat death.

"The day Tarunis managed to steal back Lopti from him, he started to lose his grip on his fame, his fear and his mind. He went berserk when he realized he had lost Lopti, and deep in his mind, he was sure it was a Russian counterpart who had stolen the pebble from him.

"Later, he spent his last days in a bunker and, in the same abode, he and his wife committed suicide.

"These powerful humans only knew one way of controlling human minds. Imagine if they had been aware that Lopti contained powers that work on every living creature in the universe, what hell they would have created. They would have made an army of ants to destroy the world. Of every man and woman who wanted to be powerful, very few use their strength to do good deeds, as mostly people just want to make other people their slaves. I'm not against gaining power; I'm against the misuse of it.

"Those people were not aware that Lopti had a limited wish circle and, if someone exceeded the use, Lopti vanished on its own from their presence. Myriad religious people were after Lopti to keep it hidden and safe from the evil humans.

"Though Satan worshipers always manage to find and get it under their control, once they learn how to use Lopti those who suffer are mostly ordinary people. They open the gates of Hell just to please themselves and gain more power and respect from nations. It's a nonstop war between snakes and humans.

"Now you're the only human who knows every single detail of Lopti and you will own it for the rest of your immortal life."

Miriam seemed scared and her eyes were stuck on Lopti as she was witnessing the Devil himself. Her face became completely pale and she grumbled to Raja, "Why do you want me to have it? I'm an ordinary human and I think you're the best guardian of such a dangerous and powerful object. Don't you agree?"

Raja replied, "Maybe you're right and I might be making the biggest mistake of my life as in the history of the first shape shifter king cobra was killed by his own love.

"He fell in love with the most beautiful girl of that time. Her name was Rsi and he trusted her blindly; the moment she gained complete control of Lopti powers, she controlled the mind of the king cobra and she killed him brutally.

"I want to take my chances as even if I want to die and I want it to be by you. Maybe you think I'm crazy or mad; I don't know why I just want the world to believe in love and I want to restore human respect in my kingdom of the snake's world.

"Just the way humans blame snakes that they are not trust worthy; because of Rsi no snake ever believed or trusted mankind.

"After the death of that first king cobra, no other shape shifters ever fell for a woman. They waited for their queen cobra, as they knew she would never ever betray them and that process was going on and on 'til I fell in love with you.

"It was the reason I took you into the cave and wanted you to see all the snakes, as I introduced you to them. I know you never noticed, but every time we went down the cave, there were different snakes, but to you as per their shapes and colors, the seemed like the same ones.

"However they are not. They keep traveling and giving chances to others and, when they come back to their abodes, they share my messages with others and then they travel. They all tried to convince me not to fall for you and, as they all were aware, I would tell you about Lopti and the details of its secret powers. And, one day or another would give you Lopti.

"They were concerned about my life because once you know how to use it, they all fear you will not only control my mind, but theirs as well and no one would be left behind to guard Lopti.

"I trust you and I love you as I told you for me love is true, solid and pure. The rest of whole world is just moving without any direction. Before you wear it, just say, these words ya push ma. These words will keep the Devil from entering your mind and taking control of your soul.

"I believe in you and know you will never ever misuse the powers and keep it safe, to use only when you feel your life is in danger. Then you know what to do. Always remember you are going to be my wife, and this journey has just started, and let me assure you it will be a thoroughly interesting one.

"I want you to be brave, and fear should not even come close to you. I want you to be such a strong-minded woman, without any fear." Raja smiled.

Miriam said, "I have no words to thank you. What have you not done for me? From a poor old woman you made me a young princess. I wish the whole world of men loved their women just the way you love me. Every day I pinch myself with the thought I'm dreaming and one day this beautiful magical world of yours will come to end, and I will be awakened in my mud house.

"The only fear I have for this dream world is, losing you. No Devil will come close to me. I want to keep Lopti with me not only because I want to show your followers that in the snake world they can trust mankind again, but I know will surely make them proud of your decision!

"However, the most encouraging fact I see from Lopti being in my control, I can keep you safe and protected." She smiled while saying those words, and he saw a new gleam in her eyes. He felt her strength and smile, which was full of confidence.

His heart was filled with joy as she was becoming independent and strong- minded soul each day. Raja was madly in love with her and against the will of every single snake in the world, he placed his life in her hands. In order to gain her trust, he kept his life on stake.

"Tomorrow I will request Ayesha to arrange me various types of crocodile leather amulets with black diamonds, emeralds and sapphires on top of the pouches and in metal. I prefer a platinum bracelet, amulet pouches sewed from three corners and one corner left open which I will sew myself after placing Lopti inside. Well, Lopti is sorted out. Now I think we should discuss something more personal and interesting about you." Miriam told him with an impish smile.

CHAPTER 9

"TIGER HUNT"

Miriam humbly said to Raja, "I always wanted to ask you something, but was hesitant and really shy, so finally I thought today's the day I should feel free to ask." Her eyes were shining and she had an impish smile on her lips. "So, you have been living one hundred-years as a snake and one thousand years as a human. How many females were in your life? Like how many snakes and how many were shape shifters or beautiful humans themselves?" Her mood was that of amusement, as today they were spending a moment all about sharing the truth.

He was sitting, relaxed and he acted as if he enjoyed her question. He held her hand and while bringing her closer to him he said, "what would you like to hear first; my life as a snake or a human?

"Before we go any further in our conversation, I want you to promise me you will never feel jealous about my past; this is intrinsically the biggest test in a relationship for respecting your loved one's past and especially when someone's sharing his heart with you. Respect that person and understand he's inviting you into his life by making you part of him.

"Look at me, I never asked you about how Alam was with you, and all your personal details. I respect your past and never asked such details; the reason is very simple.

"I believe in the future. The past simply contains some moments that happened in our lives; good, bad or ugly memories we have to live with them. The best part is when our past is haunting us we can meet a person who has an ability to heal our soul.

"It's much better to bury the past and move forward in life and enjoy the moments, which are blessed with the one who was simply born to be your soul mate.

"Now I need a promise from you that whatever you will hear today we are never going to discuss in our life again."

Raja moved his hand toward her to seal the deal in a handshake.

Miriam smiled and told him, "I promise you, my love, that with what you are going to share with me today, I will not be jealous. I promise I will never raise your past or discuss again what I will hear today.

"I love you and every second I spend with you it is true you have never discussed my past life or asked me a single question about my other relationships. I truly pray God will bless every girl in this world with a man like you. Please just share your soul with me. I really am interested to know more about you.

No matter what you share with me, I honestly promise I will just listen as your best friend rather than a lover as in that scenario I will not only understand you but will deeply sense your beautiful soul; rather than judging your character in any manner."

He was proud of the way Miriam was progressing with Ayesha as she started speaking more like an intellectual individual, one who contained the treasure of knowledge deep inside. Within a few months she had caught on very fast and was able to have conversations in five different languages and her accent and style were brilliant.

No one in this world would believe that just a few months back, she was not even able to write her own name. With the gift of youth he also broadened her mind, making it a hundred times faster to learn and absorb things compared to a normal human being.

Miriam was not only elegantly beautiful, but a very humble soul. The main reason that had him feeling even crazier about her was that she remained a simple girl with a heart of gold.

He was aware what money could do to a human mind, and how people totally forgot where they had come from and suddenly start considering themselves as gods, treating other people with hatred and making them feel small.

Miriam was the most kindhearted person he had ever met in his life. She continually asked the house staff about their families and, to his surprise, would tell everyone working for him to send their children to the best schools.

She would offer to pay for the fees and yearly expenses, in addition to their salaries. With the help of Ayesha she personally visited the best school in the city. For those who were alone with families in a different city, she would arrange for the best boarding school for their children.

Her approach was honest and wise, as she believed every child in this world deserved the best education. If all the rich people in this world would support ten children's education it would be a much better place.

Raja loved her gestures and now could relax as she took control of the house. Every member of the staff was in love with her, even to the point as Raja soon became aware of that they would even take a bullet for her.

Kindness has its own language, and any good deed that is done without any acknowledgement can make strong bounds between humans, regardless of wealth.

All Miriam's actions were visible, however she never wanted any one to thank her. The staff would keep coming and all she requested of them was to pray for a long life of Raja as their boss.

Miriam said, "You can start telling me about your life, and your love stories the way you want, I'm all ears today!"

"Well, let me start with my life as a snake. Perhaps I will take you from my birth and proper introduction to the life of a king cobra. After that, I will share my life and love stories with you. Will that be okay?"

"Yes, that would be perfect" Miriam lay next to him and kept her head on his chest listening to his anecdotes with complete concentration and excitement. When you love someone, all you want is more knowledge about that one person, so during your time together, you make sure you understand every little tidbit about your loved one.

Raja said, "Since from the beginning of the world, the total species of cobras were more than sixty-seven. However, as the human population started growing, other species started vanishing from the world.

"I have no idea why they are always after the biggest beast. There was one that ruled the sea and was known as Yucuk. It was a twelve-headed cobra and was seventy-five feet long. He was the protector and guardian of sea treasures. When humans started exploring the sea, the first thing they did was kill the poor creature.

"Then there was another six-headed cobra that was around thirty feet long. They killed him as well, and that poor fellow was not even venomous. He was the protector of hidden treasures buried under the many Hindu and various temples on earth.

"Well, as far as king cobra's lives are concerned, they are shy creatures and always try to be in their own world. Since you are going to marry one, you should know every detail about my kind.

The king cobras prefer a climate average temperature usually 95°F and are mostly found in Central and Southeast Asian rainforests. Our habitats are mostly on the edges of the forest and also near rivers and swampy areas.

"As you were concerned about sex, our sex lives starts after we are four years old and we only mate once a year. The female lays about twenty to fifty eggs. The hatching period is seventy to seventy-five days. When the eggs hatch our length starts from twelve to twenty-five inches and when fully grown, we can be from twelve to eighteen feet in length and adults weigh about twelve to twenty pounds (six to ten kilograms). Our fangs can grow to half an inch. We are born with the same amount of venom as an adult king cobra. The sad part is very few survive until adult age, as many predators such as certain birds, monitor lizards, crocodiles love to eat our young ones.

"Also I would like to share that we are the only snake kind that builds a nest and guards the eggs until they are hatched. As you have seen, we are carnivores and mainly eat other snakes, sometimes lizards, frogs and small mammals. Our average lifespan is only twenty years.

"Humans are our top predators, as are mongooses and sometimes even birds of prey. The worst are honey badgers. They don't only kill snakes; they have a strong appetite for snakes. And once a snake is caught, he will start eating it from the head. They are immune to snake poisons. Even the poisonous snakes, such a puff adder's bite, will just make them unconscious for two or three hours then they return to consciousness and will start eating the rest of the snake.

"The way human populations are growing and rainforests are being cut down, I can see our habitat will soon be taken over by humans.

"Returning to your question, I mostly lived alone as a king cobra, as that is how we are designed to live. I mentioned earlier we mate once a year; I had mated with a couple of females and the saddest part is the female also mates only once a year. Let's say, if she mated with me and later some other king cobra tried to mate with her, she won't let it happen. In his rage, the male cobra will kill her, as we are not immune to our own venom. The male king cobra will bite her to death.

"When I became human, I was in South India and in the center of a deep forest in Malabar, which was ruled and run by the Dhera Dynasty.

"The first girl I met was from India. She was one of the daughters of the Dhera Dynasty and her name was Durga Devi. Durga was twenty-one years old when first we met.

"That day was a beautiful sunny day and Durga was out in the jungle for the tiger hunt. All the monarchs were fond of hunting animals and then turning their kill into a trophy by turning it into a decorative piece.

"Like all blue bloods, hunting was one of her passions and a favorite sport. Durga, with her bow and arrows, was riding an elephant along with fifty servants on foot; some played drums and a few had sticks and made various noises with their voices.

"The whole scene felt like a carnival was going on. It was my seventh day as a human, and I was meditating in my cave. I was shirtless yet was wearing some very antique and expensive jewelry around my neck and arms. Since I lived all my life in jungles and various forests, this was nothing new for me."

Raja continued, "My only concern was not to be disturbed by anyone, although I was fine with noises around the jungle. All I wanted was to stay isolated, as I was preparing myself physically and spiritually for the human world."

Miriam interrupted, "What did she look like? Was she very beautiful?"

Raja smiled. "Lord, you girls are only concerned about how the other girl looked. If you let me continue, you will know everything about her."

Miriam said with a smile, "I apologize for interruption, please continue."

Raja said, "Durga was one brave soul. She was leading the hunt on her elephant and her mahout was a petite man known as, Venu. He was her personal mahout and, since the age of eight, when she joined her father for hunts, Venu was with her. Durga felt the elephant was not in his element that day. The journey from the palace to the forest was normal, however now in the deep forest he was acting strange, as if something was bothering him.

"Elephants are basically calm mammals, but if they go berserk then there is no stopping them. They are known as masters of destruction because their size and power is divine. That day Durga and Venu were on the elephant and suddenly the elephant went berserk. He started running on his own and poor Venu was trying his best as per his experience as a mahout.

"However, the mighty giant was uncontrollable and Durga was struggling to maintain her control on the seat. Somehow, the elephant managed to throw her from her seat into the deep forest. Her bow and arrows remained on the holder next to the seat. Durga was left alone in the deep forest as she ran after the elephant, but within a few seconds, Venu and the elephant vanished from her sight.

"The fall gave her some serious injuries, including a broken ankle. She was a strong girl and was trying her best to deal with her pain. My cave was quite close to where she fell and I could hear her yelling at the elephant and advising Venu to just stop and control the elephant.

"Suddenly her yelling turned into deadly screams and abruptly the forest became alive as a tiger was close by and because of her noises he started to chase her. When I heard the roar of a tiger, I figured her life was in danger and the hunter herself was about to be hunted.

"I came out and it was the first time I laid eyes on her. She was around five foot eight and her skin was light brown. Durga body was simply mesmerizing. Her long, silky hair was a mess and I saw fear in her big dark brown eyes. The tiger was about to attack her, as tigers are very calculated hunters. They study their prey and plan every kill. They are blessed with speed and power.

"There is no chance of changing his plans. If a tiger has made up his mind to kill something, he will never change it. Within no time I was standing between her and the tiger, and as I have this ability to speak every living creature's language, the tiger recognized the beast in me and was afraid to see me interfering with him and his prey.

"Most of the people in this world don't believe in reincarnation, but the truth is that the same tiger, a hundred and fifty years back, had been a human and professional big cat hunter. He was very well aware Durga was there to kill him. Tiger shared his heart with me and I assured him I would try my best to turn this girl into someone who would love animals and value their lives.

"Durga came and hugged me from behind, as for her I was some angel who had come to protect her. Without even knowing me, I was the closest man in her life now. Durga was surprised that the tiger was scared and was not attacking me, as I was empty-handed and shirtless.

"The tiger appeared scared while gazing into my eyes but he remained completely still. He was standing firm. Durga was not able to listen or understand our conversation, as we animals can speak from our eyes and can share our thoughts we want to discuss. Tiger paid me respect and was on his way to from where he came.

"As I turned around to see Durga, she fainted right in my arms and I carried her back to my cave. I knew she had broken her ankle while falling from the elephant. My cave was designed with a bosky entrance that made it almost invisible from the outside view. No human could sense or see that behind these huge bushes and trees that a cave full of treasure existed

"The encounter with the tiger, my appearance, and the freshness of her wounds, made her forget the severity of her pain. I made her lie down removed her hunting armor and made her relax while I concocted a paste of herbs which I applied to her wounds. Then I made her a dressing with huge leaves filled with Alum stone powder mixed with tree glue, as the combination of both can stop bleeding immediately and fix any fractured bone within a few days. Besides her dressing, I wanted to make sure she kept lying down to have proper rest and avoid any movement and pressure on the wounded ankle.

"Once her wounds had been dressed, I looked at her with complete peace of mind. It was my first such close encounter with a human. While gazing upon her I understood why God made humans superior to all the living creatures he had created. God had given them his face, his presence and his grace. Other creatures were left to serve and be of use to humans. I was just sitting and paying my humble gratitude to my lord for giving me a chance to enjoy life as a human.

"Durga was a goddess and her royalty, elegance, and beauty were casting a strange spell on me. Even though she was unconscious, her grace and gorgeousness were still hard to resist, and I couldn't remove my gaze away from her. Now the voices in the jungle were different, as more fear and frustration was included. I was aware of the reason. Durga had vanished from the face of the jungle and she was nowhere to be found.

"Her senior and junior staffs were all concerned about Durga's safety, as some of them were whispering, 'Durga was attacked by a tiger and she had been eaten alive'. Others were voicing their own concerns, wondering whether the ghosts of the forest had swallowed her.

"In those days, people were extremely superstitious and for them it was easy to blame the forest's spirits for having eaten her alive.

"Above all, the fear of her father was making them urinate in their lungis it's like a man skirt. Durga's father was from the 'Dhera Dynasty' and even in today is known as Thaskara Bavi Narman I. They all were aware the moment they returned without her that the king would turn the palace upside down. When he got mad he would simply give serious, insane commands. They were scared he would have them skinned alive.

"Durga was his only child, as two of his sons had lost their lives during a battle two years before. Durga was very dear to him. She was his heart. He lived and would die for her.

"Twenty-four hours passed and she was still unconscious. While trying to escape from the tiger she had run into a plant that had thorns filled with poison, and the poison had spread in her body.

"I inserted leaves of that same plant which worked like an antidote. The leaves managed to cure the poison; however it made her unconscious and I was aware it would take time for her to regain consciousness.

"I was sitting and watching her closely, never wanting her to wake, as it was my first encounter to see such a gorgeous human. Finally, after forty-seven hours, she woke. First she seemed scared as she examined her location. Then she saw my face and abruptly, she relaxed.

"Without saying a single word and in an elegant way, she paid me humble gratitude for saving her life. Then in a pompous style she introduced herself as a princess and said how much she wanted to reward me. She was still semi-conscious and passed out again. I was quietly nodding while I understood her sign language."

CHAPTER 10
"BUDDHA"

Durga scrutinized me and tried to understand my status. Was I a commoner or a blue blood? I was reading her thoughts.

Her gaze was stuck on the jewelry I was wearing and deep down she assessed that I was not a commoner, she was a princess and no one in this world could recognize the value of jewels and precious stones better than royals.

She was vastly intellectual and was aware of how Prince Siddhartha, widely known as Buddha had left everything and gone into the forest to find his inner peace. That's how she was measuring me. In her mind, she was sure I was a prince who was meditating and finding my inner peace like Buddha, alone in the jungle.

"Did Ayesha share any wisdom of Buddha with you?" Raja asked Miriam.

"Well, I knew the name, but don't know the whole story and who he truly was. I would be interested to know more about him," Miriam hesitantly replied.

"His teachings will appear further along in this tale of Durga. Ayesha will teach you a complete history of him and you will know him properly. However, I will give you some relevant short details about him. Buddha was born in Kiratdesa which today is known as a country called Nepal, and the location was the garden in Lumbini. Until the age of twenty-nine he lived in his palace in Lumbini. One night he left his palace and was out to explore the world to find his inner peace. He is one of the most famous spiritual leaders in the world.

"Buddha's teachings and guidance are wise and sensible. I'm going to share the tale of the connection we snakes have with him. While Buddha was doing his spiritual meditation in the sitting position with his eyes close under the Bohdi Tree and on completion of his four weeks, the skies were darkened for seven days and a huge storm started so that it rained for seven days.

That was when Mucalinda, one of the largest king cobras, surfaced from the deepest part of the earth. Mucalinda coiled his body seven times around Buddha, to keep him warm and provide comfort. Mucalinda then placed his hood on his head to protect him from heavy rain. For seven days Mucalinda stayed in the same position, as did Buddha.

"After seven days, the rain stopped and Mucalinda transformed into a young man and paid his humble respects. Mucalinda was honored to serve Buddha, because his teaching was all about not harming any single creature on the face of the earth. All the creatures in this world love souls who care for them. This is a natural act and they can sense if someone will hurt them," Raja explained to Miriam.

"That is a very deep and wonderful approach one can enlighten herself with. His teachings really seem educational and I will ask Ayesha to share his story with me. So, what happen next with Durga?" Miriam asked him while looking deep into Raja's eyes.

"Durga was finally conscious had regained her full senses, and started her conversation with me in an elegant manner." Raja replied.

"Durga shyly told me, 'I have to pay my humble gratitude to you for saving my life. As for me today you came like an angel. I have never seen you in my state before and I have to admit you're one of the most handsome looking males I have ever seen. However, I am so impressed with your bravery. For me you stood bare handed and faced the tiger and even the tiger was scared of you. It's not only me; the tiger was surprised to see the bravest form of mankind.

"'I know you are not an ordinary man, you are a prince. And in this jungle, if I'm not wrong, you are finding the inner peace just like Prince Siddhartha. Please tell me everything about yourself and my father will be glad to make your acquaintance. I want to invite you to my palace to be our guest. I'm Durga and would you be so kind to introduce yourself and tell me your name, please?

"'My name is Raja'" I introduced myself. 'I would suggest you keep lying still, straight, and relax yourself, as your wounds are still fresh and even a slight pressure will injure you again. You also scratched yourself with the thorn of a poisonous plant. I have already given you antidote and now the poison had been cleansed from your blood and flesh.'

"While she was unconscious, I arranged some fruits for her. Durga was listening to me very carefully and trying to find signs of bruising or scratches. Her eyes were wide open after she heard about the poisonous plant, and she was looking a bit scared.

"'You're fine now, Durga. You've nothing to worry about. Just have a little rest and you will be as good as new.' I told her while keeping my eyes on the ground. I was trying my best to not look at her so she couldn't see my eyes. "'I know, your highness, that the cave is not as opulent and comfortable as your place.'

"She replied elegantly, "'I'm a princess. There is no doubt about that, and I have all the riches of the world under my feet. However I have never felt so glad the way I feel now being in your presence. I have strong feelings you are one interesting man to be with, and seem to be one who is blessed with wisdom and knowledge.'

"Durga said, "'I can assess from the jewelry you're a prince yourself, aren't you? Would you like to share with me what you were missing in life that brought you to this jungle to be isolated from the rest of the world and live alone in this beautiful cave? I can see the entrance seems tiny, but from inside I can view various directions and passages. How big is this cave, and are there any dangerous animals inside those passages? Have you cautiously checked all the passages and found out how long this cavern is?'

"I said, "'please, just relax. There is nothing to fear about in this cave. There are no animals and even if there were none would attack us. Always remember animals only attack humans when they are scared of them. I have no plan to harm anyone; they sense danger more easily than humans. They basically don't attack, just try to defend themselves.

"Sometimes in life we have to do things in which we can truly find the answers to our existence. You've read about Siddhartha, the prince who left his opulence just to find his inner peace. Women and a comfortable life bored him, so one day he quietly left his palace and started walking empty handed towards an unknown destination.

"Imagine how lonely he must had felt, how empty his soul would have been, what was disturbing him and what was he really missing in his life. He, being a prince, left his kingdom and went to find himself while the whole world has just seemed concerned about making a fortune.

"How come he went against the world, while the whole world seeks a life such as his, full of lavishness?

"The answer is simple, to find satisfaction of one's mind, body, heart and whole soul. In this journey he did not only find satisfaction, but perhaps a complete understanding of his existence and the values of life. It is the same path I'm trying to walk and, honestly, it's not easy. Imagine if you have to stay alone in this cave and, while you are meditating and spiritually involved in your own world, you have no idea what kinds of evil might come and try to disconnect you. While saying this, I looked toward her.

"Durga said, "'I have read about Buddha and his teachings; to be honest I really am very impressed by your wit and wisdom. The truth is, first Buddha left everything to find inner peace and the second person was you. Maybe tomorrow the whole world will have people following you building temples and worshipping you.'" While she said those words, I felt her mischievous smile. "'I'm extremely sorry that because of me you had to leave your spiritual meditation and save my life.

"'I want to know more about you. How long have you been living in this cave? Where are you from? Who else has tried to disturb you? As you were mentioning earlier, apart from me, other forces tried to interrupt your meditation. Tell me, have you found satisfaction and spiritual wealth so far?'"

Raja said, "I told her, 'I have been here for nine days as the plan was to do spiritual meditation for thirty days. No water or food and sitting in the same position as Buddha to focus my mind toward the higher power. The transmogrified moments are when your eyes are closed you can clearly view everything around you. The depth of your vision goes beyond closed walls.

"'On the third day I viewed one beautiful girl completely naked entering my cave. She tried to distract me by making some noises and started moving around me but she never came close nor touched my body. Her voice was sweet and seductive, however I knew the tales of sirens; I knew she was not a human, perhaps was a ghost of the forest. While she tried her best to gain my attention she was not able to break my spiritual meditation and, as a result, turned into her real shape, as she was succubus.'" I looked toward Durga, who was listening to me with great attention and I asked her, "'you know what succubus means, right?'"

"Durga responded, "'No, I have never heard of this word before, educate me as much as you can. Were you not afraid of her presence?'"

"I told her, 'A succubus is the name of a female demon who is believed to have intercourse with sleeping men. I believe we have to die one day, so why worry about something which is not ours. I mean life is temporary and life after death is the true reality, and that is what I'm here for, to find the truth about being a better human. Serve the world in the best way I can and keep humanity as my priority rather than wealth, sex, greed or power.'"

"'I'm not afraid of anyone, humans or creatures. The day I have to die, no one would be able to save me from death, that's the reality of life and is the truth. Imagine you came to kill a tiger, what could that poor animal have done wrong to you? Only he's wild, beautiful and dangerous. You would have killed the amazing animal and then made him one of your decorative pieces, in your palace. Have you ever thought about how you would have felt if she was a tigress and pregnant?

"'Durga, if you had read the teachings of Buddha then you would have known even hurting an ant is a sin. They are living creatures as you are. What would have happened to you if I hadn't interfered between you and the tiger? Would you have been able to survive him hunting you down?

"'I know Buddhism is not your religion and I'm not Buddhist myself. Religion is a gift we receive when we are born from our parents. As we grow and become wise, we have a choice to investigate other religions as well. I know the religions we're born with are in our blood; however sensible people collect all the wisdom and gather all relevant knowledge from other religions, knowledge that makes sense and makes you a better human. So later they can serve humanity magnificently and simultaneously make their way towards Heaven after death.

"Durga was lost in my words, essentially it was the first time someone had chastised her. She had been born as princess and all her life not a single soul had ever spoken to her sternly and loudly, even though my voice was not that loud. However, I was angry because what gave human beings the right to think they had a right to kill innocent animals? She was quiet and her beautiful eyes were downcast as if she was trying to find something deep down in her thoughts.

"She replied, 'I never thought that way before and all you said was hundred percent right. Who am I to take anyone's life? In fact, being a princess of the state, even the animals are my responsibility and, as per our family's manner all my life I had been following my father and my late brothers. I never felt ashamed about myself. However, today you woke me, and just the thought of what I have become has made me feel miserable. With your words I can simply understand, if the higher power made me a princess, it's my test to look after other people and serve them to best capabilities. Thank you so very much, and I promise you not even my father will ever hunt any living creature while I'm alive. I will make this a law of my state.' Durga ended her emotional speech in a very promising manner.

"Night was falling so I lit the fire inside the cave as the forest was growing dark. 'I asked her, "'Are you feeling better or do you still feel pain or lethargy? If you are hungry, please do let me know, as I have plenty of fruits for you. At the same time, you have to forgive me for I'm not in a position to offer you a royal meal here.

"Durga replied, "'I have a slight pain in my ankle but the poison's effect seem better now. When do you think I would be able to move back to my palace? I humbly request you to please come with me and I promise you can make yourself the same sort of cave as this one for your spiritual meditation. The truth is, I have never been this close to any man before. I really don't know why, but something about you attracts me and the way you speak makes me feel intoxicated and under your magical spell. One more thing, I have never seen such eyes as yours. Something is different about them. What it is I'm still trying to figure out.'"

"I responded to her, "'I'm honored by your offer. I can be your friend, however I never want to meet anyone apart from you. This is my palace and you can visit me whenever you feel like it. Please don't get me wrong I never wanted to be rude or proud. Just understand I have left the world to be by myself and the truth is I also enjoy your company. There is something special about you and it's not only your eyes, but the aroma from every part of your skin, is simply heavenly. If I have to start describing your beauty I have to find words to do you justice. Let me start with your soul. Have you ever noticed the magic of your spirit? You have a strong ability to capture any man's mind with just a simple conversation.'

"While listening to these words, her face started to blush. She became crimson all of a sudden. She approached me and I stopped her right where she was.

"'Please do understand I'm still under my spiritual meditation during this period of time,' I told her. 'I can never think sensual or sexual thoughts about you, even though my soul is in strange war with my body. My soul is stopping me from getting close to you while my body is ready to break all the laws and just live for the moment, right now and right here in your arms, exploring every part of your body and giving you the pleasure of my existence. However, this is not what we are made for. Sometimes feelings control minds and most of the time our minds control our body. I just want to be your host until you're cured, healthy and you can return to your palace safe and sound. You're a princess and much better off if you're with some prince. I'm just a lost soul who's trying to find the purpose of his existence, and my life is always going to be in caves and forests. How would you be able to cope with a man like me?"'

Miriam said, "So you never made love with her and you never let her close to you?"

Raja replied, "If you let me finish, you will get all the details and you promised me you would not be jealous. Kindly, if you would allow me, may I continue?"

Miriam said, "Yes, please, however understand and forgive me, I really am crazy about you. I'm not jealous, but something pinches me deep inside, so understand me too. It's very difficult for me to share you, because you belong only to me and I will never let any-one touch a hair on your head. However, I know you are sharing your past. I'm listening to you like your best friend, but your crazy lover inside me goes berserk. Please don't mind my foolish inter-fering, and the truth is I truly am enjoying your interesting tale. Kindly carry on, continue with what happened next."

Raja spoke. "I know you love me madly as I do you. What I'm sharing with you are some chapters of my life; however you will learn a major part of history in these tales. Since you are studying major subjects with Ayesha, these stories will help you to under-stand the history and some major dynasties who ruled these lands ten thousand years ago."

Miriam said. "Yes I'm very keen to educate myself and gain all the relevant education you would give me. I know one day or an-other I will make myself more knowledgeable and be better able to present myself as your wife."

Raja said, "Thank you my love. So, coming back to my conver-sation with Durga, I managed to make her understand I could not have a physical relationship with her, however I would respect and love her in more spiritual manner. Durga was completely fas-cinated, since all she wanted was to be with me for rest of her life. I was not ready to have a relationship, as my plan was to prepare myself as a human and gain confidence in interacting with normal human beings. Durga was my first contact and I was relaxed and satisfied with my progress so far. As I mentioned to you earlier, no creatures are as cruel as humans.

"I was calculating and was not interested in taking any risks. However, simultaneously, my plan was to gain a powerful position and hire people to deal with other humans, who would have been a better choice to have on my side other than the princess herself.

"I had saved her life and in her eyes all I saw was mad love for me. Please don't ever think I tried to manipulate the princess. My intentions were honest and simple. I truly liked her. Even in the form of a beast, I would have appreciated her beauty.

"Durga acted like a rude princess to the rest of the world, but I truly brain convinced her, and made her a humble human being, and she sensed every detail required to make her path toward Heaven smooth, without question.

"Durga was lying next to me and we discussed every major subject. She also asked me about my life and whether I had concubines when I was a prince. I simply denied it, as my requirement was to find inner peace, not my sexual desires.

"Durga also shared information about the princes from the other dynasties with me, like the Dholas and Randyas who were chasing her. The truth was, at that period of time, of only three dynasties who were ruling, the Dholas were the biggest and most powerful among the three of them in the south of India.

"I asked Durga, why she was not interested in those princes?

"Durga's answer was simple. She didn't find anything interesting in either of them. They were proud princes, from what I had heard from my closest sources. They had chosen dalliance, and both of them spent more time with concubines than educating themselves or preparing for wars."

"She added, "'I don't like men who are always lost in wines and concubines. As for me, I'm still a virgin and kept myself for the one who has the same thing in mind: to find love and then enjoy sex. Tell me, what is sex without love?' Durga gazed deep into my eyes.

"I told her, "'See, that's your philosophy. They are princes and for them that is their lifestyle and don't you think whoever you will marry will follow the same custom? He will later be a king or, let's say, even a prince, yet he will have his concubines. You know about your father, right? He must have a great collection of concubines for himself, am I not right?

"Durga was quiet for few a minutes. Again she was staring at the ground, which was a sign of her confusion.

"As far as sex without love is concerned, on this issue I totally agree with you. It's not only sex, but a magical connection between two bodies. The mind plays the biggest role of a stimulator," Raja replied.

CHAPTER 11

"ASTUTENESS"

Miriam while listening to Raja told him, "I really do admire your thoughts and decent soul. I also like the way Durga valued herself as a woman, I surely can imagine it must be teaching of her mother. Only a good mother would develop well-mannered and respectable daughter, please continue what happen next."

Raja said to Miriam. "Durga truly was decent girl no doubt about it and she was enjoying every single second knowing more about him.

Durga smiled and told Raja, "I truly wished, after meeting you I could also leave the palace and could join you. However, you're also not interested in allowing me to stay with you, even just as your humble maid. One who follows your orders and looks after you, such as when you are busy doing your spiritual mediation so no succubus will bother you."

Raja replied, "My friend, I never stopped you from being with me. I just want you to understand and feel my immanence; I have huge respect for you in a beautiful way. You are the only friend that I have ever had in my life. Trust me; I have never been this close to anyone before. You might think I'm an extrovert but intrinsically, all my life, I have been an introvert. See now, this is your magic, and don't get me wrong here. I'm just an ordinary human, I am sure even the stones must have been telling their tales in your presence."

Durga just laughed and her smile changed entire atmosphere of the cave. It sounded like music from Heaven, as if suddenly someone played a chord on a harp.

While looking toward Miriam, Raja explained, "As you know, snakes are famous for their fondness of music and they dance to the music of a flute the one which most of the Central Asian snake charmers play.

"The fact is, we love music and we always enjoy various kinds of tunes. Some instruments are our favorites, such as a snake charmer's bin flute. That sound turns us on like sensing the essence of a female around us. There are many rumors that snakes are deaf and they only dance to a flute tune because their focus is on the movement of the snake charmer's flute while he is playing.

"Reality is different, as the method by which we hear is intrinsically referred to as bone conductive hearing. We can pick up even the elusive vibrations through our jaw bones and are blessed with a pair of cochlear or snail-shaped, structures in our head. All these vibrations are transmitted to these, and as now I'm human, the same cochlear structures are in my own ears. The brain feels the nerves when vibrations hit that area; they are transmitted along nerves right into the brain and vibrations are interpreted as sound. Through this effect, our jaw serves as our 'ears'. Our auditory structures compared to a human's ears are many times more sensitive.

"We can detect a charging elephant from a distance to a tiny mouse creeping along the grass. We also can detect hissing of other snakes, as that is what plays a major role in the mating habits among some of our species. This hard-to-believe stage of sensitivity makes us swift and effective hunters."

Raja completed his sentence, held Miriam's hand and continued, "You must be wondering why I share so much detail about snakes with you? The answer is very simple, my dear. I just want you to know both my worlds and you should never hate or be scared of snakes. The world always quotes, 'Even if you feed milk to a snake he will still bite, because betrayal is in his nature'. Snakes see things from a different perceptive. The second they feel threatened or that they will be harmed; that is when they attack."

Miriam said, "My love, I can truly understand and you have no idea how much I enjoy the detailed information you shared with me. Sometimes I think I should be sitting by you with a pen and papers; especially when you tell me tales of such significance, so I can write down all those magical words full of wisdom. Later on I could educate the whole world with the knowledge and insight you provided!

Miriam continues, "Imagine how many people in this world want to know the interior life of snakes? No human can become a snake to go deep into their world and study their everyday lives. I felt so thankful to my Lord for his blessing and for choosing me to gain such pearls of wisdom from you. Even if people go into the depths of the sea; they can never find such treasure.

"As a human I consider myself responsible for passing on my knowledge so they can truly value and understand the meaning of being human. Lord gave us the first rank over all the creatures on earth and in the universe. Instead of being responsible we are on a different level of life."

Miriam said, "Love, I have experienced enough melancholy and with you now I see radiance and elation in my life. What I truly love about you is that you have not only shown me the true meaning of love, you have made a mission of your life to educate and help me gain wisdom.

"If I look back on my previous life, I was in complete darkness, not because I was poor, but because I was uneducated, and education is true light. My love, understand me, also I'm a desert and need the rain of education as much as you can pour on me.

You will still find me thirsty all the time. I never enjoyed anything in my previous life, as all my life I was busy making other people happy. First was my husband then our children and later on their wives.

"When they were killed, I was left with their memories and was just counting my days to die and to be with my family. As you know, my first husband was nice however his heart was stuck on his previous love. The same goes for my children. Once they got married, they were busy and lost in their wives. I had always been alone all that time.

"Sometimes, in the middle of the night, while lying next to you, I wonder if maybe my first life was my dream and this is my true life. I really am happy with you, darling. I don't even have words to say thank you for what you have done for a lonely soul like me.

"I was not only a lonely soul; I was blind at the same time. Imagine life without education and in complete darkness. I know the world is full of people just like me, who are born as a servant and die as a servant. Everyday so many children are born and they live lives like mine, no wishes, and no personal desires. All our lives, we are busy following orders. The rich never want the poor to be educated because they know that education teaches you the difference between right and wrong. I feel so sorry for those poor fellows who are not even aware of what is going on in this world!

"What is love, fashion, style, luxury, traveling, feeling free, being happy, studying other religions, humanity, respect, honor, loving animals, thinking like a leader?

"Nothing, they know nothing at all, and don't even want their daughters to go to school as they consider them burdens, and all they want is as soon as she is of age, to get her married.

"People with powers use them as their tools; some in the name of religion, some in the name of politics, and some in the name of providing them a better life or future. Rich people need poor, uneducated people for many reasons. They want slaves and later, they want their daughters to be prostitutes for them and their sons. Poverty is a curse and I will do my best to find as many people so I can to help them accordingly.

"The only way I see an end to poverty, is to educate every child in this world.

"I want to study every subject, even about stars, the moon and the complete universe. I really am interested in investigating all religions, every prophet who walked the face of the earth, and not only three holy books, however I want to go beyond boundaries. I am totally interested to study the teachings of Buddha and Hinduism.

"I don't want treasures in the form of material things. I just want wisdom and knowledge, my love. I hope you felt my starvation for education and knowledge, so please never think I'm not interested or will ever get bored.

"Now, let us come back to the subject! So, you were portraying Leonardo da Vinci, Mona Lisa smiles." With an impish smile, Miriam taunted Raja. "Oh I mean you were giving a complete description of Durga's laugh."

Raja replied, "I like your spirit. If you keep the same spirit one day the world will treat and worship you as a spiritual guru; Knowledge and wisdom don't only give you a chance to know the world and universe, but make you feel closer to your higher power. It does not matter, whatever religion you follow. Investigating other religions would make your mind positive and kind.

"I'm just being honest about my description and memories from my previous life. Her laugh was magical, and there was no doubt about that. Every human possess some quality that is attractive.

"Durga was extremely beautiful, however her laugh was honest, innocent and pure. She might be a rude princess to the world, yet with me she was really kind and was one humble soul the world was about to meet and know. I sensed and felt she was much better, and all I was waiting was for her to walk, so we could start a journey toward her palace.

"Durga, after a healthy and beautiful laugh, asked me, "'So, you think I'm that beautiful, that the stones will speak to me or my company is that interesting even stones will enjoy being with me?'"

"'The thing I really don't know is why I feel like I know you from somewhere and from some angle we are connected. Why doesn't it feel like you're a stranger when we just met for the very first time? I'm the princess and you are in my state; instead of being nervous, you're sitting so relaxed in my presence.

"'In my state, not a single man would have that courage to sit in such a relaxed position in my presence. When I'm walking, all men just bow their heads down and the best part is not a single man is allowed to even glance at me. I have made the rules extremely strict now.

"'As I had been through an accident and after that I'm more conscious to not even speak to any commoner. There was this one insane young guy, I don't know how he managed to see me and start acting like he was in love with me. His name was Jay and he sent me a message by the hand of one of my maids.

"'I was surprised by his courage and was aware if this message got into my father's hands, he would arrange a ceremony and gather the whole nation in the biggest grounds and in front of everyone; have him killed by an elephant stepping on him. I never replied to him however I was anxious to see who this insane man was.

"'One day when I was out horseback riding with my guards, he suddenly stood in front of my guards and told them he wanted to speak to her highness.

"'My guards in such a scenario are allowed to kill whoever tries to interact with royals. I knew surely was Jay and instructed my guards not to harm him and to let him speak to me."

"'Jay, like a speedy ghost stood right in front of my horse and was staring at me like crazy. He was an ordinary looking, poor commoner."

"'What confused me was my curiosity to know how come he gathered such courage to face me even when he was aware of consequences. How come someone could be so eager to lose his life or maybe he was a lunatic who made up his mind to commit suicide.

"'Nothing was interesting about Jay. He was grotesque, four-foot eleven tall, and extremely skinny, however his eyes were powerful as if there was some kind of insanity lurking there, and one could feel it just by looking in his eyes. Growing up as a princess, in many of our lessons, one learns to read another person from head to feet.

"'Personalities can be easily read and understood. There are a few points you have to notice, and you can sense every detail of a person sitting or standing in front of you.

"'As I read their minds, just in few a seconds, I could size up and looking deep into his eyes I was sure this guy might be small in size, however he could go to battle with my entire army just to have a word with me.

"'Poverty is not a crime for me; however as royals we have to honor our monarchy. In public we can never show our excitement. While looking at Jay, I don't know why I just wanted to laugh. However I controlled myself.

"'He entertained me in some way, and honestly, I never wanted any harm to befall that poor little creature. I felt his madness for me and to be honest, I was a teenage girl at that time, and I enjoyed the attention.

"'Who would not like such a thing? Princess or commoner, all want the same thing, people going crazy for them. Every girl seeks praise; even a tree, stone or wall could praise them and they will feel flattered. This is how excited girls can be.

"'Durga took her horse a little further so her guards were not able to hear their conversation and in a strict tone she asked Jay, "What do he have to say? He should better keep one thing in his mind one wrong word and he would be a head short in his height."

"In a very teasing, innocent manner, Raja asked Durga, 'Were you in some way attracted to him?'

"Durga's face turned crimson, and she said, '"No, never, not at all, I was concerned about Jay's life, as he was not aware what he was getting himself into."'

Jay replied, "With huge respect your highness, he would speak humbly, honestly and bluntly with her and kept his matter in her kind presence and hope for a positive response. He knew he was a commoner, had no fortune or status but what should had he could have done; as he had lost his heart to Durga. He love her and wanted to make her his. She could give him any quest or exam he would fulfill and would not disappoint her.

"If she wanted him to go and speak to her father; he was ready to do that. All he wanted was to marry her. His love was honest and he really was crazy about her. He was aware, he was not a prince however; he would honor her more than any prince in this world. He would care for her for the rest of his life. He would even dedicate his life to her. The day she asked him to finish it he will. Give him one simple or critical reason to prove his love for her. He knew many princes would have told her this but his attention was honest and very serious.

"If she wanted him dead for what he had told her, she could go ahead give the order. As he had misbehaved so he deserved to be beheaded. One more thing she should never forget the King himself had announced if any commoner needs anything he should ask him or his children; as per king's kind heart his announcement was for the whole state and his sons were killed so the only child left was princess Durga.

"What the state will think about her, a poor man kept his simple request and she got him beheaded. The whole state would be against her kingdom, as he mentioned to her earlier he was all set to give up his life for his loving princess."

Durga replied, "'I felt he was not insane or in love with me, however one perfidious, cunning little guy who was dreaming to become a prince. His stupid ideas would take him on excursions he would not be totally aware of. He came prepared to face any kind of consequences; with his own volition he put his life at stake. As you know, we are trained to handle these kinds of people in a good manner. Greed is like a disease and deep down it eats you in its own way, and the best part is greedy people can never sense they are inviting death each day. The fact is there is a reason the higher power blesses special people with felicitous influence and opulence.

"'It's a serious test one needs to go through and they have to be kind, responsible and caring. Royals have to be very careful and eschew any kind of injustice with our nation.

"'As per our Hindu scriptures, if the person, who is blessed to be a king and chooses to follow the Devil, does things to make him happy regardless of higher power's teaching. The afterlife for such a king is decided in the shape of a punishment and we strongly believe in reincarnation. The transmigration of the soul reborn in form of human or animal, seven times until the unity of soul with its creator. I just don't want to end up being a slave or a prey for various predators as a punishment. As a soul can transform into any living creature, it's not necessary that I become a human after my death.

"'Like my father, in this life he is a royal and in his previous life he was a bull. No one ever knew this. He only shared with me and even showed me a hole inside his nasal septum. He still sees some reflections from his previous life, where someone is hitting him with a stick while he is pulling a load. Strange isn't it? And that is the reason he is strict and he really doesn't want to be. However just to keep his name alive he acts as if he is stern. I know in his heart he is a kindhearted man and never ever wants to hurt any other human."

"'He is the one who gave me all the knowledge of reincarnation and gave me a script to study the details about the whole concept. Imagine me being a deer and then later hunted by hyenas. They are specialized in giving agonizing death, as they start eating their prey from the stomach while the prey is still alive. Therefore it can feel every inch of their teeth, biting deep inside their stomach and in this scenario even death comes slowly.

"'Keeping all the details in mind, I planned to teach Jay a lesson, one he would never forget and would tell others to stay away from greed. He was talking constantly, while deep in my mind I was considering what lesson would be suitable for him.'"

CHAPTER 12

"THE STONING"

While kissing Miriam passionately he told her, "Love, you know me, I can go on sharing these tales with you for weeks; however I want you to have a rest. Six hours' sleep is necessary for a human body; even though you are immortal, still when it comes to your beauty, I will not take any chances." He chuckled while telling her.

Raja carried her in his arms and went to the bedroom.

It was still dark when she startled awake, after she heard someone knocked at their bedroom door. It had never happened before and Raja was already at the door.

Miriam heard Ayesha asking for her.

Miriam ran towards the door and asked, "Is everything okay?"

Ayesha replied, "You need to come with me right now to the sitting room. Do you remember the old lady from the village named Fatima; she has sent a young boy with a message for you. It's extremely urgent!

Miriam briskly went down with Ayesha. The boy was sitting on the carpet rather than the sofa and was shivering and seemed really scared. When he saw Miriam approaching, he quickly stood up and, while saluting Miriam told her his name was Babar. Then he started crying like a child and was at Miriam's feet. With tears in his eyes he begged her, "Please save my sister, she is innocent."

Miriam held up the boy by his shoulder and made him sit on the sofa and requested the maid 'Hera', who came running.

"Hera, kindly get this boy some water and bring him some food, he is famished." Then she hugged the boy and told him, "Please stop crying and tell me, is Fatima okay, and from whom do I have to save your sister? But first I want you to drink water and feel like you are at home. Relax and pull yourself together."

Babar was barely a sixteen-year-old boy and even a blind person could figure out he was from a poor family. The maid brought juice and some food for him. Miriam took the tray from the maid's hand and served the boy herself.

Babar drank the juice as he has been thirsty for ages. He refused to eat but Miriam insisted and started feeding Babar with her hands. He was looking at her as for the first time; he had never met someone so kind and her presence made him believe she truly was an angel. Miriam's love, care and kindness relaxed and calmed him. She further requested he share everything from the beginning.

After a long sigh, Babar said, "Madam, as I already informed you, my name is Babar and my parents were at the landlord's farms in the next village. Malik Omar is the name of the landlord; he is known for his cruelty and torture on his workers. Omar is more than fifty years old and I really don't know where he had seen my older sister, Zakia. We are our parents' only children and she is only a year older than me. Zakia is a very obedient and respectful girl. The whole village knows she is very religious and offers prayers five times a day. As I was telling you, I really don't know when Omar saw my sister. Yesterday he instructed my parents to bring, Zakia to his farm house, as his wife needed some help and other girls were also going.

"My parents are simple people. Madam, they are aware of Omar's bad habits, but as he used the name of his wife, they took my sister with them; my parents went straight to his farmhouse. He himself answered the door and gave orders to my parents go and work in the fields, and to come back after ten hours and take their daughter home. My father requested if he could say hello to his wife, and Omar started abusing him. Madam, I don't know if you can understand, being poor is the worst curse in this world." His tears started rolling again.

Miriam hugged the boy again and replied, "Trust me, no one can understand that more than me, please tell me what happen next."

Babar continued, "Madam my parents spent the whole day in the fields but they were extremely worried about my sister. When they finished work, they started walking briskly towards the farmhouse. On knocking at the gate my sister came out screaming and while hugging my mother, cried. "'That beast raped me!'"

Omar raped my sister several times. Her clothes were torn out and my mother covered her with a shawl. My father ran inside as he was extremely angry and wanted to kill Omar. His servants started beating my father and Omar never showed up and stayed inside.

"While hitting my father, all those goons informed him he should better keep his mouth shut otherwise they would tell everyone that their daughter was a prostitute and had come by her own choice. Another loyal servant of Omar, while slapping my father told him he would inform the whole town she had committed adultery with him and is in love with him. The name of that servant is Kalu, as he is an ugly looking man. He was a loyal dog and the right hand of Omar; he could kill and can give his life for him.

"My mother went straight to the landlord's house and told everything to his wife. Instead of supporting my parents, she abused my parents and started blaming them by saying, that my parents had taken Zakia to the farm house on purpose so they can make up a story about her innocent husband. When the landlord found out that my parents had complained about him to his wife, he became more furious. First thing he did, he banished Kalu and sent him to some other village and went straight to the mosque and involved Maulvi Hanif the mosque's cleric. The cruel cleric gathered everyone in the mosque and gave a verdict against my sister, which was that she had committed adultery with Kalu and her punishment as per Islamic Sharia law was stoning.

"I was totally unaware of the entire incident and Auntie Fatima sent a message to me and when I went to confront her, she shared the incident details with complete wisdom and sensibility. When I knew the entire story, I wanted to kill Omar. Auntie Fatima, in a very wise manner, made me understand. On my own I won't be able to do anything against all those crazy people. At present, the entire village voted in the favor of Zakia's stoning. Tomorrow, after the Friday prayer, they will stone her. Auntie Fatima gave me some money for a bus ticket along with your address. She strongly believes in you and told me you are an angel of Allah and will certainly help my family and me. I promise, madam, I will be your slave for life. My sister is innocent, and I beg you to save her life."

Miriam looked at Ayesha and gave her the signal to get ready and get the team of guards ready. "We leave right now with Babar." Then she hugged the boy again and told him, "My child, you did very well coming straight to me and without getting yourself involved directly, as your parents are already going through hell.

"The landlord's people would easily have killed you, and that would have destroyed your parents completely. Now, listen to me carefully, your sister is my daughter and no one will touch her that I promise you.

"We are leaving with you right away. Just give me time so I can inform my husband and we will make a move, all right son?"

Babar was at peace and again touching her feet, thanked her; deep in his mind he was surprised the way Miriam was acting; as she seemed only two or three years older than him. However, her approach of speaking and dealing him was as if she was from Auntie Fatima's age group.

Miriam, after giving instruction to Ayesha, went running to the bedroom wanting to bring the matter to Raja's knowledge and inform him that she was leaving for the village. In her mind, she was thinking of using Lopti, as she knew what kind of monsters people became when it came to killing someone innocent.

Raja was already up; she was surprised to see him getting ready, and before she could tell him anything, he kissed her and told her, "My love, do you think would I ever let you go alone among those wild dogs? I'm coming with you. Don't even think about using Lopti; it's a small matter and I will take care of it in my way. I know everything and I'm with you to sort out this issue. You have promised the boy that nothing will happen to his sister; no one in this world will even lay a finger on her. Your given word is my responsibility and now you please just relax and stay calm, all right my darling?"

Miriam hugged him as tightly as she could and kissed him madly. "I love you, my darling and truly am proud of you." She started getting ready but deep in her mind, she was missing her friend Madhu.

Times had changed. Before Miriam had been old, poor and weak, and was unable to do anything to save Madhu when those goons were killing her.

Now the story was different; she is a queen and her husband was the most powerful king who ever walked the face of the earth. It was not his war, it was Miriam's, and he had nothing to do with human affairs. For her given words, he was willing to go to war with the entire world. She knew he loved her, but to such extent even she was surprised but enormously happy and proud of him.

Raja drove and Miriam sat next to him. Ayesha and Babar sat on the seat. It was the first time she had seen Raja driving the jeep;

it was a beautiful early morning and just another day for the world that was unaware of a group of people planning to take the life of an innocent girl, and thereby commit an atrocious crime.

The guards followed in an assortment of cars and jeeps. Babar sat quietly, as he seemed impressed by Raja's personality. Few men existed in the world that had their own presence when they entered a place. Raja's presence was not only felt, but his persona made people bow their heads in front of him.

Even a stranger would understand and sense this man was from some royal family and was a true warrior; even the bravest fighters would think twice to challenge him.

Raja didn't ask a single question from the boy or show any kind of sympathy towards him; he was driving, and his facial expression was one on one could read or understand.

He had given Miriam a comprehensive lecture on facial expressions, and he had clearly explained to her that the greatest human weaknesses were the visible expressions. "If someone is angry, his anger will start showing on his face; on the contrary, if his sadness is evident. At the same time if excited, his expressions will make his excitement noticeable. Never show your expressions, because that allows others to judge you easily. You should always carry calmness on your face; even when you have a storm brewing deep inside you. Those who can control their facial expressions will never lose any war in life, because not a single person in the world would be able to study them.

"The art of controlling your facial expression is the first step toward winning the world." Raja told her.

That is what Miriam was doing today; inside her she held a volcano full of anger; however from her exterior, was calm and like ice. After five hour of driving, they finally reached Fatima's village. Sunshine was making the day bright and spring breezes were allowing everyone to feel wonderful and enjoy the weather.

As they entered the village, there were noises of children running after the vehicles. The whole village started to gather around them, Fatima ran toward her car. Miriam briskly stepped out and hugged her; Fatima's emotions were visible as her eyes were paying great gratitude on her arrival.

Fatima, while crying, told her. "I'm truly honored that you are here my child. Please, we don't have much time, and we have to reach the next village as after Friday prayers. They are planning to start Zakia's stoning."

The next village was a ten-minute distance by car. Miriam said to Babar "Sit with the guards and stay inside the car until we manage to rescue Zakia."

Babar nodded and briskly ran toward the guards' jeep.

Raja was wearing his sun glasses; when Fatima entered the car she greeted and thanked Raja for coming, in return he nodded.

Fatima told Miriam, "Thank Lord you came. I hope Babar had told you everything in detail. The last update I heard was Maulvi Hanif, the cleric of the mosque, is forcing Babar's father to throw the first stone at Zakia. He has threatened his father if he doesn't throw the first stone; his house will be burned and he can no longer live in this village. Omar's men have already captured the father, mother and daughter. Even though the whole village knows Omar's hideous character, they are still following and believing the evil cleric. One of the God- fearing men came to me yesterday and he told me, the way he ignited the villagers against Zakia was phenomenal.

"Maulvi Hanif made her look like the biggest sinner of the whole world and for every respectful Muslim man to teach a lesson to their daughters and all the women in village. They have to stone her, so every single girl the in village fears the consequences of adultery. Now the whole village wants to finish Zakia as she is a curse on the village. All the men want to stone her. Those who know she is innocent are scared; if they interfere, all the fanatic men will turn against them and they might face the same fate as Zakia."

Miriam held Fatima's hand and told her, "No one can escape sin. One day or another, they have to repent of what they have done. Today sins of this cleric and the landlord will end. I know and have seen such kinds of men; it takes them a second to turn from humans into wild animals."

Raja drove quietly, showing no emotions, no anger or rage. He was calm, as if he was going on a picnic. As they reached the next village, they saw a huge crowd gathering, and Raja stepped on the accelerator to reach them faster. He broke his silence and instructed Miriam, Ayesha and Fatima, "All of you will stay inside the car and no one will come out."

They all nodded.

Raja drove right into the center of the field; the entire gathering was surprised by their entry. Miriam was reading their facial expressions as they were surprised by uninvited people in the jeeps and seemed concerns who are they?"

The scene was dreadful. Zakia was buried in the ground from below her shoulders, in a standing position, and two men were throwing mud on her. While this happened, a man with a beard was haranguing a skinny old man, Miriam figured out he was Babar's father, as he was crying and the fear of death was quite visible on his face. Everyone stood still with their arrival, as Raja got out of the car, as did the guards from the other vehicles.

Miriam lowered the window slightly so she could hear his conversation and her pulse was racing. Ayesha seemed worried and tense; tension was at a peak inside the jeep.

All of a sudden there was a pin drop silence as the crowd gazed at Raja. He approached a middle-aged short man, Miriam figured out he was Omar. Just one look at him and she felt the evil inside him. Omar seemed scared and concerned on their arrival. He knew by viewing their cars, the man who was walking toward him was not an ordinary guy. Raja's personality was felt tremendously as he towered over every man gathered at this horrific scene. All carried various sizes of stones they had been intended to strike Zakia's face at full strength, as if she were not a human, but an object for target practice.

Raja, while looking directly toward Omar asked him, "What is happening here?"

Instead of Omar, Maulvi Hanif replied proudly, "We are stoning an adulterous girl; her lover managed to escape but, by the grace of Allah, we managed to catch her," He grinned and evidently expected that Raja would be proud of him and offer some sort of reward for such a brave act.

Raja turned around to the crowd and shouted, "And all of you carrying stones, what the hell do you think you are doing here? All of you who have read the Holy Quran raise your hands!"

The whole crowd briskly raised their hands, including Hanif and Omar.

"All right, you can lower your hands and now tell me how many of you read about the Prophet Jesus Christ (May peace be upon him) raise your hands." Raja asked firmly.

Again all raised their hands; this time Omar interrupted them and shouted, "Who are you and why are you here? This is our village's internal matter and no one is allowed to interfere. I suggest wherever you came from and whoever you are leave in peace, otherwise you will be in a big trouble." While saying this he looked toward his men, who were also carrying weapons.

Raja answered, "Whoever I am, that I will tell you later. Let me tell the crowd something. First of all, just like all you people, who are gathered here to butcher this girl. Stoning is a tradition set by Prophet Moses and was strictly followed by Jews. Later Muslims started following the same tradition. Jesus Christ came in times of Jews and stoning was very common in those times as well. One day while he was preaching, the biggest rabbi of that time; brought a prostitute to Jesus Christ and told him, that she had committed adultery and, as per the laws of Moses they had been told to stone her. What do you say?"

Jesus Christ wrote something on the ground with his finger and then replied, "'the one who has never committed any sin, may throw the first stone at her.'"

The angry stone-carrying crowd was reduced to a humble audience. Miriam eyes were glued on and Zakia and she could see even Zakia's gaze was riveted on Raja. Miriam knew Zakia deep in her mind was witnessing Raja as an angel sent by Allah to save her life.

Maulvi Hanif clearly wanted to say something, but Raja stopped him there and told him, "I'm coming back to you. Hold your peace for a few minutes and we all will listen to what you have to say, but first let me finish."

Raja faced the crowd and said, "Now I asked all those of you; who never committed any sin or crime, please take five steps forward. However, look deep inside your souls and think twice before you take those steps, as I swear Allah is watching you right at this very moment. You can cheat me but remember we all will die and you all know those who cheat His name will go to Hell. Now the choice is yours, to take the steps!"

Apart from six men, everyone stayed where they were and Maulvi Hanif and Omar were the first to take those steps forward.

Maulvi Hanif shouted. "Don't teach us Christianity! We are not interested."

Raja turned toward Hanif. "Now I will start with you. Let me tell you something about our saint friend, Maulvi Hanif. He is a child molester, as many children complained, but all you stupid illiterate parents kept sending them to him to learn the Holy Quran. Imagine if he was a man of Allah he would have supported Zakia; instead he gave orders to stone her."

Maulvi Hanif again tried to say something, but Raja removed his glasses and placed his face near Hanif's and told him, "Shut the hell up."

Maulvi Hanif fell on the ground, his complexion turned completely pale. He didn't get up and judging by his reaction, everyone standing there must have felt what he had seen in Raja's eyes, and it had scared the life out of him.

Now the crowd turned serious as they understood, Raja was an angel of Allah. Raja turned toward them and spoke, "Ali and Assam, please step forward. Just last year two five-year-old boys' bodies were found near the forest. Some man brutally raped and asphyxiated. They both were your sons and also students of this devil Maulvi Hanif right?"

Ali and Assam started crying loudly and were at Raja's feet. "Yes, sir, Ali shouted, they were our children and you truly are an angel of Allah, we both beg you, please tell us who killed our sons?"

"Even that time your holy Maulvi Hanif misguided you that some stranger; would have done such an evil act. For a few months' all of you kept searching for the rapist as a stranger and with the passage of time, each of you got busy in life and totally forgot the death of your own children. Even your wives and the mothers of your boys were sure it was Hanif, as both the boys, in their innocent manner told their mothers about how Hanif was touching their private parts. That time even your wives ignored it and, when looking at their dead bodies, their heart sank as the boys had been brutally raped before being killed."

Then Raja turned and looked at Hanif and ordered him, "Tell everyone the truth."

Hanif was still on the ground, lost and scared. Hanif started yelling, "Please get me out of here and yes I have kill those boys and raped many other little boys."

Both Ali and Assam moved to jump on Hanif, and even the crowd wanted to kill him. Raja stopped everyone and again shouted, "Stay where you all are including both of you. There is one more devil we need to discuss here."

Raja smoothly turned toward Omar. "So, my dear landlord, would you be kind enough to start sharing your raping adventures or should I start opening up your account?"

Omar was speechless; even he must have understood that Raja was not an ordinary man.

"Yes, I have raped her forcefully. She is an innocent girl; she begged in the name of Allah and Holy Prophet Muhammad but the Devil took control of my mind."

Then Omar looked at the crowd and called out the names of eight men and asked them forgiveness for raping their daughters and threatening them to keep their mouths shut. While saying that, Omar started crying out loud like a little child.

Raja again turned toward the crowd and shouted in anger, "All of you stupid people, when would you wake up? Those who murder your children, rape your daughters and wives; you stand with them to kill innocent people. When will you stop disrespecting your religion and making fun of yourself in front of the whole world? No human has a right to kill another human. Life and death is in the hand of Allah, not yours; just remember that!

"Now I will leave these two, who are your true criminals. They deserve to be stoned in place of Zakia. However I still humbly request you hand them over to the Police. I will inform the director general of police myself and a top lawyer will represent your case. Trust me, I will make sure they get the death sentence."

Raja then went to Omar's guard and told them. "Throw away your weapons and support your poor brothers and make sure you handover Kalu with these two bastards."

He told the crowd. "All the men listen to me carefully. "I want all of you to respect all the girls who have been raped by Omar, and I will consider those men brave who will marry those innocent girls. I assure you they are as pure as your mothers, sisters and daughters. The real brave men are those who give honor to women. I promise all my support to those men. Just tell Fatima all your needs and she will inform my wife. Their wishes will be fulfilled accordingly."

He looked at Zakia's father; who was stood with a victorious smile on his face and with joined hands as he thanked Raja. "What are you waiting for? Take your daughter out from that grave, and cover her body with a big shawl."

Raja knew that Zakia had urinated in her clothes, so great was her fear of death; he didn't want anyone to see her in that condition. He gave a signal to the women in the car to come out and help Zakia.

Miriam, Ayesha and Fatima came running from the jeep; Babar was already helping his father to dig out Zakia. Fatima put her big shawl on Zakia and as she came out, she hugged her father and brother.

Then Babar told Zakia briefly about her rescuers and introduced her to Miriam and she showed her gratitude and held Miriam's feet, while thanking and praising her. Miriam hugged Zakia and they both shed tears but her their tears were of joy and victory.

All those gathered apologized to Zakia, and Miriam took leave from Zakia and told Fatima, "Let me know if Zakia's family needs anything, I will send some money for you." While looking at Zakia's father, she informed him, "Buy some land and start agriculture with your son; support your family and stay happy."

Raja was back in the jeep, Miriam went and sat next to him, and placed her hand on his hand, from depth of her heart, she told him, "I love you deeply. Thank you for what you did today. You made me very proud, my love." Raja smiled and told her, "My pleasure, my darling. Anything for you, just seeing you happy made my day."

They both smiled and started driving toward their home. In the back seat Ayesha smiled, while watching those two madly in love.

Miriam's soul was in peace and, as they were leaving the spot, she saw Madhu standing in a white sari smiling at her. Miriam was shocked to see her; she wanted Raja to stop the jeep. However when she looked back again Madhu had vanished, Miriam shed few tears.

Raja felt her surprise and, with a smile, told her, "See, even your friend is proud of you."

Shocked, Miriam wanted to ask Raja if he had also seen Madhu, but he placed a finger on his lips.

From the back seat, Ayesha asked Miriam "Is everything okay?"

"Yes all is good," Miriam replied.

Once they entered the house, Raja and Miriam both went straight to the bed room, where Miriam hugged Raja and said, "Thank you sweetheart, for what you did for me today. I have no words to describe how proud and happy I am."

Raja hugged her back and said, "Love, this is nothing. For you I can go to war with the world. Have some herbal tea and just relax, as I know you been under great stress today."

"Yes, my love, that is so true. I was really worried today. Before we hit the bed, tell me one thing. What did Maulvi Hanif see in your eyes that made him so scared?" Miriam asked him with a peaceful smile.

"Well, in my eyes he saw himself in my cave full of snakes," Raja replied while smiling.

"Oh my God! That is why his face turned pale!" Miriam chuckled.

CHAPTER 13

"GODDESS KALI'S HIDDEN TEMPLE OF SACRIFICES"

"Please tell me, what happened next with Durga. Her story is still stuck in my head and I am wondering how she dealt with Jay," Miriam asked Raja innocently.

Raja replied, "Sure, but you better lie down and keep your head on my chest and I will continue. I want you to relax your body and soul."

She immediately followed the instruction and Raja started telling her the rest of the story.

"As I told you earlier, Durga made up her mind to teach a life-long lesson to Jay; so let me take you back to my cave and continue from where we stopped.

"Durga while twisting hairs in her fingers continued, 'If I asked him to swim in the river filled with crocodiles or fight a lion, I knew just to please me, for a moment he would say yes. Then, being a cunning man, he would give me a million excuses regarding circumstances and consequences of the fight and at the end would blame me for keeping a bet that no man would be able to fulfill.

"'He was praising me like a poet, saying things which would cause any ordinary girl listening to, fall in love with him. I was just enjoying the entire situation, and I really wanted to educate myself with such a character. I was aware of his lack of audacity and that he would eschew any strong task that was out of his reach. My mind was all set to edify myself with his test, and give him an impossible task.'"

"Sometimes when you are with a person, with whom you can share and say anything and everything. In that instant you completely ignore your surroundings and the whole world. As one's universe is right there in that very moment, the same thing was happening with both of us. We were lost in each other, sharing thoughts, minds and enjoying conversations with complete freedom. I was a new-born human and king of all the snakes and she was a beautiful princess. She was one of God's creations, was blessed with beauty and brains. I was truly honored to be around her. She was full of life and one heavenly soul.

"We were in the most dangerous forest in the world, filled with the wildest creatures. We were simply enjoying all the unusual sounds coming from the forest. As for us it was music, a sound of peace and relaxation with spiritual healing.

"The cave's surroundings were more comfortable than any room of her palace and, above all, she was starved of communication with someone who possessed peace of mind, someone who would not judge her comments about herself and later not to spread any rumors about her.

"My abode was nothing less than a heaven for her. I was also enjoying her company and, from her, I was observing the gestures humans made while speaking to each other. My confidence soared after I spent time with Durga.

"As you are aware, I'm capable of communicating with every living creature on this earth. I gave instructions to a team of monkeys and their job was to provide various kinds of fruits and nuts. They never entered my cave, however once they started bringing the supplies, they left all goods outside of my cave and signaled me about a food drop.

"I also spoke to the king of buffaloes and we set a signal and, upon hearing my signal, he would make sure a female buffalo stood outside waiting for me so I could drink milk. Animals are very devoted and loyal; once they agree to do something they will never turn back.

"All the snakes brought various types of eggs for me; food was not a problem at all. Apart from animals, the spirits of the forest were kind and full of hospitality, and kept offering me various kinds of delicacies. I'm not that big of a food fan, as you know me."

Miriam asked, with wide eyes, "What do you mean by, the spirits of the forest?"

"Every forest in the world is ruled by its own spirits. They are creatures from a different world, not visible to humans. However all the animals can see them and can feel their existence. There is a party in the jungle on every full moon; I took Durga to one, which I will share with you later in the story, and also will give you a complete description of the creatures.

"I mentioned to you earlier, I was newly transformed into a human and I focused on only one thing, and that was to gather as much knowledge of human behavior as I could. It was my great chance to gain more knowledge. Learning human manners from Durga was something to which I truly looked forward to. I wanted her to teach me various subjects, as much as she could. I was keen to know Jay's mind and to what extent people like him could go," Raja replied.

Miriam said, "I look forward to hearing details about the party in the forest, and I can understand, you were just like new-born baby and were on the right track to understand the living standard of humans."

"I told Durga that I was deeply interested in hearing the whole tale, how she had handled such an evil man. I was keen to study human personalities and on what stage of mind, they became worse than animals. As for me, I left everything to find peace for my soul and Durga's tale would educate me in some way so I would be able to help someone else whom I found stuck, in a similar scenario as Durga was. Greed is a disease. What made people like Jay think they could win over humanity? I understood people like Jay needed to learn a lesson, so they could set an example for others to avoid greed.

"Durga replied with a beautiful smile, '"Sure! You saved my life and it will be an honor for me to share this strange tale with you and I'm honestly sure you will learn a lot from my experience with Jay and how I handled him with my wisdom and knowledge.

"She returned to Jay flattering her with his words, like, '"I can do this for you. I can give my life for you. Name it and I will do it for you to prove my devotion towards you.'" With the tone of princess, she told Jay, 'Stop this nonsense of you dying for me! What is the value of your life if just on my one signal your soul would leave your body and travel back to where it belongs?'

"Durga told Jay she valued people who had courage to speak their minds and that he had shown interest in her. However she wanted to meet him the following day and would tell him her wish. Durga continued if he manages to fulfill that she can speak to her father and he will happily make him a prince. She could have given him her wish right now, but the reason she delayed was so he can come to his senses and never ever show her his face again. He had twenty-four-hours to come back to his senses and vanish from the face of earth. She really don't know what suicide mission he had selected for himself and why he was in such a hurry to leave the world. Next time when they meet, he was bound to accomplish her command, and remember he had to fulfill her wish. Even if it's the most daring mission he will hear and would be bound to fulfill it. Remember if he say no or give her any excuses; he will be disqualified. On accepting her wish, she would provide all necessary requirements, and will provide all he would require to complete her wish. As Durga's believes in a fair deal she would give him extreme freedom to demand his needs for making her wish come true. Keep in his mind and just remember if he fails, she will make sure his head would be removed or she would throw him in a cave of her lions and would watch him being eaten alive."

Jay displayed his ugly dirty teeth and replied, "He accept her challenge of her wish which he would be waiting to hear tomorrow and he promised would fulfill every single wish of her; his highness."

"One thing was bothering her. Why was he so confident? Were there any gods who were supporting him or did he practice black magic or have control over some evil spirit? Durga never saw any commoner ever raise their head in front of her, and Jay was standing staring at her with such confidence.

"As he left her presence, she called her closest guard, Veer, and gave him a mission to investigate more about this man, who he was, what kind of people he has acquaintance with. She especially instructed Veer to find out if he was involved in any sinister activities.

"Then she went back home and waited for Veer to come back and give her a complete report on Jay's movements. Veer took almost six hours to return and, as he entered the palace, he informed one of Durga's close maids of his arrival. Durga had already told the maid to bring it to her knowledge as soon Veer was back in the palace.

"She went out and took a walk with Veer in the garden and they sat down. She asked Veer, "'so, what details do you have for me about this character Jay?'

"Veer kept his gaze on the ground and told her about Jay. 'Your highness, because I found out some unusual details about him, I think it would be wise if we get the king involved in this matter. Right now since we have to take a serious action against him, otherwise we will be too late. He is not an ordinary man. I agree he looks like a normal, poor commoner, but he truly is not. I followed him and he went straight to a cave that is near the village. I managed to follow him inside. What I saw there is really quite hard for me to share with you. I know you are a brave princess, but still I believe some issues exists that only men should handle, and this man, Jay, is far beyond your reach. Only our king knows how to deal with this kind of evil man."'

Raja continued, "Durga's eyes widened with surprise, as she knew Veer was one of the bravest soldiers in her army. He had been trained to kill ten to fifteen men with his bare hands. It was the first time she had seen fear and concern on his face, as if he have seen some monster. Veer was an extremely strong man and thinking about Jay's personality compared to his, made her more worried. How come a man like Veer was scared of an ordinary man like Jay? What had Veer seen in that cave that had provoked him to involve the king in such a small matter? She made up her mind. Whatever creature Jay was, she would deal with him in her own way. She gathered all her courage and ordered Veer, "'there is no need to inform the king. I want to deal with this matter on my own and you must share everything explicit with me, as to what you saw in that cave.'"

"Veer told her, 'Your highness, as I entered the cave, it was full of big rocks and, in the middle, was a vast, empty space, just like your dining room inside the palace. On walls I saw torch holders and he was lighting every torch on the walls. Then the cave view became like it was daylight inside there. Everything was clearly visible and the next thing I did was to find a place to hide, behind a huge rock so no one inside the cave could be aware of me being there.

"'At the inner edge of the cave, I saw a statue of the goddess Kali. I had never seen such a real statue of the goddess Kali, as if she were alive and present herself in that cave. Then as I observed Jay, he went and bowed his head and kissed the status's feet.

I noticed at her feet a huge tub made of fine marble. When I tried to look at what was inside the tub, I saw it was full of bloodstains.

"'Jay then started talking to the statue. I was not able to hear; however what surprised me was, it seemed as if the statue was replying to him. Sometimes he cried in front of her statue and sometimes he started laughing like a serious lunatic.

"'For a long time, his conversation went on with the statue, as if he was sharing some story with her and seeking advice. A few times I felt he was begging her for something and she is saying no to him. He kept trying to convince her.

"'What I really found weird inside the cave was that the light of the moon started touching the statue and Jay. The cave was deep inside the mountains and from where the moonlight was coming. I truly was not able to figure out.

"'One thing I know for sure is that it was not a holy place; something tremendously evil was present in that cave. Every single stone reeked of the horrors that had taken place in that cave. What had really happened there no one knew apart from Jay. The marble tub filled with bloodstains was a mystery in itself. It didn't take me long to figure out this was not a cave, but a temple of sacrifices!

"'While I was assessing the temple, what I witnessed next was the shock of my life. From the middle of nowhere twelve men appeared all of a sudden. They were midgets and all wore long black robes; even their skin was jet black. What gave me a chill was when I tried to see their features so I could remember their faces so later I can find and arrest them. All midgets had no features, like no nose, no eyes and not even a mouth. All those twelve midgets were faceless men and I knew they were some kind of evil creatures. They all bowed their heads before Jay, as if he was their god. One of the midgets started feeling here and there, as if he felt my presence. I sensed they must have had some kind of powers to track me down and I quietly left the cave. When I had been following Jay, I had marked my route and memorized all the locations. The worst moment came when I left the cave and turned to memorize the location, I was in a complete shock when I realized there was no sign of any cave. The mountain had become plain and had changed from what I had seen before entering the cave. I returned back and tried to search for the cave, as my plan was to come back with few guards and arrest Jay and later investigate the entire area.

"'The entrance had vanished from the mountain, as if there had never been a cave. If I would have just viewed the entrance from a distance and later was not able to find it, then it would have made sense. The problem was that I spent hours inside and saw all of what I told you. I spent another half an hour just trying to find the cave which I was not able to find. I don't know what type of opaque they created and I kept roaming like a mad person.

"'From the mountains I went straight to the Durga Temple, as you know your highness; the Durga Temple was created by your great grandfather and is one of the biggest and oldest temples in the state. I went and knocked on the priest's door. He was surprised to see me in such a ghastly condition; I discussed with him in detail and he was surprised by my story. I asked him if he knew Jay and he told me he did know him but his gathering is with a strange kind of crowd and they all were disciples of the goddess Kali and were involved in various kind of evil acts. The priest also told me, people were scared of Jay and there were several rumors about him. Some said he possessed evil powers; few said that goddess Kali had been seen with him on various occasions. I spent some time praying to goddess Durga then came back to the palace.'"

"Fear and concern were visible in Veer's eyes, and Durga told Veer, "'Listen! Do not discuss with anyone what you saw and I want you not to worry about anything. I promise you, I will sort out this man in my own way. Leave it up with me until I give you any further instructions.'"

Veer bowed his head and humbly replied, "'I'm at your service, your highness, and my life is always at your disposal. Please just be careful and I will be waiting for your further instructions.'"

"Durga told me, "'the next thing I had to do was to visit Guru Das. He was a hundred and four years old and one of my father's advisers.

"'Guru Das was a true sage, a man of wisdom and an extremely knowledgeable soul. He was capable of predicting the future, as well as sensing an evil presence within a second, and always had been my guiding angel.

"'Guru Das was strictly against my father the king and my brothers going to lead the army. He begged them not to go that day and to rather leave after two days. But no one listened to him, as he secretly informed my father, that his sons would be killed on that very day. And that day I lost my two brothers. My father ignored his advice and so did my brothers and they were brutally murdered. After that, my father never made a single decision without consulting Guru Das; he was like a father figure to me and simultaneously he treated me as a daughter and a close friend.

'Guru Das was in great health, as he spent most of his time meditating. Not only was he our spiritual guru; he was also our medicine man for the family. He was gifted with healing powers for any cure; he had great knowledge on various herbs and how to use them.

"'He saw me coming and as I neared him, I clearly viewed his kind smile, as he was aware of why I was there and what I would share with him. I sat close to him, and it was just the two of us, so I started my conversation.

"I asked, "'Guru, you know the secrets of one's heart and you can read the mind too, so what do you think about this man Jay?'

"Guru Das replied, "'Durga, I have given you enough knowl-edge of how to judge people, read their eyes, body language and the way they speak. What is your conclusion about Jay? I would like to hear your views first and then I will share mine,'

CHAPTER 14
"VAHUS"

R aja continued, "Durga told me that Jay was a sweet talker, no personality and she clearly felt something about him was malicious; she did take her own time to figure it out, while he was trying to capture her soul with his saccharine words. However, she sensed from what he said that all he wanted was to be a prince, gain power and rule the state. Jay was a commoner, still she felt deception in his eyes and she told him that the following day she would present her wish to him and if he fulfilled it, she would marry him. What bothered her was Jay's confidence. How could a commoner be so sure to take such a big risk?

"What happened to his cognizance and why was he not scared of death? She sent Veer to gather his report and he followed him into a cave and she shared all of this with Guru Das, about what was told to her by Veer and what he had witnessed in the cave.

"Guru Das listened to every word with complete concentration, and responded that Jay was essentially an ascetic of goddess Kali, who was famously known as the goddess of time, change, and destruction.

"He was one of those people who were known for giving religion a bad name, as they picked up all the worst aspects and add their own doctrines and create their own cults. The strange part was people started following such fanatics who were so blind in their faith. They believed goddess Kali's blessings were with them and they could do and achieve anything they wanted. They practiced some evil acts too.

"The worst and most devilish act they had been committing was sacrificing children, on the darkest nights, when the moon had vanished from the skies. Their belief was that by committing such sacrifices they could gain enormous powers. Maybe from Jay's appearance Durga thought of him as a commoner but intrinsically he was not.

If Durga concluded that he saw her and fell for her, the fact was, it's not as if he jumped on her as a fool. Jay had planned the whole game and had been honing his skills and powers since the day Durga had been born.

"He wanted to gain power not only of the state; in fact he wanted to control Durga's mind too. Being a commoner, he had approached her when he knew more than fifty soldiers always guarded her and on Durga's one signal she could have easily had him killed. He knew and was aware she wouldn't do anything such like that. He had his own team with whom he shared his plans and concerns. Every move he made was very well calculated.

"Just as Durga and Guru Das had been discussing as one team, on how to handle him and tried to find his weakness. He was aware of Durga's weakness, which was kindness and he took full advantage of her.

"He did have his own team, consisting of nefarious people. They were all disciples of the goddess Kali and they all knew and believed that by offering sacrifices to the goddess Kali that she in return, would fulfill all their dirty desires and wishes.

"They all had evil knowledge which could harm not only Durga but the entire kingdom. Their constellation consisted of not more than twenty disciples, however they were all extremely powerful. Now

Guru Das was concerned of Durga's safety and if they shared this incident with her father, he would definitely order guards to kill Jay.

"Durga's father would not understand that Jay was not easy to be eradicated, as he would control minds of the guards as he controlled Durga's.

"He worked his invocation on Durga, and one could only imagine how else such an ugly man could have spoken to Durga and she would have listened to him. How is it possible that Jay held his wish of marrying her and telling Durga that he loved her?

"It was a conspiracy to gain power; he was an extremely greedy person, and if he managed to marry Durga then he would set Hell free on earth.

"They had no knowledge of the blessings of goddess Kali; she blessed her followers with changes. As far as destruction was concerned, she only killed the ego, lust, greed and all types of bad habits within humans.

"People like Jay always give religion a bad name and turn a positive approach into a negative one, so their wishes may come true as per their negative thoughts.

Durga responded to this by telling, "Guru that as per Veer's details, she thought the mysterious hidden temple inside the cave was used for sacrificing children.

"How was it possible that no one in the states knew about child sacrifices, these people performing such evil crimes and how come not a single parent had complained about the loss of their children?

"Guru Das replied by saying that people like them were very cunning, sharp and smart. They calculated every single move of their crime. Secondly, ordinary people were always scared of such people because, as you know, they are superstitious meager people and are always scared of curses from 'holy' men.

"Guru knew most ordinary people in the state who were acquainted with such people always considered them ineffable, highly knowledgeable and powerful. He had strong feelings they had to have been kidnapping small children from different states and then, on the darkest nights, they performed sacrifices. Jay had imbibed the blood of children below five years of age.

"He had been part of all types of serious cults. Since young age, he had spent time with Agoris. They are devotees of Lord Shiva and they were famous for eating leftover from dead people's flesh. They wear ashes from a human pyre and drink from human skull, which they used as drinking and eating bowls also known as ka-pala. Agoris mostly lived near Hindu cremation grounds, a place avoided by many. Among all the sects in Hinduism, the most feared ones are Agoris. They believe nothing is unholy, and in everything god can be found. In their eyes even a cow dung or animal urine and is sacred too. Agoris have to leave their families, friends and all loved ones. They travel freely, without worrying about food or shelter. They drink wine and smoke opium on a daily basis; they use mud pipes and believe they are following Lord Shiva. They are also strong devotee of the goddess Kamakhya.

"Jay did all this for gaining various powers. Any crazy or insane ritual he came to know about, he got involved in, experimenting and becoming more powerful.

"Like all Agoris, he had been drinking his own urine, keeping the head of a live chicken in his mouth and then tearing the head off from its body with his teeth, later drinking the blood of the chicken. People like Jay performed such kind of acts with other animals as well.

"Guru told her not to worry, as nothing bad would ever happen to her while he was alive in this world and that even if he died, he had trained her well to protect herself and her family too.

"Durga asked innocuously whether anyone in this world knew about those faceless midgets, the way Veer described them.

"Guru said that yes, Veer had described them in complete de-tail. They were faceless yet they were the most terrifying creatures in the whole universe. They all stay together in groups of twelve. Finding them in this world is not only difficult, but almost completely impossible. Those faceless creatures are called Danwals. There is only one way to find them, by finding at special tree.

"That tree is full of only green leaves but once in three years, for only two days, twelve leaves will grow purple. That is the sign and the person with knowledge will figure out that below the same tree is the abode of Danwals. Guru knew the only way to capture Danwals is to hold one purple leaf in your hand, as that is when you are able to see Danwals. Once a day, one or two of them will come out of hidden doors of the tree and that is the time you have to catch it by its neck. While holding that purple leaf, you are invisible to their eyes; there is no other way you can ever touch Danwals.

"If you manage to catch a Danwal, you become the owner of all twelve, and they will be your slaves for life. They do look faceless but their mouths are in their stomachs. After slaughtering those innocent children in the goddess Kali's hidden temple they offer the blood to the goddess, which people like Jay later then lick from her feet and the bodies they serve to the Danwals as meal.

"They even devour the bones, hairs, nails and teeth of those little children. That is the main reason no one had ever been able to find those children's bodies. Danwals do have the powers, to give answers to all questions, and they can always be with the person who owns them. Guru suggested that when Jay came to talk to Durga, even at that time Danwals were his protectors and they have the ability to control other people's minds.

"The reason they were not able to control Durga's mind was because she was protected by the many prayers Guru had offered all the time. Jay could have as many evil powers as he wanted, but Durga was the Lord's chosen one. Together with Guru Das, they would beat Jay at his own game. Guru told her to wear a locket around her neck, while he removed one of his own from his neck.

He kept it in both hands, closed his eyes and prayed over the locket. Then he placed the locket around her neck.

"Guru made her promise she would never take it off. The reason was that sometimes people like Jay got help from Danwals to travel inside a person's mind. They tried to find weakness, and the first one he had found, he had taken advantage of her kindnesses! So, he was aware Durga would not harm him in anyway. Now when Danwals tried to look in Durga's eyes, Guru had blocked them from entering her mind and finding another weakness.

"Durga wanted to know why Veer was not able to find the cave's entrance which led to the temple of goddess Kali.

"To this Guru said that again it was the Danwals. They could build a shield around the cave so it became invisible to human eyes. However they would find the temple and this was something she wouldn't have to worry about. First they have to sort out this devil servant, Jay.

"Guru wanted to know what wish she had thought of. He wanted her to share it with him and to let him see how strong the wish was and then he would guide her. He had to be sure the question she kept in front of a person like Jay covered all details that would capture the essence to defeat him. Guru Das spoke while looking into Durga eyes.

"Durga responded by sharing her plan for sending Jay on a quest and that he needed to go and find the Vahus; the color changing stone from the cave of the lost souls, which was situated in mountains of Lanka. He must return with Vahus and use its magic to control a soul. She would have given him one month to complete the quest and would provide him all necessary requirements for his journey, along with her two bravest soldiers to accompany him, as she wanted her deal to be fair and honest.

"Guru Das told her she was ready to rule the world and he could feel she calculated all the relevant details while finalizing such a crucial task. The quest she had selected was not only extremely dangerous, but no man had ever been able to get his hands on the Vahus.

"He really liked her idea and, for a man like Jay, nothing would have been better. The best part would be a journey and the mission, and he could see it was evil versus evil, and he would not be able to gain possession of great Vahus.

"The reason was simple the souls inside the cave, knew the powers of the Vahus and would try their best to protect that stone. If he managed to get hold of the stone, all the lost souls would enter his body and he had no idea what they would do with him. This was not a mission for anyone to even consider. Such a quest was plan a trip to commit suicide.

"Lost souls knew the powers of that stone. By keeping that stone in any dead man or woman's mouth, he would capture the soul of that body and make the soul his slave, and would use it to get the soul to do evil work. Lost souls would never let it happen, as they are protectors of the dead and know the catastrophe this one soul is cable of once captured.

"Guru was extremely proud of her and he could see she was all set and ready to win at life. What surprised him was that he had told her about the Vahus color- changing stone's powers when she was just a little girl. They had never discussed anymore about that stone and now she planned to use the impossible mission for that cunning Jay.

"Guru was entirely sure Durga would beat him at his own game, as Jay had a reputation for verbosity; Durga's quest would make him quiet right on the spot. He had challenged her reputation and

Guru Das knew Durga would set a new example in teaching Jay a lesson by creating an example for others. The world should understand her credence and people like Jay needed to cower once Durga's name is mentioned, which should make him snivel all his filthy life.

"Guru Das added that they had to make sure this whole issue would be handled in great privacy. In case Durga's father found about this, it would be a big problem for both of them, also as it was not the right time to get Jay killed in public. The following day, Guru Das would go with Durga so he could see if the goddess Kali or any evil shadow stood next to Jay.

"If Jay was completely dependent on Danwals, then he has no idea they would never make it out of that cave alive. All Guru Das's life he had done spiritual meditation and he had been in that cave and spent thirty-two days there. He never went for the stone; rather he had been there to gain strength and wisdom from the lost souls. He assured her even a mighty heart would lose his mind in that cave.

"Initially the cave had a small entrance and then inside it was a different world and one could simply feel movements everywhere, as if you have entered a new city. That one little tiny stone Vahus was alive.

"As it was shy of any living creature, it remained invisible to any living human and no one could find that where the stone was located.

"When Guru had completed his seventh day of prayers inside the cave and had been sitting in one position without food or water. Even with closed eyes he felt the rays of those magical lights gave him strength.

"Once he felt the rays touching his body, the cave suddenly became alive. He felt the presence of thousands of people walking around him and they were busy doing their normal day work.

"It seemed as he was in a new country, with men and women from various races. Some were extremely well dressed and they seemed like people from the West. A few seemed as if they were ancient warriors. Some were giant humans and a few were midgets. They were all different from present-day humans. They all respected and regarded each other like good citizens. Guru Das never heard any strange voices or saw any of them fighting with each other.

"The scary part of that cave was not only the human souls that resided there; various creatures' souls guarded the Vahus. Even if someone managed to control the human souls, they would need a lifetime of experience to handle all those monstrous creatures' souls. Even a steel-hearted person like Guru Das got scared the first time he saw her coming toward him. All the creatures addressed her by the name shebuf, the soul sucker.

"Shebuf was half buffalo and half woman. From her head to her stomach she was a woman and the rest of her body was a buffalo. Guru Das had never seen such scary eyes in his entire life. The color of her eyes was orange. Her full body was obese and jet black, with thick curly hairs covering her face, and all he could see were those horrendous eyes. They were not only vast, but they possessed the power to suck your soul within a second.

"Most of the corpses Guru Das saw were of soldiers and sorcerers, however one thing was common in all those corpses in that cave; their mouths were wide open and it didn't take him much time to understand that their souls had been sucked out by shebuf. Even from the corpses their fear was felt, the way they died with their mouths widely open. There was also a very big problem; even the bravest hearts, who somehow managed to keep their senses calm in her sight, went insane once she started screaming.

"Her voice had a strange melancholy and extreme anger, that made you feel like someone started inserting millions of needles into your body.

"The second-most brutal monstrous creatures' souls were the hyben. There were more than ten hyben in the lost souls cave and they always stayed in a pack. They had an upper body of a hyena and below, the legs of a human; they have the ability to walk both ways, sometimes like humans and sometime on their four legs.

"They were nine times larger than normal hyenas and were enormously dangerous. Well, when it came to capturing and hunting intruders in lost cave of souls, their hunting procedure was similar to normal hyenas. They also start eating their prey from the stomach and, in that scenario the death was excruciating and slow. However, their style was little different, they would open the stomach with their sharp teeth and then the whole pack would go for a trip, leaving the prey screaming with agonizing pain.

"Then they would come back and will take a small bite and again would go away. They want the screams to be heard throughout the whole cave. The pack would make sure the prey remained alive for as long as it could, as they ate very slowly. It's a legend about hybens that they are hell dogs and those who lost their lives fighting against powerful creatures in hell, their souls were transferred to the cave of lost souls.

"The king of all monstrous creatures is Angion. Guru Das never saw him but he knew he existed, as his presence was felt deeply in the cave. An Angion was four times bigger than a lion and had wings, so he can fly. His features were the same as a lion, however the wings gave him a mighty presence. Angion only appeared when the rest of the cave was unable to stop intruders.

"As all the souls, including humans and creatures, kept themselves busy in asking forgiveness from the Lord, they could all easily feel the presence of man of God. That was the only reason they let Guru Das stay there and let him finish his fasting for thirty days.

"When he completed his spiritual meditation, he felt the various types of lights and rays which were touching him before, then started entering his body. All those lights were coming out from Vahus, as the stone was blessing him with hidden powers.

"Any additional knowledge, wisdom or power makes your confidence stronger but concurrently adds another burden on your mind and soul. That makes you more humble, kind, and you don't see the world through your eyes; you can see from your mind, Guru Das told Durga.

"Durga asked whether he spoke to someone inside the cave, as she felt someone had told him about the Angion.

CHAPTER 15

"CAVE OF THE LOST SOULS"

"Guru Das, while smiling, told her that the king and queen of lost souls had visited him to introduce themselves. No one in the world could tell they were just souls; he felt as if they were alive and they truly were in their full glory. The name of the king was, Hukush and he introduced his queen by the name Ziyush.

"Hukush was good-looking man and he still wore the attire of a king, and Ziyush was one of the most beautiful women Guru Das had ever seen in his life. Their appearances suggested that they both seemed kind and loving, however they held secrets in their heart only God knew and that is what they both shared with him. Their tale was thought provoking and the message they taught him then became the essence of Guru's life and teaching.

"First they arranged food for him, he had never tasted such delicious food in his entire life. They knew he had fasted for thirty days. Physically he was weak but mentally and spiritually he was far too strong. They insisted on what he would like to eat and he was amazed by the manner of their asking, as they were still in their kingdom. Humbly he thanked them for letting him complete his spiritual routine then replied and told them he was a vegetarian and only preferred vegetables, lentils, and fruits.

"Hukush, without turning around said, "'you heard the man. Serve him as per his wish.'" Within a second, a table covered with vegetarian food was set in a corner. He didn't know where the table had come from and the food seemed as if it had been freshly cooked. Hukush and his wife joined Guru Das and, with a pleasant smile, he started eating. He knew offering them food would make no sense. First he thanked them for their hospitality and while eating, requested whether he could ask them few questions.

"Hukush with a pleasant smile agreed, and Guru Das asked why their souls were there?

"Hukush told him that their kingdom was vast and spread over the entire west. He had been in love with his queen and the whole kingdom was happy and prosperous. He had been fifty years old at that time and Ziyush thirty-four. They had been blessed with everything and they both were God-fearing people. His Ziyush had just one simple wish, which was to have a child. She had been treated by the finest herbalist from around the globe; but no one was able to solve their problem. One day, Hukush's wife told him she had arranged with two virgin girls that they would give them a child. All Hukush would have to do was sleep with them. He was not interested in her proposition but she insisted and, being madly in love with her, after all he was forced to say yes to his queen.

"Ziyush knew if he did not have an heir, after his death, his own cunning advisers would take over his kingdom and his name would be completely removed. Hukush was less concerned about the kingdom but he was not able to see heartrending face of his wife. Her health started deteriorating and all she wanted was a child. Finally he had to say yes. The poor girls were not in position to say no to a queen, so they were happy to serve their king. Ziyush promised both girls that once either one of them bore a child, she would send them and their family away and would settle them for life, with fully furnished houses, with land ownership, and a huge quantity of gold.

"Both girls got pregnant at the same time and the king and queen announced in their kingdom that the queen was pregnant. There was a great ceremony for a week. The whole nation was celebrating; in every corner of kingdom people enjoyed carnivals. Everyone danced, drank, and there was a nonstop feast, along with the celebration. Everything was going well and Hukush was happy and so was Ziyush. When the girls completed six months of their pregnancies, Hukush started noticing strange variations in his wife's moods.

"'A woman's heart is truly deepest than an ocean,' whoever said those words truly was a genius. Hukush wanted to know what was bothering his beloved wife, one beautiful evening when the clouds were playing hide and seek with moon.

"Ziyush was standing on the palace terrace and was observing the clouds and the moon. Hukush went and hugged her from behind while he kissed her neck softly and whispered, "'I love you madly. Tell me what is disturbing you, sweetheart.'

"Ziyush turned around, looked deep into his eyes and said, she wanted to share what is killing her inside, but was aware of his kind heart and beautiful soul. She was afraid Hukush would never agree with what she wanted to ask him.

"All his life he just loved her as her most devoted, humble servant and friend. What was it she wanted? He gave her his word he would agree to do whatever was on her mind. It had been her wish to have children from other women. He had followed her like a lamb, who even knew his master was taking him for sacrifice, but walked the path with complete honesty.

"Ziyush explained her wish, she didn't want those girls to be alive once they gave birth to his children. One day or another they could raise their voices and if that day came, they could lose everything. What she feared the most was the way the world would look at her. Everyone would make fun of her and she imagined, they would even consider Hukush as a liar.

"She could see the world destroyed rather than Hukush's head bowed before anyone; she couldn't see and would prefer to die before such a moment occurred in her life. She loved him madly as in him, she'd always seen her God. She asked him to consider it the madness of love and begged him to support her and promise that the day they give birth to their children, they would kill them right that very moment. For this they would not include anyone else. They had to do the killing themselves together.

"Hukush was quiet and he tried to see deep in the eyes of his love; she was totally a changed person standing before him, trying to seek the answer in his eyes. He felt the Devil was talking in her that very second. His kind, loving queen, who couldn't bear to even see a single tear in the eye of a commoner, that day her new image scared him. What to do when you love someone? Your heart beats for the one you love and his life was in her. He had already given her his word and agreed to her unthinkable wish. Sometimes being a king gave a feeling, that you are the god in yourself and who can touch or stop you for doing good or bad? The Devil was transferred from her into Hukush. Finally, the day came, that both girls gave birth to his two sons. Those girls happily handed a part of their soul. He was looking in their eyes and was able to find the strange distressing as they were in horrible pain, but still their eyes were filled with joy while just looking at the babies.

"Hukush and his wife slaughtered each of the girls. They were weak and were already in immense pain and they cut their throats. He still remembered those eyes with millions of questions asking, why and for what reason they were killing them.

"What wrong had they done? They had fulfilled their wish and just wanted to return to their families and they were killing them. Not a single word was said but their eyes were doing the talking.

"Those eyes 'Oh my Lord' still haunted Hukush and Ziyush. Later they fed the bodies to their pet lions, and they devoured the corpses and with the passage of time, the couple completely forgot about those girls. The whole world came to know that Hukush's wife had given birth to twins. Again it was a huge celebration and a very grand one too. Many kings and queens traveled from different continents to participate in those most joyful moments of their lives. The arrival of their sons made Hukush the happiest man on the Earth, and his wife was extremely happy and alive again.

"One year passed, and it was their sons' birthday, and the palace was filled with guests from all around the globe.

"In life the one thing they ignored completely was God, who had been watching. One of Hukush's advisers, name Aumash had been after his kingdom and Hukush was entirely ignorant about his conspiracy. Aumash turned out to be his regicide, and had been planning to kill Hukush's entire family.

"That night, Hukush and his wife had both been drinking far too much, and later they both started to feel lightheaded. They excused themselves to their royal guests and went to rest in the royal chamber. Hukush awoke when he felt extreme pain, someone was slitting his throat and when he turned his eyes around another man was doing the same with his wife. That night they were killed, Hukush's adviser didn't even spare Hukush's innocent children. They were also killed brutally.

"Hukush's soul was released from his body and he watched everything and later his wife's soul joined him. The agony of being helpless and watching one's children brutally killed was the most horrible pain anyone could ever go through. Then they both saw a beam of light and both girls came in the shape of angels to them that they were in Heaven and had come to take their children with them. Hukush and his wife's souls would be stuck in the cave of lost souls and where they could pray for forgiveness, and maybe you would get a chance to join them in Heaven. Then both girls told them their souls had been assigned to protect a special stone called Vahus. They also informed them with a pleasant smile that they had forgiven them for what they had done to them, because that was what their Lord Jesus Christ's teaching was all about.

"Hukush cried remembering the words of Jesus Christ, in which he clearly said, 'for all who draw the sword will die by the sword.' He totally had followed his lord all life and could not understand how he had become so blind and had ignored his teachings and guidance. Few words they may seem, but the wisdom of the world was hidden in them; he clearly advised those who killed others would be killed in the same manner. God can forgive all sins but when it comes to murder, it will not go unpunished. That act makes God very angry and we humans keep repeating it again and again. God blesses us humans with the biggest gift in the form of life. God is the owner of our lives and only he has a right to take a human's life.

"While Hukush told his story, Guru Das saw tears in both their eyes. He controlled his emotions and start telling Guru Das again that all the souls in the cave were of murderers and torturers, only those souls who took the life of another human. Could he imagine all of them had been brutally murdered the same way they had killed others. If you looked back into history, even the kings who were untouchables, even when in power were also killed like ordinary peasants. What happened to their securities, cornucopia of power and wealth? They all were killed by ordinary, unknown people. Give a name of one prophet who predicted and warned humans about such a reality? Imagine how strongly Jesus Christ instructed all mankind but when they were alive. No one listened and this became their destiny and all of them now, their souls were stuck there to protect Vahus. Various faiths, different views about life after death, but the honest truth they only discovered when they died. Hukush knew Guru Das was not a Christian, but begged him to pray to Jesus Christ for their forgiveness. The Lord always listened to holy men like Guru and maybe they would be given another chance so their souls could join their children in Heaven.

"Guru Das requested Hukush, to tell him more about Jesus Christ and then he shared Jesus Christ's life story. He told Guru Das how incredibly his birth had taken place and how he had accepted a harsh verdict and even being as innocent as a child, he had suffered and had been given death on a cross. He had died and he sacrificed his life for all the sinners of the world like us. Jesus' story was a life changer for Guru Das. He told Hukush he would offer his prayers directly to Jesus Christ, and he spent the next two days praying with them. During their prayer breaks, Hukush told Guru

Das about the lost cave, and the creatures inside. He told Guru Das many secrets that only the dead knew but were forbidden to the living souls. Hukush was the one who told me about existence and presence of Angion in the lost souls cave. In some of his details, he tried to give Guru Das hints to educate people as much as possible so they could prepare themselves to meet God after their deaths.

"What Guru Das really would have liked to know was the mystery of the Vahus; he was very keen to go into greater depth on the history of this magical stone and was deeply interested to know the true origin of the Vahus was. With a trembling heart, Guru Das finally asked Hukush, about the origin of Vahus and where this stone had really come from and what it's true history was.

"Hukush was quiet for a few seconds then he started gazing toward the cave's ceiling and in a strong voice replied, that before Adam, God made angels, and one he really made very beautiful and his name was Lucifer. He was God's closest and favorite angel; Lucifer, like all other angels, was a true soldier of God and always followed his orders. When God planned to make Adam, Lucifer was the one who was totally against such an idea and tried to convince God, not to make humans by saying that if God created someone with his face and mind, the first thing he would do was disobey God. Man would make God ashamed of his own creation. God's mind was set and he really wanted to create his magnum opus. In the form of Adam, he created the first human. Lucifer started feeling jealous, as God was spending most of his time with Adam. God was in love with Adam and he was happy and proud of his own creation.

"On the other hand, Lucifer began a conspiracy among other angels. He felt angels would be left just to serve humans and, as for him, he wanted humans serve angels. Most of the time, he requested God to make humans the slaves of angels; in that way, angels could control and keep them on track. However, God was madly in love with Adam and rejected his proposal and clearly informed him that not a single living soul was above humans, even angels would have to serve them and look after them.

"Then God made Eve and, after some time, Adam and Eve both committed the first sin in Heaven. God was furious and that was when the first conflict happened in the universe and in Heaven, between Lucifer and God. As that was the moment which Lucifer had been waiting for God to regret his creation. Lucifer, with his team of rebel angels, went to God and Lucifer started telling God that he wished God had listened to him, as he had never wanted God to be sad about His creation.

"God became angry, as he still loved mankind but wanted to test their loyalty and dedication to him. He punished Adam and Eve, threw them out of Heaven. God made Earth for humans, as he always believed in the human race that one day or another they would ask his forgiveness. God didn't selected time limit of human life, because when he had made Adam, he had made him and Eve immortal. However after committing sins, God divided body and soul. Human bodies expired but the souls remained alive for eternity. God introduced them to death and limited their life.

"God set a plan for humans; for the time they spent on Earth they would be judged by their good deeds. Those who feared Him and obeyed His laws, He would welcome them back to Heaven. Lucifer went against God for showing such kindness again toward humans. He challenged God, that not a single human soul would be clean, as they would all turn into sinners. God was tired of Lucifer's hatred and enormous amount of jealousy, and casted him out of Heaven. The lost cave was the place where he fell and that was where the archangel Michael followed him and tried to kill him and his soul. He somehow managed to escape from the archangel Michael, however during their fight Vahus fell, which was actually a button from the heavenly dress of Lucifer and from that day 'til now, the war is still going on. Slaves of Lucifer keep trying to steal Vahus and what God did was ordered the most evil souls to protect Vahus. It was like cutting iron from the iron.

"Guru Das had been given a task to spread Hukush's message; to inform humans about not killing each others. Guru Das tried his best to share wisdom with everyone. The first one to ignore Guru Das's prediction was Durga's father and look what happened, he lost his two sons. It was Guru Das's loss as well, as he had loved those boys madly. He devoted his life to serve Durga and raised all three of them. He tried to teach Durga's brothers never to kill anyone, but when they were still young and hot blooded. They started killing people and the result as per Jesus Christ's warning, they died the same way. Their death devastated Guru Das, which was basically his greatest failure in life. Imagine even though Durga's father was a king and Guru being a scholar, they still lost them.

"Power is a strange possession, Guru Das said, as being human when we came into our senses, we started seeking powers from every aspect. When Guru Das was Durga's age, his only fantasy was to become the most knowledgeable man on the planet. Now, at this age, when he looked deep inside himself, he saw nothing but knowledge, wisdom and unlimited powers. Still he felt all that he had gained in his whole life was just only a drop out of the sea.

"Imagine with only a drop of wisdom, he had been urged to stay isolated from the rest of the world, in order to keep all relevant details to himself. He couldn't even have a decent conversation with an ordinary person, because all they spoke and wanted to know was how to be rich, how to hurt or control others and how they could become the strongest and have more concubines.

"He told Durga that when she enough wisdom within her, the only person she would enjoy having a conversation with was someone who held and valued knowledge deeply. Guru Das wanted to talk, and he always enjoyed conversation, and all his life he had spent time with older people. They always guided him and gave him some kind of knowledge. It was hard to imagine that these days hardly any young ones wanted to spend time with their elders. They thought, 'What do they know?'

"Apart from Durga's father and her, no one was interested in understanding the reality of life and the truth. Guru Das had transferred most of his knowledge between Durga and her siblings. She knew Guru had never married nor had any children of his own. All his life he had loved Durga as his own, and when her brothers had been killed, his soul dead with them.

"The only reason he wanted to stay alive was to keep Durga safe from people like Jay. Doing that made his heart truly happy. He felt Durga was ready to become a stronger queen, he would not die until he witness her coronation. What worried him was the man who would be her husband and he told her, as per my knowledge, this man honestly required the heart of a lion to walk with you. Guru Das looked toward Durga with serious concern.

"Durga responded with a smile by saying that Guru Das didn't have to worry about that man with a lion heart; if there was one for her he would appear automatically. Otherwise she would easily manage the state.

"The following day they would meet Jay and give him the quest and they would see what his reaction would be then. As far as Durga understood, he would ask advice from those faceless creatures and they would surely inform him not to travel toward that side of the world, as that cave could mean bad news for his life.

If he still insisted he wanted to accept the challenge and let the journey begin for Jay and his faceless creatures." Durga finished firmly.

CHAPTER 16
"RAMA'S BRIDGE"

"So, how are you enjoying my life story so far?" Raja asked Miriam.

"I'm so lost and even in my dreams I feel I'm in Durga's palace and watching every single scene you depicted in your tale. All I knew was that old people are the only ones who are great story tellers, but my love, you truly are the master story teller. I don't want you to stop; I really am on a cliffhanger and eager to know what happened next!" Miriam said while holding his hand.

"Your wish is my command, my darling. I truly am glad you are enjoying the tale. There are many reasons for why I wanted to share all these details. One of the main reasons is, since my transformation into a human; all the knowledge and the wisdom I gained with it, I want you to have it and the life I led without you. My love, you have all the right to know each second of my existence!

"According to your wish, let's continue the rest of the tale," Raja replied.

"Guru Das advised Durga that if Jay traveled and managed to find the cave, Guru Das and Durga would get all the details of what occurred. He said that if she sent her men along with Jay then she should strongly advise them not to go inside the cave with him. Durga's men needed to remain at a reasonable distance from the cave and give Jay twenty-four hours to complete his mission. If, within that period, he didn't find his way back, Durga tell her men to return home.

"Durga replied that she thought it's fair enough and agreed with Guru Das completely. They would not risk a single life of their men. She had thought to send Veer with him, but guessed he was far too scared of Jay, so now they needed to select two other brave soldiers.

"Guru Das disagreed, saying that Veer was still a better choice and he was brave enough to go with him. Guru Das advised Durga to have a word with him one more time. If she found even a little bit of hesitation in his eyes, then she should let Veer decide and select two other men he thought were capable for such a task. That night Guru Das would create a hidden map for Jay; there would be some guidance for him to find the exact tracks. In the map there would be directions toward Rama's bridge, which would start from southeastern cost of Pamban Island, which is also known as Rameswaram Island, and lead him straight to Mannar Island, off the northwestern cost of Lanka. The map would be invisible to read the location of the cave, as Guru Das wanted him to use his mind or the hidden powers of Danwals. The only way to read the map was one needed rain drops on that codex, as Guru Das would write on a leaf of a special plant called Revix.

"The beauty of a Revix leaf was, it one could write hidden words on it, as this plant only survived on rain water and contained a magical combination once rain poured. Normally the leaves were plain and seemed as if nothing was written on them. However, once seen after a rain shower, every single word was visible on the leaves. Guru Das guaranteed that with this map they would give Jay the time of his life; if he thought he knew everything, they would show him that they also knew a thing or two.

"Guru Das would give Durga two lockets which she had to give to their men with a strict instruction, not to take them off until they returned home. Guru Das was aware Jay might try to control their minds and would use them as bait to understand the dangers of the cave. One more important thing was that, if Jay managed to find his way to the cave, as to whatever will happen inside, Guru Das would get all the details as he had a spiritual connection with Hukush and they spoke to each other from time to time.

"This night he would inform Hukush about Durga, as well as Jay's greed. Durga might think it was unfair to Jay but they had strong control of the senses of human souls, and even if someone said the name of the cave, the spirits of the cave were aware of that person. Guru Das just wanted to be informed about what happened inside with Jay; in that way Durga would be well informed about Jay's fate. Even though Guru Das had a source, they would be aware of the whole quest, which he would share with her later. He suggested that she needed to have some rest and that first thing in the morning they would do their final preparations for their meeting with Jay.

"Durga touched Guru Das's feet, which was part of her paying respect to him as per her Hindu culture, and after wishing him good night, left his presence. The first thing she did after going back to her chamber, was to send a message for Veer with an order to come and see her right away. It was already late in the night but she wanted to get everything organized before the sun hit the sky and a new day started. Soon Veer stood right in front of her waiting to hear what his princess had to say to him.

"Durga said to Veer that they would meet Jay the following day at the same location where he had addressed Durga directly. She had already selected a quest for Jay and wanted the deal to be fair and wished for two of her men to go along with him to help him complete his mission. There was one cave that was in Lanka, known as the cave of the lost souls, which is where she'd be sending Jay and she honestly wanted to ask Veer whether he was willing to be part of this mission. Before he gave her any answer, she wanted to inform him of the quest's simple rules. Firstly, Veer would just escort him until the time he reached the cave. Secondly, Veer was not allowed to go inside the cave with him.

"Durga gazed at Veer's face and advised him to keep a decent distance from the cave. However, she wanted Veer's camp to be in a position where he could view the cave entrance. She wished for him to keep an eye on the cave. Even though Jay would try his best to control Veer's mind to escort him inside the cave, Durga would give each of them a locket. Wearing that locket would keep Veer's mind immune from Jay's magical spell, if he tried to use one on him. Durga knew she couldn't risk their lives but Veer was the one, she truly was confident would enjoy this epic journey and return to share the adventure. This would be a different experience for Veer; however he was free to withdraw himself from this quest and prepare two brave soldiers and guide them as per Durga's instructions, which she had briefed him.

"Veer told Durga that he did not lie, what he'd seen really had frightened him for a while, which she needed to understand that all this was totally new for him. If she sent him to fight against an army he had no fear of men. These satanic people and their magical rituals could scare even a man like Veer. However it was for only the time being, and he felt honored if she still had faith in him. Even if she ordered him to jump in a river filled with crocodiles, without even giving a second thought he would jump. He was her soldier and as for a soldier, his job was to follow orders, without thinking about the consequences.

"Veer's mind was all set to serve Durga and he had no more fear of anyone or anything. While keeping his gaze downcast, he requested that she count him in and he would select one brave soldier to join him. He assured her, they would simply follow

Durga's instructions and would help Jay with honesty. If Durga wanted the deal to be fair and honest, Veer would make sure they kept it according to her mindset and standards. Veer would be in his abode and would start preparing for their journey. He would inform his fellow soldier to start packing for the quest and would only share with him what he needed to know, nothing more or less. Veer stated that he had been born to serve her and that was the purpose of his existence. He would not ask her more about the cave; all he knew was if Durga had selected that cave for a criminal such as Jay, it must be according to his evil standards and not an easy one to come out from. He trusted all Durga's judgments and supported her decision. He reassured her that everything would be fine."

"Durga told Veer that she was proud of him and that he should start preparations for the journey. She would request a list of Jay's requirements and Veer could make sure that all his needs would be fulfilled!

"Raja paused his story telling and, after kissing Miriam passionately told her, "My love, let me tell you some more about Rama's Bridge. I think it will be interesting for you. I know in your previous life you attended Hindu festivals and you grew up with your Hindu friends and must be already aware of their gods. Well, I know how the world works. Most of the people are not interested in investigating other religions, and without any know how, they think their religion is the best. As I mentioned to you earlier, I want you to be equipped with knowledge about all the religions, their relevant histories and details.

"First let me share a bit of Hindu mythology; according to their mythology and beliefs the world is divided into three parts.

"The first part, 'Heavens', ruled by 'Devas', mean gods. Bliss and merrymaking is the life style in Heaven. Gods drink for their enjoyment and there is no hunger, thirst, old age or death. Gods were bored of the easy access to everything and they wanted to find peace and true happiness, so they decided to speak to Brahma to tell them how they can be eternally happy.

"The master and the creator of these three worlds, is known as Brahma. I will show you his imaginary portraits when we visit India. He is an old man with a white beard and three faces, one facing front and the other two facing left and right. Brahma has four arms.

"The second part, the Underworld, is ruled by Demons, who specialize in terrifying humans, as they are never happy. They would always sit together and discuss with each other that although they were powerful, feared by all however they were still dissatisfied, and they decided to meet Brahma to ask him to guide them to the way to find inner satisfaction.

"The third part, Earth is inhabited by humans. The earth is ruled by humans and they are never satisfied and always seek for more. The humans' biggest problem is they always asked for more than what they get. For example, the farmers painfully ploughed the land and after sometime with hard labor they harvested. Humans' main worries and concerns were birds, which were destroying their fields. They also made up their mind to speak to Brahma, and ask him how they can be satisfied and happy.

"Finally, the gods, the humans, and the demons, gathered around Lord Brahma and told him they were deeply unhappy. After saying that, the leaders of all combined parties humbly requested of Brahma to please guide them as to what they should do to accomplish gratification and peace of mind, so they could remain happy for the rest of their lives.

"'Brahma was silent for few seconds then uttered Sanskrit single syllable, 'DA' and he disappeared. Everyone was perplexed as he left all three races to keep guessing. What did 'DA' mean? All of them understood that Brahma had given them a code and wanted them to find their own answer in the single syllable 'DA.'

"The Gods were back in their world and one of them shouted with joy, and told everyone he knew what 'DA' meant. They all started inquiring of him, "'what is it?' "Well, he replied, it meant 'Damana' or 'Restraint.' The father wants them to enjoy their pleasurable lives that he provided them and, at the same time, they should work on their self-restraint. This would provide them the contentment and happiness they had never experience before.

"On earth, the farmers, as before, were complaining about the birds eating their grain. When an angry farmer suggested killing all the birds, his companion responded by saying that he'd managed to understand the meaning of 'DA'! It meant 'Dan' or 'giving away' and not to hoard selfishly. If humans started practicing charity, they would experience a satisfaction they could have never imagined before.

"In the Underworld, demons returned to their work of petrifying humans. While one day when they were practicing terrifying humans, one of them said, "'Wait, I understand the meaning of DA. It means Daya or Compassion.' They immediately let their victims go and they felt happiness, when they saw joy on the faces of their victims. Their hearts were filled with happiness they never experienced before.

"In this study, we learn about three great virtues and divine qualities:

Self control, charity, and compassion as it's a knowledge and wisdom on its own.

"Coming back to our main subject, Rama's Bridge also contains an interesting story, as per Hindu mythology, and the details written in their holy book Ramayana.

"Let me start with the basic facts, such as Rama's Setu-bridge was not the first name of the bridge. The first name, as per ancient history, was Nala Setu. Nala was the name of the engineer who designed and constructed the whole bridge, with the help of the Vanara Army. Because of the people's love and veneration for Ram, it was changed to Rama's Setu. Later it got the name Setu Bandha-that which joins two lands. In the eighteenth century, the bridge got a new name and it was Adam's Bridge.

The length of the bridge is thirty-five kilometers and the width is three and a half kilometers.

"This story revolves around five major characters, their god Ram, his wife Sita, Ram's brother Lakshman, Ram's loyal monk Hanuman-the Hindu monkey god and the biggest villain in the history of Hindu religion called Ravan.

"In Hinduism there are basically three main gods, you can say. Brahma is the creator of the universe, Vishnu the caretaker who governs the universe, and Shiva the destroyer.

"Ram and Krishna were two of the seven incarnations of the god Vishnu.

"Hinduism is based on three major scriptures, the Bhagavad Gita, then Ramayana and the third is Mahabharata. Hinduism does have more books, but the most important and famous are these three.

"Ram was a human incarnation of Vishnu and the son of King Dashrath. Ravan kidnapped Sita in order to take revenge for the insult of his sister, Surpankha. Lakshaman was injured in the battle.

"Hanuman was the greatest devotee of Lord Ram. He was a monkey-like human with super powers. It is said that he flew from India to Lanka in order to convey the message of Ram to Sita. He had also burnt the golden Lanka.

"It is said that Hanuman is still alive. Lord Ram prayed to the lord of the ocean to let his soldiers cross the sea. The lord agreed and promised that every stone that would have Lord Ram's name written on it would float on the water.

"Therefore, Ram's army wrote Ram on thousands of big stones and threw them into the water. Thus, Ram Setu or the bridge was formed.

"As I told you, Lord Vishnu has seven incarnations. The most interesting thing is that six of them had taken birth and died but one of them is yet to come, according to Hinduism. He is known as the Kalki Avatar.

"Ramayana and Mahabharata are completely different. The first one is about being a perfect man. It describes the complete life of Lord Ram. He is known as purushottam Ram, which means he is the best man. He had been the perfect son, brother, husband and all. Also the highlight of Ramayana is the battle between Ram and Ravan. Ravan was a very wise, powerful and wealthy, man but all of it was destroyed just because of his one mistake and never-ending ego.

"Mahabharata, on the other hand, is all about fight, politics and the triumph of right over wrong. The main character Arjun is guided by Lord Krishna-the one who is related to Dwarka-to win the battle against his own cousins. It is the most amazing story that you could ever read. Trust me, it is out of this world.

"Gita is related to Mahabharata. It consists of all the teachings and prose that Lord Krishna gave to Arjun about life and war. One who could follow the teachings of Gita can really excel in his life." Raja gave a long sigh, having completed his lecture.

Miriam replied to him, "There is only one Allah and no one before or above him. The Lord is alive, and worshiping a false Idol is a sin, as per the teachings of Islam. Praying to any statue or picture, in my religion is idolatry, and such practices are strictly forbidden, and are considered unholy, accordingly to the teaching of Islam. I never knew they had such a deep and interesting history. I have truly grown up with you, as far as being open minded and not being too judgmental about other people or their religions.

Raja said, "I believe we are no one to judge or criticize other religions. See, every single human being is born alone and will die alone. It does not matter whatever religion he or she followed; at the end he will go in his own personal grave. Not a single loved one of his or her will join them in their grave. Now, keeping all this in mind, what an individual needs to focus on is his own moments in the grave and life after death.

"No one is Jesus Christ to replace their sins and accept death right? I would suggest we leave the world religions to their believers; everyone gets a message of truth, but we can't force people or tell them we are the best, when we are not. Everyone's life is full of sins; we all do dirty and insane things and then we try to become wise men and start interfering in other people's lives, religions and businesses. All they simply need to understand is one humble philosophy: 'live and let others live.' Humans basically need to improve themselves in every possible manner, rather than to always find fault in other humans.

"Sometimes they have issues with others' race; some think their skin color gives them the right to rule over other skin color. How can they forget every human is equal, despite their race or culture? Given a chance to understand and respect other people's beliefs, you will feel peace in your heart. The biggest religion of all is humanity. Any religion that teaches us to keep peace within, and learn to love other humans, that religion deserves respect. Corruption and flaws are manmade and as you know, humans are masters of interpreting religions, as per their own minds, desires and wishes.

"If we look deep into the history of Islam, again you will find many sects in Islam itself; the majorities are Sunni and then Shias. There are many other sects that come under the umbrella of Islam, such as Ismalis and Ahmadiyyas. Sunni don't consider other sects proper Muslims. Ismalis are much more modern minded and their places of worship are very similar to Protestant churches, where men and women are free to worship together.

"For example, imagine the rituals of Shia on the tenth of Muharram their mourning and practicing self-flagellations. What do other religious people think about those rituals? For them it is hard to understand why they are hurting themselves. However, on educating themselves with the knowledge, what happened to their prophet's family made them understand that they remember the pain the prophet's family went through.

"The world respects other people's beliefs and whatever traditions they follow. It's very important for humans to give space to other people and let them breathe the way they want. Islam has its own beauty, and we all should respect that. Those, who are honest and truly value humanity, as per Prophet Muhammad (May peace be upon him), I love one of his quote in which he clearly mentioned. 'One who treads a path in search of knowledge has his path to Paradise made easy by God' (Riyadh us-Saleheen 245). I don't believe in debates. I believe in peaceful discussions. You are at the stage of perceiving the reality of how human brains love to corrupt things that are pure and full of virtue. Well, it's such a contentious subject and I can go on and on." Raja kissed her lips and while gazing at her smiled.

Miriam kissed him passionately and, with a beautiful smile, asked, "I know there is so much I need to learn and understand, and I truly am at your disposal. You are my sage and I am deeply in love with you. Why is it that the better I know you, the more intensely I fall in love with you?

Miriam further asked, "My love please tell me what happened next in Durga's story."

Raja replied, "I love you too, my darling, and as always your wish is my command. It took me one-thousand years to find my peace and, trust me. nothing can heal your soul more than being with your true love. Imagine how alone I was and now with you all I want is to transfer all the knowledge and wisdom into you in one day.

"I have a sea of love in me and I truly want to make you ready to be loved the way no woman has ever been loved before!" Raja smiled and hugged her.

CHAPTER 17

"ART OF BEING A SKILLED WARRIOR"

"Let me take you back to Durga's story," Raja continued from where he left the tale.

"That night was one of the toughest nights for Durga to fall sleep. Her mind was asking millions of questions and her soul was doing some planning on its own. Deep in her mind she was discussing all the aspects of the upcoming meeting with Jay. The best part of all this drama was that Durga was not scared of him.

"Like most of the royals, deep down somewhere she had a serious gambler in her. The only difference about this bet was that her life was at stake.

"She wanted to play the same game, the way he had started. Her plan was to be less emotional, as he would try his best to read her emotions. Jay would try to dig deep in her mind, as he knew Veer was her man whom she had sent to spy on him; he wanted to read her face. He wanted to read her eyes and what she held in them for him. Was she scared, angry or is impressed by whatever details she had found out about him?

"He would do his best to discover her reactions toward him, so he could use her weakness against her. In Durga's mind, she wanted to be one step ahead of him and hit him there where he least expected; in a way she was enjoying this whole battle, as for her it was something new and, for the very first time, she was deeply involved in such an event.

"Sleep is a strange goddess. It does not matter if you are lying on nails or suffering massive pain or your brain is surrounded by millions of worries; sleep will take control of your body and will take you into the world of dreams.

"That is what finally happened with Durga. Her eyes automatically closed and she was lost in the world of her dreams. It's a saying what goes in life or whatever circumstances you are in, your dreams also show same things from the same events.

"In her dream she woke up in the Cave of Lost Souls. As she walked a little further inside the cave, she was welcomed by Hukush and Ziyush. It took her a second to recognize both of them as per the depiction provided by Guru Das; they both were the most glamorous and beautiful people she had ever met in her life.

"Ziyush held Durga's hand and made her sit by her, while Hukush just sat with a gentle smile and gazed at her.

"Ziyush, with a loveable voice, told her, 'Listen, my child, we got the message from Guru Das. There is nothing you should be concerned about; we will deal with Jay, as we are expert in handling such kinds of monsters beneath human skin.'

"Ziyush told her what would happen to him, and from every corner all Durga heard was heart-wrenching screams, and they grew louder and louder until she woke up.

"The moment Durga woke up, she felt relief and relaxed. Her soul was fresh and so was her mind, not tensed at all from what was going on. Today was the day; she was in complete control of herself and that was the beauty of wearing confidence beneath your skin. Confidence not only makes you see things which are invisible to normal souls, it gives you a boost which you highly need to make decisions, which are extremely important for your life.

"The first thing Durga did was go out to study the weather in the shape of investigating the day ahead. She was surprised to see it was a cloudy day. Finding the weather dark, cloudy and with chances of downpour, brought a smile to her face. As this was her favorite type of weather. She was in love with cloudy and storming weathers. She prayed to her gods to show a sign for day to be in her favor.

"Since childhood, Durga had been a strong believer in her gods, as for her they were her friends and according to her belief, if she asked gods to show her some sign, such as how the day was going to be, they never disappointed her. Understanding a sign of gods is a silent language only those who honestly believe in them can speak and understand. Those individuals are owners of strong faith and they truly believe someone is out there listening to their every request. It's an education, a craft, and only those who have pure souls can gain possession of such command.'

"One of her maids handed her a pearl white velvet amulet. For a second she was surprised and wanted to ask the maid who had sent this. As the amulet came into her hand, she easily felt with a touch that it was from Guru Das. According to their discussion the day before, Guru Das had sent his blessed pendants for her soldiers. Durga took a nice, relaxing bath, which had been set for her, and all her maids were around her. She wanted to enjoy the day as a true fighter who was excited to be part of the war, despite of being concerned by the ugly sides of the wars. One of her maids came and told her the king was waiting for her at the breakfast table. Durga went straight to see her father. The king was waiting for her to start the breakfast and, as she entered the dining room, he smiled at her and Durga after touching her father's feet, sat quietly next to him.

"Parents are blessed with an instinct to read their children and sense something is wrong or they are stuck in a serious problem. It took a second for Durga's father to understand she was going through some serious struggles. To ease her mind and not wanting to forcefully or directly ask her what was disturbing her, instead he asked her how was she. Durga was trying her best to pretend everything was normal and this was just another ordinary day. She respectfully answered that she was doing fine. Her father gave a long sigh, and continued the conversation by saying that if there was anything he could do for her, he could sense she seem disturbed by some issue. 'I'm your father' he told her, 'and always remember never hide anything from your parents.'

"Durga felt so much love for her father that very moment, all she wanted was to hug him and request his blessings. However she controlled her emotions and innocently replied that everything was fine and she truly loved him. She was aware of his kindness and he knew it well, that if there was anything she wanted he'd be the one she came to ask. She told him not to worry, and if she were ever perturbed, he would know it without a second wasted; she would come visit him and bring any issues to his knowledge."

"'Good.' the king replied, 'and she should always remember, I'm here for you.'

"Durga, after spending some quality time with her father and finishing her breakfast, went back to her room and from there she sent a message for Veer to meet her near the royal garden's fountains. After dressing in her finest attire, she was all set for the day. The beauty of being well dressed is wearing a strong confidence within yourself, knowing your worth and who can present better then a princess. Durga wanted to make no errors as far as her expressions were concerned; she knew Jay would be seeking her weakness, through her face and personality expressions.

"As she neared to the fountains, Durga noticed a tall well-built soldier obediently standing next to Veer. They both bowed their heads and paid her their respect, Veer introduced, Gopal while keeping his gaze downcast. 'Your highness,' he said, 'please let me have the honor of introducing you to Gopal. I have trained him myself out of your myriad soldiers. Gopal can fight bare handed with more than ten people who are fully equipped with swords and blades. I have trained him myself and he is from your special squad. He was born for only one reason, to serve you and die for you. He will accompany me on the quest.'"

"Veer took a deep breath after finishing his briefing and Durga told him that she was proud of both of them and assured them this journey would give them a unique experience and a different exposure to marvel their skills and to understand the depth of good versus evil. She trusted their judgment and told Veer, just for his information, in case the king would require his assistance, he would be informed by Durga that he had taken a vacation. She hoped he had informed Gopal what to do and what not. Then she gave them blessed pendants that contained powers to keep them both safe. No black magic would work on their minds or souls, and they would remain in their senses until they had safely returned home. She reminded them not to remove their pendants at any cost. Even if they heard screams or some evil visiting them in the form of a sage or beautiful girls, under at no circumstances were they allowed to enter the cave. Durga hoped she had made herself clear!

"Veer confidently assured Durga they would make her proud and would treat Jay fairly and provide him full support until he entered the cave. Once he entered they would wait outside. If he didn't come out as per Durga's given time period, they would return home accordingly.

"Durga informed them that Guru Das and three of them would attend this meeting. She didn't want a whole army with her. She wanted their meeting to be fair, with no pressure on him or on them.

"'As you wish your highness,' Veer replied.

"'Let us go and give the devil a task according to his dirty mind,' Durga ordered and then requested to bring the horses, so they could make their way to the meeting.

"Veer briskly went to get the horses, and in few minutes he was back and brought her personal horse. They started riding toward the same location; Durga knew Guru Das would already be waiting for them at the meeting point. As she reached the location, the first thing looked for was Guru Das, and he was there on his horse, waiting for her. When she neared him, they both just smiled at each other with no words exchanged. Then she looked around and there was no sign of Jay. She searched Guru Das's eyes for an answer as to what had happened to Jay. Guru Das smiled again and told her he would be here shortly.

"'Jay was trying to make the princess feel he was worth waiting for, and he really didn't care that she was a royal. After ten minutes she saw him coming and he was not alone. Two extremely scary-looking men were walking behind him, at a fair distance as if he was some kind of prince and they were his devotees. Durga gathered all her required strength to control her facial expressions and emotions. As he drew closer she saw his same ugly, disturbing smile, as if he were already a champion of the quest. He, without bowing his head to her, greeted, 'Hello, your highness, how have you been? Hope you selected an easy task for me. See, I'm here, and I hope you can see my determination to ask for your hand.'" Jay showed his dirty yellowish teeth. His gaze passed over Guru Das and humbly he bowed his head and offered Namaste to him.

"Guru Das nodded as he responded to Jay's greeting.

"Durga with emotionless face was keen to discuss only business, nothing more and nothing less, and in a pompous tone she started her speech, "'Jay, I have selected a quest for you, I want you to go to Lanka and I want you to bring me, Vahus from the Cave of Lost Souls. You are free to demand your requirements for the quest; two of my finest soldiers will escort you during your quest. I will provide you the finest horses, food stock and, if you require any other things, you can give the list to Veer. He will make sure all your demands have been well taken care. As I told you, I want the deal to be fair. I will also provide you a map, however how to read the map that you have to figure out. If you have any questions, you are free to ask. If you want to withdraw then, I have a right to take your life.'"

"After hearing about the quest, Jay kept his sight on the ground and started murmuring. It was not difficult for her to understand; he was talking to someone on the ground. Durga's focus was entirely on him; she knew it was the Danwals he was speaking to. Jay seemed concerned and worried, from the answers he was receiving. Then, suddenly, he looked toward the sky and again started muttering, as if he was having a conversation with someone in the skies. The whole process took him two minutes; it was complete silence during that time. She studied his facial expressions. The reply from Danwals was not supporting and Durga read that from his expression. However, the reply from the sky made his concerns vanish and his expression became completely normal. Durga understood he was speaking to goddess Kali.

"'I accept the quest your highness,' Jay told her. Kindly give me the map for the Cave of Lost Souls. As per your given time period, I will bring you Vahus. Thank you for offering me men and other relevant supports. I'm a poor man and don't have such resources, so will accept your goodwill and kindness. Within two hours, we will start our journey and rest assured, I will complete my mission according to the time frame you have given me. I want to remind you, I have to come back with Vahus within one month. You must wait for me and during this month, you will not fall in love with anyone or get married. If I don't return, you have all the right to make a choice. I believe in my gods and firmly know we were made for each other.'" Jay displayed his ugly teeth to her again. He was confident and his voice was firmer this time.

"'I promise you, one whole month, starting from tomorrow, I will wait for you as if I belong to you. I will not fall in love with any man nor would marry, I give you my word; will not even die in this month,' Durga told him in a rigid voice.

"During this whole conversation, Guru Das quietly listened to both of them.

"Durga told Veer to take care and from now on, be with Jay, and fulfill all his requirements for the quest. She informed Jay that his time would start from the following day as of this day, as half of the day was already gone. She believed in a fair deal; for her his time would start from the following day. Then she requested that Guru Das kindly give the map to Veer so they could depart from this place. Lastly, Durga gazed at Jay and asked him whether there was anything he wanted to ask.

"Jay smiled and told her no, and that he would see her after one month and that she should please stay safe for him.

"She looked to Guru Das and told him that they should go, and they both left the meeting spot.

"While riding at a slow pace, Durga asked Guru Das, "What he thought of Jay? She suspected that when he was looking down and murmuring, he was speaking to Danwals, and when he was speaking to the skies, her guess was that he was having a conversion with the goddess Kali. However she would love to be enlightened by his observations.

"Guru Das explained that Jay exceeded his expectations. The way he presented himself, no one was able to see his semblance to cruelty and evil acts. Jay was not an ordinary human. It was the first time Guru Das had met a man who was under the protection of a bizarre shell. He needed to crack the code to enter Jay's mind; it was easy to know what his type was before seeing him. However, people like Jay always existed under various layers. He was a master of deceit and the face and body which he showed Durga, that is not who he truly was. 'Jay is older than me,' Guru Das told Durga with a calm smile.

"'What? Seriously who is he?' exclaimed Durga, whose eyes widened with surprised.

"'My child,' Guru Das told her with a mischievous smile, 'there is nothing to worry about; he is just an ordinary wizard. In reality he is a thousand times uglier than what he showed you.'

"'Please, Guru, my life is at stake and you're enjoying the entire situation. Don't you think this is the moment we have to be very serious about?' Durga complained.

"'My child let me teach you a great lesson today,' Guru Das told her. 'Life basically is not as serious as it seems; problems, worries, concerns and dangers are part of it. These are the type of adventures one should be thankful for, to the higher power. The reason we learn and gain knowledge from such type of experiences, imagine you are a princess; what worries do you have? None! I guess, and this is a perfect moment to celebrate and accept the adventure that came into your life. Enjoy the felicity of this wonderful task and what you will learn in these thirty days, it will help you to acknowledge the strength of your soul, mind and body.

"'Every other step of life is a challenge and you will meet worse creatures, who are ravenous to eat you alive and takeover your place as a princess and whatever is yours. To survive, consider life as a war, a battle you play with your mind, rather than arrows or swords. Weapons make a mind weak and what really happens is when we know we are carrying a weapon, we start relying on it more than our own brain. And later when we lose the weapon, our mind becomes weak and we end up getting killed by our enemy for sure.

"'We prefer to give up easily, however when we rely on our mind, we calculate every step and path we plan; concurrently we are aware of every step our enemy will take to beat us. The enemy will come up with the finest weapon to defeat us, already considering himself a winner. That will be his biggest mistake and at the end, his over estimation will get him killed by his own hand. Life is all about understanding the right paths. Stay humble as much as you can, and keep your mind open to accept challenges and experiences of life on a high scale. See, when we are born, the higher-power sends us into this world as infants. We have to rely on our parents. The only reason he sends us innocent is because he knew our parents would go through their test. Raising one's child is a serious test for parents, what you teach them and make them acknowledge is the existence and blessings of a higher power.

"'If the children turn evil because of the ignorance of their parents, they will have to answer for that on Judgment Day. The higher power knows all the details of what will happen next. The Lord selects hard times and good times for us. He wants us to know that He exists. Imagine if everyone had a blessed life, no worries or problems. Who would pray to the higher power? Humans are the most selfish creatures in the universe. It's in their blood to forget, if someone had been nice to them or someone provided them with food in times when they were hungry. The moment they are settled, they will forget about all the people who were on their side, when they needed someone of their own. I share with you an interesting tale of human nature.' Guru Das looked toward Durga while she listened to him, but not with complete concentration.

"'I know, my sweetheart,' Guru Das told Durga, 'all you wanted to hear is about Jay. Trust me, I'm coming onto his topic and, believe me, we will discuss him in depth. However, what I'm telling you, it's all related to your training and skill, as you already started a war today. However, you are using your mind to win, and that is how skilled warriors accept challenges and beat their opponent with their own strength. So would you be interested to listen to the tale of human nature?'"

"Durga responded to Guru Das, 'Sorry, forgive me please. See on one side you tell me, he is not who he seems and behind his face there is another person. Then you leave me on cliffhanger with millions of questions, and you share your sense of humor. I have this much right to be upset, don't you agree? I know and that is why I love you, you are the reason I took such a bold step in my life. I'm humbly honored for all the wisdom and love you share with me. Now please tell me the tale of human nature.'"

CHAPTER 18

"TWO TYPES OF ADVERSARIES"

Raja asked Miriam, "Love you understand the way Guru Das educated Durga? See he was helping her but simultaneously made her a sensible warrior. Any act in anger is an act of Devil and Guru Das knew it well.

Yes my love, kindly continue and tell me, what Guru Das taught Durga next. Miriam asked anxiously.

"Guru Das said, 'Now we are talking, and this is how I love you to be, always happy no matter how life treats you or even if you are stuck in horrible circumstances; always keep a smile on your beautiful face. That is the best way to embrace life, the way it comes to us.

"'Seventy-four years ago, I completed my spiritual meditation on mountains of east. Guru Das with a deep sigh continued, I was only thirty years old that time, and was returning to populated villages. After a long period of isolation, I was really interested to see some humans and have a decent conversation; at the same time I was starving for a good simple meal. It was getting dark when I reached the village, and my heart suggested that I knock on the first door on my way. The house was quite huge and I knocked the door.

"'A middle-aged servant answered the door and asked me, what I was looking for. I politely requested that as traveler and holy man

I would be thankful if I could have something to eat. A man from within the house inquired who was at the door. The servant obediently replied that some sage asking for a meal. The man within the house responded that he should bring the guest inside and arrange meal for him and that he would join him shortly. The servant opened the door and invited me inside the house. I quietly followed and sat at the indicated spot, where I closed my eyes and started thanking my Lord for his blessings, my host, his family and his house. Hardly after seven minutes, I heard Namaskar. I opened my eyes and responded. "My host informed me that his name was Kumar and that he humbly welcomed me to his house. He inquired what I would like to eat.

"Guru Das thanked him, and told him his name and that he was a vegetarian. He was fine that whatever was leftover in Kumar's house would do for him. He never meant to disturb or bother Kumar. He could feel Kumar had been highly blessed by higher power and he told him that the presence of a higher power was easily be felt in Kumar's abode; Guru Das could also see with his powers that Kumar had seven children; six daughters and one son. He also informed Kumar his fifth daughter was a special child of the Lord and that if it were possible, he would like to meet her. At the same time, Guru Das wished to bless Kumar's whole family.

"Kumar's eyes widened with surprise. He truly felt Guru Das was a sage and touched his feet, started worshipping him and thanked Guru Das for choosing his house and blessing it with his presence. The Lord had been very kind to Kumar and yes he did had seven children. His fifth daughter's name was Nemi and since the day she was born, the Lord had highly blessed Kumar greatly. His family had gone to attend a function nearby and would be returning home at anytime. Kumar humbly requested that Guru Das let them have the honor of being the host and serving him for this whole night and have some rest. He also requested that if Guru Das could please stay as long as he wished and consider this house as his own. From now on, Kumar wished that Guru Das consider him and his family as his loyal devotees.

"Guru Das felt that Kumar had been honest in his offer and devotions toward him. Kumar was a handsome, noble man, with a god-fearing heart. Guru Das accepted his offer and told him that he would stay two nights with him and his family. The servant brought a meal, which Guru Das shared with Kumar and they discussed various things. Within half an hour, Kumar's family was back and it took Guru Das a second to recognize Nemi. She was one of those with whom you really feel connected. Nemi was blessed with large eyes and her smile was as honest as life itself. She surely was greatly blessed by the presence of the Lord to make others feel relaxed and happy. Such a charming and an obedient child you could hardly meet in this world. All of Kumar's daughters were blessed with beautiful features, however Nemi was innocently beautiful. From her eyes you could feel she not only had a good spirit inside her but one that would never ever hurt any living soul.

"Guru Das added that Nemi's other sisters were nice and obedient too. He was aware that time would change their hearts. Kumar's son was quiet and decent, the one who mostly believed in minding his own business. Kumar's wife was a happy woman, who truly did her best to serve Guru Das. He spent two great days with the family and then, while leaving, he offered the family many blessings and prayers. He did promise he would keep visiting them.

"Many years later, Guru Das was on the same path where their house was, so he went to meet the family. Most of the daughters had been married; the son had also married and he had moved in with his in-laws, leaving the parents alone. The eldest daughter had selected her own groom, against the will of her parents and later she had found out, that he was a good for nothing gambler. So she kept returning to her parents' house to ask for money. The second daughter had married a man, who was engaged to her aunt her dad's younger sister. Later, the family found out the man was a fraudster. The third girl was married in the family and later she found out, her husband was a womanizer.

"Nemi was married to a decent young man, who even though was poor at the time of marriage, still refused to accept dowry from Kumar. He humbly requested for his daughter's hand and told Kumar, if the gods would be kind to them, they would bless them with all the prosperity and happiness to their family. He would work as hard as he could, to provide all the happiness of the world to his wife. He seemed a determined and focused gentleman and Kumar accepted his honest proposal. As Kumar was a self-made man, he valued the young boy's spirit.

"The last two sisters were also married, the second last married to a man who was nothing but full of loquacity. The name of the second-last daughter was Sumi. Her biggest problem was that she was more interested in gossiping than taking care of her own family affairs.

"With the passage of time, Nemi's husband progressed and became a successful merchant and had huge stock of cattle. Nemi was the only child, who was taking care of her parents properly. The rest of the children were always begging their father to help them. Nemi was helping her sisters as much as she could; however deep down, all of them were extremely jealous of her. The sisters cursed Nemi all the time, when they were together and wanted to exchange their lives with hers.

"Nemi's husband bought her huge collection of jewelry, which she used to wear on various wedding or family gatherings. One day, her sisters planned to steal her jewelry so they can pay off their huge debts, as their husbands borrowed from various landlords who were seriously hunting them. 'When the Devil takes control on your mind, the first thing he does is make you ready for a smaller crime. The crime looks so minor, deep in our heart we feel this is nothing, just a small robbery. We humans don't understand even an infant is born out of tiny drops of sperm and then later turns into a baby and finally grows into a complete man. Sin is similar to a sperm drop; it takes a tiny drop and then you have no idea, what kind of circumstances sin will get you involve in.'

"That was in Kumar's daughters' case. They planned a small robbery, which later turned into something indescribable. On the other hand, poor Nemi, asked permission to give her savings and jewelry to her sisters in need. Her husband was a big hearted man and gave her permission to help her sisters. A day before the family reunion at their parents' abode, Nemi handed over her jewelry and savings to her father.

"Kumar was not in favor of what Nemi was offering, since being a self-made man, he sincerely wanted to see his sons-in-law to feed their own families. Instead of sending their wives to knock on doors, they all needed to set a plan and work things sensibly; rather than look to Nemi's or someone else's wealth. Nemi's plan was to hand over all her valuable assets at the next family reunion; on the other hand, the cunning sisters made an extremely horrible plan for their innocent sister.

"First, the elder sister, who was master of seduction, in some way managed to seduce the village's most handsome young man, Alok. She told him to meet her at an isolated location, where she gave Alok a poisonous drink, and the poor fellow died on the spot. The sisters made a grave for him and quietly buried his body. This they did entirely without their husbands' knowledge. After finishing Alok, they returned to their father's house, where Nemi had already arrived with her husband. Their plan was to give small portion of the same poison to Nemi and later take her out of the house and at the same location where they had killed Alok, they wanted to kill her and bury her next to him. Later, they wanted to spread the rumor that Nemi was cheating on her husband, and was having an affair with Alok, and that they had both run away together.

"Their plan was lethal and well calculated, yet they had bad luck. After they mixed poison in her drink, Guru Das entered Kumar's house at the same time. He sensed Nemi had been poisoned. Kumar was happy to see Guru Das and Guru Das briskly instructed Kumar to bring Nemi to him. Kumar was not able to understand why Guru Das's facial expression reflected concern. He ran quickly inside the house unknowingly about the poison, which was already spreading through Nemi's veins.

"Now sages don't carry any money or food; all they carry with them is a decent quantity of herbal medicines. Guru Das sack was equipped with various types of dry herbs in original and some in ground forms. He quickly took out a dry herb and inserted it in Nemi's mouth. She was not able to speak but still had all her senses; the poor girl was not even aware whatever was happening to her, which had basically been done by her own blood. Guru Das managed to save Nemi's life; even Kumar was looking at Guru Das for answers. What exactly had happened to his beloved daughter?

"All the sisters were acting strangely, as they were extremely worried about what had happened to Nemi. Guru Das saw fear in their eyes, but when evil overcomes our soul, he teaches us various tricks. They were all wearing various masks, pretending they were kind, caring and loving souls. Some were crying and some running here and there, asking Guru Das what had happened to their sister. Nemi's husband was seriously worried, as the man was deeply in love with his wife. Guru Das told him to relax and that nothing was wrong; it was just a food poisoning. Guru Das had given her medicine and within few hours, Nemi would be totally fine. Guru Das now experienced a great test of time, as he didn't believe in back stabbing and disclosing other people's crime. Guru Das believed in giving a chance, but the problem with giving them a chance was the following day, Kumar was supposed to hand over the savings and jewelry to cunning sisters. Nemi was such a kind soul; she would never imagine in a million year that her own sisters poisoned and tried to kill her.

"Kumar was at Guru Das's feet and asked him, whether he would please be so kind as to share the truth with him. What had really happened to his child? Kumar had raised Nemi from the cradle and had never seen her like this. She had been sick various times but never so serious. This was no food poisoning, Kumar's child had come back from dead. If Guru Das had not come on time, his daughter might have died. Kumar started crying again.

"Guru Das responded by saying that he would tell Kumar what had really happened, however he had to make a request of him. Kumar affirmed that Guru could ask anything and could kindly give him an order, as he knew he was his loyal servant and honest devotee. Nemi had brought all her jewelry and savings, as she wanted to distribute them among her sisters. Guru Das would tell her himself not to do that and Kumar would support him in his decision.

"Nemi was like a daughter to Guru Das and she truly was the Lord's angel on earth. She always looked after Guru Das, whenever he had a chance to stay at their abode. While he had his memories of his sweet child, someone brutally knocked on the door. A servant went running to answer the door to find Alok's mother there. Her tone scared, she requested to see Kumar, and the servant came inside and informed them about Alok's mother. Kumar requested that Guru Das excuse him and he went to see the woman. Alok's mother was extremely worried and asked Kumar whether he or his elder son-in-law had hurt Alok, as he had been missing for a long time. Kumar seemed surprised and asked her, why would they hurt Alok?

"His mother started shouting, that someone had seen his eldest daughter flirting with her son, and now he had been gone for a long time. Her son had never stayed away from her for such a long time and it was the first time since his birth. She begged him to understand that Alok was her only son and if anything happened to him, she swore she would burn herself alive in front of his house. As fast as she had arrived, in same momentum she vanished to search for her son.

"Kumar came straight to Guru Das and asked him to kindly tell him what was going on, first attack on Nemi and now Alok's mother asking whether Kumar and his eldest son-in-law had hurt Alok. Kumar then went to call his eldest daughter Bindu and Guru Das wondered what he could do to help poor Kumar. Bindu came with her father and he made her sit next to them; Kumar had always considered Guru Das as a member of his family and he asked Bindu about Alok.

"Guru Das read Bindu's facial expressions and as Kumar spoke Alok's name, she became pale. As Guru had mentioned to Durga, once people started committing sins, they become experts in lying and covering up their crimes as in Bindu's case. She controlled her expression and replied that she had met Alok and he was trying to be licentious, upon which she had scolded him and that was all there had been to it. She was curious and wanted to know what had happened to him. She had returned to her innocent mode and Guru Das considered how good she was a liar. Kumar thought Bindu spoke the truth and innocently told her that Alok's mother was spreading rumors everywhere that you had been flirting with him and that someone had seen her doing that.

"Kumar thanked the Lord that Bindu's husband had not heard her conversation, otherwise it would have been a big problem for Bindu. Guru Das quietly listened to both of them then requested that Kumar allow him speak to Bindu, and also send the other four inside. He would like to speak to all of them together. One by one, all five sisters stood before Guru Das and he told them to take a seat. He told Bindu that he thought it was much better if she confessed and let him find a way to help her. The problem with all of them was that they had honed their skills in lying and Bindu pretended as if she was not aware of anything. What Guru Das truly wanted was for them to confess.

"Bindu while smiling weirdly asked, what you meant by this question, as they were confused by what he wanted them to confess to. Guru Das gazed right into her eyes and firmly asked again. Whether they wanted him to tell them every single detail of what they needed to confess. Fine then, he said. How about poisoning Nemi? Why they all killed Alok? Just to make up a story that their sister had run away with him and she was having an illicit relationship with Alok, what kind of devil was controlling her mind, because of greed how could they sink so low in their lives. What wrong had poor Kumar done to them that had stooped to such a low level to destroy his respect in the whole village?

"It was their duty to figure out their husbands' problems and they should have cleaned up their personal mess themselves. They had taken a life of an innocent person; the second life he had saved was their sister. They had given her poison so she could die and they could have stolen her goods and make it seem as if she was of bad character.

"Guru Das said, 'Let me tell you something about your kind sister, who always loved all of you and in every possible manner, always tried to help all of you. Even she brought all her jewelry and savings to be distributed among all of you, so you can payoff whomever you owe. Instead this is how you have returned her kindness, by poisoning her. Here I give you a chance to repent; one of you will accept the murder of Alok and she would surrender herself to the village court or otherwise all five of you would be considered equally guilty and will be charged as murderers. You all choose to be in such a predicament by yourselves. Now volition is yours and according to the crime, I give you two minutes to decide with each other!'

"Instead of discussing this with the other sisters, Bindu started to lure Guru Das while offering a lascivious wink. He scolded her and told her time was passing and she should make a quick decision. Apart from Bindu and Sumi, all the others were aware that their secret had been unveiled and shuddered in horror. Still, Bindu and Sumi tried to convince other sisters to stay firm and keep pretending that they were innocent and knew nothing about what this 'stupid sage' was talking about.

"Within a minute, the three sisters were at Guru Das's feet begging him to forgive them. They all burst into tears and started blaming Bindu and Sumi; it was their plot and they had gotten them involved. Bindu was the one had poisoned both Alok and Nemi; the three sisters claimed they had done nothing they were innocent. 'Please do help us,' they pleaded. If our husbands will find out, they will leave us and even our father will disown us.' Bindu and Sumi were pale and they were really scared, as they gazed at their sisters in disbelief.

"Now, even Sumi joined rest of her sisters and they all started blaming Bindu. Guru Das looked at Bindu and asked her,' "so, are you ready to accept your crimes?"'

"Bindu replied, 'I will not hand myself over alone. They were all part of this whole conspiracy, and deserve the same fate as mine.' Bindu's cunning soul was visible and now her sisters looked upon her with great surprise. A long story cut short, Guru Das somehow managed to make Bindu realize, she had committed a murder and this was the opportunity for her to save her afterlife, otherwise her soul would return as some detestable animal which humans loved to hunt and eat. It was time for her to save her sisters' lives by accepting the responsibility of the crimes they had all committed together. At least she would have a chance to make one thing right; the rest was her choice.

Bindu understood that she was left with no choice and she stared at her sisters for one last time then left the house. She went straight to Alok's mother and took her to where she and her sisters had buried his corpse.

"The very next day, the villagers buried Bindu alive with Alok's pyre. Guru Das was sad to see Kumar's face; the poor man was not even aware why Bindu had committed such a cruel act. Bindu's husband was simply surprised that his wife was a killer.

"Nemi was much better and when she came to know about Bindu's death, she was tremendously sad.

"Kumar instructed Nemi to take her assets back with her, and let his other daughters find their own way to sort out their problems. Guru Das left their house and after that, he never had a chance to see the family again.

"The moral of this story was, in our life we are targeted by two types of enemies. The first ones are people like Jay, who come and challenge you to your face for the war while giving you the time period to prepare yourself to deal with them.

"Guru Das told Durga, the second type known as, the invisible enemy; they are more dangerous and come unwarned to attack you. They can be anyone, your closest individuals, friends and sometimes your own siblings!

"Durga told Guru Das that she loved the moral of the tale. Now she understands why he wanted to share this story with her before discussing anything about Jay. She had truly enjoyed hearing the tale, and it was difficult to hear that even one's own sisters could be one's lethal enemies. She guessed that was why she didn't have any sisters. She added, teasing, 'Now this is the first time you mentioned some girl flirted with you. I would like to hear more stories about girls flirting with you.'"

"Guru replied, 'You're seriously naughty girl! See, your mood has changed now; you are not tense anymore and you're back in life. There is no need to be serious and filled with extra tension to win a war. The wise king will always keep himself as relaxed as he can, to study his moves and find options for winning a war. Now, let me enlighten you, with my personal study of this Jay."

CHAPTER 19

"RQUI"

"Durga politely asked Guru Das whether Jay really was older than him. She wanted all the details, as what he'd seen and found in him with his hidden, visionary powers. Durga desperately sought answers from Guru Das."

"Guru replied by saying, 'Well, my child! As I mentioned to you earlier, he exceeded my expectation about him. He is more malicious than I considered. Guru Das researched his persona without seeing him in person. Now that he had seen him, it had given him a good chance to go deep inside his mind and view who he really was. Well, people transform. The only way to find out about their true identity is by entering their mind and, once you are there, the first thing you see is their soul.

"'The body can hide behind a different entity, but the soul always remains the same. When Guru Das was in his mind, he saw who really Jay was. Jay appeared to be twice as old than in reality; he is uglier than what you see at present. He is a wizard, drinking children's blood and having a strong alliance with the goddess Kali. He managed to wear this mask and he has been given only a year to stay in such a form. He swears in front of the goddess kali that once he becomes the king, he will serve her and offer her sacrifices every day.

"'The goddess Kali simply informed him she would not provide any kind of help to make him a king. He will be totally on his own. That is when he started searching for Danwals, since being an experienced wizard, he figured out the way to catch them, which he finally did. Now the deal between him and the goddess kali was simple. In case he wasn't able to be a king, once he completed this year, he would return to his old form. His powers would be taken away from him and he would be just an ordinary dying, sick old man.

"'When she first described him, he managed to look into his life and was able to see the ugliness of his life in progress; however with the help of Danwals, his transformation was blocked. I was only able to view how he was involved with various cult followers, and how he had been sacrificing innocent children. I already mentioned you earlier, the time he spent with Agoris. Today, while meeting him in person, I was able to break the barrier and enter his mind. I have not tried to control him otherwise Danwals would have felt my presence and escaping his mind would have been a problem. He managed to show the commoners how sanctimonious he was and they all respected him.

"'My child, there are two types of people those who consider themselves still learning or humble students. Even they possess the knowledge as massive as the sea itself. Others, who manage to collect a few drops from the ocean, they start posing as masters of the universe. Jay is the second type, with little knowledge however pretending with huge display. However, what you have demanded from him, it's a serious task. I was observing him and sensed, he was speaking to Danwals. What I saw was they were trying their best to convince him it's a suicide mission, not only for him, but for them as well. They offered to make him vanish and can take him somewhere safe and faraway from Durga's state.

"'He totally ignored them and spoke to the goddess Kali. Again he requested her help, for one last time. She reminded him about their agreement, that she will not provide any kind of assistance for him to be a king. Jay is a clever fellow and he managed to convince the goddess Kali that he had managed to gain princess's intention and all she wanted was a stone from the Cave of Lost Souls. The goddess Kali gave some instructions to Danwals and vanished from the skies. After that Danwals agreed to help him to get the Vahus. I know you saw a dream in which you were in the cave with Hukush and Ziyush. They are waiting for him and now, when we reach the palace, I would like to show you something.'" Guru Das sighed deeply.

"Durga thanked Guru Das, and said with a smile, 'Now my soul is in deep peace. I'm relaxed and I wish I could see what is going to happen inside the cave with Jay.'"

"They reached the palace and Durga went straight with Guru Das into his chamber.

"So, what do you think of the story so far? I know somethings you will understand and few you will not. Don't worry about it, feel free to ask about what you don't understand, ask me my darling," Raja said while looking at Miriam.

Excitedly, Miriam replied, "My love, you are such an amazing story teller. When you speak your voice takes me into the world of Dugra, Guru Das and Jay. Your voice is enough to enchant me with your magic. Now imagine when you start narrating Durga's story, I just feel everything is alive and I'm right there among them. I just feel myself lost and present in Durga's world watching every scene with my own eyes. My love, please continue and don't stop telling me what happened next. I really love you and every second I spend with you is like living a whole life full of happiness. Tell me what happens next, what Guru Das wanted to show Durga. Please take me back from where you stopped!"

"Raja replied kindly, "The purpose of my life is just to serve you and make you happy. I'm glad you are enjoying the tale, as all I want is for you to understand some of the realities and mysteries of life. What you will hear in these anecdotes, one day could be seriously useful for your everyday life. I know you want to help others and there is no better way to help starving souls. Knowledge will prepare them to survive in this cruel world, and protect themselves and the ones they love. Money can finish anytime, but wisdom will go with them to their graves. Let me continue from where I stopped and take you back in the world of Durga.

"As Guru Das entered his chamber, he opened one of his sacks and took out a piece of black cloth. Nothing was printed or written on it, and Guru Das spread the cloth and it became a huge shawl. He closed his eyes and recited few words while holding the cloth next to the wall. Within a second, the cloth flew on its own and stuck on the wall, as if someone had glued the cloth on the wall. Guru Das again recited a few words and suddenly the cloth turned into a screen. What she saw next was Jay with his two devotees, who were the same men who came with him for the meeting. Veer and Gopal were quietly following them; they were close to entering Rama's Bridge. It was already getting dark and next thing they noticed, all of them stopped to select a space for camping, as they planned to rest and move forward in the morning.

"Impressed, Durga asked Guru how it was possible that they could see all the travel and action." Durga jumped from her seat and hugged Guru Das.

"Guru Das replied with a naughty smile, 'My child, don't be excited. These tools will all be yours shortly. I never used the cloth and I kept it for some special occasion, and what can be more important than watching your first war. You are not only going to view the entire journey, however you will hear every word they will speak. Would you like to have hearing with what you're viewing?'"

"Durga excitedly replied, 'Yes please, I want to observe every detail of this trip and want to hear every word they speak during their trip.'"

"Guru Das told Durga, 'I desire to view their travel for little while as I wish for them to be in the middle of Rama's Bridge, where I have a surprise for them. Since I want their journey to be filled with surprising elements, after every five hours they will face a new challenge. I want his two devotees traveling with Jay to beat him for putting their lives in such danger. I really am looking forward how Danwals will react to those surprises and how far can they go to protect Jay. Later, I want you to take Rqui, the magical cloth in your room, and view the whole journey from there.

"Durga wanted to know what Rqui is and where he had found it, and he told her that Rqui had been gifted to him by a humble sage. 'He was about hundred and ten years old,' Guru Das said, 'and I met him in the depths of a forest. I was extremely thirsty and was dying for a drop of water. While I was walking, I started hearing the voices of many people from a distance. I started following the direction of the voices and I ended up standing in front of a strange cave with an extremely narrow entrance.

"'Saying hello into the cave, I entered where I was surprised by what I saw next. Rqui had been hung on a wall and all the voices were coming out of it. I stood in shock to see strange, small people stuck inside Rqui. All of a sudden, the people disappeared from Rqui and I heard a voice from behind asking me who I was and what was doing there? I quickly turned around and saw an old man lying relaxed on the floor. I asked forgiveness for entering without permission and introduced myself by telling my name. I humbly stated that I was a traveler and would like to have a glass of water.

"'The old man introduced himself with a kind smile and said that he was Indir Jogi and that I was welcome to come sit next to him. With a smile, Indir Jogi asked me whether I was on a quest to become a sage. Guru Das, in respect touched his feet and sat next to him and told him that I sought people like him from whom I could gain pearls of wisdom." With a smile, Jogi passed me a glass of water. From where the glass had come, I had no idea; however he offered it with great hospitality, which I humbly accepted. The water was sweet, mild cold and refreshing. I had never had such delicious water after that.

"'He asked me if I was hungry, and I nodded obediently. I'm not a big fan of eating however this day I wanted to enjoy food, because I had company and it'd been more than two years since I had spoken to any living person and almost a month I had eaten a single grain of rice. Indir Jogi asked whether a vegetarian meal would be acceptable and I responded by saying that I was a vegetarian. He added that he have no idea why do people ate dead animals' meat, and that they thought its good for their health, would provide special powers and make them strong.

"'Those fools, he told me, had no idea the real power was all about controlling your mind and soul. Once you could control those, you gained strength through your soul and in that scenario, a body automatically became twenty times stronger than an ordinary human. Once you ate dead animal's meat, people contracted various kinds of diseases, poor folks had no idea about.

"'Two trays of meals were sitting next to me; again I was surprised where the food came from. One thing I understood for sure, Indir Jogi was a truly knowledgeable sage, blessed with hidden powers. We both had the meal together. I hesitate before finally asking who those tiny people inside the wall were and what world they were from.

"Indir Jogi, while gazing into my eyes, told me he had been watching the future. This was not an ordinary cloth I was looking at; it was a magical mirror that could hear your order and show you a time or world that you wanted to view and hear. You could choose past, present and future; it all showed exact events that had happened, were happening or would happen. He asked what I must be thinking why Indir Jogi would share details of such a valuable item with me. Maybe greed would overcome my soul and I was stronger than him and could easily kill and steal Rqui yes, that is what it was called.

"Guru Das said, keeping his gaze modestly downcast, 'You're my host, my respected sage. You provided me water, shelter, food and above all, your wonderful alliance. You're kind, wise and what you shared with me and as I have witnessed by my own eyes, the true magic of Rqui. I truly don't want to be rude, however it hurt me that even being so wise you doubt my character. I know you were educating me and were giving an example. My hunger and need is different. I want to view the world using my mind, not my eyes

"Indir Jogi begged Guru Das to accept his humble apologies if he had offended Guru Das in any manner; it had not been his intention by any means. In fact, the truth was, he had honestly looked for Guru Das's arrival. Since he had been in this place for more than two years and he had been instructed, the first human to come visit him, he would hand Rqui to him. It's just a magical object to view what our world is all about and what is happening and what will happen in future. Imagine if this goes in one wrong hand, how that man can manipulate the whole world. Only a sage like Guru Das could keep it safe and for his eyes only, and he would share it with eyes he trusted with his heart, mind and soul. Indir Jogi had known Guru Das would have millions of question about Rqui, from where the water and food is coming and who he truly was. He invited him to feel free to ask him.

"Guru Das replied, 'I am out in this forest to find hidden secrets and gain knowledge and wisdom. Yes, it truly is the first time I have seen something like Rqui. I had never heard of it and never seen something like this before. I have spent time as devotee for some extremely powerful sages. If you feel like sharing your wisdom, I will consider myself lucky and blessed. Please accept me as your loyal devotee. I would also like to add, I will keep all the wisdom to myself unless I find the right devotee to transfer the pearls of wisdoms. I assure you I will always make you proud, as your loyal devotee.

"Indir Jogi said, 'Fair enough, my friend, as I mentioned to you earlier, you have been chosen by gods, and I was only playing the role of guardian of your treasure. You asked me about Rqui, and I am honored to share Rqui's story and what the origin of this magical cloth is.

"'Sixteen months ago on a sunny, beautiful afternoon, I was practicing my breathing exercises. Suddenly, my gaze landed on a beautiful pink little bird. I have lived in myriad forests, and had never seen such kind of bird in my life before. I forgot my work out and started staring at the bird. She was tiny and I noticed that tiny bird's every move. Each move was different from other birds I had studied before. It all seemed as if the tiny bird was extremely busy investigating the surroundings, the wild flowers, and various plants. My heart stopped when I saw a hawk, like me he was also observing the bird's moves. I knew any second the hawk would attack and that is exactly what happened next. My heart was in of the mouth. I didn't know why all I wanted was to save the little beautiful bird. I recited my spell and the air moved the bird into my cave. My next spell was to create a magical shield around the cave once the bird had entered, so the hawk was not able to follow the bird deep inside my cave.

"'The bird saw the hawk briskly flying toward her. A gust of air surprised her more, pushing her toward the cave. The pink bird flowed with the air and ended up in my cave. The hawk seems seriously determined to catch her. He kept trying to enter the cave and was surprised that he was unable to enter. If I'm not wrong, the hawk tried more than hundred times and was not willing to give up. I have seen many predators and was aware they charge their prey only once. If their prey manages to escape, they easily change their minds and wait for other prey.

"'However, this hawk was as if from some other world; he was not interested in giving up on pink bird. After more than hundred attempts, he was exhausted and took a break, while sitting at the edge of the cave. His actions seemed as if he would not leave unless the bird came out. He had figured out there was no way he could enter the cave, so he sat guard at the entrance.

"'The hawk was least bothered about the surrounding or who was around. He never even noticed me nor any other living creatures; the whole event a few minutes ago, had made all the birds aware of the hawk's presence and they had already vanished from their abodes. Even the crawlers were silenced in the presence of this strange hawk. I never noticed silence could be so haunting in the forest, as houses and caves could be quiet but a forest no way. During the day, noon, evening or night, the forests are always alive; weird voices from every single corner always keep the forest alive. Sometimes when predators hunt or kill their prey, the noises during those moments turn deadly. Monkeys start screaming and birds start flying toward unknown destinations. While the prey is dead and eaten, the forest life returns to normal. Now, all of a sudden, not even a single insect made a sound. Silence has its own language, which in some way can be extremely daunting, and that is how the forest was at that moment.

"'I started walking toward cave and my attention remained on the hawk as his was on the cave. One thing I knew for sure was that the hawk waiting for pink bird was not an ordinary hawk. Something was seriously strange about him; all of his actions were making him suspicious. The hawk was not interested in me at all; he didn't even notice me when I walk right in front of him and into my cave.

"'The moment I entered the cave, he attacked me, as that is when he noticed me and became furious. How come I entered the cave and he couldn't. His voice changed as he started screaming; I turned around and gave him one last look. My heart almost stopped with fear. As a man almost ten feet tall was punching the diaphanous shield. He was extremely well built and his head was of a hawk and his body was of a human. He was shirtless and below wore a black and gold kilt. On his wrists and neck he wore jewelry studded with precious stones. I was not scared of him; however I had come to realize that I had involved myself in something exceptionally serious. I was certain that even a bigger surprise was waiting for me inside my cave; it was obvious I would not have to worry about catching the pink bird it would be waiting for me.

"'There was no sign of pink bird; however my cave was extremely bright as someone had lit a bon fire. Exactly where we are sitting right now was the place the lights were coming out of. I had hold up both hands to keep myself from getting blinded. All of the sudden I heard a sweet voice.

"'Remove your hands, my savior and friend.'

"'I quickly followed the instructions and what I saw next, that I don't even have words to do justice to describe her. She was the most beautiful girl I had ever seen in my hundred plus years. For few seconds, my breath stopped and my heart skipped a beat; concurrently I was speechless, as I was born dumb. She was between twenty-seven to thirty years old. Her hair was golden and her eyes were like sapphires. Her smile was so alive that she could easily raise the dead. She was more than six feet tall and towered over me. As you can see; I'm a short man; her presence was so strong, made the whole room glow. She hugged me and kept thanking me for saving her life.

"'I have no words to pay my gratitude to you,' she said.

"'I had totally forgotten who I was and where I was, and was even not aware that I was a sage and had taken an oath to stay away from women. Women have a strange effect on men's minds; even as a monk and sage, all my life I try to control my weakness I kept my eyes on the ground to avoid any weakness taking control of my mind. I know your mentors must have taught you the way mine did; it's much better not to look at any woman's face. We have been told that if you don't know the pleasure, you stay away from sins. It was the first time I felt I have been a fool all my life. I can gain all the knowledge, serious wisdom; the reality of feeling a true joy is only in the presence of women. After a minute or two, I finally was able to get my voice back and keeping my eyes downcast, I told the girl she was most welcome. She stated that I must be surprised how a pink bird could turn into a girl like her and with her magical smile, she tried to make eye contact with me.

"'I felt the pink bird was in danger and all I wanted to do was to protect her. Used my knowledge and the little thing or two I knew." Indir Jogi replied her in simple manner.

"She told me she was a fairy and was in our world from Fairyland in the shape of a bird. She was a princess of a place called Azus and her name was Bazgen but that I could call her Baz as all her family and loved ones addressed her by her nick name.

"'Holy God, those dimples, when she smiles could turn any believer into non-believer,' Indir Jogi said. 'I knew in her presence I was losing my mind, all I want was time to be stopped and I keep looking at her. I never knew what a woman's beauty could do to a man like me. I was possessed; my heart, soul and mind completely lost their direction. I even forgot about my own existence and the reasons of my decisions I had selected for myself. Leading a life to support other humans, gain wisdom, and all my life I meet weird creatures. I had never met anyone like Baz; she was truly a heart stopper. In my heart, I was really angry with the gods. Why had they allowed me to meet her when I was a hundred above? I don't know how but somehow I managed to control my emotions, desires and the urge to be an ordinary man. I was again back in my world of being a monk, and kept my downcast and started a proper conversation with Baz.

"'It's an honor to meet you princess Baz,' Indir Jogi said, 'first of all, sorry that I brought you into this cave without your permission. The reason was simple, because I noticed the hawk was studying your every move. I figured out he would attack on you and all I wanted was to save your life. I covered the cave with an invisible shield so the hawk was unable to enter. I was surprised by how determined the hawk was; now he is waiting for you outside, but he is transformed into a strange creature. The face is still that of a hawk however the body is of a strong man. If you don't mind me asking, who is he and why is he chasing after you?'"

"'We live in Fairyland,' Baz said, "The creature you saw attacking me and now transformed into his original form basically is from land of others. In the land of others, all living souls are mostly the way you have seen standing outside. They can transform their bodies into humans; however their faces remain the same, according to their true identities. They want to come and rule your kind and the humans' land, and for that they need complete transformation. They knew humans are weak and they can easily control them. Fairies are their only option, and once they marry a fairy, only we can give them exactly what they want. He is outside waiting for me, so he can abduct and take me to the land of others. The name of the demon ruler is Belphegor. He is better known as the Seven Princes of Hell. All the monsters are like the one you saw, with various animal faces and human bodies. Even their women are the same, which is why it's Belphegor's plan to improve his nation's looks.

"'We fairies are always in favor of humans and their land; we like to visit sometimes to view your beautiful land. We are not permitted to travel alone; I was stubborn and came on my own. If you would have not helped me today, he could have easily abducted me. Please feel free to wish for any desire you have in your heart; if it's in my power, any word out of your mouth will be fulfilled. That I promise,'" Baz replied.

"Indir Jogi dreamily said to her, 'All I want you to stay with me; I want to spend rest of my life just looking at you. I don't want any material things; I don't want any knowledge or wisdom. I know I'm ugly old man, however please do think I do have a heart and the poor thing never beaten so fast as it did today. I was not even aware I'm a man, as all my life I was busy finding wisdom, knowledge and mental strength. Only today I came to know, nothing is more pleasant than being in the presence of a beautiful woman like you. I would not be able to find my peace without you, as my soul is at the place where it never had been before. Even a second without you, I have no idea how would I be able to breathe. I assure you I would die, the second you leave me. I could never rejoice again and for my remaining days, I will miss you every second as if someone has given me a cruel punishment. Can you stay with me forever; can you fulfill this humble wish of mine?

"Baz replied, 'Oh my dear savior, only this is not within my powers. However, I have a gift for you and that will surely make you forget about me. Just remember me as one of your dreams you had once in your life.

"Then she swung her pretty arm and, in the next second, Rqui was in her hand. She taught Indir Jogi the codes and the magic of it. He was able to sit, relax and watch with his own eyes, the present, past and what was going to be happen in the future. Imagine being able to view one's own death and how one would die. The way she was depicting Rqui, the details truly amazed him and her beauty started to vanish and again the sage in Indir Jogi returned. The quest was on, to find out what more treasure of wisdom he could gain from her.

"With a laugh, Baz told him. 'I would also like to bless you with a gift of wishes coming true. All you have to do is wish whatever you need and within ten seconds it will be fulfilled. Rqui is for your entertainment and wishes come true is for your everyday needs. One more thing it is not like a magical lamp, that you have to rub and a Djinn would come out to ask your three wishes. This one is different; your mind would be your lamp and at the same time your Djinn. Now you can give a try and make any wish you want.

"The first thing that came to my mind, Indir Jogi simply wished for it. Once he completed his wish, he informed her that he had made his wish, what was next?

"Baz informed him that his wish was already complete; he could go outside and see for himself.

"He went running outside and was surprised to see the hawk creature had vanished as if he had never existed. How had that happened, he asked Baz surprisingly.

"Baz said, 'You wished for the hawk to vanish and he did; all your wishes would go through my mind into the wish-making planet. That planet has their team of invisible creatures who make things happen. Their wish-completing time period is different from normal human beings. Let's say for them one second is like your one year and two seconds are like two of your years. When they fulfill your wish, for you it's a quick action, however for them it's a long period of time. Imagine how many people make wishes every day. Some big and some small, some wish for material things, some for love, and a few for health. Mostly, the rest of the world just wishes to become rich over night. I know what you will wish for is going to be food, water and staying in good health.

"A material thing you already have wisdom, to find and be rich, however those don't interest you and that is what makes you an interesting man on another planet. The honest truth is no one likes greed; creatures from the other planet support each other and never want to supersede each other. They believe in equality and team work. That is why all the planets are organized and in peace. You will never see them fighting with each other; it's only humans who are always killing each other and want the best for themselves, want to rule and make other humans their slaves. You always have done well in life and still you go through hardships each day. That is the reason I'm standing right here with you and blessing you with the gifts for life. Even if I wanted to live with you for rest of my life, I can't. The problem is fairies can only survive for forty-eight hours on human planet; one second over that time would kill us. I would be grounded once returned to fairyland, and would be banned for rest of my life to return to your beautiful land"'

"After her answer she kissed him on his cheek, hugged him and then vanished from the face of the earth. His heart sank with sadness, he lost the purpose of his existence and all he wanted to do was to end his life. He was truly in love with her, and before finishing himself, he wanted to take a look at Rqui. Once he started viewing the world inside Rqui, he became addicted and thought to himself that Baz was right. All these years he was just relaxing and watching the world studying the history; getting to know about kings and queens from various countries; learning languages. It made him lazy and everything turned out to be easily accessible. He just had one simple request to Guru Das, to use it when he needed it, otherwise he would be stuck in one place and he didn't need anyone interfering in his life. Concurrently, Indir Jogi was blessed to make as many wishes as he wanted; his food came at his command, and so did fresh juices and water. Baz had been absolutely honest with him forgetting about her; she was lost somewhere deep in a corner of his mind.

"Guru Das said to Durga, 'Now you know, my child, what the mystery of Rqui is. I never misuse Rqui. According to the wisdom when someone warns, always take it seriously; such as Indir Jogi warned Guru Das about using Rqui carefully, he took it seriously. I would request the same what Indir Jogi warned me about, not to be addicted of Rqui. Watch what you need and shut it down right away. My child, sometimes too much information is also not healthy for the human mind; it can leave horrible scars on your mind.

"Durga responded, nodding, 'This was amazing tale; I promise you Guru, I would never misuse Rqui.

CHAPTER 20

"THE PRECARIOUS JOURNEY"

R aja said to Miriam, 'My love, I share detail philosophies of those sages, the reason I want you to understand moral of each anecdote. The wisdom and the message hidden in these stories, I know you are the right candidate to share and educate humans in your own way.

Miriam seemed still lost in her own imaginary world of Durga's tale, replied efficiently, "Love you know I am coming from simple ordinary background, your world and Durga's anecdote is not just only a tale for me. I believe this is pure treasure and should be preserved for generations to come, so they can value simple meaning of life and its understandings. Please continue, what happens next?"

Raja said, "Durga looked at Rqui. The dawn was taking over from darkness, and she heard Jay instructing everyone get ready to initiate the journey. Guru Das took leave from Durga and went inside for a short rest. Durga ordered her breakfast and she watched every move they made towards Rama's Bridge. Jay was looking expectantly toward the sky, while studying movements of the clouds as he searched for something. Durga soon figured out that by the help of Danwals he was able to crack the code, and managed to navigate to the final destination from the map. From the movement of clouds and by his reaction, now he was waiting for the rain. She understood Jay was seriously dedicated to completing his quest, and Danwals were so far guiding him in the right direction. They were riding and Rama's Bridge was visible from a distance.

"Jay smiled while looking towards his associates, and said, "'I promise you, once I become the king, you both will be right and left hands, and together we will conquer the whole world. I want to be the king of the world and the most powerful man on this earth. For that reason, I need honest devotees, just like both of you. You will be free, to do whatever you like; you can continue kidnapping children and continue sacrificing them to keep our beloved goddess Kali happy. If we have her on our side, nothing is impossible, my friends!"'

"Veer and Gopal were quite far on a distance from Jay and his devotees. However, they were looking firm and obedient to support Jay in his quest. Durga understood it must be Jay who had instructed them to keep a distance so they wouldn't be able to hear their discussions or planning. Teja and Danu, Jay's two devotees, were well aware of caves, mountains and hidden temples in Lanka and, like Jay they too were devoted worshippers of the goddess Kali. Five years before, both had been kidnapping and sacrificing children in Lanka, and when all the surrounding villagers gathered together to catch the culprits, they escaped Lanka and came to the south of India. Like Jay, they were also addicted to drinking children's blood, as for them the only way to be immortal was through sacrificing to the goddess Kali and drinking human blood.

"Jay said, 'Can you believe, the old man, Guru Das thought we won't be able to crack his code? Such an old fool! The problem with old sages is they just think they are the only ones who know everything. Teja, do you guys remember the way he was looking at me during our meeting, as if I'm just a fool and signing my own death wish? I knew he is the one who told Durga about the Cave of the Lost Souls. The fool forgot one simple thing; everything is possible in this world, if a man is determined and seriously dedicated to making it possible. I honestly feel pity on all of these sages, who believe that what they know, no one else knows in this world. He might be a man of wisdom; however he should have respected and honored my bravery. If he had hidden powers, I think by now he would have figured out my real age. Then instead of supporting Durga, he would have been rubbing his head on my feet to know the secret of my youth. As per my knowledge, the old man is just a con man taking advantage of a simple royal family. As soon as I become the king, his old ass will be the first one to be fired and later thrown in a cage of hungry lions.'"

"Guru Das entered the room and sat next to Durga. '"I heard Jay cursing about me!" He said to Durga with a kind smile.

"Durga told Guru Das, 'Yes, he thinks you are a con man and an old fool, who was not able to sense his real identity. He is older than you, which is the main reason, why he's extremely proud, that you were not able to recognize his actual age. If you were wise, you would have respected him and for gaining the knowledge of youth, he wanted you to beg him to know the secret.

"This again was one of the biggest subjects human can learn, considering other people lower and talking low about them. If you want to judge the class of a human, watch his mouth and the words coming out of it. Oridary people are always concerned about other people's life; on the contrary, those who are focused on their own lives are never interested what others think about them. Since they are busy thinking only about themselves, and they are so focused, you will hardly see them wasting their time on small talk. We are born only once in this world and life is limited and short; better to use in progressing yourself.

"Guru Das said, 'He can make as much fun as he wants of me; this again depicts that he truly is a low-minded man. Even if he becomes a king, he will still act like a beggar. A real king is someone who, if you take away everything from him, will always act like a king. It's human nature; once you have a mind of a beast, you can never turn him into a human again. Few things people can never understand; with the possession of power and money, you can control people, you can scare them, however you can neither gain their respect nor win their hearts. In the end, it is one of their own personal attendants who will cut their throats. This is good for us, as he is proud and still thinks he is in control of everything. In his mind, he is sure that he will complete the quest and, as he thinks we know nothing, again the whole scenario goes in our favor. Remember one thing, having confidence is great but being over confident is an open invitation to suicide. His over confidence is what got him into such a path, which only leads to a horrible death; he can't even escape now. I sometimes pity him, but the problem with people like Jay is they are so stubborn and are so involved in their own world of greed and over confidence. They are blind and deaf to admit the reality. He would have never thought in a million years about doing good deeds for humanity with his knowledge or hidden powers, and I know for sure he never will. Well, time to give him some action, as I have already arranged some surprises for him. The first one will get started any minute.' Guru Das turned his full attention toward Rqui.

"Their full concentration was on Rqui. Jay and his devotees were leading and still keeping a great distance from Veer and Gopal. Suddenly Jay stopped, and so did his devotees and in the distance, Gopal and Veer stood still exactly where they were. Everyone watched something that was blocking the road quite far away. Jay's eyes widened with surprise as Rama's Bridge was in the middle of the sea; what was blocking the road and now was approaching briskly. Jay was finally able to see what was running toward them; from appearances they seemed like crocodiles but twenty-five feet tall. Jay was shocked to see crocodiles running on two feet; this was completely new for him. All his life he has seen crocodiles, but never such gigantic, aggressive and dangerous species.

"Jay, without wasting a second, closed his eyes and started reciting a spell. Next thing, Danwals appeared from nowhere, and it was the first time Durga had seen them; her mouth became dry and her breathe was on hold. Danwals truly were midgets; Durga jumped from her seat in response to what she saw next. The midget Danwals started growing tall and within a few seconds, they were more than thirty feet tall. Durga was afraid to finally see the Danwals' identity; she held Guru Das's hand tightly and did not even blink, as she was involved in watching what would happen next on Rqui. The Danwals were really horrible-looking creatures; even when they were in midget form, no one would have the heart to go near them. As per Veer's portrayal, they wore black robes; it was not any kind of robes; basically it was their skin. Veer and Gopal drew out there swords and they were ready to fight the crocodiles. However, they stood where they were and did not move a single inch. Durga knew Veer was truly scared of Danwals and now encountering those in giant shape had frozen him. The horses seemed really scared and were difficult to control. Veer and Gopal somehow managed them.

"The sea became alive and the sun hid behind the clouds. The day lost against the darkness. Durga deep in her mind asked herself what had happened to the weather so suddenly. Soon the creatures might clash or the Lord would create perfect weather for the deadly war. The total numbers of crocodiles was equal to the number of Danwals; they charged and wasted no time attacking the Danwals. The next scene amazed everyone, the five people on Rama's Bridge and the two of them sitting at the palace watching the war through Rqui. Danwals turned out to be fast. Each successfully caught a crocodile by its neck, and started devouring it. Their mouths in their stomachs opened wide, around six to seven feet and their teeth turned into grinding machines.

Within few minutes, there was no sign of a single twenty-five foot walking crocodile.

"Danwals ate them all; crocodiles are not easy animals to fight then eat alive. They are built to kill, and those were not ordinary crocodiles. They had been extremely gigantic and dangerous. Ordinary crocodile skin is like armor and the walking crocodiles' skin was ten times thicker than normal. The way the Danwals had eaten them, they proved themselves as truly the most dangerous monsters that had ever walked the face of Earth.

"Jay and his team were still standing at a distance, but Jay's yellow teeth were visible even from afar. The Danwals started approaching him and, as they took five steps, they returned to their original size. Once they drew near, all twelve of bowed in front of Jay and vanished. The sun came out and the day became normal, as if nothing had ever happened on Rama's Bridge. Jay seemed disappointed that the sun had regained control of the sky as he desperately wanted rain. He turned around and gave instructions to everyone to continue the journey; they all got back on track on their unimaginable quest.

"'Have you seen that, those midget creatures turned into giants?' Durga asked. How is that possible? Who were those walking crocodiles? Those creatures were there to hurt Jay and his devotees or could they have harmed our men as well? I really am terrified; what I saw seems like things are going in their favor now.

"'What is going on? Lord! I really am scared. What if Jay managed to bring the Vahus? I swear, Guru, I will kill myself rather than marry Jay. Have you seen how easily Danwals ate those deadly crocodiles, as if they were some ordinary worms?' Fear was visible deep in Durga's eyes and her face had become pale.

"'My child,' Guru Das said, 'you have to be patient. This is a war and in war, we should always remember our enemy also came prepared to win. Essentially it's your first war and that is the reason you are far too excited. I want you to learn every detail. This was beginning of the war and they are not aware, it was just a small test to assess their strength. See, with this attack on them, we simply understood the reason why Danwals agreed to support Jay.

"'You remember in our meeting, they simply refuse to enter the Cave of the Last Souls. In their own words they warned Jay; to escape from the meeting. Now everything is clear; the goddess Kali has blessed the Danwals with the remarkable power of increasing their height to thirty feet. Danwals are blessed with a power to do the impossible and increasing their heights which was totally out of their reach. Once they felt the power of increased height, they said yes! I feel sorry for those walking crocodiles, they were our warriors and they sacrificed their lives as brave soldiers for us. They were following Hukush's instructions, as now it's not only our war. It's matter of Vahus and since Hukush is the king of the lost cave, he will keep testing the strength of his enemies; while attempting various attacks.

"'As I have clearly mentioned earlier, you can count the people who know about Vahus on both your hands. Any corner of the world, if anyone even says a word Vahus, his face and mind comes under strict scrutiny by Hukush and his special team. Within a second, they can find out the person who took the name Vahus and their plans towards it. Hukush and his team are well prepared for Jay and his devotees. The reason our men are protected is because the team is aware who is planning to come inside the cave. Anyone who is just simply accompanying the culprits would never be harmed, unless their intention is to enter the cave and do evil. Our men's minds and consciences are clean and clear. They are just following instructions of their princess and being her loyal obedient soldiers. Trust me, they will return the same way they left.

"'My child, we are fighting a war and not for a second should weakness control you. Take fear out of your mind. I know you are brave and this all is new to you. Don't for a second consider yourself an ordinary soul; there is a reason God has chosen you to be a princess. When you are a royal, it's your responsibility to protect your nation, your territory and your crown. You're my child! How could you even think I will let anything happen to you? I have told you many times; while I'm alive no one can even harm a single hair on your head. If you ever doubt or feel fear again, I will never talk to you again.' Guru Das stared into her eyes.

"Durga hugged Guru Das then replied, 'Forgive me, Guru. I have no idea how fear entered into my soul and made me skeptical. I agree, we are in a war and Jay has all the rights to use all his tools, to win this battle. I know we are far too strongly equipped with blessings and alliances. I have seen the Cave of Lost Souls; it was even in my dream, but I know it's not a joke. I have no words for your love and kindness toward me. I promise I will never let you down again. My reaction was stupid and amateur. Therefore you will never see me weak again. You know well that I'm closer to you than my father; the honest fact is that you are the best father a daughter could ever dream to have. God has been extremely kind to me by blessing me to have you as my guardian, as one of the biggest privileges of my life. This is my first war, however not the last. I know people like Jay will keep coming in our lives. I truly love you Guru and please keep your faith in me and never leave me or be angry with me.'"

CHAPTER 21

"THE SIRENS"

Miriam with an excitement told Raja, "I really like the way Guru Das guided Durga. When you tell his parts in the story and the way he loved and cared for Durga, he reminded me of my father. My father was a man of principles and few words, however his eyes were alive and they always speak to me in abundance. He truly educated me to be a better human and standby to my principles. How to live gracefully in poverty, he taught me well. I really am in love with Guru Das and his wisdom.

"Good if you feel his wisdom and love for Durga, you truly would understand essence of his knowledge in much positive manner. Human's parents never die my love, in fact they live deep in your soul, watch and pray for you to do good deeds. As I was telling you Durga and Guru Das started watching from Rqui, as Jay and his team were getting closer to the land." Raja told Miriam.

"Jay was able to view the greenery of Talaimannar, in the Mannar Island of Lanka, from a distance. Again he looked up in the sky and tried to read the movement of the clouds; the sun was still in control.

"'Let's camp here and we wait for the rain, otherwise we will just be wasting our time wandering around the woods. I need to warn all of you, the rest of the journey is not going to be easy; be ready to face extreme dangers around every corner. I want each and every one of you to be fresh, be relaxed and prepare yourself for the upcoming battles. One more thing, I want all of you to sleep with your one eye open. Danwals are here just to guard us, but still stay alert,' Jay instructed his team, including Veer and Gopal.

Tired Durga said to Guru Das, "I go to have some sleep and as soon I wake up, would come and have breakfast in your chamber so we can continue watching their journey together."

Guru responded, "I want you to sleep peacefully, as nothing has happened, and it's just another ordinary day. Life is all about enjoying sleep, without considering worries about a day, week or month. Sweet dreams my child, stay blessed and safe." Guru Das placed his hand on her head while offering prayers and blessings.

Durga was feeling tired and the first thing before going to bed she took a nice hot bath. She followed Guru Das's teachings and took the idea of the war out from her head and was feeling fresh. As she hit the bed, she was in the world of her beautiful dreams. She woke late from her usual routine and she felt herself charged and all set for the new day. She ordered her breakfast to be served in Guru Das's chamber and went there.

"Good morning, Guru." She approached and touched his feet in the ritual of paying respect to one's elders.

"Good morning, my child. I can see from your face you had a good sleep. That is a good sign, as now you understand the art of being in control during war. Never let worries control your mind; bad times are like a storm. The harder it comes, in the same way it vanishes, as if it's never existed," Guru Das informed her, with kind gaze.

"All the peace I have in my soul is because of your wise teaching. What are the latest updates and news on the journey?" Durga asked him.

"No, my child, I was waiting for you to arrive so we can watch it together. Let's see what's going on with our enemy. One thing I know, the land of Lanka is full of mysteries the thick jungles, the hidden palaces and imperceptible creatures existing there. I can imagine a journey toward the cave would be an interesting one," Guru Das replied with a smile.

Jay was walking in the depth of jungle and it was raining. He had managed to read the map and was now moving briskly in the right direction leading to the Cave of Lost Souls. As his speed picked up, it was clear from his expression that he was in such a hurry. All that was on his mind was to find Vahus and finish the quest and marry Durga, finally be the prince and rule her state. Teja and Danu were leading, Jay was following them, and Durga's men maintained a distance while they followed them.

Everyone was walking quietly, but then suddenly the sweet voices of girls singing in the jungle stunned them all. From the beach all the way in the depth of the forest, they had not seen any village and had not even encountered a single human soul. Where the songs were coming from, they were trying to figure out; however they started feeling the advance stage of inebriation. Jay quickly figured out something was not right and these voices were distractions, as even he would not able to control his steps.

Veer and Gopal noticed Jay and his devotees started acting as if they were intoxicated. Because of the locket Guru Das had given them, they were immune. Veer played smart and winked at Gopal, to pretend they both were intoxicated as well and they started walking like Jay and his devotees. The singing was highly seductive and the voices were getting closer and closer, now that they were in deepest part of the jungle. The bushes were tall and filled with thorns for those three who were asleep, walking with their eyes open. They lost their senses; they were walking without even feeling that the thorn bushes were poking and scratching their bodies. Because they were under a spell all they wanted was to reach the singing girls, after crossing a huge muddy swamp surrounded by big thorn bushes. They ended up right in front of a beautiful lake; on the right was beautiful water fall. Under the water fall was an opening of a cave. The voices were coming from the cave and Jay and his devotees without even a thought, jumped in the lake and started swimming toward the cave.

Veer and Gopal stood there and confusedly watched them. They knew something was inviting them and whatever sounded like those girls, they knew were not humans. Gopal's screamed so loud it made the whole jungle alive. He started pointing toward something gigantic under the water coming toward Jay and his devotees. Veer pressed his mouth by his hand to refrain himself from screaming. Jay and his devotees were still intoxicated and swam toward the cave. They seemed as if they had totally forgotten who they were and why they had come to Lanka.

Jay seemed like the walking dead and so did his devotees; they were all desperate to reach the voices, as if those were not voices, but the serum of life. This time it was screams of Danu, as he started swaying toward the skies in the maw of a forty-five foot, three headed python.

The python tried to position Danu so as to swallow him whole; the other two python heads started attacking Jay and Teja. Within a second from the depth of the lake, Danwals started rising and shortly they were thirty feet tall. Briskly they rescued Danu from one of the head, and the other two Danwals carried Jay, Danu and Teja to the cave's entrance. They returned and joined other Danwals, who were busy fighting the three-headed python. The python had already squeezed five of the Danwals, and he was trying to bite and eat the others. Danwals were trying to get hold of python's heads so they could start eating. The Python was not only strong; however was fighting well with good tactics.

Danwals manage to break Jay, Teja and Danu's spell and they returned to their senses. They were surprised to find themselves under attack; all three of them started religious mantras. The intoxicating singing was still heard, however thanks to their mantras, they managed to avoid the intoxicating spell. On the other hand, the python had captured a Danwal in one of his maws, and within a few seconds he devoured it alive. Watching one of the Danwals eaten alive made the other eleven furious; one jumped on the python's tail and fixed the tail on his stomach. The mouth on Danwal's stomach opened and the teeth started working like a grinding machine. Now Danwals started eating the python alive and feeling such a pain, the python's grip became weak and the five who were being squeezed in its coil were released. Instead of attacking the Danwals, the python wanted to free its tail so he could escape. The python was slashing its tail wildly; however the Danwal's mouth was glued to the tail. The Danwals' anger had reached a different level, they were enjoying by giving python an agonizing torture. The other three managed to keep python heads on their mouth; all four Danwals started eating the huge python. They decreased their teeth's speed; the python was suffering a slow and painful death. After eating the heads, they left the remaining pieces for the rest of the Danwals. All eleven shared the forty-five foot python and demolished the entire giant snake. They gathered and hugged each other as one; it was the first time everyone heard their voice while they cried. Everyone kept hands on their ears, as the cries of Danwals were horrifying and hurtful to their ears. For a few minutes their cries were heard then returned to their normal size. They ran to Jay and were at his feet, and again started crying, but this time the cries went unheard from distance. Jay placed his hands on their heads and all eleven Danwals vanished.

Jay looked inside the cave where the singing could still be heard. He wanted to go inside. Once and for all, he needed to find out who those girls were. He signaled to Veer and Gopal to swim across the lake and join him and they followed his instruction and started swimming. As they emerged from the lake and approached Jay, he started hurling abuse at them.

"You idiots, why were you both on the other side of the lake while the three of us were on this side? You were sent to be with us and support us during my quest, not to be our audience. I know you would not join us inside the Cave of the Lost Souls, however before we reach the cave, both of you have to act like you are warriors, and fight with us," Jay told Veer, while trying to control his anger.

"We were seduced and inebriated like you guys, beside you instructed us to keep our distance. We only followed your instructions all the time and on daily basis. When we all became intoxicated with the girls' singing, we started walking toward where the voices were coming from. Your creatures broke our spell, and how could we cross? There was a huge war going inside the lake, between that giant three-headed python and your monsters!" Veer complained to Jay.

"Okay, from now on you walk with us and we all will enter inside this cave. I want no further distractions during our journey. Let's go together and find out the mystery of who these singing girls are?" Jay lit the torches and started to lead the team.

Durga was stunned and by the grisly scene she had witnessed. The three- headed giant python had finally managed to kill one of the Danwals, which made her happy. Simultaneously, she was impressed by Jay's determination and had to agree that he in some way was a courageous and focused man. The day before, Guru Das's teachings had opened her mind and she started to see her enemy from various angles. Her vision was not block anymore; the fear had completely vanished. Durga understood war was an art and which she could easily win, if she overcame and controlled her fears. However, she had never seen this much action in her entire life, the way Danwals and all those creatures were attacking each other. One thing was clear all the creatures were sacrificing their lives to keep her safe.

The cave's opening was quite wide and the voices were getting louder with every step they took. Suddenly the cave became silent, which confused Jay and his team tremendously. Inside the cave all they were able to see was only a single species of a plant, and it was everywhere. All the way in every corner of the cave and even on the cave's ceiling, the same ugly plant was visible.

"Where did the girls vanish?" Jay asked his devotees surprisingly. They all seem concerned and were in shock as well; everyone was trying to find some secret door which lead to where the girls were hiding.

Jay closed his eyes and started coordinating with Danwals; within few minutes his eyes opened and he smiled while looking at everyone. "My friends, there are no girls here. In fact, they have never been here!"

All of them start looking at each other, trying to figure out what Jay was talking about, as they had all heard seductive women singing songs.

"What is going on, whose voices we heard and followed?" a wide eyed Teja asked Jay.

"Look around and what you see is what was singing and seducing us," Jay told all of them while smiling.

"All we see here is only this plant covering the entire cave. Oh lord, please don't tell us that, these plants were singing?" Veer asked him this time.

"Unfortunately yes, you got it right. These are not ordinary plants! They were raised on the blood of sirens. I know you are not aware what does sirens mean and who they were. Sirens were sea creatures, which were able to transform themselves into beautiful girls; their voices were full of seduction and intoxication. The crews of all the ships which used to pass by heard their voices and were lulled into a deep sleep. Once they were deeply asleep, Sirens climbed and took over their ships and killed everyone.

"Their actual appearance was a combination of half woman and half bird, however only few were able to see them in their actual shape. Those were ten brave soldiers, who represented the king of Lanka. When more than ten ships were found crewless, the king raised his eyebrows. As his trading business was affected, so he ordered his team of ten intelligent men to investigate and solve the mysteries. The king's wizard was a beautiful young girl, who managed to see in her crystal ball and figured out, it was the sirens that were hunting the crew. With her magical powers, she soon understood the sirens' vocal seduction, these sirens created the seductive voices to hunt their preys. She made a potion with various herbs to which she added the dust of some dead reptile's bones.

"The wizard notified the power of the potion and gained the king's permission, which he happily granted. Then she made those ten men drink the potion. After drinking it the men were immune to the sirens' seductive singing. The wizard provided a map by which they were able to track the sirens' abode. This cave and few nearby caves were where those sirens lived. When the ten soldiers attacked sirens, all of them managed to escape toward the west. Only one was caught in this cave, where you see all of these plants. She was brutally killed by the men and her blood spilled on the soil inside the cave and these plants were born from her blood cells, as they acted like seeds to give birth to these ugly plants.

"I hope now you can understand these plants contain blood of the same siren and these plants are the reason for those seductive songs. This plant is avenging revenge of the siren's death and they invite travelers inside the cave, which they can only enter once they have crossed this huge lake. When they enter the lake, they become prey of three-headed python. All the sirens managed to swim toward the west. Not a single incident ever took place on these shores after the killing of that one siren. Let us burn all these plants so they don't distract any more travelers in the future."

While finishing the tale, Jay started burning the plants and the others followed him accordingly. The plants' cries were heart wrenching and extremely melancholic.

Once the fire took control of the cave, they all were surprised to discover the hidden doors inside the cave. However, Jay was not interested to investigate further; what the secret behind those hidden entrances were. He was focused on finishing his mission and returning to collect his prize. They left the cave, swam back across the lake then took their positions on their horses. Jay sped up the journey as he followed the map's directions which led toward the deadly Cave of Lost Souls. Jay had known this journey would be a tough one, but he hadn't seen these attacks coming. Since he had stepped on Rama's Bridge, the creatures he had encountered had not been ordinary. How many soldiers and scholars had traveled the same path to achieve the great Vahus and not a single one had been able to get past the walking giant crocodiles. However, if someone had crossed their path, he would have fallen prey to the three-headed monster python.

Deep in his mind, Jay was preparing himself for more attacks before reaching the Cave of Lost Souls. He gathered all his strength and looked up at the sky and start reciting mantras. Jay couldn't risk more Danwals before completing his mission. He had decided not to camp or take a break now; he wanted to reach the cave as soon as possible. After reaching his destination then camp and rest for a while before entering the cave and participating in the greatest battle of his life.

Jay stuck to his plan and traveled non-stop toward his final destination. During their journey, things went well no attack and not a single encounter. Jay's confidence was not eroded in any way; in fact it was getting stronger. On the full moon night in the depth of the Lanka forest, it was the fourth night after last attack had taken place. The horses suddenly stopped and refused to move further; they seemed really scared and started making strange noises. Jay briskly recited his mantra and the Danwals appeared. He was not in a mood to waste any time to investigate what would appear next. The Danwals started growing tall as they figured out whatever they were going to face was not small.

Jay shouted to his team, "Take charge and be ready, we are under attack!"

CHAPTER 22
"THE UNIMAGINABLE QUEST"

The voices from the sky gained everyone's attention. The voices seemed like huge birds were flying and approaching them. First it was hard to figure out what type of birds were those, but it seemed like sky was filled with birds. To everyone's surprise, as the birds drew nearer, the light of the moon revealed that birds were giant, blood-sucking bats. Their jaws were visible, and no one had ever seen such terrifying giant bats before. The Danwals made a circle around Jay and his men and mouths in their stomachs were open wide.

The bats launched the attack and the Danwals started catching them and briskly eating them, one by one. The quantity of the bats was more than thirty; however the speed of Danwals was amazing. They were wild and hungry as for them it was matter of taking revenge on all creatures. Within fifteen minutes they had cleared the sky, and not a single bat was left alive. Once they completed their job, Danwals were back to their normal size. They bowed in front of Jay and again vanished, as if they had never existed and nothing happened few minutes earlier. Jay instructed everyone to setup camp and sleep for a while. Now that the attack had taken place, for few hours they would have time to regain energy after having some quality sleep. All the men were dead tired and so were the horses. All of them had a peaceful sleep for almost ten hours. Jay felt revived and his mind, body and soul charged to continue the journey.

They were back on track, following the map that led them to the Cave of Lost Souls. It took them another week and finally Jay was standing right in front of the Cave of Lost Souls. He told his team to relax and instructed Gopal and Veer that they were free to camp wherever they wanted or at whatever distance suited them. As agreed, he reconfirmed with Veer and Gopal that if he didn't show up within twenty-four hours they were free to return home.

Teja and Danu were fast sleep and at quite a distance so were Veer and Gopal. Jay sat and offered his prayers to the goddess Kali. He kept checking the cave's entrance; not for a second would he change his decision. His faith in goddess Kali was on extreme level and he truly was her most devoted monk. Jay's gaze remained on the cave's entrance as he was able to see everything inside just looking at the entrance. Calculating enemies inside and studying their strength and weakness, people like Jay seemed to be so focused on their cause it was difficult to read his emotions and facial expressions.

After an eight-hour rest, Jay walked into Veer and Gopal's camp. He reminded them that their twenty-four hours would start right from the moment he set his first step inside the cave. They both nodded and watched him join Teja and Danu. Veer kept his eyes on three of them and as they neared the cave, Jay turned around and signed that they could now start keeping an eye on the time. All three of them vanished inside the cave. He didn't know why, but Veer felt his heartbeat increase with a chill.

As Jay entered the Cave of Lost Souls, he sensed the smell of death all around. The cave was dark and freezing, and Jay took every step carefully. They lit the torch and it was not an easy cave, for it was full of weird complications; each opening was a new mystery. They could easily feel millions of eyes watching and surrounding them. Jay knew the calmness in the cave was the signs of upcoming tornado, which would hit soon. He recited the code and Danwals appeared, they protected all three men and by keeping them inside a circle.

Jay heard the voice of Hukush, "My name is Hukush and I'm the king of this cave. I will give you one, and only one chance to turn back and save yourself and your men's lives.

"I mean no harm to you or your kingdom; I'm here to take Vahus with me, nothing more because my life depends on that. I would not leave without it," Jay replied in an arrogant manner.

"You have no idea what are you wishing for, Vahus is property of this cave and you're talking about taking it from here. Let me tell you something, I don't allow someone to even think of Vahus. What can I say don't blame me later, that I didn't warned you." Hukush told him and his royalty was clear in his accent.

"I have no choice but to destroy everyone who stands in my way. In fact I warn you to save your life and vanish wherever you can," Jay replied and this time his soaring confidence was strongly felt in his voice.

"As I'm the king, it is my job to give you a chance. Sometimes, when people are greedy, they are blind and they are not aware of what kind of consequences they are getting themselves into. That is your case and one thing you have to alter from your concern is being worried about lives that exist in this cave," Hukush replied with a grim laugh.

Once Hukush was finished, the cave came alive. It felt as if they were not in some cave; however it seemed like a vast battle ground. Jay looked around what he saw made him seriously concerned. His team and Danwals were surrounded by thousands of warriors. They were all from different part of the world and they were mix of men and women of various races. It seemed as if they were up against the world's most deadly killers and trained warriors. Their faces were brutal and dead serious, Jay knew they all were masters of killing humans in the most painful manner.

The Danwals created a shield around the three of them, and after providing them complete protection, they started growing tall and launched the attack on the warriors. On other side Jay started searching for Vahus. He was not able to find it on the battlefield. The cave was filled with layers and he was trying to use his third eye, to help him to decide whether to go below the cave or choose the lead going toward the next level above the battle field.

The war was on, Danwals were trying to eat and kill warriors who were already dead. The warriors were equipped with the most deadly weapon Jay had ever seen in his life. Jay was making way toward the lower section of the cave, as his instinct were telling him Vahus was hidden somewhere down in the lowest section of the cave. He knew the cave was full of sections and every corner was guarded by the world's deadliest warriors.

On other side the warriors were attacking Danwals from all the corners. It just seemed as if elephants were under the attack by lions. The warriors were fearless and highly skilled in creating, an excellent attack strategies. Danwals created a shield and caged the entire warriors' souls behind that shield. They were not able to cross over the shield and the Danwals started escorting Jay toward the cave's lower section. This time, the Danwals were leading as they knew the location of Vahus. The lowest section was incredibly dark and Jay again lit his extra torch. The temperature was dropped in this section; all of them were still inside the protected shield and saved from the freezing cold.

It was quite dark but with the help of Jay's torch, he kept moving forward. In Jay's mind, he quickly wanted to get hold of Vahus and move out of the cave.

One of Danwal's scream froze everyone where they were. Jay moved the torch toward the direction from where the scream had come from. What he saw next was one of the Danwals head was in Shebuf's mouth. Teja and Danu's screams made the cave alive, the torches on the wall automatically were lit and the whole cave illuminated. Jay himself was surprised to see a half-woman and half-buffalo, while staring all three men Shebuf throw the headless body of one of the Danwals. While walking toward them, she started chewing the head; her orange fiery eyes made Danu beg Jay to save his life and get him out of here. Jay searched for the rest of the Danwals. The remaining ten Danwals were in the distance trying to capture Shebuf in their cage of shield. The Danwals were aware that nothing could kill or hurt Shebuf, as it was just her soul. How could one kill someone who was already dead?

The Danwals were risking everything for Jay and trying their best, to fulfill his wish. Goddess Kali gave them power to increase their height and Jay had promised them that once he gets hold of Vahus, he would free them for good!

The Danwals were aware this trip was suicidal for him, and they honestly tried their best to make him understand. Jay was far too stubborn and greedy to becoming a king; his madness had taken the life of two Danwals. In the world of monsters and creatures, Danwals were well known as immortal monsters. After a great struggle, Danwals were able to capture Shebuf's in a shield cage. Shebuf's tumultuous screams were enough to make any living creature go mad, they would only escape by killing themselves. All the human souls were trying to break the shield and the Danwals were aware of that they can't hold them in that shield cage for too long.

All of them shivered with the howling they heard, and the howling became louder and louder. As some big dogs ran toward them, Jay and his devotees' protective shield was removed by Hukush. Jay and Teja took cover behind Danwals; however Danu was confused and scared, so he started running in the opposite direction. His painful screams drew all the attention towards him, as he was lying on the ground and one of the Hybens had bitten his stomach and opened it wide. As they were preparing their attack while surrounding Danwals. They totally ignored Danu's body as his agonizing screams echoed in the depths of the cave. Danu was lying trying to look at his stomach, at what the Hyben had done to him. Jay was surprised why Hyben were not eating or finishing him, why they had left him to suffer. One of the Danwals managed to create protective shield for Jay and Teja, and later he joined his team who were already fighting the Hybens. The Hybens attack techniques were worth watching they divided into groups of three and acted as if they would attack each Danwals individually. However instead of fighting one on one, the group of three attacked single Danwals brutally. One jumped on its face, another snatched his arm and the third one grabbed the Danwal's leg. Within a few seconds, three of the Hybens had torn three Danwals. The other seven were not able to understand the speed of the Hyben attack, while the three torn-up Danwal bodies were laying next to Danu's body and their screams merged with Danu's.

The whole cave was filled with excruciating screams, but Jay remained focused on finding Vahus. He knew the Vahus would never share a single ray of light as it was human shy. The Hybens' next attack killed Danu and all three injured Danwals. The remaining seven Danwals manage to capture the Hyben in shield cages. The Danwals start marching toward the location of the Vahus, and while they were running loud roars froze them immediately. The roar was so powerful that it shook the walls of the cave.

Something gigantic flew from the highest section of the cave, and landed right in front of all of them. It was Angion, the flying lion. His presence made everyone appear tiny. Angion was more than thirty-five feet tall and was more than fifty feet in length. As Angion landed on the ground, his wings vanished inside his skin; it was the first time the Danwals start running backwards. Jay was shocked to see how Danwals were afraid of something.

He started reciting his mantras and begged help from the goddess Kali. Angion was an aggressive lion and began to hunt every Danwal. Angion single paw tore a twenty-five foot tall Danwal into two pieces. The Danwals were unable to fight Angion; all they were trying to do was escape him. Within less than ten minutes, the remaining seven Danwals were turned into pieces everywhere on the ground. Hukush, Shebuf, and all the souls were free from the shield, and so were Hybens, and all of them slowly moved toward Jay and Teja.

Time stopped inside the cave, and from nowhere the goddess Kali appeared and in her six arms she carried swords. The goddess Kali charged at Angion, and the rest of all souls left the ground, made a circle and became an audience to witness the war of the Titans. Angion jumped on the goddess Kali and from the angle of his attack, it was clear his target was the goddess's neck. Jay seemed happy to see that the goddess Kali had come all this way to participate in his war.

For him it did not matter whether he collected the Vahus or died inside the cave. She had won his soul and he watched her, fighting to save his life. Goddess Kali's swords managed to injure Angion, however his wounds healed automatically. Their fight continued, and no soul interfered or attacked the goddess. As warriors they understood the principles of a one on one fight, until one of the fighters gave up. All of the sudden, the goddess Kali pushed Angion away and spoke to him, and he stood right where he was.

The goddess Kali then turned toward Jay. "The reason I came here is not because I want children sacrificed or that I support such things. I came here because you are my son; like every mother I always loved you. No mother would ever admit her child is the most evil soul that ever walked on earth. How could I? I love you with all yours goods and evils that reside deep inside you. I was motivated by your prayers and your love for me. My child, you have chosen a path that was not meant for you. I supported and protected you. See, for you I even fought the mighty Angion. He is not my enemy; however I wanted you to know that I love you and would always love you. I want you to pay full attention to what I'm going to tell you, my son.

"Now, here is what is going to happen next. I want you make your heart, mind and body strong. In a few seconds I will vanish from here, and the souls of your Danwals will kill you. I want you to ask for forgiveness for all your sins and especially from all the parents of all the children you sacrificed. They are waiting for you in Hell so prepare yourself to be killed every other day.

They would drink your blood and you will feel the pain. The saddest part is in Hell you die every day, and yes, my child, the suffering is never-ending. Those souls you see here, they all have a chance to enter Heaven, as once in life they did something good. Jay, my child, there is not a single act you performed which could have given your soul a chance to find your redemption in this soul. I would keep you in prayers, may the lord give you a chance!" With those words, she vanished.

Vahus came alive and its rays spread colorful light in the cave. Jay saw Vahus. Instead of praying and asking forgiveness, he ran toward Vahus. His feet struck something and he fell and when he looked around it was the Danwals all twelve of them. The Danwals were at their actual height and seeing them brought a smile to Jay's face. As he had found a life line, Jay showed them Vahus. In a way, he was trying to tell them that he had finally found the location of the Vahus and he wished for them to bring it to him so they could leave this cave.

Teja's screams brought him back to his senses. Hybens had opened Teja's stomach then left for a walk and left him screaming. Jay remembered the words the goddess Kali had told him before vanishing "he would be killed by Danwals". It was the first time he understood this main problem had always been his greed, what brought him to this point. With his last thought, he saw one of the

Danwals holding his head and placing it right into his stomach. With his last sigh, his body vanished from the Cave of Last Souls. The cave went into complete darkness, so did the life and greed of Jay.

In the darkness Hukush spoke, "Once again, the death of this man witnessed and glorified the words of my Lord, Jesus Christ. Jay, for all his life, used Danwals to kidnap and kill other humans and whoever challenged his authority. Today he was killed by his own weapon, simply the same way he killed others."

Durga, after a long sigh, smiled at Raja and told him, "This was my tale and experience of a man in my life. After that incident, I instructed all my maids and guards that if any men tried to contact me in a romantic manner, to give his details to Gopal or Veer right away. Can you imagine at such a young age that I managed to see creatures and monsters from the hidden world? What about you, have you ever encountered any such creature that I mentioned in my anecdotes?"

Raja replied, "No, never. I think I would be extremely scared if I ever had such an encounter. I have to say this was one astonishing anecdote, extremely magical and adventurous. I guess your Guru Das would be well aware where you are right now. I can clearly assume he would be watching us on Rqui, if I'm not wrong?"

"Yes, he is, and don't worry. He knew you saved my life. Guru Das would have found a way to convince my father that I'm safe and in good hands. By now Guru Das would have been in love with you as well," Durga told him.

"I just have one simple request," Raja said, "I truly am a private person. I left the whole world to find my true self. Kindly never force me to meet anyone, unless I feel myself ready to enter the world of humans. See, being alone in this cave, which is located in the middle of nowhere, not a single human would likely travel through such a deep forest to find me. Now, imagine this. If I were in my own world of wealth, would I ever get a chance to hear such a fascinating story such as yours? This is what I'm seeking knowledge, exploration of the world, secrets hidden from most people's eyes and ears. I believe we all are free and we should have a choice of whom to talk and meet. I truly enjoy your company, as I'm able to read your eyes. You mean no harm to me, as you can see same in mine. I truly like to share what I have learned so far and what you shared with me was out of the world. Human minds can be so deceiving. I was surprised to learn; people like Jay are so lost inside their shallow world. He even ignored the advice of the goddess Kali, who came especially for him like a mother to try make him a normal human. However, even she couldn't figure out that he was a soulless devil, and nothing in this world would ever take the greed out of him. Concurrently, the moral of your story teaches a great lesson. When a human is blind in his greed, he doesn't even listen to his gods or goddesses."

CHAPTER 23

"CORRELATIONS"

Miriam startled awake, as she had been fast sleep and lost in her world of dreams. "My Lord, now that was one splendid anecdote. If it was not you telling me, this whole tale seems like a fairytale. It truly seems like a work of fiction, however it's you who are telling me such an amazing tale; as with us our tale is like one unusual love story. If I share my tale with someone who would believe me, it's hard to even imagine or believe such myths truly exist in our simple world of human beings. Who would imagine, you are one thousand years old and, in a previous life, you were a king cobra. Still, you can transform yourself into one. Look at me I was seventy-four and am now sitting here as eighteen-year-old girl. This hidden side of your world I find truly mesmerizing and extremely magical. Imagine Jay could have asked any material happiness he wanted. His greed was only able to satisfy him to be the most powerful and rich man of the state. He became so lost in achieving his goal, insanity surpassed all the limits and made him completely blind. Durga really seemed in love with you. What happen next and what happen to her?" Miriam asked Raja while gazing into his steely eyes.

Raja answered, "Durga's wounds were finally healing; however she wanted to spend more time with me. The honest fact, I truly was enjoying her company and wanted to keep her just for myself. Yes, I have no idea what she liked about me; in her eyes it was easy for me to read that she was in love with me. I guess living in her own shell, the experience with Jay somehow left her isolated from the world of men. She was not able to trust any man.

"Within in few days, she educated me on various subjects, which only princes or princesses are aware about. If those royals could share only five percent of their education with commoners, humans would easily able to create a wealthy, healthy and peaceful environment. Those who are born with silver spoon usually think they are fortunate to born in royal or wealthy family. In some way they are and on the contrary in some ways they are not. They are basically two types of heirs in this world. Number one is the type of royals who prefer to take their heritage to a different level. They want to conquer the states, what their forefathers were not able to do. As they are extremely dedicated, they somehow manage to surpass their elders. From their childhood they understand the worth of discipline, responsibility, and the difference of their existence, lifestyle from the commoners. The second types are the ones who believe wealth stays forever and they don't have to make much effort. At an early age, when they are meant to gain education, their main focus is leisure. That's where their problems start, as they have no knowhow on how to run things. The moment their parents pass away, people take control on their dynasties. They suffer the worst in this world, as the rule of the world is simple; when you're rich everyone is your friend. The moment your crown is taken, the closet friends are the first ones to vanish.

"Durga turned out to be a true harbinger; her personal war with Jay made her mature. Durga started to spend more time getting involved in various types of educations that included spending more time with Guru Das, and learning various advance fight skills from Veer and Gopal. Sometimes, when we keep our mind focused on various things, deep down somewhere we start becoming isolated within ourselves. Durga was stuck in some moments of tempestuous monotonous of renunciation, and now meeting me, she had finally come out from those dull moments of her existence. With me, Durga was alive again; she finally met the self she had buried somewhere while taking responsibilities as a true princess. With me she managed to culminate and ravage her inner isolation. At the end she was girl who needs to feel happy and loved.

"Even though I only offered my close friendship, she accepted with grace. However, it was obvious from her expression and gaze, she was in love with me. On the other hand, I truly liked her. Durga's presence was highly intoxicating. Her face, eyes, smile, body, hands and her feet; how I controlled myself only I know. Durga piqued me; I was not ready and still wanted to study and understand human physical interactions. Even if it has been ages, I still am not able to sense why I never wanted Durga to know my true identity. Now, as I have lived a thousand years, met myriad of humans, I come to one simple conclusion Durga was truly the most humble soul, who would have supported and loved me; even if I would have shared my true identity. I guess with Durga my anecdote, Lord written in a strange way." Raja in mesmerizing voice told Miriam.

Miriam, while holding Raja's hand, softly told him. "I have to make an honest confession, when you started telling me about Durga, I truly disliked her. It has never happened before that I abhorred anyone; I guess when you love someone, it's truly hard to share your love. I know not everyone is open-minded as you're on this subject. However, for people like me, I definitely needed a tale like the one you shared to be given a chance to listen another person's story rather than living in a fake world of jealousy. I understand it's much better discussing people you have relationships with; in some good or bad manner they participate in our lives. All

I have now is huge respect for Durga; she truly was princess who knew the art of living in people's heart. I really want to know every single detail about her. What happened next? I am dying to know."

Raja replied, "Thank you, I agree with you that it is the best approach one should keep for the people you love. The past is just a mystery and life is now. However, what is life without the past and the history of our existence? What can be more interesting than the people we lived with and spent moments of our lives? We believe in them as they were our loved ones, our own, family and friends. We shared a decent part of our life with them; deep down they are always there somewhere in one of the hidden corners we hardly like to visit. Who can be closer than the person we are with and the person whom we are choose to love, for the rest of our existence?

"Jealously is like a critical disease; once it enters your mind, forget about it ever leaving unless you're dead. Now is life and this is the moment we are alive, you and me looking at each other. We can kiss and we touch each other. What can be more magical than this moment? The people we are talking about they are long gone, however you asked me to open the book of my life, without mentioning few people's names, my tale is incomplete. Durga, she did far too much for a beast like me, I could had made her the love of my life and she would have still been alive and with me. My heart never accepted her. I respected her more and in my own way I did love her. However, I knew being with her would have left me empty and her too.

"The reason was simple. Even being with her, I would have been seeking you in this world. People can love each other and can even compromise in relationships. I wanted to find you, the one for whom you can wait a thousand years to be with. True love is insanity, dangerous in its own way. We both handover our lives to each other, like you met me the first time and, without your permission, I turned you eighteen. While I have shared with you the secret and the only way to kill me, is in the shape of Lopti. If this is not madness, then what is it? Like we met and felt, we're one soul in two bodies. Now if that is what you call true love then I'm happy with you and there are no secrets between us. You love me for who I am and I don't have to pretend to be someone I'm not. This chemistry that we both have, I was not able to generate with anyone. Love is all about being connected emotionally, mentally and physically. If a single element is missing, that relationship is built on a castle of sand; and can break any time. How I spent time it's sometimes truly hard for me to find words to explain to you. Every second without you is like a thousand years for me. Now you are highly literate and can do the math."

"I know, my love, I feel your seconds without me and now, as I'm finally with you, I promise the rest of your life that we celebrate and live like it's a thousand years. I love you and really do. Please share what happen next between you and Durga," Miriam asked Raja while kissing his hand.

"Durga and I exchanged words of wisdom with each other; her wound was better and she was able to travel. Durga simply was not interested in going anywhere from my cave. All she wanted was to stay with me for the rest of her life. Durga tried her best to make me understand that it was first time that she had finally found peace deep inside her soul. Durga was not shy at all; she was blunt and fearless in expressing her feelings toward me. Accepting her was not easy for me, as my life journey as a human had just started. There was a list of things for me to do and on top was to find trust worthy humans, who could represent me and look after my daily affairs. Like my right and left-hand people who as per my instructions, setup my trading business.

"Durga taught me how things work in the human world. I clearly informed Durga I would never return to my family. I had unlimited access of gold, diamonds and other precious stones. I asked her how I could buy a palace and which state she suggested was weaker, where I could make my own palace and start my own kingdom. On my asking, Durga laughed and, while laughing, told me that was the easiest thing for her to do for me; she could make me a prince within one day. In her way I didn't even require treasure. 'Keep it with you,' she said, 'because all you have to do is to marry me," Raja explained to Miriam. "And you know what, we both laughed at her suggestion.

"Further, Durga told me, "'I promise to be your humble servant for life in the shape of your wife. I will worship you day and night. I beg you, please don't keep me apart from you. I know I would never ever be happy again. I know true love happens only once in our lives, and you are the love of my life. My heart is set on you, and would remain yours 'til the time you finally don't accept me as your servant and wife.'"

"I was able to see her commitment and deep honesty in her eyes. However, I was not in a position to marry her and expose myself. Without revealing my truth, I never wanted to cheat her or take advantage of her. How would she have reacted knowing that I was a newborn human and beneath me lived a king cobra? Maybe she should have started worshipping me as a god. Imagine what would have happened to our love story? I know all those wizards, rich moguls and evil worshippers who want to take away my place; they have no idea what they are getting themselves into. With every pleasure follows the pain, 'til the time you were not in my life; I was living a cursed life. Sad and lonely, what can one do if he or she is alive for rest of their lives? 'til Jesus Christ comes back and the judgment day get started. I lived in palaces, surrounded by luxurious goods, did all those things made me happy? Obviously not, I can appreciate great painters' work and his skills of art; for how long can I keep looking at them? Such collections are just good to impress other rich folks or with the passage of time, those art collections are your assets. Collection of cars, even the finest car I have driven I always felt alone. You sitting next to me, holding my hand now that is what makes a car seem like a magical object from a different part of the universe. Now that is what we call the effect of being in love. You came and with your presence all these material things seem alive now. I truly love you my darling," Raja told Miriam while looking deep in her beautiful eyes.

"I love you too, my life," Miriam replied with a smile.

"Coming back to chapter of Durga, I managed to convince her to go back to her palace. She agreed on one condition, that she would visit me every day to which I agreed. I walked her near her palace and then she insisted and even begged me to come to meet her father. Durga was sure her father would be happy to meet me because I had saved her life from the tiger. Cared and cured Durga and later safely escorted back to her palace. I humbly reminded her about my privacy and finding my inner peace. I still was not ready to mix with anyone apart from her. I don't know why she cried while being leaving me; she was teaching me an important lesson about human emotions.

"I stood right where I could see her go, she kept turning around and looking at me. Finally her guards saw her coming, they came running toward her and that was the moment I vanished into the forest. That whole night alone, I missed her and concurrently thought about all the possibilities and planned my life ahead. I knew Durga was the only soul who would move things for me, without any expectations or greed. I was humbly thankful to my Lord for bringing Durga into my life and planned my existence as a human. If Durga were not in my life, things would have been quite impossible for me to get started. Finding trust worthy people in this world is the hardest job. All the staff you see work for us at home. Their generations have been tested and judged in the most critical way possible. Durga was a princess and in her blood honesty and loyalty existed. She supported me enormously. During that night without Durga, I knew what favors I needed to ask her to build my own, untouchable empire. Next early morning,

Durga entered the cave. She looked elegantly beautiful, and was dressed in an expensive traditional red dress. Durga was fresh and excited; I guess she was desperate to share with me what had happened back in the palace. Then she started telling me how the palace reacted when she returned," Raja, while slightly smiling, told Miriam.

"'As you saw,' Durga said, 'the guards started shouting the moment they saw me. In a second, the news spread in the whole palace and went straight to my father. I knew my father loved me, however that moment melted my heart. I never saw my father crying, even at the death of my brothers; my father didn't shed a single tear. He came running toward me and he was literally crying like a baby. He held me in his strong arms and I felt his immense love. He was checking me from top to bottom, scrutinizing whether I was harmed. I hugged my father tightly and bravely told him I was fine and totally safe.

"'Then he started asking me millions of questions, like what happened, where I had been all these days, had someone kidnapped me or held me hostage? I knew Guru Das had managed to convince my father I was fine and had no need to hurt the staff or send a search party for me. I told him how I had fallen off the elephant and managed to find a shelter in a cave. I never lied to my father. I simply explained him the fall I had got me injured so I took a refuge inside the cave for all this period 'til the time my wounds were healed and I was able to walk back home. I was dying to share every single detail about our meeting. I wanted my parents to know about you. How brave and how wise you are and how you left your kingdom to find your inner peace to be a better man. I know they would have loved to meet you and paid a special gratitude for saving my life. I know you're the only man on earth; they would let me marry you, without getting in your complete background about your family. I know and am a true witness of your charisma; something is unique and extremely appealing about you. A personality that attracts others to blindly fall in love with you and I know for sure your magic would have easily worked on my parents. Then I went to see Guru Das, he start smiling from the distance when he saw me. I touched his feet and sat next to him. I don't know why I felt shy around Guru Das; for the very first time in my life," Durga explained.

"Guru Das smiled and told Durga, "'I know where you were, my child. It was not easy to stop the storm in the palace. Your father was seriously mad at your guards and he wanted to severely punish those poor people. How I made him understand you have no idea that you are fine and would be back. I can see you are happy. All I can say is that man is not an ordinary man; respect him with all your heart. You're lucky to be in his presence. Learn as much knowledge as you can from him. I know one thing, he would never harm you, however he will always be your protector throughout your entire life, my child. If he doesn't want to meet anyone, don't force him. Some people presences are worth only for us rather than putting them on display for the world. He truly is a gem and you value the moments you spend with him. I always knew you are truly blessed, my child and a chosen one to witness the truth about reality.

"'Thank you, Guru," said Durga. "'I have a request, and hope you are not going to say no to me. I want Rqui as tomorrow I have to go back to him and I want to give him a gift. I want that when I'm not with him he can keep watching me as his eyes only seek me in this entire world. I don't need Rqui for myself, as he live in my heart and I can feel him connected to my soul. He is not interested in gold, diamonds or any material gift. I think only Rqui would be a gift that can make him happy, so kindly don't say no.'

"'How can I keep an eye on you that would be my only concern? Rqui is yours my child and do what pleases you," Guru Das told Durga while getting up and walking toward his things.

"'Here you go!' Durga said while handing me Rqui. 'Please don't say a word, like you don't need it or what are you going to do with it. As I clearly informed you, what I told Guru as well, you would be able to watch me when we are apart from each other. I want to know your eyes are always on me and you are there to protect me if anyone attacks me. I think in such way there might be a chance that someday a spark of love for me will wake in you.

"'So, you want me to be your guard, I asked Durga?" Raja said.

"She responded, 'What if tiger attacked me again? Secondly, value the heart of a giver, never the value of the gift. I want you to have it; I will feel safe if it's with you.'

"'Thank you, I promise would keep your gift always closer to my heart,'" I told her, while accepting her gift. That day, Durga was in a very good mood and I thought it was the right time to speak about my needs and requirements with her."

CHAPTER 24
"ART OF REVENGE"

I humbly requested that Durga suggest a location where I could buy or build a palace so I could start my own empire. I sought an isolated state where I could maintain low profile, and gradually, with the passage of time, start progressing. I requested her to guide me on a path to successfully complete transactions, a complete cost of how much gold and what types of precious stones were needed to convert them into buying coins. I also requested that Durga to guide me with regard to the noble businesses in which, I should involve myself in order to increase my wealth.

Durga was more than happy to help me providing her complete support. I was truly impressed to find out that not only was Durga a princess, she was a sharp business minded woman. She knew everything about trading, investment and the property business. We both spent a whole day together discussing various business opportunities. After a long discussion and planning, we came to a conclusion that Durga would find me four men squad to work for me. I told her I wanted one man to take care of all the business deals and transactions for me. One I wanted to be head of my security and later hire team of staff as per his experience. The third man had to be a good cook, to make food and entertain guests in the house. The fourth and final person would be the one required to be caretaker of the house, like a professional butler.

My only requirement was they should all be people who followed orders and were loyal staff. I told Durga, I didn't mind paying them three times more than what they had been earning in their previous jobs. Durga suggested that she would find all the details of the royals in south and would find land free from any kingdom. She also promised me to provide me with complete information on the linking states and relevant details about the neighboring rulers. Durga was so involved in helping me; for her my requests seemed like a mission. She did take some time to work out everything in a proper sequence. Durga selected a number of skilled men and asked me, how I would like to meet and finalize their selection. I requested that she first help me to exchange my treasure. I wanted everything sorted out for me before I started hiring people. I was aware it wouldn't only be hiring staff; it would entail being responsible for their whole families as well. Durga educated me about how a staff residence area should be; according to their job descriptions we had to provide them housing. Palaces basically had to have a separate section only for servant quarters. Durga, after a complete investigation managed to find me a remote palace in north. Durga told me the legends and reality of the state, as the palace was incredibly haunted. Durga started telling me about some history of the state and an incident that had occurred in that palace and nearby land. The Maharaja Divesh was the owner of that palace and he was one of the cruelest kings, who had ever walked on the face of the earth. There were many hidden dungeons in his palace.

Since one of his favorite sports was torturing men and women, he paid a huge amount to the torturers, who could come up with new way to torture the human body. He used to attain orgasm at human tumultuous screams; no one could ever understand what kind of peace he found in hurting other people. Like most of the kings, his other interest was women.

One day he saw a young beautiful girl walking in his palace. She was daughter of one of his gardeners. King Divesh, couldn't stop looking at her, she was devilishly beautiful. Something was different in her walk and even in her poverty, she shone like a diamond. He held her hand and took her inside and told everyone he wanted to marry her. No one was able to say a single word; even the father of the girl bowed his head at the king's decision.

The girl's name was Diyva and the moment king married her he made Diyva his queen. Diyva fell madly in love with the king, as she had always wanted to be a princess. Diyva was extremely fond of expensive jewelry and the entire palace was surprise king Divesh had fallen deeply in love with Diyva. He started spending most of his time with Diyva and the whole nation was happy, as the sport of torturing had ended completely.

The neighboring king passed away and his young son became the king. The name of the young king was Arum, he was hot tempered prince and wanted to conquer entire world. However, his father had never permitted him to go on wars and takeover other kingdoms. Now that he was king, the first thing he did was challenged King Divesh in war. The king accepted his challenge and he prepared his army and went to war. Queen Diyva cried the day when king Divesh left. He promised her he would return and once he got hold of King Arum's kingdom, he would lay all Arum's treasure at her feet. Queen Diyva smiled at proposal then happily sent him to war.

After three days, one of the war messengers returned to the palace and briskly gathered hundreds of King Divesh's queens, and informed them that king Divesh was killed in battle. The messengers also informed them that King Arum was marching toward the palace. The queens started moaning and started killing themselves. Some hanged themselves, a few slit their throats and others jumped from the top of the palace. Death overtook the palace screams and painful crying could be heard from a distance.

Queen Diyva was the only queen who took the news without fuss. She chose to stay alive, entered her royal chamber, and locked the door from the inside. When she came out, she was dressed in her best costume and prepared herself for King Arum.

She was extremely beautiful, however she was equipped with the most sensual and passionate charms any queen had ever possessed in this entire universe. On King Arum's arrival, she threw rose petals on him and with her charms, full of seduction she managed to capture his heart. The same moment King Arum married her and made her his queen. He quickly figured out that Queen Diyva's weakness was jewelry, so he started showering her with jewels.

Almost six months had passed, and King Arum had gone out hunting, when one of his closest bodyguards returned badly injured. His screams were heard in the whole palace, as he was crying and shouting: He is alive and he killed King Arum. The staff gave the bodyguard water and, in the meantime, Queen Diyva ran up to the guard and asked him who was alive and what happened to King Arum.

"Your highness, King Divesh, he is still alive and brutally killed King Arum. He is carrying King Arum's head and with all of his loyal soldiers, he is marching toward the palace. He strictly ordered to open his torture dungeon that's the first order he gave. I beg you, please kill me, I don't want to die painfully! The extremely frightened bodyguard begged Queen Diyva between with broken breaths.

"Nothing will happen to anyone," Queen Diyva told him with great confidence, "start the preparations to welcome our king."

Queen Diyva briskly went to her royal chamber and got dressed. When she came out, she again was in her best costume and delicate jewelry, on top of which she wore her mesmerizing smile, full of seduction.

King Divesh entered the palace with a blast; he seemed extremely strong, well built and rough. He was holding head of

King Arum; the whole palace felt his machismo. Harsh times had wrought mysterious changes in him; his eyes were full of fire. With his other hand he held arm of Queen Diyva and took her into their private chambers. He threw the head right in her feet; she was able to see fire in his eyes.

Then King Divesh politely asked her, "Why haven't you killed yourself? When all my queens even those with whom I slept only for a night, took their own lives in the most painful manner, how could you be still alive, when I loved you the most?"

With a seraphic smile, queen Diyva confidently explained, "My Lord, I wanted to protect your legacy; I accept I was left with no choice but to marry king Arum. I swear my body was with him, however my soul was always connected with you. Deep down somewhere in my soul, I knew you were alive and that was the main reason I stayed alive. So, when you return I could welcome you with my open arms."

King Divesh was surprised, back in his mind he wondered why she was hyperventilating. In a strange tone he told her, "You like gold, jewelry and precious stones. I have something special in my mind for you. A gift the whole world would remember a king gave to a most loving wife!" While completing his sentence, he departed from the royal chamber.

He instructed his closest adviser, "I want the finest craftsmen in country. Get me the top goldsmith, precious stones fitter and top of the line sculptor. I want them here in the palace within two hours. If a minute late, you better give me your head or otherwise I will take it off myself. You know me; it would be in the most horrifying way."

The adviser vanished as if he had never existed in the palace; within one and half hours, all three artists were standing in the king's court.

"Take all these artists and Queen Diyva down to one of my torture chambers," a furious King Divesh instructed his adviser.

Within a few minutes all the artists and the queen were in his dungeon.

King Divesh went down to the dungeon and studied Queen Diyva who was standing motionless. He was unable to read her, as she was not afraid, crying or happy. Queen Diyva stood still, without remorse.

King Divesh turned toward the artists and started instructed them, "I want all of you to measure every single part of her body. Now this is what I want you to do." While looking at the gold smith, he told him, "I want you to measure her whole body and melt the gold for the sculptor."

Then King Divesh looked at precious stone fitter, "I want you to fit sapphires in her eyes; replace her lips with ruby, I want her nose to be made of tourmaline. Her ears I want you to replace with emeralds."

Finally King Divesh turned toward the sculptor. "I want you to make her face, with diamonds and the whole body with gold.

"Now listen all of you carefully, what I'm going to tell you next is the most important part of this complete transaction; for my beloved ex-queen. As this is the best test of your mastery of your work, I want you to fix the eyes last. I want you to keep Queen Diyva alive, as long as you can. I truly want my favorite queen to see the creation of my final gift to her." King Divesh, instructed everyone.

Queen Diyva remained standing and watched him like a statue. Some people in this world were extremely difficult to understand; Queen Diyva was one of them. Her reaction surprised King Divesh as he was master of understanding people's reactions. She was the first and only person who did not beg for her life. Most begged him for pardon, others for life, and some for a quick death. Her silence haunted him; however he remained standing and staring at her.

All three of artists started taking her body measurements; then they tied both her hands and feet with chains. They fixed her head in a metal block so she doesn't move it, and they started with her lips. After delicately cutting her lips, they cut her nose, ears, and then they started peeling the skin on her face. Her screams were loud and they all knew the intensity of the pain Queen Diyva was going through. They were surprised she did not beg for mercy or life; even though the goldsmith gave her a hint to give it a try. Queen Diyva turned out to be the most stubborn soul, who had ever walked into the King Divesh's torture chambers. She took extreme torture and in the most painful way, her soul left her destroyed body in peace.

King Divesh kept her statue in his court; he never married again. However, he became completely irrepressible and kept torturing innocent people for minor issues. He ruled for another ten year and then one of King Arum's cousins from the east launched an attack on his state and managed to capture him alive. King Divesh was brutally tortured nonstop for thirty days and was then publicly executed. He refused to beg for mercy and accepted the cruel suffering. The witnesses in the arena heard his last word and that was name of Queen Diyva.

With a smile, Durga told Raja, "I guess both were different kind of lovers, who liked to accept and give extreme sufferings. I guess some love stories are hard to understand, as their situations need to be studied and to comprehend human psyche. 'To what limit humans can endure pain, to tell someone they love them without saying a single word'. Well coming back to the palace, whoever tried to live there, they were found dead. Their bodies were later discovered, in one of King Divesh dungeons. Rumors had it all the people who were tortured, their souls were still alive and living in the palace. I did my job and shared the whole legend of the palace, now it's simply up to you. If you ask my advice, of course I would say no. However if you want I can speak to Guru Das and we can find a solution, to clear the palace from the presence of killer souls."

Raja told Durga, "This is exactly what I wanted. No need to involve Guru Das. I have something which you have to give to my right hand man, whomever you select. I will give you the instructions later, once I hand you the object. Trust me, there wouldn't be a single evil spirit in that palace, this I will take care myself. Take complete possession of the property; later I want Gopal to make sure the whole palace is cleaned up neatly. I want him to feel that is he is in charge of the palace and he should sort out all required retentions, according to his mind. I will meet him there, and provide him my complete support. Kindly please start the process, and I wait for the results." Raja told Durga.

Durga insisted on buying the palace for me, as a gift. I refused and threatened to vanish from her life, if she committed such kind of stupidity. I in a humble way explained to her, that I felt truly blessed with her love and kindness for me. I valued her just the way she was, without reminding her she was a princess. I told her I felt comfortable around her and considered her my own in this strange and mysterious world. I made myself clear that she was under the wrong impression of my huge ego. Durga and I were spiritually close to each other; I was her own in this world and so was she for me. Durga's only concern was me to be close to her; she insisted I stayed in her state. The good thing about royals, they don't get emotionally involve when it comes to principles. As I shared my plan with her, that was simple and straight forward. I informed her that she needed to start growing her kingdom in the south and on the other hand would start capturing the north. She atones on my suggestion, and started working through my basic list of requirements. Durga used all her powers to move my treasure and started working on the projects I had requested of her.

Durga told me she had decided that Gopal would be my right-hand man, because he was the only person, she already tested with her quest. He had encountered various creatures and monsters;

a haunted palace would not be an issue for him, as I had assured would take care of insidious presences in the palace. She instructed him to be my shadow and face. Gopal was a brave loyal soldier, happily married and with two-year old daughter.

He was a man who had loved only one woman and hardly had any weaknesses. Even the bravest and strongest men had lost fortunes because their flesh was frail. Covetousness took control of their minds and they became slaves of lust. The greatest weakness of a man was woman; those who could control their lust were truly the ones who ruled the world. As they knew once they had power and money, they could have anything they wanted in this world. They looked at the bigger picture rather than remaining in moments of illusions full of lust. Gopal, I strongly believed and knew he would turn out to be a solid man without any weakness. People such as Gopal were not for sale and would never be intimidated by lust or material things. I valued Durga's judgment and selection, even though I had been precise in providing my personal details.

Durga somehow managed to move things quickly. Gopal had already left for the north with a batch of skilled body guards. Durga was well aware of the journey and various tribes' bandits on the way. Gopal knew about the legends of the haunted palace, even though he had never visited the palace personally. Like all other children, he had also grown up listening to the tales of King Divesh and his cruelest way of taking revenge from his favorite Queen Diyva. Despite being vacant from such a long time, the palace was still in good condition; however without human's existence it seemed ruined. Gopal considered it as a new adventure, since after the quest, ordinary jobs no longer excited him. He was excited to discover the palace's secrets and was interested to visit the infamous torture dungeons of King Divesh.

CHAPTER 25

"SATI"

Miriam broke her silence and told Raja, "King Divesh was the cruelest man I have ever heard about. The people who killed my family and Madhu, I always thought they were the most brutal people I had ever witnessed in my life. However, after hearing the way King Divesh took revenge from his queen, made me understood the depth of cruelty that humans hold inside them and it's truly unbelievable. King Divesh palace would have been full of evil presence, were you not scared and why would you want to buy a haunted location?"

Raja replied, "Nothing in this world can scare me, secondly now you would be surprise to know that nothing would scare you too. The power of life is stronger than the darkness of the death. Evil or bad spirits only attack and feed on weak and scared souls, not only we are alive but immortals. Life has all the powers that you require to scare evil souls, always remember that my love.

"God blessed humans with the most precious gift of life, he kept the limit short for life, however it's still long enough to make a choice of living wisely. Intrinsically gift of life by God is just a simple trailer of what they would get after dying. The reality of life starts right after the moment when people die. As you can imagine people like King Divesh, think they are immortals and would live forever. However the problem occurs when human like him die, they are stuck between hell and earth. His soul was left to feel the emptiness of his crime, while he being himself still thought he do have power to scare people. Which he managed to do to weak hearted humans, however he himself was scared every second of being stuck in between both worlds.

"Human cruelty would surprise you at every stage of your immortal life, I know you have the most caring and loving heart, however I suggest it's time to make it as strong as you can.

Miriam replied, "I wish I can make my heart strong, however please don't forget I am still a human. We came in two packages, cruel and caring. I guess my type is the one with kindness. Tell me what happen next after you bought the palace?"

Raja replied. "I was sharing the feelings of Gopal, as he was excited to investigate King Divesh palace. During the quest he had been following Veer's instructions and this time it was a chance for him to lead. He had no desire to pass up such a privilege to shine by serving his princess. Gopal had great respect for Princess Durga and believed in her leadership; he devoted his life to her. Gopal knew the king she had selected for him to serve, truly must be a brilliant man. The reason after the quest, Gopal had proved his loyalty to her and had been considered one of her most trust worthy staff.

Time passed quickly after that; within two months Gopal managed the palace. The day before leaving, I spent a whole day with Durga. I thanked her in every possible way, she was sad and crying hysterically. I promised her I would be watching her in Rqui every morning and evening, that day I truly understood the beauty of being human. The emotions they have, their brain work on different scale and being sad is a strange mystery. Despite moving on my own and planning to run my own kingdom, I was honestly sad to be away from Durga. With her love, care, friendship and her huge crush on me, in a way it made me closer to her. I knew it would take me ages to be close to someone, the way I was with Durga. She was the owner of a great heart, pure, simple and innocent. Still I'm not able to understand what made her so sure that one day or another I would accept her as my lover and wife. Durga's soul was filled with strong confidence about me, as I was her man.

Confidence basically is a tricky human armor, it can help you conquer the world or lose everything.

I never interfered with her belief and confidence in us; Durga had a full right to be blissful in whatever pleased her. I guess in her own world I was the reason of her contentment.

I was aware the world's most expensive sculpture Queen Diyva's was buried in one of King Divesh's dungeons. That palace was like a cave full of hidden treasures, however it was still untouched; it had not been possible to find with human eyes. In the mean time I dug out all the hidden treasures in Durga's state and gave them to her as a humble token of our friendship. Durga was the right candidate worthy of such treasure; she would use it to build a powerful prosperous nation. Durga did not accept my bequest; she kept arguing with me that I needed it more than her; since I was establishing myself. I told Durga there is no need to be preposterous; I finally succeeded her keep to the treasure. She told me would accept only on one promise that if I ever needed anything, that I would only asked her. With a smile I promised her and she hugged me and softly whispered, "You truly are a Raja. Only a man with heart would offer such a gesture; this is the biggest gift I ever received in my life."

"You did a good thing," Miriam told Raja. She was addicted to Raja's storytelling in his mellifluous baritone; Miriam was keen to know every detail of Raja's life. His story telling was helping her to know him and understanding the essence of his persona. The people who were part of his life, he started with telling a story of Durga and she seemed really amazing. All the characters in Durga's story, intrinsically each chapter contain a hidden message and taught her powerful wisdom.

"Durga seems like a great princess and I hope she had turned her nation into a united and a peaceful community. I really wish she lived a great and wonderful life. I really am interested to know further details about King Divesh's palace. Was it really haunted? Did you guys see something? What happened next when you moved there?" Miriam anxiously asked Raja.

Raja in explaining manner replied, "One day while I was on the verge of moving to my palace, Durga came and she was sad. On my asking why she told me, 'her father, the king was not well.' It was new expression of human emotion, her love for her father. He was in tremendous pain and she was feeling every bit of it. Humans are blessed with understanding relationships and emotion on a different level. Durga told me her father's only concern was her safety and prosperity; that day I started to had huge respect for humans. That day I came to know depth of the relationship between a child and a parent is above all the relationships in the world. Durga truly was my coach and from her I learn human sociology and I have no words to pay my gratitude to her.

Tears started falling from Miriam's eyes, when she told me, "I agree with you. Imagine a mother who raised a child inside her for nine months. For nine month, she doesn't even sleep well. In her mind, she is always concerned about the safety of her child; even in a deep sleep she is unconsciously afraid of not to roll over on her child. Because you have seen how poor mothers are, as they don't have fancy cribs for their children, so the babies share beds with their mothers. When alone, she talks to her unborn child in extreme excitement, as he or she understands every word she says to them. While giving a birth, only a mother can suffer indescribable pain. Only another woman or mother, who had been through such a process, can understand. The biggest weight on a human heart and soul is when they carry the dead body of their child. I know and I have been in that place where those fanatic animals brutally murdered my children right in front of my eyes. Within a few minutes, their souls left their bodies and went to Heaven and left me alone to cry for them every other day."

Raja kissed and hugged her and with a smile told her, "You promised me my love that you will never ever cry again. I can understand the depth of your pain. Please remember they are with the Lord and are in the best place. If you cry then I will not share with you what happen next in the palace and the rest of Durga's story. Always remember I'm your family now and you are my responsibility. It hurts me when you cry my dear, I truly feel sad.

Miriam stopped crying and with a beautiful smile replied, "Sorry and forgive me my darling. I was lost in memories. What happened next? I really want to know and prefer to keep my mind busy. I love to be lost in your world; even though there are other women, I still find my peace in them. I love you honey; I live and die in your arms. You filled my lonely life, my darling and you introduced me to real happiness."

"That's my girl, Raja told her with a smile. To return back to the tale, Durga started spending most of her time looking after her father. Once a day she visited me, and I offered her my full support to be with her, and planned to delay my traveling to my palace. Meeting her made me understand not everyone could be a prince or princess. Even though I knew she needed me the most; she still insisted I should make the move and take complete charge of my palace. Durga told me Guru Das was with her and he was doing his best to cure her father. She was more concerned about me and instructed me to be careful of the palace's evil entities. I made her laugh the whole evening, as it was my last night in the cave. I reminded her about how she had fallen from an elephant; I told her still the tiger must be cursing me for taking away his lunch. We discussed Jay and his greed about becoming a king and making her his Queen. Within a few minutes, she was in great mood. While looking toward me in a poignant way, she told me it was going to be hard, not to see me every day. She really did love me and that I should care about myself and stay safe. She would come and visit me soon, she told me with an ocean of love in her eyes. "Please do that, let me serve you as a true princess, because here in this cave I was not able to treat you the way you deserve; your highness," she said. With lots of love, prayers and tears in her eyes, I left the cave early the next morning.

As I reached the palace, from the distance I knew I had truly found exactly what I had wanted for an abode. Gopal was a doer, and he made the palace alive. A guard stopped me at the gate. Gopal, as per my instructions, had hired good amount of workers. The whole lot seemed to be active, aggressive and highly trained.

At a simple glimpse I figured out all of the staff was honest and loyal. Some went running inside the palace and informed Gopal, and he came briskly and bowed his head.

"Thank you, Gopal, you did a great job with the palace. Tell me is it still haunted or everything is under control?" Raja asked him.

"Your highness, first of all welcome to your palace, hope you find everything according to your standard. The first day I entered this palace, even in the air I could smell death. The palace was alive with unseen souls. Even the walls were talking and instructing me to leave and run away from this place. I had never seen such a haunted palace before; anyway, it was not easy. Somehow I managed to keep the symbol given by 'her highness Durga' in the center of palace. All of the sudden, the whole palace became quiet, as if not a single evil spirit ever existed here," Gopal informed me while keeping his eyes on the dark green marble floor.

"Have you brought your family?" I asked him.

"Not yet your highness, I was waiting for you and wanted to finish my job first. I would like to give you a complete tour of the palace. For staff we have huge servant quarters and can easily accommodate more than thousand servants," Gopal informed me.

"Great, let us take a tour. How about we start from the torture dungeons? How many are there in total?" I asked him in a way to make him relax.

"Five in total your highness, I have to apologize, as they have not been touched yet. I left them as they were, I wanted you to come and let me know what we should do with them. Clean them up or shut them down?" Gopal replied.

"Let us take a take look and then I will decide. Shall we start the tour?" I asked.

"Sure your highness, please this way." Gopal replied and start walking slightly behind me, while guiding me downstairs.

While I observed the palace I consider human sociology. When they were alive, all they wanted was to impress others with material things, like all the wealth King Divesh kept on display ostentatiously but possibly never actually even looked at.

More than two centuries ago, King Divesh's great-grandfather had established the palace. Later, his father had increased the structure, however King Divesh had renovated on a different level. King Divesh's existence was felt at every corner of the palace. Apart from his evil side, he truly had been a man of taste, elegance and class.

The palace screamed King Divesh's ownership on his two centuries old abode. The opulence could easily be felt, even after all this time; the craftsmanship was visible on interior, walls and ceiling. Myriad people tried and somehow succeeded to step inside the palace, but they never came out. The word was out that King Divesh still tortured and killed those who tried to enter his palace. All the palace's valuable items were still in their location.

The dungeons were four floors below the entrance of the palace. Gopal gave details of various torturing equipment. I finalized the biggest dungeon and planned to turn it into my kingdom of snakes.

"I want you to close all the entrances; however I want you to build a connecting door from my bed-room. The door should be built in such a way; that for outsiders the door to be invisible. I never want anyone to go down and let us close the palace's dark chapter. Make sure the architect you hire for this job never shares or discusses what he had done in my palace. I don't mind you paying him extra. If he opens his mouth, your relationship with me and your princess Durga will be over," I warned Gopal.

"I can understand your highness. I was informed by Princess Durga that you are a private person. I assure you 'til I'm alive, I promise you will never fail you," Gopal replied.

"Thank you, I really do have high expectations of you. From now on, you will be representing me. I will only meet selected people, rest of all the dealings and state issues, you will take care. What tactics you would use to maintain my low profile? How would you handle inquiries, concerns and questions about me? That I simply leave upon you, however, remember one thing for me it would be a test of your sharpness and leadership skills. I want to remain private and with the passage of time, you will understand I am different from all the kings you have served before. One more thing, bring your family and the next big mansion of adviser is yours from now on," I instructed Gopal.

He responded, "As I mentioned to you earlier, I came equipped how to keep you safe and protected; my humble request is to trust me. If I ever let you down, you have the right to take my head in exchange. I give you my word; I have devoted my life to serve you, my king."

"Great so we are settled," I replied.

Gopal truly was a man of his word. He took complete charge of the state. Within few days, the torture dungeons were closed and the architect linked the dungeon entrance to my bedroom. The door was designed in such a way that not a single soul was able to find it with their human eyes. One night, I entered the biggest torture chamber and invited all the snakes. Shortly, the cave started to fill with various types of snakes. Even though I was transformed into a human, all the snakes were my responsibility, as I was their king. Secondly, they were my eyes and ears on the planet. The possibility of human betrayal was always present, however I knew snakes would give their lives for me. The dungeons were treasure hub, and shortly I managed to dig up Queen Diyva's jeweled sculpture.

Time passed and Durga's father became more ill, as both his kidneys had failed. The Dhola dynasty started rolling over the states; they managed to take over the Mandya's kingdom. Durga turned into a true matriarch and was devoted to protecting her kingdom from the Dhola dynasty. Rundara Dhola came to know about Durga's father health and since he was a valiant conqueror, he sent a request to visit Durga's father to ask after his health. He had heard the rumors about Durga's beauty and knew she was a goddess in human shape. Finding all the circumstances in his favor, he managed to get a chance to visit the dying king. Durga was not happy with her father's decision to allow King Rundara Dhola's visit at their palace. She wanted to go to war with him. Her father was sick and knew King Rundara Dhola had already become a powerful king. His army was twenty times bigger than Durga's, and sending his only daughter to war with them was madness.

Finally the day came, King Rundara Dhola arrived and at her dying father's request, she welcomed him according to royal traditions and gave him a complete protocol.

King Rundara Dhola sat next to the dying king and whispered, "You know why I'm here? My visit is simple, either you let me take control of your kingdom or I challenge you at war. Or I have one more option, you give permission to your daughter be my bride, your kingdom will fall under Dhola dynasty, however you and Durga will still own the state. I'm sitting here and need your answer right now.

"I accept your proposal and we can arrange the marriage," Durga's father replied in a weak, shivery voice, "just a humble request, kindly please let me have a word alone with my daughter!"

"Thank you for being kind and accepting me as your son. I provide you complete privacy to have a word with your daughter princess Durga." King Rundara was escorted into the next chamber to wait for the king to see him again.

Durga had heard every word discussed and agreed upon between her father and King Rundara. She had already made up her mind what her answer to the dying her father would be.

Durga's father said, "My daughter and my princess, I know in my whole life, you never let me down ever. I know I will die as a proud father, whom the Lord blessed with the greatest daughter ever born. My child, as my heart beats for you as your father, concurrently my soul lived for daughters of our state and nation. If I refuse his offer, the Dhola's would launch an attack on our nation. They would kill all the men and make all the women their slaves and concubines. I could sacrifice my only daughter and my own blood to save thousands of my other daughters. I want you to think like a princess and not like an emotional daughter. If you think my verdict is not acceptable, I take my word back and let us have a war with them. King Rundra seemed like a good man and I can see in his eyes he honestly likes you and wants to marry you. Always remember what I have taught you. The reason the gods made us king is because he believes in us that we will never be selfish while making our decisions. I await your verdict, my child."

Durga responded, "Father, if you have given your word, for your word I can easily give my life. I say yes and you're my father and your pride is above all things. I love you and I am proud to have a wise father like you." While saying those words, Durga hugged her father and shared millions of unheard screams and invisible tears.

"The marriage took place the same day and two days later, Durga's father passed away. King Rundra loved Durga immensely; she accepted her fate and served him as her king and husband. She tried her best to please him and gave him the same amount of love he showered on her. However Durga's soul was still connected to mine and I was the only man she had truly loved.

One day, when King Rundra went to another city, I entered Durga's room. She act normally and she didn't ask me how I had managed to visit her without being getting caught by one of King Rundra's guards.

"I know now you're married, and I have no right to enter your room like this, however I wanted to pay my condolences on your loss. I truly am sorry about your father's death," I told her. "I know your pain is indescribable. If there is anything I can do, please feel free. I know it's a painful moment, however congratulation on your wedding, I truly wish you a blessed life!"

"Thank you for coming and for condolences and congratulating me on my wedding. I only would beg you to forget about me. I won't be able to meet or see you again. You're the man I always loved and even dreamed as a little girl to marry one day. However, life is not how we want it to be. It works as its own master. I wish you a wonderful, successful life. Goodbye." After saying those words, Durga turned her face away.

Whatever happens in life, good or bad, time kept moving on and Durga produced a healthy heir whom she named, Maharaja. The truth was that she pretended to be good a wife and a very supportive Queen. Deep down her soul was empty, she was not able to forget me. Durga's suffering devoured King Rundra. He pretended to show the world he was happy, but deep down he was gradually dying each and every day.

How poor could a man be, someone should have asked King Rundra; though he ruled the biggest state he was not able to win the heart of his wife. He became a true example of a man without love. The moment a person comes to know that the one they love the most, doesn't love them back; that person's heart breaks into uncountable pieces.

One day he took his own life by drinking poison. Overnight Durga had become from his wife to his widow. As per Hindu culture, King Rundra's family announced that Durga would become Sati. This meant that the widowed woman immolated herself on her husband's funeral pyre. It also meant that when a wife's husband died, she had no right to live in this world. They both should die together and remain with each other forever.

Durga handed over her only son, Maharaja, to Guru Das and requested that he would make him the world's greatest king. At least his father's soul could be happy for once, as she had never given him single shred of happiness. Guru Das convinced her he would help her escape and they would go somewhere far and live peacefully. "There is no need to sacrifice your life for some religious ritual," Guru Das said, and he even gave her examples of Jay who had followed a bad religious ritual and now Durga was doing the same. "What is the difference between both of you, tell me?"

With a lost smile, Durga replied, "Both were hopeless romantics and fell for wrong people. Jay believed he loved me and would easily win me and make me his wife. I believed the same for someone and was not able to give my hundred percent to my husband. He was kind and great man; he truly sensed my heart and never complained about anything. His death was result of my insincerity to him so at least let me die in peace with my husband and look after him eternally."

The next morning Durga would be burned alive as a Sati with her husband's pyre. That night I entered her room; it seemed as if centuries had passed since I had been alone with her. Her condition was indecipherable; her blithe soul had vanished from her lustrous eyes. Durga wore white sari; I had never seen her without colors before. According to Hindu tradition, once a woman was widowed. All she could wear was white nothing colorful, no bangles or jewelry. Even in such simplicity, Durga's gorgeousness and elegance were visible.

"Burning yourself alive with your dead husband, are you bereft of your senses?" I asked Durga while gazing at her. "What are you doing? Are you crazy? You are a mother; how will your child survive without you? Apart from you I have no one in my life. What will I do without you? I know you loved me madly, and because of your madness, you have been unable to focus on your husband. What is my fault in it? Tell me and you know what you are to me. I also loved you, I told you millions of times, in a different way and however you never listened to me. I knew King Rundra would truly do his best to win your heart. You turned out so stubborn. Now let me take you from here. Even if I have to fight your whole army, I'm ready. Get one thing straight in your head, I will not let you burn tomorrow."

"It's no one's fault, Raja. Truly, love is really a brutal killer. Please understand me, I have given my word of acceptance, and I will never back out from that. It's not only my word; this time my father's respect is at stake. I can burn myself a million times for the sake of my family's tradition. When every single widow can burn to death with her husband, why can't I?

"See, life always plays opposite of what we dream and think, as we planned to rule the world. You and I as a strong king and Queen, look at us now we both are sitting here empty and lost. I will find my peace. If you ever get a chance, please help Guru Das make my son the strongest king in the world. Now you go, and I pray you find true love. I wish you love and happiness. Goodbye!" Durga turned her face from me.

I vanished from her sight, and that was the last time we spoke to each other.

There was no way I was willing to give up on her stupidity. I knew exactly to whom I needed to speak to convince Durga. Guru

Das was staying at King Rundra's palace to attend the ritual, and I was aware in which chamber to find him.

"Hello, Guru Das, I hope there is no need for me to introduce myself. In this whole state you're the only person, who knows the truth about me," I told Guru Das.

"I know who you are and I wish we could have met in a different time, so I would have considered myself the luckiest man on earth," Guru Das told me. However, you are aware of the circumstances. My child has made up her mind to die tomorrow. I know you love her and you want me to convince Durga, to change her mind. Trust me, I begged her to change her mind. I know we both would not be able to live without her. She made me the guardian of her son. Life for her son Maharaja is going to be so difficult without her. I have to stay alive with such guilt for the rest of my life. I have used all my knowledge to convince her. I have known her since she was born; that child is a determined soul. It's good we finally met; in fact, I wanted to meet you as I have a simple request. If anything happens to me, please look after Maharaja. I know with your presence in his life, I would be able to make him a king. The whole world will remember until end of the time. In this way, we both can show our love and gratitude for being in presence of our beloved Durga." While saying those words, Guru Das controlled his emotions, though tears were rolling down his cheeks.

"I am not only disappointed in myself, the way she spoke about you and loved you; I came with hope you would be able to help me." I said to him. "I can understand you are in more agony than I am. Now tell me what should I do? It's killing me to even think she selected the most painful death for herself. How could you just stand and watch her burn to death tomorrow?"

"I am an ordinary human," Guru Das explained. "Since she was little, I never said no to her, and this was the last time she asked me something. I looked in her eyes and I know you did the same;

her soul has vanished. I think she would find her peace in going with her husband. Like every other human, in some way, one day we all die. When we are young, we never even give it a thought, that one day we have to face death. With the passage of time, we understand everyone's biggest fear is death. No one knows when and how they will die; she controlled her fear of death. She selected her own pain; mentally she prepared herself to face the agony.

"Death has its own claws and when it pulls our soul out, it does hurt in most painful way. Imagine you are a king of the world, only I know what kind of chaos you can create. Tomorrow morning only I can understand. Let us value her memories, because when a person dies, it's only his body which vanishes from our eyes. However they always stay alive in our hearts and minds. She is my beloved child, and I would never let her memory vanish from my mind."

"You were her guru," I told him, "She was my guru and I have to respect your wisdom. Please understand, she helped me to be a human. Like you, she will always stay deep in my heart, 'til I die. I will be in close contact with you; my support and love is there for her son. I am with you in making him a great king. Trust me, nothing will happen to you." After paying my respects, I removed myself from his presence.

The next morning I was there among the guests who acted as if they were there to pay their condolences. I knew all they were interested in was to watch Queen Durga burned alive. Such an inhumane act was about to take place and there was not a single man or woman who could stop this complete madness. They wanted to view the game of death; all of them wanted to enjoy her pain and screams. It was so easy for me to give just one sign and, within few seconds, the whole palace would have been filled with snakes of all shapes and forms. My soul was feeling a strange kind of pandemonium; it was the first time I had felt completely helpless.

Even the day was dark and ugly. Durga had always studied the morning to understand how her day was supposed to be. I was missing her madly, and deep down I was extremely angry with her. I saw the preparations get started.

As per schedule; King Rundra's family started the ceremony of his funeral pyre. They placed wooden logs and rested the king dead body. Then Durga walked in the midst of a group of middle aged women, wearing a white sari. There was no fear in her pompous walk; she was perfectly in her senses and her presence represented royalty. She quietly approached the pyre and, when she reached it, she calmly lay next to her husband. The priest and family members started piling wood on both of them. The priest started his prayers and mantras, performing the religious rituals, then lit the pyre. When I heard her first scream, I left the site as quickly as I could. That was the last time I heard her voice. The whole state heard her screams while she suffered terrible pain, however not once she begged for her life.

I kept an eye on Durga's son Maharaja, and he truly became the most famous king of his time. He spread his kingdom from Central Asia to Far East Asia. He shocked the world with the temples he build; even today's architects are researching. For instance, how come forty tons of granite were brought to the top of the temple? Even today's experts are trying to figure it out, what types of tools were used to carve, write on and craft those temples. Even today, if you go to the south of India, you will find Maharaja's temples. In one of these you will find a pair of male and female, half-human half-snake sculptures. There is a hidden chamber in one of his temples, where you will find picture of Maharaja and Guru Das.

Guru Das lived another century and we both shared a great relationship; he truly was a wise and kind man. He taught me well about human minds and he died healthy and peacefully while sleeping. How those temples were built, only Guru Das and I know, let us not go there. Let all the credit goes to our wonderful king Maharaja." Raja hugged Miriam while sharing Durga fate with her, as he tried to find peace for his soul in her arms.

CHAPTER 26
"MYSTERIOUS DESTINATIONS"

Miriam, while wiping her tears, complained to Raja. "My Holy Lord what a tragic end for a beautiful soul like Durga! That such a painful and agonizing death would be the fate of exuberant Durga; I never expected such a poignant end to her story. If you would have given me a single hint, I simply could have requested you to stop telling me any further. I am angry with you. Durga was not a girl whom you should have betrayed. She gave her soul, her heart to you. Why didn't you marry her? Imagine if you were her husband, nothing would have happened to her.

"Durga could have lived a peaceful life the way she wanted. I can feel her melancholy and later the unbearable painful death she selected for herself. Durga was exceptional. I love her for her kindness and the way she cared and supported you. Her love for you was real, pure, and simple just as her innocuous soul.

"I know and can understand your concern for me; it's not only you. Anyone who would come to know about Durga's tale would definitely consider me the biggest criminal during our relationship.

"There are some relationships which blossom during their own times, as every love story in the world does have its own ending. Durga's fate was written in such a way; you think I never loved her.

I told you myriad times I loved her in my own way. If it was within my power, do you think I would have let her suffer? The Lord has his own plans. For the time being, we don't understand however with passage of time everything makes sense.

"The Lord wanted the world to remember her, through the success of Durga's son. If it was within my powers, do you think I would have let you marry Alam? When the whole town was killing your family, why did I never show up or try to save them? Your fate was written in such a manner that you have to go through tremendous torture and pain.

"Even if I used all my powers and strength, Durga's tale was written in such a way that no one in this world was able to change a word of her story. I know her soul is happy; she felt proud of what her son has achieved in this world. As I mentioned to you earlier, his thousand year-old portrait was found with Guru Das in one of his temples and when he was alive, he instructed his literate staff to write down every detail about his dynasty on the wall of his famous temples. Trust me, if she somehow knew her fate too, her soul was dead long ago. I tried millions of times to resuscitate her soul, however she became stubborn and gave priority to her cultural pride.

"How difficult it was for me to let her go; she was my friend and only human family. The day before her live burning, Gopal asked my permission to invade Dhola's kingdom. Durga's army was prepared, and until the last moment Veer had been begging Durga to let him attack and rescue her. She sacrificed to keep the pride of her father and the whole nation. Her honor was more important to her than anything in this world. I know her memories would haunt you all your life, which is the effect of my dear Durga. I never wanted to go there, however I guess it's right in some way. You deserve to know about the people who were special in my life. How about we change the subject and let me tell you something entirely different?"

Miriam requested, "Yes, please. Something unique and different which would make me forget about her sad tale. Otherwise, I won't be able to sleep the whole night; her thoughts would keep me thinking about her."

Raja told her, "Let me share with you some of the most mysterious locations in this world, which are infamous and related to reptilians and serpents' presence. When we start traveling around the world, I would love to take you there. The world is full of mysteries and I know you would love to know every single detail about them. How normal humans are still trying to figure out details, through scientific and physical investigations; however they are not able to find answers!"

Miriam replied, "I never dreamed that my life could change in such a dramatic way. Since the day you came in my life I truly have witnessed unbelievable events, heard the most amazing and unusual stories. My life had been simple and I was always thankful for the blessing, my Lord provided me. I never complain about poverty and my treasure was my children and family. Life with you is on a fast track, which is filled with bounteous adventures, mysteries and a world of hidden wisdom. Every night before going to sleep and on waking in the morning, I praise the Lord for choosing me as the love of your life. I want to be with you everywhere, around the globe. Show me what you think can help mankind in some way. I want to be a link between your world and my world, and want to share wisdom and knowledge, without disclosing too much of our information. Please keep educating me with all your knowledge and I am excited to know about the mysterious locations of the world."

Raja replied, "Sure my love, and let's start with continent of Australia!"

Australia, "Kalkajaja" The Black Mountain.

"Kalkajaja, or Mountain of Death, is located in the continent of Australia. The mountain is seriously one of the world's most mystifying and ominous geological features. It consists of enormous black granite boulders, piled precariously one on top of the other that stand nearly fourteen hundred feet high," said Raja.

"Mountain of Death is considered a cursed and evil place, with his numerous dark passage ways and cavern.

"Australian researchers predicted the mountain is an entrance to the underground empire inhabited by unearthly race of evil monsters and lizard creatures.

"Australia is a country owned by Caucasians, however still in such a modern country exist a tribe called Aboriginal. They are brown-skinned people and mostly look like a mix of Africans and Central Asians. They have a strong belief that the Rainbow Serpent was the one who created the world. They worship him as a god and originator; they powerfully believe he is the one who has authority over life, as a giver and taker.

"If by any means furious, he can turn into a punisher for those who have stepped out of line or sometimes can even devour humans too. The Rainbow Serpent has the power to bring chaos and destruction; concurrently they consider it an extremely awesome force!

"Kalkajaja is important to them because they believe the Rainbow Serpent lives beneath it.

"Kalkajaja is also known as Black Mountain and it is strictly avoided by the natives. The surrounding is not only avoided by humans; however birds and small animals stay away from it too. The mountain is known for devouring any living creature that tries to make its way in. Myriad humans have been vanished, some were trying to explore the mountain, some were in search of solving the vanishing mystery and some tried to investigate the mountain!

"The reason it's known as the Mountain of Death is because whoever tries to explore those big black stones; vanishes from the face of the earth. There are myriad incidents recorded by the authorities. A cop was chasing a thief and the thief went into the Black Mountain. The cop followed him and they both disappeared.

"Gold prospectors vanished, so did stray cattle catchers. Finally two brave policemen entered the cave. Only one came out and he was scared and unable to tell what he saw inside!

"There are various legends about the strange black mountain; some believe the mountain is the abode of huge snakes and reptilian people. They control the world from that mountain, and they don't like human interference.

"The Aborigines don't call them aliens; they also call them demons or spirits!

"The truth is that the caverns end at a hidden entrance that leads you into the centre of the earth, from where the reptilian people operate their kingdom. They are called Aeksious, a dangerous species and not from this world, and the difference between them and us is they don't believe in God.

"However, they do respect us and we respect them, as we both are aware our ancestors were the same. In a way we are related to each other, that's the reason they fully support us ruling the world. Aeksious consider humans as the weakest creatures on earth and they will bring nothing but a disaster on this planet. They are on the mission to transfer valuable mineral resources to their planet. Almost all of the powerful governments and kingdoms are aware they exist and they had been experimenting on humans since the world came into existence.

"As I mentioned to you, most of the world is owned and run by various powerful species. That's why no one has ever heard why they are here. If by mistake, some ordinary folks enter Aeksious territory, they are never seen again. Imagine humans can reach the moon, how is it possible no one is able to tell the truth about this Black Mountain?

"I have visited their empire once, and on our travel to that side of the world, I would take you with me. There are certain places that even I can't do justice in describing to you. It would be better if you view them yourself."

Miriam asked, "My love I don't know why, but this place seems really dangerous and I certainly would like to visit with you. The comical thing is since you came into my life, I have no fear of anything at all. Good or evil place, I know if you are with me, I would learn something new from visiting. Tell me about some more mysterious places."

Casal Paula, Malta

Raja replied, "The next one is near the small village of Casal Paula, on the island of Malta, where one of the world most notorious cavern entrances is located. Built on the Corradino plateau, this village overlooks the capital of Malta, Valletta, as well as Grand Harbour.

"The infamous labyrinths became known when they were discovered by excavators. This is the Hypogeum of Sal Saflini. In which archaeologists discovered the bones of thirty-three thousand people who had been brutally sacrificed by an ancient pagan Neolithic cult.

"There are various legends about who the ancient pagan Neolithic cult was actually offering human sacrifices. According to historians they were offering sacrifices to the Devil and others researchers have their own side of fable, that they had been offering sacrifices to creatures beneath earth.

"The fact is the pagan Neolithic cult was worshiping a race of humanoid reptilians. Their faces were covered with long hairs and they were masters of controlling climates. They were obsessed with human sacrifices and for them this was a kind of entertainment. The name of the race is Bekazish.

"Like humans, we reptilians are also divided into two categories, good and evil. One is like me, who believe in God, and the others believe they are loyal servants of the Devil. Bekazish were factual and sincere followers of the Devil. All they wanted was the destruction of humankind. They played the same game that Devil plays every day with all of us, being nice and making people greedy for glittering material things. In such ways a few humans lost their minds and they thought the Devil was on their side, and all those who are within his power follow the Devil's weird instructions. Thousands of years B.C. that is what was these ancient pagan Neolithic cult were doing, offering their own race to please the race of Bekazish. In return, Bekazish promised them a long life, glittering stones and materialistic treasures.

"Until the world ends, the cruelty of devil worshipers will remain; they do not value the life of other humans.

"Myriad incident occurred after the cavern and catacomb were opened to public in Malta. The first was a teacher organizing a school trip and who took children to the Hypogeum. The teacher and the children happily entered the cave and then they vanished. The parents went inside and all they could hear was the cries of their children from beneath the cavern. The cavern is multi-leveled and later a brave diplomat from the British Consulate paid a huge price for a guide to escort her into the cave. The guide agreed and when she entered, she went further and guide was left behind. The diplomat slipped into the lower part of cavern. There she saw humanoid reptilians whose faces were covered with white hairs. When they felt her existence in their surroundings, one of them raised both his arms and created wind. Then he vanished and she felt something slippery touch her body. She then ran back and finally managed to find another guide and made her way out of the cavern.

"After her testimony, the British government sealed the cavern and 'til today it's sealed for the regular public.

"Malta is basically one of the most ancient countries of the world, with a history filled with myths and legends. Essentially, it was the centre of ancient civilization and the worshiping of various gods and demons.

"Even today Bekazish live beneath that cave and from time to time, the powerful leaders of our world offer them human sacrifices!" Raja took a breath.

"What happen to those children and their teacher?" disturbed Miriam asked.

Raja responded, "They had been sacrificed and later eaten by Bekazish! The reason the leaders keep making sacrifices and feeding them was, they knew that if the Bekazish came out from beneath the ground, it would be the biggest chaos in the history of the world. The abduction of children and teacher only happened because the leaders delayed their supply of human sacrifices and Bekazish took complete advantage of the school trip in their territory."

Miriam demanded, "I want to know about more locations. This seems such an interesting topic."

Raja saw excitement in her eyes; he was able to make her forget about Durga and got her interested in mysterious locations, he continued with another mysterious location.

Ellora Caves, India

"The next destination is located within one of my favorite historical locations in the land of mysteries, India. Known as Ellora or the Ajanta caves, situated North West of the city called Aurangabad; located in the Indian state of Maharashtra.

"Let me give a rare overview about this mysterious archaeological site. The site contains all together thirty-four caves and temples. The twelve Buddhist caves from one to twelve, seventeen Hindu caves from thirteen to twenty-nine and five Jain caves thirty to thirty-four. Built in propinquity, these reveal the religious harmony prevalent during this period of Indian history. The temples and caves represent the epitome of Indian rock-cut architecture.

"Even today scientists and architectural geniuses are researching who made those temples and how they did so. More than a thousand laborers scooped and carved the caves and temples out of the vertical face of the Charanandri hills. It took them two centuries to complete their work.

"The Buddhist caves were the first ones to be created, and the magnum opus among Buddhist caves is cave number ten, widely known as the Carpenter's cave. Beyond its grand multi-storied entry is a cathedral-like stupa hall, whose ceiling has been elegantly carved to give the impression of wooden beams. The main attraction is a fifteen-foot statue of Buddha seated in a preaching pose, right at the heart of the cave.

"The Hindu caves section starts from twenty-one to twenty-nine. It's worth spending a quiet moment in each cave as now you possess the power to see, feel and sense things that are impossible for ordinary humans. The first thing you see while approaching cave twenty-one is the sculpture of Nandhi the bull. Lord Shiva rides on Nandhi and it was his protector and defender.

"In Hindu mythology animals play huge part. For example, Lord Shiva wears a cobra around his neck. His son Lord Ganesh was half human and half elephant. Lord Hanuman was a monkey god. The list goes on and on.

"The Kailasa Temple is the biggest question mark for human minds. The craft is beyond imagination, turning Rocky Mountains into the most mesmerizing temples ever been created. The craftsmen sculpted Ramayana on those hills.

"What I really want to share with you is Nagas and two other celestials' existence in human forms, residing with Buddha, Hindu and Jain gods. They were the owners, protectors of their gods, as the upper part of temples were for various gods and kings. However the basement and underground world belongs to Nagas and two other celestials. Their job was to care for the temples, gods and kings.

"The complete description of the caves which I have provided you, now that is what's visible and every living creature can witness the beauty and mystery of caves. The world mostly focuses on how those were created and who were those masterminded people, who did the crafting.

"Now as you are immortal and with the passage of time, you will develop your powers. One of the main powers of being immortal is when you visit ancient locations and, by reciting a code, your third eye will open and you will be back in whatever time or year you want. The best part is, no one would be able to see you while you visit those ancient times and locations.

"I would take you back in time and we will visit these temples. I want to show you one cave and especially when it was alive and in full form. There is sacrificial alter outside that cave and you will see with your eyes what happened on that altar!"

Miriam replied, "The locations are educating, your cadenced story telling makes them more interesting to my ears. In my previous life I never even in my dreams had imagined such things. I will go with you into the past or future but never alone. The reason is simple, if you are with me I have nothing to worry about, otherwise how would I come back into the present time?"

Raja briskly replied, "Love, nowhere without me. We go together."

Smiling Miriam replied, "I know love, you would never let me go alone. I was just joking with you, as I always seek your attention and love for me. It would be an honor to accompany you to such fascinating temples. Educate me more about such locations, love."

The Snake Island

Raja replied, "Sure, let me tell you about an island filled with various legends, myths and mysteries; the Brazilian locals have been warned for generations not to step there. One of the most famous legends about the island is that pirates from around the world hide their treasure there. They were the ones who brought the most venomous snakes from the world, and set them free on the island.

"On the coast of Brazil, this island has been abode for more than five thousand most venomous snakes. The strange fact is that this is the only island on earth were you can find unique golden lance head viper or Bothrops insularis.

"Let me tell you about Bothrops insularis. It is a deadly snake whose poison can kill a person in less than an hour. It exists in just one place in the world, the island of Queimada Grande. Legend also has it that the lighthouse there was built in 1909. There is no such record; however it is the fact that there was attempt to create better living conditions on the island. But, it was verified that the best solution was just to automate the lighthouse.

"In 1920, a lighthouse keeper lived there with his wife and five-year-old daughter. All three of them were found dead; there was no one to take them back to the mainland.

"Cautions were posted for travelers to look ten times before taking a step and hundred times where to place your hand. That island is only for people with present and extremely focus mind, other precautions are required to be kept in consideration.

"The species of snake, the golden lance head viper, is not only unique but surely does carry the world's most potent venom, which can be used for the most critical illnesses in the world."

Surprised, Miriam asked, "Why didn't you set up your own kingdom on that island?"

With a smile, Raja replied, "Well because I am not a snake any-more. Secondly, my job is to restore lost humanity among humans and look after treasures of the whole world not only an island's treasure."

Miriam replied, "The world is full of so many hidden secrets; instead of exploring and decoding them, we are stuck in our own conflicts. Educate me more about such locations so I truly can help my own race. So what is next?"

Temple of Hathor, Egypt
Raja replied, "I know, love, you would be a great leader. Let me share the details of our next location with you.

"Egypt is one country from which humans think they have managed to understand the history of the world. Trust me, they have dug nothing yet.

"The Castle of the Sistrum or house of Hathor is a perfect university to understand the domination of king cobra. All the hieroglyphics carving and art depict the wisdom, prosperity, knowledge and healings through snakes. The temple gives signs in every pictogram that show the way to find long life and wealth.

"The goddess Wadjet was the protector and guardian of the ancient civilization of Egypt. All the pharaohs were selected by goddess Wadjet, who herself was a cobra. The cobra symbol was a compelling emblem in the crowns of pharaohs, as the emblem represents the pharaoh's dominion and godly authority in ancient Egypt and all around the world.

"Only a few living souls have witnessed a cobra standing on its tail, and you have seen me standing in that position. Now only you and me know the cobra that stand on tip of his tail is a shape shifter.

"In Hathor's temple, wisdom is left behind in shape of art, and the king cobra is shown standing on its tail. In that era, snakes were controlling humans and building history. They taught humans how to command critical issues.

"Hathor temple has many hidden chambers where some of the most significant secrets buried, and I know they are not for human eyes. Some secrets should better remain hidden, otherwise the chances for chaos in this world would take humans to end the world before Armageddon."

Miriam, while smiling said, "I should honestly be thankful to you for giving me immortality as a gift, because living a normal life I could never have done justice to the way I want to love you. Also, I really want to see all these places, understand the myth about life and things that I can convey in easy manners to bring sense for humanity. The more I know about the world, the clearer I understand the importance of king cobra in our world."

Raja replied, "Ninety percent of the world is totally unaware of the truth. Medicine started because of snake, Asclepius, who was son of Apollo also known as the first doctor. One day, when he was visiting a friend, a snake entered the room. Asclepius with help of his friend killed the snake, and within a few minutes another snake with a herb in its mouth kissed the dead snake. When the herb entered the dead snake's mouth, it instantly invigorated. That was the moment and birth of Asclepius, medical proficiency. He somehow managed to steal a sample of that herb and, after a dedicated search, he found the herb. He started practicing with the snake and few other herbs, and Asclepius became a master of medicine and started bringing people back from death. One of patient's was Hippolytus, who was wrongly accused of the rape of his stepmother Phaedra.

"Hades was the soul collector and was not happy with the dropping numbers of souls in his collections. He complained to his brother Zeus and explained to him that if all the humans become immortal, they would never respect the gods. Zeus killed Asclepius with one single thunderbolt, however Zeus was inspired by Asclepius' talent and honored him by placing him as a thirteenth zodiac sign in the stars.

"Ophiucus was the thirteenth zodiac sign; in ancient times better known as Serpentarius which means, the serpent holder. Ophiucus is described as a man handling a serpent; his body divides the large snake into two parts. Actually, he is patterned after the original serpent holder, Enki, a Sumerian god. Even today the world of medicine honors Asclepius, in sign of Caduceus which is represented by a winged staff with two snakes wrapped around it."

Miriam replied, "This was deep but very interesting, the whole story about medicine and how it got started seemed really magical.

CHAPTER 27

"WORSHIPS AND MYTHS"

Raja further explained to Miriam, "Life is not what you believe or think; it is not about us. Life is all about how we can help each other, be there for each other in times of need, despite various excuses, such as not being of same religion or race or color. To love each other is one of the reasons why we are here in this world. God from time to time, tests our humanity while sending natural disasters. He judges all those whom he has given in abundance and what they do for mankind.

"I know, for humans material things are keys to happiness and make them feel different from others. People make money so they can live in palaces and mansions, even their family consists of four, and other unoccupied rooms are only for spirits, who often come to sleep on empty beds. Trust me on this one, if you have empty beds at your house that is what happens on them. Think for one second about those people who are homeless lying somewhere in extreme cold or heat.

"Humanity is all about feelings and being an owner of a vigorous heart; if you don't have feelings, how can you sense other people's pain? If you don't have an enthusiastic heart, how can you hear people's cries?

"Nothing makes God happier than hearing the laughter of humans. As for God, that is the music he loves the most.

"The story of our existence starts with five main characters, God, Man, Woman, Devil and Snake.

"For some the Devil and Snake are one, while for few, Snake was simply one of God's created creatures whom the Devil chose to complete his mission. That is what the truth is because the Devil was fascinated by the way God had formed snakes.

"Until today, the Devil has used Snake as his symbol; the interesting fact about the relationship between The Devil and Snake is he added death in the shape of poison in their fangs, while God gave wisdom to mankind to use that venom and turn it into life-saving drugs.

"The world is divided and truly is confused about the existence of snakes, few believe in killing them on the sight, while some had created temples and do worship them as their gods.

"What I am going to share with you next are the facts of how, in some cultures of the world, they have their festivals, temples and ceremonies for snakes. They are worshipped and considered gods, messengers and creators of the world, while for most of the religions and cultures, they are considers as demons. I would love to take you to world ceremonies of serpents, where people pray, worship and honor them. I really am not exaggerating; such occasions occur in this world and they are true. I believe the world should be free to make a choice, worshiping what they believe in. If they find peace and harmony and are not hurting any living creature, sooner or later they will find the truth of the real Lord!

"Those ceremonies are colorful and worth attending; to see a deep combination of faith and devotion is always fascinating. I know as per Islam for you it's a sin to even think about such beliefs. However, I know some places where even Muslims are convinced that those reptilians they visit do have some spiritual existence. I humbly request that you see the world with open mind; don't judge or try to own other people's lives. The moment humans try to control other people's lives and think they can show them the right path toward Heaven, which is when they start moving away from Heaven themselves. All they truly need to understand is that every single human came alone in world and would die alone. Each of them has to face their own death and later judgments according to the life they lived.

"We all are born free in this world and let people live just the way they want. It's easy to call rest of the world wrong and our own self right, one must investigate the depth of the world. Believe me, some facts would give you reason to rethink about what the truth really is!

"Time is the honest cruelty and reality for humans to understand. God exists and He is watching every second of how you spend your life.

"We have all the time in the world and I would make sure to show. We will attend most of the ceremonies, however today I would just share with you the essence of some of those places, because if I start sharing every single temple or complete details, then we will both be lost in this never ending subject," Raja told her with a smile.

"I know and can understand the biggest problems with ordinary people are that their minds consist of limited knowledge. However, when you travel and meet wise people and see historical places that are staring right back in your eyes and asking you, you better believe it, my dear. The human brain is maturing and progressing with the passage of time; they are making ways through science to investigate the possibility of impossible accomplishments. I truly wish if they can just take a deep interest in historical places in the world, their forefathers had left knowledge for them and all they could need for making the world a better place."

Nag Panchami Festival, India

"In India, Nag Panchami is one of the biggest holy festivals. There are various myths and legends about Nag Panchami; in country like Nepal they have their own version of the legend, while in India Hindus have a few of their own. I would share few with you," Raja said.

"As legend recalls, the earth belonged to and was ruled by Nagas (cobras) before the arrival of the men on earth. The Nagas consented to allow the men to use the land for cultivation, except the one day, the day of Nag Panchami. A peasant forgot the restriction and that day the mother cobra and her infants came out of their burrow, considering no danger outside. Without realizing it, the peasant committed the unforgiveable sin. While working in the fields, he killed a baby cobra, totally unaware of this sin, peacefully finished his work and went home.

"The mother cobra waited to take her vengeance, and in the darkness of the night she entered the peasant's house. She killed the peasant and the next morning went into the house of his daughter. The mother cobra was surprised to see the act of the peasant daughter as she was offering and worshiping effigy of the king cobra, and her devotion calmed her fury.

"The mother cobra spared the life of the girl and left in peace. Ever since, the women of Hindu faith wait for the sacred day of Nag Panchami to offer flowers, milk and honey to cobras. Hence, throughout the centuries this ritual brings prosperity and protects their families from the cobra bites. During this holy day, humans invite cobras into their communities, to pay their gratitude and show how vastly Cobras are respected by humans. The very next day of the Naga Panchami the cobras are released at the same locations from where they had been caught.

"The other version of legend goes something like this, during Amritmanthan certain poison was spilled by king cobra or Shesh Nag. This poison could have easily destroyed the world, but Lord

Shiva drank that poison and saved the world. Nag Panchami is celebrated on that day only according to the Indian calendar. Every year in India, people celebrate the Nag Panchami festival, where people preach to snakes in order to save themselves from the anger and poison of snakes."

St Dominic (951-1032), Cocullo Snake Festival, Italy
Raja continued, "If you think such cults and beliefs only occur in Central Asia, you will be surprised the whole world is full of such rituals. Europe, Italy, in the village of Cocullo, villagers have perpetuated an eleventh century pagan ritual. The anecdote recalls how the Benedictine monk St. Dominic who saved the people from a terrible invasion of snakes.

"St. Dominic of Sora was born in Foligno, Italy. He devoted his life to God and became Benedictine monk and founded a number of hermitages in central Italy. He was blessed and well renowned for the gift of performing various miracles, however the miracles for which St Dominic was remembered included cure of snakebites.

"Inhabitants known as Marsi, from the same town, were snake charmers. They were devotees of serpent Goddess Angitia. Even today their passion for snakes is still alive.

"St. Dominic is also known as the protector against snake bites. St. Dominic's day still occurs once a year. The ritual started with his statue, which is carried through the village, with the snakes coiling around the statue and its bearers. The squirming mass of snakes is released back into the forest, leaving the villagers supposedly immune from snakebites for another year.

"Around six weeks before the procession, on nineteen March St. Joseph's Day, snake handlers start collecting snakes from the area around the village. They mostly try to catch non-venomous snakes, such as four-liner rat snake. Even though knowing the snakes are non-venomous, their fangs are still removed. The snake handlers keep them as pets, until the day of procession on the statue.

"Centuries ago, this ceremony was the cruelest ritual festival for snakes. After the procession's end, all the captured snakes were supposedly collected cooked and eaten. Today they are released back into the forest, where the poor creatures have to wait for another year to grow back their fangs. The menu has been changed; instead of snakes, the people now they eat sweet, ring-shaped bread resembling a baked coiled snake." Raja studied Miriam's facial expression.

Miriam replied, "Human behavior toward all living creatures bring nothing but shame to me. I can simply seek forgiveness on behalf of my fellow kind. All the powers you have blessed me with would be used to educate people. Baking snakes, seriously, the things people do to pleasure their inner demons. Love, please prepare me and educate me more on the same subject."

Hopi Snake Festival, North America

Raja continued, "The Native American Hopi tribe is one of the most ancient, dexterous and astute people in the world. Ancient tribes follow what they have been taught by their ancestors, which is basically difficult for the normal world to understand. The Hopi tribe understands their knowledge is enough for them to survive well in this world. One of their most famous rituals is the Snake Dance, which intrinsically is a sixteen days celebration. The ceremony is a kind of a prayer request for rain to the underworld, where they believe the gods and spirits of their ancestors reside. As the tribe treats snakes as their brothers and according to their belief, they rely on them to offer the prayers together. The sightseers who visit to see the Snake Dance are simply interested in the demonstration of it, rather than the belief that it has power to influence the weather.

"The dance is performed by members of the Snake and Antelope clans from all three of the mesas in Arizona, where the Hopi's live.

"On the twelfth day before the ceremony, the Snake priests leave on a mission to gather snakes, often taking young boys from the Snake clan. Those boys have been blessed with a gift to capture and handle snakes without any fear, since the day they were born.

"They first start the dance, while carrying the snake in their hands and later in their mouths!

"The whole dance is well organized; the high priest who carries the snake is escorted by an assistant and they both dance around the plaza. Each pair is followed by a third man called gatherer, whose only responsibility is to make sure when dancer drops the snake it doesn't go into the crowd.

"The Snake priests keep a keen eye on every single snake; in the end, all the snakes are carefully carried and dropped off at special shrines, where they are released. The final prayers are offered from the mouths of the priests to the underworld whereas per their belief, the rain gods live.

Once all rituals are performed, the dancers drink an emetic, and this is believed to purge them of any dangerous snake charms. Later in the day, dark clouds will form and rain will follow.

"During this huge celebration, not a single snake is hurt and they are safely released where they were caught.

"It's not only this ritual; they are often visited by flying serpents. These are huge and hardly visible to ordinary eyes. The problem with the world is they only believe what science and media show them. Tribes such as the Hopi are blessed with wisdom beyond imagination. Even today when lifestyles have changed completely and modernization has taken control of human minds, the Hopi are well equipped with an ocean of wisdom. They don't need to seek from the books what the world is offering!"

Shrine of 'Manghophir', Karachi, Pakistan
"I know even being Muslim you're not aware of this mysterious Shrine of Manghophir. As you know, Muslims strongly believe in shrines of

saints, right? They believe conveying their problems and worries to a dead saint, is like conveying their message to Allah. Muslims believe saints are closer to Allah as they are a shortcut to Allah and true messengers of their prayers. The legend revolves around a famous Hindu dacoit few centuries ago. His name was Mangho and he was famous for looting traders' convoys with his gang.

"The traders and all travelers were really tired of being robbed continually; they hired a skilled team of brave soldiers to kill Mangho. During the confrontation, the soldiers were no match for Mangho and his gang.

"The most often robbed traders were Arab Muslims and one day they took complains to a Muslim saint named Shah Farid. The saint understood the pain and losses the traders were facing and promised to speak to the Hindu dacoit on their behalf.

"On meeting with Mangho, the old saint sensed a decent saint hidden in the Hindu dacoit. He managed to make Mangho understand the beauty of humanity and afterlife rewards for doing good deeds in this life. Manghophir accepted Islam and devoted his life to do good deeds.

"Saint Shah Farid became his mentor and after watching his devotion and services for mankind, he added Phir (saint) to his name.

"One day, Manghophir saw two crocodiles that had lost their way from river and ended up near a big pond next to where Mangho Phir was meditating. The villagers wanted to kill the crocodiles, as they were scared of them. Mangho Phir took complete responsibility for the most dangerous reptilian species on earth. He assured the villagers that those crocodiles were now his pets and that they or their generation would never harm any humans. The villagers knew of Mangho Phir's connection with Allah and they honored his words.

"Seven centuries have passed and today, from two crocodiles there are more than a hundred crocodiles in the same pond, and they have never hurt a single human.

"Healing fountains are next to his shrine, where thousands of people suffering from various skin diseases can take a bath and be cured.

"Millions of people visit the shrine and they pay huge respect to those crocodiles; some bring Central Asian sweets, a few shower them with rose petals, and others bring chickens and goat for them to eat.

"That's the only shrine which fascinates the entire world with the calmness of crocodiles, otherwise wherever crocodiles exist, human death tolls can easily increase!" Raja told Miriam.

Islamic Exorcism with sacrifice of a poisonous snake, Middle East
"As you are already aware in the Holy Quran, the snake is considered a devil and the main culprit of human émigré from Heaven." Raja explained.

"In Morocco, the snake charmers do have a second serious job, and that is where they actually make their decent living and earnings. For their living and earnings, a venomous snake has to sacrifice his or her life. The tribe is known as Iasavi. Their expertise includes exorcism and healing possessed sick individuals.

"The tribe's job is to cure demon-possessed humans. And they consider venomous snakes as evil and Jinn. According to their belief, the only way to cure a possessed human is to kill a demon in his or her presence.

"The sacrifice of a snake is the only cure; the killing of snake is death of the demon residing in a human body.

"The family members arrange a ceremony where the ritual, healing of a possessed person begins. It seems more like a festival where neighbors and close relatives come to be part of the ritual.

"The Iasavi tribe brings musical instruments, as the whole tribe consists of professional showmen. They create a mesmerizing atmosphere with their dances and stunts; within a couple of minutes the whole crowd is part of the trance.

"The tribe leader cuts the snake head and later skins it. While performing the dance he starts eating the same snake. Some of the members of his tribe join him to take a bite to create a more gruesome atmosphere. During the process, the tribe gives drugs to the possessed person. The effects make the person calm.

"The family members and relatives believe the tribe has done their job; no one knows that they fed the possessed person, and the drug is so filthy even the evil spirit leaves the body of the person," Raja told Miriam, with a smile.

Feather Serpent Temples.
"In Mesoamerican religions, one of their important supernatural deities was called Quetzalcoatl among the Aztecs, Kukulkan among the Yucatec Maya, while Q'uq'umatz and Tohil existed among the K'iche' Maya.

"Aztec and Mayan temples all over South America are witness of the glory of snake god feather serpent, who was also considered and known as master of clouds and rains. All corn-growing nations in South America worshiped the feather serpent. As per their belief, when the clouds were red, it was because he was bleeding. His blood turns into nourishing rains and the rain enable the corn-fields and humans to flourish. Still, in the those temples' scriptures it is clearly mentioned how high priests of those temples open the chests of humans to take the beating heart and place them on the gods' altars.

"Actually, the rulers of that time found the human sacrifice a kind of an event to keep the nation's spirits high. The feather serpent had nothing to do with those hearts; nowhere is it written or it can be found in any ancient manuscript that the feather serpent ate those hearts, drank human blood or ate headless bodies.

"Humans always find excuses to create a world where, they can set up a circus to kill other humans. Nothing excites human more than watching death of other human, in the most gruesome way.

Even now that the world has been educated, they still are not able to figure out why the feather serpent would ask them to take other human heart. He was a god and if he wanted, he could have eaten whoever he liked himself. Those high priests made their kings happy and the kings kept their nation happy, while organizing such brutal killing events," Raja explained to Miriam.

Miriam replied, "Why am I not shocked that humans enjoyed watching other people suffering, because I have been the victim of such a crowd."

Temple of Python, Quidah, Benin Republic
Raja explained, "I know love, the reason I share all this with you is so you can understand you are not the only one who has been through the human circus of death. Let me tell you little more about some interesting temples.

"Quidah is a centre of Voodoo practice in a country called the Benin Republic, located in continent of Africa. In 1717, Houeda, now known as Quidah, was defeated by notorious Ghezo warriors. King Kpasse, ruler of the kingdom of Quidah, fled the town and tried to find refuge in the deep forest. Myriad pythons came and protected King Kpasse of Quidah, from getting capture.

"They save the king and that is when the adoration of pythons started after the war. The king decided to commemorate pythons by building three huts in that forest. Since that day they are known as royal pythons and have been worshiped in Quidah."

Arjuna's Penance, Mahabalipuram...India
Raja continued, "The map of truth and divinity can be evidently found on Arjuna's Penance a legacy created by the Pallava kings, as they left two serious hidden messages in their glorious colossal uncovered bas-relief monolith.

"The first message is about the self-mortification pose of Arjuna Mahabharata hero shown fasting and standing on one leg. He is determined to receive the powerful weapon from Lord Shiva. Celestial creatures, various gods and dwarves are on top of the rock, while below you would find ordinary South Indian everyday life in full glory in the vicinity of the portrait. Various birds and animals are also pictographic to keep the balance of life in every form.

"Coming back to the first message, to win in life it's important never to give up. Humiliation, controlling ego and staying honest to your desires, basically help you to achieve what you want in life. Arjuna set an example for all human kind to understand the strength of devotion; dedicated hearts can mold gods.

"The second message is about serpent gods, as they are emerge from the deepest part of the earth. They are centre of attraction and their existence is crafted elegantly in a higher grace. Even being strong deities, their humility is well presented as they are emerge placing their hands together in a sign of modesty. So the second message is all about being humble in life.

"There are myriad more temples, I would keep informing you from time to time. Meanwhile, we should start planning our wedding. Anything special you want, feel free to let me know," Raja told Miriam.

Miriam replied shyly, "I only have one humble request and that is, if we can call an Imam a Muslim cleric to conduct our wedding."

Raja firmly replied, "Sure we can have both weddings, Muslim and Christian, first with Imam and later with a Christian priest. I want just a simple ceremony at home or if you want grand function, we can organize accordingly!"

Miriam replied, "No, love, a simple ceremony is fine. My whole world is you and my family is Ayesha and the household staff."

Raja replied with smile, "Great, so our wedding is planned and settled then."

CHAPTER 28

"THE WEDDING"

As Miriam was becoming intellectual, she figured out that Raja discussed his wealth modestly. Miriam came to know the delegations that came to visit the house, were attaches of the most powerful leaders, kings and presidents of various countries. Raja had devised the most effective method to maintain low profile, as it was the best way for him not being visible to the eyes of the world. No one noticed small delegations moving in and out of countries or cities, however if a powerful leader planned to visit any country, it was a completely different story.

One evening, Miriam asked Raja, "You know all our leaders who are rulers of ours and other countries, right?

Raja replied, "A few acquaintances not that a strong relationship or any kind of friendship with them. The people who run countries, top businessmen or dictators, they all have more enemies than friends. Any person seen with them also ends in a similar way as they do. One thing you need to learn is keeping a balance between staying alive and staying in control. The ends of the rich and famous people lives are always awful. The reason is they are watched by millions. The moment they gain upper hand on other humans, they start thinking they can play God.

"The problem is everyone wants to play God, but they don't know how to act like humans. One more thing rich people might like you or be your friends, however they will never make you rich. They will only give you this much, which will keep you with them or follow them just like an obedient dog.

"If I was close to leaders or kings, I would have been killed before I even existed. There is a group of people who make and break leaders; I am part of that faction. However, I work according to my terms and conditions. They all know I am an investor who donates large sums of money, and that's all. Only a handful of people know who I truly am. The rest all know I exist, and am one of the anonymous investors. The people who run the kings, presidents and leaders are anonymous people. No one knows who they are or where they live, however they control the economy of the world."

Miriam asked, "You are a wise, clever and well calculated man. Why did you select me from such a big world? I would not even consider myself ordinary, because even those people do have some sense. All I knew was my children and serving my first husband as my owner.

"My first life was filled with smiles and innocent laughter of my beautiful children; even in the poverty I was the richest woman on earth. The definition of love one can only understands when a woman becomes a mother. A child she has inside herself and can you imagine, there were so many moments when I wanted to turn side while lying on bed but I never did. One simple thought, that my turn or wrong movement would hurt my unborn child.

"Those people, without giving a thought, killed my children right in front of my eyes. As if their lives were not worth anything can you imagine my pain? It was so profound that my screams were lost deep down somewhere inside my soul. I begged them to kill me with my family, and they laughed and left me burning in a pain of the never-ending fire.

"Suicide is a sin in Islam and I was not able to even take my own life, because I knew if I committed suicide, my Allah would never forgive me, and my final destination would never get to be with my loved ones. My abode would have been Hell, so I chose to spend more time in hell on earth and waited for my natural death," Miriam told Raja while teardrops fell from her eyes.

Raja replied, "I know my love and I can feel every inch of your pain. See for you I was born and I had been selected to become a human. It's all God's plan and His mysterious ways of taking care of things. When we think we have lost our whole world and everything that is when He wants us to believe in Him. Yes, that very moment He is there and listening. As He want humans to rejoice and praise Him and pay humble gratitude for His blessing and all of His kindness. I know you must be thinking how one can thank Him when He took their children from him or her. Well that is what God is all about, He wants you to find your peace through Him, as he is your Lord, father and your own in this whole universe. He wants us to give Him all our pain, yet have you ever considered when you try to carry something heavy and you feel like you can't do this alone? You seek someone to help you; your pain is the same as that burden; He wants you to place all your pain on His shoulder. Give Him a chance to show you, He is there to carry all suffering with love and a smile.

"In return, He has an everlasting gift of life for you with all your loved ones. That gift is eternal and all those people you loved will be there to love you back.

"I really do feel your pain. You miss your children every second and the only way to cure your pain is to love you. I never ever want to replace your children's love from your soul and heart; they belong there and truly are part of you. They are with the Lord and are in a much better place than we are. In so many ways this pain is your power to help people, educate them and help them to be human again.

"Imagine how many mothers you can save from the pain you suffer every single second of your life. The teachings of the Lord Jesus Christ; love your enemy and forgive them. It needs courage to forgive someone and I know you are the bravest soul I had ever seen in my entire life," Raja explained while wiping away her tears.

"Love is the most beautiful gift God has blessed all living creatures with, what is the true meaning of happiness, only those who felt love can understand. My Lord has been extremely kind to me; gave me life to feel and sense the beauty of His magical creation of this world. I had always been thankful to Him; it's the first time in my life I am being unthankful for all this blessings.

"The reason I think even the immortal life is not enough for me to love you! Imagine the moments being alive are only those when I am with you, rest I feel every single second is waste of my life. For me the definition of love is being at my final destination like home; where you feel safe, relaxed, happy and complete. For me that place is being in your arms. This is why all the poets have written about love, how highly toxic it is.

"Tomorrow is our wedding and this night I don't want us to sleep, I just want us to sit outside under the full moon, let the moon witness what we share and discuss tonight. I know you had a family before they all claimed they loved you. I know once you were a little girl and your parents loved you, so did your brother and sisters.

"I know deep down somewhere you have always been alone waiting, dreaming and imagining a world of your own, full of madness, adventure and a man being crazy about you. Your first husband Alam loved you in his own way and you never complained to him. You have been a good mother and when your sons got married, they totally ignored you. I was aware of your unheard cries.

"When the whole world slept, enjoyed beautiful moments in their dreams, you were lying in your bed crying. Life without love is like a sleep without a dream; even you think you are in peace but you are not.

"I know even you had a whole world of people around you, who claimed they were your own and loved you. Let me assure you something today, I want to play the role of all your loved ones. I want to be your mother, father, brother, sister and friend too, a whole group of relatives, who made you happy whenever they visited your house.

"I want to be the friend you always wanted, with whom you can share every ugly, dirty secret you have always been too shy to share with others. I want to be your lover, who dedicated his life just to make you smile and keep you blissful. I want to be your husband, who devotes his life to serve, protect, respect and honor you for rest of your life.

"I want to be the man who is your protector, consider you as his country and always ready to go to war with the whole world to keep you safe. I believe in the madness of love and that is all I have for you, with my each heart beat and with every breath I take, your name will be on it; my eyes will seek and search only for you.

"The day someone is born, all his or her life they just live on with only one hope to find happiness. For some finding happiness is only through being rich, all their life they keep finding a way to be rich. In the same circle, one day in their life they finally find a way to be rich. Guess what happens next, instead of being happy, they start being depressed about getting old, death starting to close in and now they have money and they don't want to die. Imagine the money they made all their lives, now someone else will enjoy the ride on their money. While on the other side, the maggots will be enjoying their flesh deep down in their graves.

"It's not material things that can provide peace for your soul, yes maybe good for your eyes or make you look good in other people eyes.

"Humans don't understand one simple philosophy about life, everyone in this world is born to love the one person who is born for them. Life is worth living and finding that one soul.

"I lived for thousands of years, as a human only for one simple hope to find the one. I can happily live rest of my immortal life with you; we do things together that God wants us to do," Raja explained.

Miriam replied briskly, "I really did something wonderful which touched the heart of my creator and He blessed me with you. I wish from the bottom of my heart, that all men in this world honor and love their women just the way you do."

They both hugged and in the atmosphere, it was strange tranquility. As serenity of the night was signing and glorifying their madness of love, the moon was witnessing the whole scene and glowed with harmony.

The following day was the big day of Miriam's life, while the beauticians were preparing her for the wedding, with elite makeup and expensive jewelry. Deep down in her heart, she was thinking of joy and happiness. Today was the biggest day of her life, she was getting married to a man, who not only loves her but in his own way, he worshiped her.

Miriam felt the presence of her children, her boys sitting next to her smiling while their honest delight was visible in their eyes. Far on the edge of the door, she saw Alam staring her with strange eyes. In his gaze she could read millions of questions, like seriously you are young again and are you not scared of this monster?

Miriam was also able to see weird jealously in his eyes, for a while, then all of the sudden he gave her an honest smile as if he was blessing her, for a new start of her life. She nodded toward him, while acknowledging his blessing and in her own way thanked Alam. Her sons were still sitting next to her; Miriam hugged both of her sons and started crying, "'Please, never leave me again.'"

The eldest son spoke to her, "'Mother, we are happy for you. Please always remember who you were and you are the world's greatest mother. Always remain blessed and remember we love you and are proud of you.'"

Ayesha's voice brought her back to the real world. She was still surrounded by dozens of maids, who all were busy fixing her makeup, jewelry and dress.

Miriam briskly hugged Ayesha, and while crying asked her, "'Oh, Ayesha, why are our lives so complicated? When we are celebrating the biggest joy of our life, we still feel so empty and lonely deep inside.'"

Ayesha, while hugging her firmly, replied, "Please don't cry. I know and can understand your pain. Every second of our lives are predestined. See this moment right now, how I am trying to comfort you. There would be times when you are going to hold and comfort me. You know Raja can't see a single tear in your eyes and so do I. Now he is your world and you're going to be his. Wipe away your tears and give me your beautiful smile."

There were two simple ceremonies; the first one was Nikah, an Islamic cleric went and while Miriam was behind curtains, Raja was able to only hear her voice as they both were in different rooms.

He asked Miriam, "Do you accept Mr. Raja as your husband?"

Miriam, in a sophisticated tone replied, "'Yes.'"

The cleric asked her three times and all three times she replied, yes.

Then the cleric asked, Raja the same question and he also replied, 'Yes.'

Once the Islamic ceremony ended, Miriam wore a beautiful white dress and the pastor started the vows.

Then they got married in the Christian way; the pastor read a few verses from the Bible and asked the bride and groom if they accepted each other as husband and wife. They both replied, "'I do.'"

Right after the ceremony, Miriam went to their bedroom and again she changed her dress. This time she wore a traditional red dress, which consisted of a long skirt with short blouse that covered the whole waist. Raja enters the bedroom and first thing he did he gave her a beautiful diamond necklace while looking at her face, as it was one of the well-customs in Muslims marriage. The bride would keep her face covered until her husband removed the veil. Also, there's a tradition he should offer her a gift before doing so. Keeping that in mind, Raja placed his gift in her hand and removed the veil.

"I don't have any gift for you, my love!" concerned Miriam told Raja.

"That you don't have to worry about, my darling, however if you really want to give me something, then I know what I'm going to ask you is the most difficult thing for you to do. Still I would be happy if you give my request a chance," Raja told her.

"My love, please don't say such thing. You own my life and you don't need to request. Just order me," Miriam replied.

"Sweetheart, my humble request is that you please kindly do forgive all those people who killed your family; I know it's hard for you, but remember forgiving someone is an act of kindness. One of the messages, as I told you before from the Lord Jesus Christ is to love your enemy. That would be pure and honest love for the world. Trust me, you will find peace deep down in your soul after doing so."

Raja's face and his smile made her heart sink, to a place from where nothing resurfaced. Miriam replied, "Okay, my love, I forgive all those people who killed my family, and I also forgive all those people who killed my dear friend. If you would have asked me to take my heart from my chest and give it to you, I would have done it. I know you would only make me a much better human, and I really am proud to be your wife.

"However this diamond necklace is not what I seek as a gift. My gift would be the rest of your love stories and adventures you lived without me. Like your first century was Durga and tenth I am, still eight centuries I know nothing about your life. If you say there were no girls in those eight centuries, then that would be the biggest lie of the world. One more thing: I want you to tell me honestly after sharing all your remaining eight love stories, why you chose me to be your wife and why you have given me the gift of immortality?" Miriam asked him.

Raja replied with a smile, "God, you women only have only one concern and that is the knowledge of your man with other women. We have a long life to live, so trust me I will share every detail of my simple existence. Yes, there were women in every century, and they all taught me something I'will share with you. About your question, why you? So my love all those girls were blessed with one great quality, like for instance Durga was one of the most brave people I have ever met. What she taught me, when a woman wants to be brave, no men in this world can come close to her bravery. Imagine sacrificing herself for honor of her father, chosen to burn alive with her dead husband, really salute to her.

"While the other eight were blessed with various qualities and that I would share when tell their stories.

"Why I selected you to be my wife, so the answer, my love, is very simple. The gift of immortality I can only give to one human and that human I selected was you, because you have more than all those nine women had in them. See you are brave as you were ready to face the most evil humans, who were above to stone Zakia. Knowing them from the depth of their evil roots, you were aware they would stone you too, just for interfering in their evil actions. You risked your life and were ready to go for a war with them; now even brave men can stand motionless, but no one has courage to raise their voice. The rest of your qualities I would share with you once I start sharing my life in each century.

"Above all, God has chosen you, because no one would help the human race better than you. The biggest challenge for you is to work with new mothers of various cultures. As to raise a child to be a better human, start with character education which starting from the moment the child is born. We can only bring peace and harmony into this world when we love each other as humans. All Jesus Christ's teaching are based on loving each other, nothing more and nothing less. When children are raised with hatred in them, what outcome can we expect from them? When they are taught we are better humans and our religion is best, why would they even consider investigating other cultures or religions?

"Character education need to be in syllabus starting from third grade, I have the right person who you would be working with to promote this subject. Trust me, this would take a century or two to get it implemented, as in coming times humans would create a hell on earth, while setting a stage of death in name of religion and faith.

"Hate gives birth to aggression and violence, and invites angels of death. It's one of your responsibilities now, to find a team of people and assign them to educate young parents, despite their religions, status or race.

"Immortality is a gift but at the same time a burden to do things which can bring peace to the human race. Like in Islam, being martyr is the biggest honor for any man or woman. Now, for me, your family was martyr, because they took a stand to save lives, not taking lives. The reason they stood for the weak and innocent was because Alam and your sons believed they were on the right side. In Hinduism, any kind of human sacrifice is not acceptable and I know it would not be easy to find those parents, but you have a long life to live, right?" Raja explained to her with a smile.

Miriam replied, "I am with you, my love, and truly agree that developing character education for our future generations would be the only option to bring peace to this beautiful world. Like in a clear word you want me to work on world peace and try to find ways for humans not to kill other humans. I know it's the hardest task, because this would be a war between good and evil. My job is to defeat the Devil himself and create myriad hurdles to his work. With the blessing of the Lord and your support I will give my best, my love.

While she finished her sentence, they both heard a frantic knock at the door.

"Who is it?" Raja asked.

"It's me, Ayesha."

Raja opened the door; Ayesha asked permission to enter.

Raja made way for her; she looked at Miriam and then gazed back toward Raja.

"You can say whatever you want; she is my wife now," Raja calmly told her.

"We need to leave now. Abdul Salam's son, with help of a Greek witch named Ananke Erinyes, managed to find the head of Abdul Salam. They are extremely close to bringing him back to life and we both know he would be pure evil with much hidden powers this time. One more thing, this witch is the Queen of darkness, and she can smell you in the air. When Abdul Salam awakens from the dead, the first thing he would seek is you. I suggest we need to leave for the west right away. We need to be behind a magical shield and take shelter below your chateau!" Ayesha explained.

"Thank you, Ayesha, however make sure for next twenty-four hours I want no one to disturb us. After that we plan just the way you suggested," Raja replied.

Ayesha left the room, and Miriam remember Abdul Salam as he was the main character who allowed them to meet for the first time, and now on the first day of their marriage, his name was back in their lives.

Raja, while smiling, came close to her. "See, love, this is life. One moment happiness, the other second dark clouds of concerns gather around us. Such news gives us a reality check that we are alive and life is a constant struggle. I don't care what happen next; all I want is my twenty-four hours with you and I want to feel I am alive and loved.

"I know you must be thinking how come Ayesha knew about Abdul Salam, so my love Ayesha is not who you think she is. However all this we discuss later, because Ayesha is a complete chapter, and you need to know every detail of her. As for now, let me love my wife," and while saying those words, he kissed Miriam.

Miriam passionately kissed him back and hugged him as tight as she could. All she wanted to do was to protect him and save him from the rest of the world. As he was ready to go to war for her with the whole world, Miriam made her mind she would do the same for her love and even to protect him from hundreds of Abdul Salam's she would not hesitate. With that thought, her soul was at peace and she wanted to make the next twenty-four hours the best time for both of them.

And the journey begins…

ABOUT THE AUTHOR

A. Amos is a deep thinker with a passion for understanding the mysteries of life, love, and humanity. He has traveled throughout the world and is heavily invested in the personal development of others—with a firm belief that knowledge is the best gift that one can offer to the world.

Made in the USA
Lexington, KY
09 April 2016